The Sword of Stonehenge

By Malcom Massey

The Martin Culver Series

Volume 5

Norfolk, Virginia USA

The Sword of Stonehenge

By Malcom Massey

First Print Edition

June 1, 2017

The Fifth Volume in The Martin Culver Series

ISBN-13: 978-1505242713

ISBN: 1505242711

DEDICATION

This novel is dedicated to my brother Troy.

Though his life was tragically taken,

His Spirit is now free.

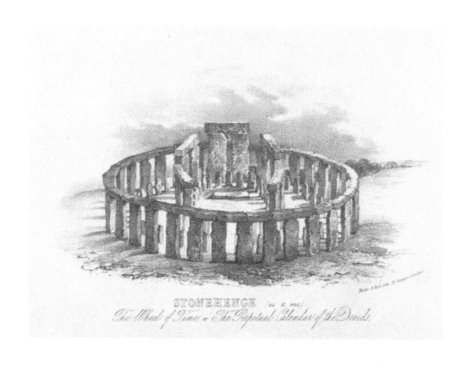

STONEHENGE (as it was)
The Wheel of Time or The Perpetual Calendar of the Druids

Stonehenge (as it was)

The Wheel of Time or

The Perpetual Calendar of the Druids

Chapter 1

Salisbury Plain, England
Near Stonehenge

The afternoon air pulsed through waning daylight, droning with the echo of heavy equipment across the rolling Salisbury Plain. Bringing to mind an out-of-breath dragon, the sound reverberated on for miles. The imposing noise reached a medieval-style campaign tent pitched within sight of the Stonehenge megaliths, delivering a rhythmic audio backdrop to the lines and images dancing across multiple computer and radar screens crammed beneath the canvas.

The steady methodical rumble of the machine responsible for such an ungodly noise served a compelling purpose. The four-wheel drive Massey-Ferguson tractor carried wireless equipment that transmitted continuous GPS coordinates from the antenna of the tractor to the tent housing the University College at London's field data collection center.

Following a pre-determined tracking pattern, each pass resulted in a GPS reading, which was then sequenced with a corresponding image created by Ground Penetrating Radar, or GPR. Passing mere millimeters above the grassy plain, the 1,000 kilo plate beneath the lumbering tractor was capable of peering a full three meters below the surface, with the potential to reveal undiscovered secrets as it systematically crisscrossed the countryside, working within a stone's throw of the ring of ancient monoliths known as Stonehenge.

The data collection tent, a hive of activity, contained a virtual bunker of latest research equipment with one very capable person at its center, operating multiple computers and data-plotting printers simultaneously.

Born Moroccan and given a name difficult to pronounce, "Pete" as he preferred to be called, was totally in his element. The young, thinly bearded grad student relaxed and leaned back in his motorized wheelchair, playing video games with one hand while monitoring the GPR data screen with the other. He clicked to record certain data points that fed into an onscreen grid glowing iridescent green. The student was, like the professor he idolized,

1

wheel-chair bound. The difference was that Pete had been born this way, having come to London from Morocco as a child for multiple leg surgeries before the age of ten.

Professor Haddad's injuries were the result of the collapse of an ancient tunnel he had been excavating on an archaeological dig in Luxor, Egypt some 20 years prior. While that accident had ended the Professor's direct involvement in field work, Pete's motorized chair could take him anywhere.

Pete was in charge of drone surveillance for the research project, launching the team video drone at intervals to pass over the area, recording their work process, as well as observing any significant readings from an aerial perspective. He had just brought the drone unit back for a data download and recharge.

Pete was aware of recent discoveries in the chalky, level plains surrounding Stonehenge, discoveries that were changing the landscape of conventional thought about the history of this enigmatic land, with its many henges, barrows and cairns. These discoveries had created an urgency to search for anything that years of detailed conventional archaeology had missed, including searching beneath Stonehenge itself.

Stonehenge proper was now known to be but one of many megalithic sites in the area, potentially dwarfed by the size and complexity of the latest findings. Stonehenge, that mysterious great Druid temple of old, was where Professor Haddad had chosen to invest his energy and efforts, his reputation, and his remaining credibility.

The research team for which Pete had been selected received funding by way of a grant approved by the UCL Institute of Archaeology. After hundreds of years of discovery and study of Stonehenge above ground, the UCL team had been selected and permitted to take a unique and different approach.

The team's mission was clear: to thoroughly canvass the Stonehenge grounds for any undocumented *below* ground artifacts and structures. Ground penetrating radar provided the in-depth view required.

The UCL research team had expected great discoveries since early in the project, but as summer faded and fall ensued, the team's enthusiasm was draining away. The Professor had dispelled the concerns of his team with wise counsel, noting that with the

2

right data, new discoveries would come. With new finds would come a corresponding bump in credibility within British archaeological circles. In fact, the team could become the equivalent of rock-star status in the stuffy world of archaeology, overnight sensations, not to mention how such discoveries would enhance one's *curriculum vitae.*

Not everyone within staid British archaeology circles had been in agreement to return to Stonehenge. Pete remembered the argument that he had heard the day Professor Haddad had invited the British Museum's board of directors to one of his lectures.

Several had stormed out after the Professor's remarks, while others stayed to argue various points of contention. Those few remaining grew tired of being reminded that they had no right to restrict the cutting edge archaeology that the Professor had proposed.

To search using the new technology, to expose Stonehenge to potential digging and disruption, to shake up conventional theory was tantamount to invading a site considered sacred to British archaeologists as it had been to the Druids and the Beaker people before them, in ages long past. The most conservative archaeological authorities outright opposed the work, including an international consortium of museum directors led by the recalcitrant British Museum Board of Directors. Others whispered their concerns in the high hallways and drawing rooms of their own academic temples.

While some members protested to disturbing Stonehenge on the basis of the hallowed, near-sacred standing of the site, others balked on the pretext that the Stonehenge site's deep historical roots and unmistakable astrological alignment made it too important to disturb. A few of the more superstitious objected based on the old Druid legends, fearing some musty pox upon those who dared probe hallowed ground too deeply.

Whatever the reasons, the result had been a permit so limited in scope that permission had been granted to retrieve data only. Even that approval came with five pages of barrister talk and stipulations. No digging. No paint marking. Not a blade of grass was to be disturbed.

Pete knew from listening to his Professor that although the team was poised to unearth major discoveries in the near term, those who opposed them were foes of change, any change under any circumstances.

"These same recalcitrant creatures would have opposed Copernicus or Newton had they existed in the age of discovery," the Professor had often repeated. "Am I to be discouraged by such opposition, from those small of mind and low of brow?"

If there was such a thing as standard truth in archaeology, the Professor had often been quoted drilling one particular thought into the minds of his students.

"Old 'knowledge' dies a hard death when so many have so much so deeply invested in their understanding the past, no matter how mistaken they may be."

Professor Haddad believed that the status quo in London's sedate archaeological societies had always been a dangerous thing to disrupt. Yet, here they were, conducting the research, attempting to prove everyone else wrong.

The Professor believed that Stonehenge had a clear purpose. His most recent lecture had laid out the elements of Haddad's theory. Pete had memorized every word.

"Stonehenge was a royal ceremonial embalming temple of enormous importance through the ages, ending with the Druids. The records of the kings whose bodies were brought here from throughout the known world, when found, will likely be recorded in the Ogham text."

"Records indicate that the great upright stones supported the physical structure of the temple at Stonehenge. Each great stone, whether sarsen or bluestone, bore tribute to the particular region where the honored deceased had originated. As such, each massive column provided a unique witness by its mute presence, the kind of powerful record that results from unified, collective action, and mutual activity, not unlike the monumental pyramids of Egypt and megaliths world-wide."

"Above the huge stones," the Professor had related to his students, "Stonehenge possessed a great domed roof, open at the center peak. The roof reached nearly to the ground surrounding it, requiring participants to bow low before entering. The walls shielded the priests within from view of fire hearths and torch-light, allowing them to mediate and focus on the study of star patterns relating to particular deaths, to record their findings."

According to what he stated, Professor Haddad desired to discover the recorded royal embalming rosters and star-chart observations above all else.

Where the Professor most greatly varied from past theory regarding Stonehenge was his wheel-tunnel-spoke hypothesis, which Pete had heard enough times during the Professor's many extended lectures about it as to write his own detailed analysis.

The Professor taught that Stonehenge had been built over maze-like tunnel structures with pathways privy only to the initiated. Having found records in the collection of the British Museum indicating that these spoke-like tunnel structures existed, the Professor claimed to have found ancient diagrams showing a deep central pit wherein resided an impressive stone altar, with rows of rising seats extending from the packed ground to the roof. Surrounding the pit, resembling seats at a football stadium, these risers gave each participant a view of the ceremonies taking place in the proscenium below them.

According to the Ogham text diagrams, passages chiseled from beneath the Salisbury plain extended from the central altar of Stonehenge in each of the four cardinal directions, tunnels that led away from the temple away beneath the surrounding fields to dark catacombs rich in artifacts and mummies.

Professor Haddad, known to have an obsessive interest in all things Egyptian, especially embalming, hoped above all else to find in these tunnels not only the mummified remains of priests of the old ways, but the mummies of kings long past, perhaps even a repository of the complete records of the star-study that had taken place here. That was the dream.

The team's mission then was simple. They were tasked to prove the Professor's theory before funding ran out or before permission to work was withdrawn. Either case would mean a disastrous turn for this type of probing research. The research team's only alternative would be to go home empty-handed and in a larger sense, disgraced and discredited before their peers.

Today's effort represented their last research opportunity. The civic push to run a motorway tunnel below the Salisbury plan, thus avoiding rushing traffic above ground near Stonehenge had gained strength.

With popular support waning, further research opportunities would be precluded should the team not make some positive finding within the next twenty-four hours. Adding insult to potential injury, the very real risk existed that tunnel engineering studies and planning might any day stumble upon the theorized network of ancient tunnels, stealing the team's thunder and their discovery.

Ensconced behind the wall of data collection equipment, Pete's eyes were fixed on the screens in front of him, his hands incessantly moving, keying. Only his twisted legs remained motionless. Pete's impressive hand eye coordination, fine-tuned by a lifetime of video gaming, was finally paying off. Research grants from the University College at London Archaeology department had also paid for his fourth and final year of university, based on his amazing ability to manage the University's complicated data collection array practically with his eyes closed.

Pete dueled online dragons on one monitor while he multi-tasked across the data collection console, monitoring multiple screens at once. Keeping one eye on the screen that scrolled GPS coordinates, he tracked the movement of the GPR tractor within the selected search quadrant on another screen. A third monitor showed a three-dimensional underground view of every inch of ground the GPR tractor passed over down to a depth of three meters. Ground penetrating radar, originally developed for military use, had come into its own in the field of archaeology, providing crisp, clear views of whatever lay below ground level, without disturbing the soil or any proximate objects.

Glancing to his smartphone watch, Pete was glad to see that their work day was near an end. The last day of field work on this project, the final day of funding for this phase of the Stonehenge research. No significant discoveries had been made since summer. With funding running out, the team's only option would be to begin the analysis phase of the data previously collected and hope to find some overlooked anomaly.

Pete was not heartbroken about those prospects. This way the work would continue indoors, which was his element and infinitely easier to maneuver. The Salisbury Plain weather was growing less pleasant by the day, bearing promise of an early winter. A constant cool breeze made the afternoons less tolerable. The sun set earlier every day, its warmth melting away with it.

Watching onscreen as the GPR tractor reached the end of its next designated run, Pete looked up just as the onboard sensing equipment signaled a major change in the ground beneath. He watched as the machine paused briefly, its headlamps abruptly flicking on in the deepening dusk as if the machine were coming to life.

What Pete could not see was the tractor operator as that individual inserted a thumb drive into the dash-mounted computer, saved the most recent data and pocketed the results.

Turning abruptly out of pattern, the tractor angled unmistakably toward the data collection tent, lurched forward with a roar and belched black exhaust. Shifting into high gear, the operator inside the rumbling glass-walled cab reached underneath the instrument console and toggled a single switch, silencing the alarm that would normally have alerted the data collection tent that he had veered off course.

With the flip of a second switch, the tractor operator smiled a grim smile, knowing that he had now eliminated the possibility of remote control override. The third switch he flipped shorted out the tractor's computer, permanently erasing the data and preventing any forensic efforts to recover it. By placing the British Museum's most expensive and potentially most revolutionary piece of archaeological equipment exclusively under his control, the operator now possessed the sole copy of the vital GPR data that the equipment had collected.

Several hundred meters away, between the data tent and the lumbering GPR tractor, a second research assistant from UCL was moving quickly from spot to spot across the flat terrain. Reading the coordinates being fed into her handheld device, Brooke Burnside meticulously placed marker stakes with orange flags at the location of promising hits that the GPR had detected, hammering them into place with a solid rubber mallet.

"Send me the next one, Pete," Brooke called over her handheld radio.

Pete glanced at the screen.

"Fifty one point six seven eight degrees North, one point eight four six West," Pete responded. "How many flags do you have left?"

"Three," Brooke answered back. "You've kept me busy all afternoon. I've been running out here for hours. My knee aches."

"It's good for you," Pete replied, ignoring her complaint. "Good exercise. You will look better in that wedding dress. Now let's focus. We only have three targets left to mark to complete this quadrant. I think the Professor's on the way back now. I just noticed that he changed course."

"Did the equipment alert you?"

"No, strictly visual. I just happened to look up and see him turn."

"Good then," Brooke said into the radio. She cocked her head to one side, looking past the bill of her cap toward the setting sun. "It's getting dark, and I have big plans for tonight. I'm meeting his parents."

"Big plans, whatever," Pete joked. "If you hurry, perhaps you can signal Professor Haddad and catch a ride on the tractor and save yourself a hike back."

"Ewww, disgusting! I don't know about that," she squealed into the radio. "He's a bit too touchy-feely for me."

"Be careful what you say," Pete cautioned. "He could hear you."

A sudden insistent beeping sound in the background made it difficult for Brooke to hear anything else. Pete turned to the monitor so urgently sounding off.

"Pete, can you repeat what you said? What is that horrid sound?"

Pete stared at the screen with the three dimensional display screens. Alarms were sounding from the speakers. The display showed something beneath the ground, an arched, dark shadow surrounded by the luminescent green of a rectangular enclosure. It appeared to be a subterranean stone chamber. The beeping sound speeded up, more insistent, as if it were a warning. Pete hands flowed across the keys to record the GPS location of the images, before he responded to Brooke's call. This was the break they had been waiting for. He had to act immediately.

"Brooke, can you see the tractor?"

8

"Yes, it's headed directly toward me now."

"See if you can signal the Professor. I am trying to maintain a connection, but I'm having some issues. Haddad has definitely discovered something there, we want to make sure it gets marked."

As Pete spoke, the data transmission from the GPR tractor was interrupted. The monitor screen went dark. Doing a quick systems check, Pete could found no obvious errors, only a lack of signal.

Brooke glanced west, noting that the sun was minutes from setting. Hearing the roar grow closer, she gripped the radio tighter, turning toward the GPR tractor. She was surprised at how quickly the machine had closed the distance.

The tractor advanced rapidly, no longer lumbering across the field. Its heavy metal baseplates flew over the grass tops, motor churning in overdrive. Smoke from the upright diesel exhaust belched skyward. Suddenly Brooke was afraid. She could not explain why, but she knew she needed to run.

Turning toward the data collection tent, Brooke ran as fast as she could, bringing the radio to her mouth to hail Pete again. The grass was damp with evening dew. With twilight deepening, visibility was difficult. Her first panicked steps found no traction.

Looking over her right shoulder, Brooke could see flickering flames shooting from the diesel exhaust amid a constant column of smoke. The tractor was bearing down on her faster than, outpacing the questions that raced through her mind.

"What the hell happened?" she frantically wondered. *"Did the Professor fall asleep at the wheel, or has he taken ill? Did he not see me in the twilight? Did the tractor malfunction in some way?"*

Brooke dodged right, making for the closest paved road. She knew there was a ditch that she would have to jump, but hopefully that would stop the tractor. She stumbled, dropping her radio, but made no attempt to retrieve it as she scrambled back to her feet.

The intense rumbling sound, the smoke and flames from the tractor's exhaust combined to make it seem as if she were being pursued by some ancient dragon, stirred from eons of slumber and now released upon the Salisbury Plain. Had that truly been the case, she would have felt no less terror than she felt at that very moment.

Suddenly Brooke saw her shadow leap long and dark ahead of her, a grim spectre of things to come. Bright lights surrounded her like the glare of a landing airplane. She had hoped for a miracle, but was rewarded with a nightmare. Hearing the heavy, wide tractor at her heels, the sound of field grass crushing beneath the heavy tires, she dodged left and right in an attempt to elude the persistent machine.

Looking over her shoulder, Brooke saw her own terrified reflection in the glass cockpit surrounding the steering cabin of the radar tractor. The glare from her reflected image prevented her from seeing the operator inside. Her face contorted in horror as she screamed. The monstrous tractor bashed into her, knocking her to her knees, pushing her backwards across the wet grass. She attempted to grab something, anything along the smooth front of the machine, but she found no solid handhold. Her right boot caught beneath the front of the radar plates and the ground. She pulled out her stake mallet and began to beat on the front grill of the tractor out of sheer fear and frustration. She did not have the strength or the flexibility to free her foot.

Brooke held hope that she might yet attract his attention through this banging noise if nothing else.

After several solid whacks against the metal grill, Brooke lost her grip on the mallet. Pain shot through her ankle as it dragged across the rough ground and was pulled beneath the machine. The sensation of fire and of crunching bone became excruciating as her foot was crushed, her screams lost between belches of the GPR tractor's grumbling motor.

Realizing that there would be little left to identify her if this continued, Brooke reached inside her jacket, pulling out her University ID lanyard as she bounced along the ground. She reached toward the tractor, stuffing the ID into the grill near the radiator. As her leg slipped further beneath the GPR plates, she let out the most intense scream yet.

Suddenly Brooke no longer had the strength to fight. The tractor rolled up and over her body, a ton of GPR plates grinding her into the ancient Salisbury plain, leaving little record of her life. A streak of lifeless bones and bloodstains smeared the tractor's heavy radar plates, ending her personal story on the same field of history she had dedicated herself to investigate.

Hearing a disturbance, Pete rolled his chair in reverse, looking up to see several geese honking as they took flight, formed into a ragged V-formation, and began to wing their way south toward France. Pete put the binoculars aside, unable to see through the darkness, or the gathering mist.

The GPR tractor had switched on a bank of overhead driving lights as it approached Brooke's position. Now the machine had turned, proceeding directly toward the data collection tent. Pete quickly scanned the horizon for Brooke but could not see her anywhere. He assumed the glare was to blame.

Although no one answered the radio, but it made sense that the Professor had swung around and picked Brooke up for the ride back to the tent. Pete wanted to believe that everything was just fine.

His gut told him something different. He solemnly picked up the radio from its charging cradle.

"Brooke, this is Pete, come in," his voice intoned, no longer expecting a response.

There was no response, only crackling silence.

"Professor, this is Pete. Do you read me?"

The tractor steadily closed the gap, taking dead aim at the data collection tent.

Pete looked past his twisted feet to the wheels of his chair, making sure they were free of entanglements should he decide to make a run for it. At the same time, he pounded the button to launch the observation drone waiting in front of him, just outside the tent. With a whir of blades and a rushing breeze the drone shot skyward, the camera and running lights flickering to life on yet another screen. The drone's camera, still set on infrared, transmitted a green glow that reflected circular patterns across the surface of Pete's glasses.

Pete looked across the field toward the tractor again, then glanced down at the monitor. The drone camera transmitted a field of brilliant illumination, the shimmering heat signature of the tractor exhaust and the pale outline of a live body inside the windowed cab.

Sprawled across the screen were horrific infrared camera images of the still-warm flesh and bones of a human being smeared along a track 8 to 10 meters long. The bones were not deep, lying just beneath the surface of the ground. A quick glance at the elongated skeletal image revealed a peculiar feature of one

11

leg, the reflective metal of an artificial knee. Pete knew that Brooke had an artificial knee on her left leg, the result of having served in Afghanistan with the British Armed Forces.

Looking up, Pete could see the lights of the tractor shining in his face not fifty feet away. Shifting his motorized chair into reverse, Pete collided with a tent pole. Before he could pull turn, the GPR tractor ran full tilt into the tent, crushing the table full of computers and monitors, pinning him beneath.

The tabletop held strong, propped two feet above the ground by sturdy equipment cases. Pete laughed, thinking that the cases had saved him. The tractor stopped directly over top of him, rear wheels digging into the ground, unable to proceed further. Pete's laughter turned sour when the case to the left of him emitted a cracking noise, no match for the weight of the radar plates. Within seconds, the table was pressed against Pete's face.

For a moment, he was able to breathe. Realizing his paralyzed feet were trapped, Pete stretched his hand down, trying desperately to yank his legs free. The clutter of crushed equipment at the base of his overturned wheelchair made it impossible for him to escape.

Straining to take his next breath, Pete found that impossible as well. Slowly, surely, the table flattened him into the ground as the radar tractor weighted it down.

With blackness flooding his senses, Pete's last awareness was the high-pitched, maniacal sound of the Professor's laughter.

Chapter 2

"Sandra, are you down there in the dark?"

Startled, Sandra Culver turned round, her eyes wide with fear. The unexpected brightness of the kitchen lights nearly blinded her.

Spotting her coffee cup across the counter, she shunned the comfort of her father-in-law's arms.

"I heard a noise," he explained. "I didn't see a light on. I didn't mean to scare you."

"I'm not scared," she lied. "I just couldn't sleep."

Sandra began to pace the floor as she waited for Jack to ask the question she dreaded the most.

"Have you heard any news about Martin?"

There it was. Her day was off to its usual start. Determined not to cry this time, Sandra breathed deep, tried to find her center. Now was no time for an argument.

"No, I haven't," she said quietly. "At this point I don't know if I will hear anything."

Jack tried again to console Sandra, reaching for her again.

"It's just so hard," Sandra confessed, stepping back from him. "I don't know if I'm doing the right thing."

She leaned against the kitchen island, taking her coffee cup in one hand, while gripping the edge of the counter with the other, like a sinner fighting altar call in a southern church.

"I just don't know *when* this will get better."

Jack leaned against the counter, then turned toward her.

"It won't get better until you hear something one way or the other. Maybe I should stay," he said in a lower voice. "Maybe it's not good timing."

"The only reason to wait would be if you thought they might find him. Am I wrong to maintain hope this long?"

Jack hesitated.

"I don't think you are wrong, Sandra, but think about Eric and Elizabeth. We've promised them this trip. Even if Martin is found, they probably don't want to be sitting around here."

"Let's stick with our plan. You have decided what to do about the International Antiquities Foundation, and we both know the kids deserve a break. Now that the legal documents are ready to complete, it will take you one week, two weeks, max. You take care of business here, then come to San Jose for a break."

Sensing Sandra was finally hearing him, Jack continued.

"When you are ready, you can come back to Virginia, make plans for a place to live. I will bring the children when you're ready. Summer is over, so staying here means they have to be registered in school ASAP."

Jack hoped his words had not been too harsh. That was his tendency, to talk as if he were still giving orders to a Navy crew.

"You're sure the school in Costa Rica has room for them?"

"Last night I talked to my friend Vicky. She is the principal," Jack assured her. "She is looking forward to enrolling them."

Sandra poured her cold coffee into the kitchen sink.

"Jack, you talk as if Martin is gone forever, like it's time for me to move on," she said quietly. "Is that what you believe?"

"You're going to have to let Martin go," Jack said. "He's my son. I would know if he survived. No one survives this long at sea."

"Well, he may be your son, Jack, but he's my husband. In my heart, I'm not so sure it's over."

"Sandra, you've lost a lot. I know it hasn't been easy. But you need to be able to handle things on your own, to be decisive, to move ahead."

They both looked up the wall clock as they heard the twins descending the hallway stairs.

"Will you be okay alone?" Jack asked, changing the subject. "Do you feel safer now?"

"After what happened at the house and the IAF, I'm still looking for a bomber behind every bush," she admitted.

"You're in a gated condo community now, Sandra. You have a good security system, a 24 hour guard at the gate. It would be hard for anyone to get to you in here."

Sandra tugged her dark blazer more tightly across her body. "That doesn't make me feel any better. I don't really feel safe anywhere, not even here. I feel like a sitting duck, just waiting for something to happen."

"You live less than two miles from work. You are only minutes from the IAF office," Jack continued. "Once you are there, you have guards and security. You will be fine."

Sandra stared at the counter, rubbing at some perceived defect in the surface.

"It's time for us to leave," Jack said quietly, gulping down the last of his coffee. "We can't be late for our flight."

Sandra did not respond.

"I'll take the twins to the car," Jack said. "I already loaded their bags."

He waited another moment.

"Sandra, if we miss our flight to Miami, we will never make San Jose by tonight."

Jack hesitated before pressing on.

"I can stay, or should I just get a cab?"

"No, I'm ready," Sandra agreed, suddenly coming to life. "Let me get my keys."

Chapter 3

The Pearl Islands
Pacific Coast of Panama

At the very limit of his picture-postcard world, the sun-burnt shell of a man knelt below a majestic, sweeping palm tree, resting his hands on weak, emaciated thighs. Shucking away a feverish chill, the man closed his eyes, praying as slight waves pushed into the sheltered cove, rocking him to the point of slumber. Reciting the Lord's Prayer, the man committed himself once again to his maker.

The warm water brushed gently against his legs, lapping away pure white sand from beneath him. The flowing brine both stung and soothed his festering mosquito bites. Between the discomfort of a rumbling stomach and his throbbing head, the man finished praying. Before opening his eyes, he calculated his odds of living to tell his story. He didn't need odds to know that his days were numbered.

Remembering why he had knelt down, the man concentrated on the task at hand. Forcing trembling, stick-thin fingers to peel layers of salt-encrusted cloth from his swollen, injured hand, the man frowned intently. His sunburned face, shaded by long, sun-bleached hair, scowled from beneath a full and ragged beard.

Pale wrinkled skin appeared, revealed a strip at a time, sickly white and shriveled in contrast to his dark, leathery forearm. He continued unwrapping the improvised dressing until his entire hand was exposed, revealing the wound at its center. He cringed to see the result of his methodical labor.

Rotating the hand from side to side, the man inspected the wound. His palm had grown hot and red, despite daily re-bandaging and frequent seawater soaks. Squinting, he brought his hand close and sniffed, bending stiff, purple fingers one at a time. Finding little control over his middle and ring fingers, the man realized that he felt a new tingling numbness from his wrist toward his fingertips. Stabbing pains jolted from his fingers to the elbow with every slight movement. He lowered his injured hand into the warm, salty water.

Rubbing his beard with the back of his uninjured hand, the man peered toward the sky, then slowly lowered his gaze.

16

How he had reached the shores of this deserted island had been a mystery from day one. The frustration of not knowing how he had come to be in this place weighed him down, draining him as certainly as the constant fever that gripped his body.

Ruined remnants of his memory wafted about aimlessly, floating like cobwebs guarding the doorway to some ancient hidden chamber. Each time he tried a little more memory returned, only to be drowned out by pounding headaches that always started in his ears.

He knew he had been shot in the hand, but not who shot him, or why he carried an empty .45 caliber pistol.

He remembered an explosion that seemed as though it would rip the world apart, deafening all sound with the emptiness that it brought, but not how long ago it had happened.

He remembered falling from the sky but not how he had come to be in the air in the first place.

He could recall struggling in the water but not how he made it to the beach.

He had no clear memory of his family, only that they had been mercilessly killed to exact revenge on him.

Names floated through his mind like street signs illuminated ever so briefly by car headlamps. Even his own name eluded him, skittering just out of reach like an elusive insect hiding from the light. He had decided that the name on the engraved pen he found clipped inside his watch band would do as well as any. Culver, the pen whispered in neat engraved letters.

Culver was a name, at least. Better than the name he felt he deserved. Better than killer, or murderer, which is how he had come to see himself since waking up on this island. A place of tropical beauty framed in elements of human tragedy, of nature at its best and worst, played out daily on a tiny circular stage surrounded by the endless ocean.

Along with an intense desire to survive, Culver maintained a strong sense of conscience. The only court of law that existed on this island, his conscience had evaluated his case, ruling against him in a clear decision. The evidence at hand conclusively proved him to be a ruthless killer. The undisputable, grisly proof of his murderous actions lay not 50 yards from where he knelt in the sand.

Culver had no means of identifying the remains, or even stating with certainty what had taken place. It seemed obvious, for reasons he could not clearly state, that his being stranded on this tropical island was directly connected with the body.

Shivering away another chill, Culver rinsed the bandage in the salty waves and began re-wrapping the cloth, moving slowly, methodically. After tying off the dressing he stood to his feet, with concentrated effort. The pain in his legs, the sight of his hand injury, the loneliness combined to overwhelm his emotions. For a brief moment, he voiced a dry, tearless crying sound, then immediately stopped.

A vibration beneath his feet halted him in his tracks.

He looked toward the thick tropical foliage and palm trees that loomed high along the entire length of the small semi-circular beach behind him. The island was too small to be actively volcanic. Early on, he had explored every square inch. He would know.

Familiar movement at the base of the nearest live palm tree attracted Culver's attention, though that had not been the source of the tremor. Through gritty, sunburned eyelids he watched hordes of hermit crabs begin their daily trek toward their gruesome feast.

Looking like an undulating shell carpet that flowed across the sand, the crabs appeared simultaneously from beneath nearby rotting palm-leaf heaps. Their busy morbid scrabbling left little doubt as to their presence, or to the presence of the rotting half-carcass that attracted them. Culver had tried to bury what was left of the body, to cover the stench if nothing else, but each time he made the effort the crabs and the wind had undone his work, re-exposing the ghastly secret for the world to see. Now his energy for such extra activity was depleted.

The sound of their shell-clicking march failed to reach Culver's ears, although watching the crabs work reminded Martin that he too was hungry. Licking his sun-chapped lips with a parched tongue, Culver felt weak. He knew he had to continue to make an effort to eat.

Leaning against a palm trunk, Culver scooped a handful of the slow moving crabs into a smoke-smudged metal coffee can. Returning to his fire, such as it was, Culver placed the container directly on top of the smoldering embers. He reverently emptied his last few ounces of rainwater from a smaller, rusted food tin into the coffee can, scarcely enough fresh water left to top the hermit crab shells. One by one the half-coconut shells comprising his rain gathering system either had cracked, or had become too infested with mosquito larvae to drink. Desperate for protein, he had resorted to drinking those as well.

Culver had enough dry wood left to bring a fire to life. Leaning close to the ground, he forced a weak stream of breath across the coals, managing at last to coax a flame to life. He sweated, improbably shivering in front of the small fire, watching until the water began to lightly boil. Futile clinking against the inside of the coffee can fell on deaf ears, slowing perceptibly before ceasing altogether. Culver pounded the crabs shells open with a charred wooden stick, allowing the hot water to reach the meat deeper inside.

Shielding his eyes against the sun, Culver struggled to his feet once more while he waited for his peculiar stew to boil, to distance himself from the choking smoke. Feeling a familiar, dizzying wave of weakness push past him like a stiff breeze, Culver attempted to remain steady. He shuffled slowly across the hot sand to a narrow strip of shade beside the rust-streaked Navy barge looming high above. His bare feet absorbed the welcome comfort and coolness he found there. Leaning heavily against the rough metal surface between patches of dead barnacles, Culver stretched his arms over his head, trying to keep his stiff joints limber.

Sitting high above the waterline in a grove of palm trees, the hulking gray military barge had apparently been pushed by great waves or high winds to its present location. Regardless of how it got there, the barge had become the center of Culver's daily life. He felt linked to it. The sun baked deck twenty feet above him was miserably hot during the day, but provided welcome warmth at night, as long as he could rally the energy to make the climb. The few items he had managed to scrounge to keep life and limb together had come from inside the pilot house of the barge - the saw blade, the empty cans, the matches for his initial fire. The webbed cargo straps that he found on the work deck made the basis for two rudimentary hammocks. The one closest to the beach had collapsed, but he still used the one up top at night.

Grateful for the shelter the barge provided, sensing that it was integral to his survival, Culver had not ventured out of view of it since waking up on this island, not even once.

Their stories were parallels, in a sense. There was no explanation as to how either of them had come to be in this place, yet here they both were. For all Culver knew, he and the barge had washed up in the same ferocious storm.

Moving cautiously, Culver sat down, keeping his eyes fixed on the far horizon. No longer able to remember just how many days he had followed the same routine - watch the sky, scan the horizon, scrounge a meal - he stared at the distant line where incredibly blue sky met intensely green sea, imagining that he saw a vessel, any vessel. All he saw were fork-tailed frigate birds cruising dark and smooth like slender black kites, high above the waves. Aiming his empty pistol at each one, he imagined what they might taste like roasted over his fire. Closing his eyes, he could smell the changing sea breeze, the same as every afternoon.

The sense he lacked was hearing. He heard neither waves, nor sea-birds, nor wind brushing through the palms. Nothing interrupted the overpowering, surrounding silence except his own pounding heartbeat whenever he tried to sleep. His rising pulse always preceded his being startled wide awake by the frightening sensation of falling backwards, weightless and uncontrolled.

The bright disc of the sun had peaked, arching steadily towards the west as dark clouds gathered on the opposite horizon. Nothing new caught Culver's attention, the same idyllic view, day after day. No ships or planes, no vessels.

Sitting cross-legged in the sand, Culver returned to his meager, uninviting stew. He removed his improvised stew pot from the fire using a bent palm spine for tongs. As he leaned forward, Culver's eyes blurred. For a moment, he felt as though he might pass out. He reached for the ground to steady himself, setting down the wavering, steaming can so as not to spill it.

Once more sensing vibration through the sand, Culver looked up, peering out past the reef and over the waves. The heavy afternoon air throbbed in a manner totally distinct from the familiar shoreline wave pattern. It pulsed through the sand, increased in intensity, alerted him to a change. Something was happening, a rhythm different from the other days. He felt it, but he could not hear it.

He had not sighted the first boat or plane in the weeks since washing up on this remote beach, yet he had not lost hope. Perhaps it was a plane, perhaps not. The real question was, would the vibration bring a rescue, or would it bring retribution for the person Culver was convinced he had murdered.

The unusual, thudding vibration ceased as a hot tremor passed through Culver's body, fading into racking chills. He scanned the horizon, then turned away from the deepening green of the ocean. His pervading thought was to get somewhere safe, to hide.

Carefully collecting his can of hermit crab stew, Culver shielded it from the view of anyone who might be looking and stumbled toward the barge's hull ladder.

With all the effort he could muster, Culver began to climb the welded u-shaped rungs one step at a time. Whatever was coming, he wanted to be as high above the beach as possible.

Culver's strength ran out sooner than usual. He stopped several rungs above ground level to rest. Rust and barnacles bit into his feet and hands. His injured hand was less cooperative, feeling weak and club-like inside the damp, salty bandage.

Fearing that he might slip and spill his precious meal, Culver paused, hooking his arm through the rusty rung facing him. He leaned back and tipped the can up, gulping down the barely cooked broth, ignoring the foul odor, pausing to roll bits of crab flesh around in his mouth as one would a great delicacy. The can trembled in his failing grip, his sun-bleached beard straining the drips that missed his mouth completely. He hated the peculiar, bitter taste, but drank it down all the same, spitting out inedible bits of shell.

Culver realized that neither his gathering weakness nor his trembling hands were a good sign. Desperate to get to higher ground, he dropped the can to the sand and stubbornly struggled on, convinced trouble was headed his way. He had no basis for paranoia other than the human carcass lying on the beach, and the haunting thought that someone, as some point, would surely demand an explanation for what had transpired. Such an explanation he knew he could not provide.

Culver focused every remaining ounce of energy to advance the last few steps, struggling to make it to the hot, high deck, his place of safety. There was no food up on the deck. All the overhanging coconuts he had been able to reach were long gone, painstakingly sawed in half to remove the juice and the meat.

Stooping beneath the overhanging palm branches, Culver crossed the deck and made it to the tattered hammock he had fashioned alongside the pilot house. He tentatively sat down before leaning back. Facing the ocean, he hoped he would yet see a vessel or a plane. He could still sense a unique vibration in the air, under his feet and through the metal deck. Reached up to touch the glass window of the pilot house with his good hand, his fingers sensed the vibration there as well.

Leaning against the pilot house bulkhead was the rusty saw blade Culver had found, wedged into a two foot long palm spine for a handle. By binding it with leather strips from his own belt, he had created a sort of sword, useful for defense as well as carpentry. Before his energy faded, Culver had practiced self-defense moves every day, as shown in the Self Defense Manual he had found aboard the barge.

Culver reached for the blade with his bandaged hand. Feeling heavier and hotter with every movement, Culver was unable to force his hand to grasp the tool. He turned to reach the saw with his good hand. The dull blade had served him well, cutting open coconuts, trimming straps for his hammock, cutting firewood.

Looking to the wall where he scratched marks to track the days, Culver made another mark, then prayed to live to carve the next one. He had no idea which day of the week it actually was, often forgetting to mark the count chart.

Feeling flushed, Culver closed his eyes and noticed his good hand now pulsing with fever as he gripped the sawblade a little tighter. Though dull, perhaps the blade might yet save his life, or his arm, if nothing else. He knew what he had to do if his wounded hand continued to deteriorate. In preparation, he looped what was left of his belt around the wrist of his bandaged hand and waited.

If the blade would cut coconut shells, bones should not be too much different. He had no experience in such things, but held onto the blade, should it become necessary, should the unthinkable somehow become the inevitable.

22

It was at that moment that a hovering, whirring shadow slowly passed over the deck of the barge, whipping away the palm fronds into a tornadic frenzy. Culver looked up in an effort to see what the disturbance was, to defend himself if necessary. He climbed out of the hammock but managed only two stumbling, ragged steps before collapsing to the hot metal deck of the barge.

Chapter 4

International Antiquities Foundation
Norfolk, VA

Behind too-dark sunglasses, Sandra Culver wheeled the Range Rover through crowded parking lot into her designated space, nearly colliding with the dawdling vehicle ahead of her. Throwing the transmission into park as her phone rang yet again, Sandra released a heavy sigh.   She glanced up at the three story headquarters of the International Antiquities Foundation. Noticing heavy, dark clouds framing the building, Sandra glanced down at her phone, shaking her head.

Three incoming calls from the IAF office since leaving Jack and her twins at the Norfolk Airport, the first two calls coming before she had even left the parking garage. Dry-eyed now, Sandra slipped the phone into the pocket of her blazer jacket without answering, pausing to check her makeup in the visor mirror. She took note of the slow moving vehicle she had passed still stalking a parking space. The neatly lettered sign in front of her, its yellow border reflected in the jet-black finish of her vehicle, read, "Sandra Culver, President, IAF".

"Not for long," she thought, shutting off the engine.

Taking in slower, deeper breaths, Sandra focused, looked one last time into the rearview mirror, then closed her eyes. She was determined to shake off the trapped, numb feeling that had dogged her daily since Martin's disappearance, the near-catatonic state that had held her captive for weeks.

The time for action had long since passed, she reminded herself. Time to sign the missing person declaration, deal with Martin's insurance, time to move on. It was time to get back to business, to re-join the world. Most importantly, it was time to decide the fate of the IAF and her part in it. Forced to face matters on her own, Sandra had motivated herself to draft a lengthy to-do list, things that she could no longer put off. Her lawyer had drawn the papers for everything she had planned. By finishing her within the week, Sandra could join her twins at Jack's condo in Costa Rica worry-free.

Standing beside the open door of the Range Rover, Sandra smoothed her skirt before gathering her leather briefcase and

24

phone, Sandra checked the skies, then stretched to search the back seat for an umbrella. Failing to find one, she locked her SUV and walked briskly toward the entrance of IAF headquarters building, hoping to beat the rain. There was no sign of the vehicle she had followed into the employee parking area.

Sandra's phone rang again. She hurried up the steps, using peripheral vision to dodge the newly installed Vehicle Mitigation System. Made up of heavy concrete barriers and planters, the VMS was intended to keep potential bombers far from the IAF building. Sandra thought they were ugly.

Scrolling down her messages, Sandra did not notice as the armed security guard stepped from behind the first brick column. In her distracted haste, Sandra nearly collided with the crew-cut, uniformed woman, the both of them caught quite off-guard.

"Excuse me!" the female sentry barked, stepping to one side. "Good morning!"

"Good *morning*!" said Sandra sourly as she struggled to tug the front door open. The guard grunted as she watched Sandra enter the foyer of the building. Remaining outside, the guard cupped her hands in front of her face, lighting the cigarette she had tucked into one corner of her scowling mouth.

Due to their abrupt near-collision, neither Sandra nor the guard noticed the vehicle on the back row in the very full parking lot. The driver sat, watching, methodically cleaning a small set of binoculars.

"Mrs. Culver, I have a call for you," Amanda called out over the reception desk as soon as Sandra entered the lobby.

"Can't they wait 'til I get in the door?" Sandra thought. Her first day back at the office was off and running.

"He says he's calling international long-distance."

"Good morning, Amanda. Get his name and ask if he doesn't mind holding a sec," Sandra said as she glanced at the sweeping staircase, then punched the elevator button repeatedly. "Give me time to get upstairs, ok?"

Sandra's mind began to race to keep pace with the morning. She hoped the double espresso she downed at airport would kick in soon. It was at that moment that she noticed Amanda's low-cut dress.

"Amanda," Sandra called out. "Call our security firm. Have that security guard replaced. She never knew I was there until the last minute. And tell them to send a non-smoker this time."

"Yes, Mrs. Culver."

"And Amanda dear, put on a sweater, hmm? You'll catch your death."

"Mrs. Culver," a research assistant called out from the balcony overhead. "I have the report on the British Museum's latest statement on the Parthenon Marbles."

"I have new details on the UNESCO conference," another staffer aide called from the second floor. "The topic was ISIS trade in Syrian antiquities," he continued. "The journals want a response from the IAF."

A third aide stopped in front of her with a stack of reports.

"These need your approval to be submitted," the aide requested. "These are the grant vouchers for Middle East travel teams to secure the Syrian at-risk sites."

"The United Nations committee on repatriated antiquities wants to know if we will send a representative to their investigative panel," another assistant shouted.

"Please, it sounds like the floor of the New York Stock Exchange in here," Sandra responded, managing to not sound as exasperated as she felt. "Give me ten minutes to get settled, people! We will meet in the library for updates. I have one hour, no more. Pass the word to the others."

"Ten minutes, library, got it," the first research aide replied.

Sandra turned away from the line of staff beginning to form in her wake just as the elevator doors slid open. Rushing inside, she waited for the door to close, looked down, then broke into an awkward high-heeled run as soon as the elevator door re-opened. Her heels tapped a rhythmic staccato across the marble floor.

An incessant electronic long double-beep tone repeatedly pierced the silence of Sandra's stylish office, echoing out into the hallway as soon as she opened her door. The sound of the phone was deeply irritating by the fourth ring.

"Call on line two for Mrs. Culver," Amanda chimed over the intercom.

"I've got it!" Sandra muttered.

She flipped on the light and dropped her briefcase to the floor. Through the long window, a threatening sky could be seen pushing across the Chesapeake Bay, dark clouds riding low and reflecting the light from inside the office against the glass window like a mirror. Sandra looked at the sky, touched the golden cross pendant she wore, praying that her children's flight to Costa Rica with Jack would take off safely and as planned.

Glimpsing her own face reflected in the window glass, Sandra winced. She had hoped that she might appear more rested. Tensing her jaw, Sandra reached for the slim black phone blinking on the far side of her desk.

"Sandra Culver speaking, may I help you?"

The voice at the other end of the line hesitated.

"Good morning Mrs. Culver, may I speak to Mr. Martin Culver?"

Sandra paused to evaluate the caller's thick British accent.

"No, I'm sorry, he is not available."

"Very well then. Is Mr. Chartwell at hand? I'm calling international long distance. It is urgent that I speak to him, or to Mr. Culver."

"No, I'm very sorry. I don't expect Mr. Chartwell until later in the week. May anyone else help you?"

"No, that's fine. I'll call back or you can tell him I will see him at the lecture I'm presenting at the British Museum in London. Thanks so much, luv."

"I'm not your ..." Sandra began, realizing she was talking to no one. The phone caller had abruptly terminated the call. Sandra stared at the phone in frustration, dropping it roughly into the charging cradle.

Sandra realized she was not alone. She turned to see Cita Tate leaning against the frame of her office door.

"Was that your favorite gentleman caller?" Cita asked, allowing a slight smile to cross her face.

"Yes, it sounded like that same chap," Sandra muttered, standing up. "The one with the British accent. Quit smiling, Cita, it's not funny. He just keeps calling, won't leave his name. He has an annoying voice, like some dull, braying donkey."

"Any idea who he is?"

"I still think it might be the same man from the Museum Conference in New York last week, the one who kept following me around in his wheelchair."

"I remember you talking about him," Cita replied. "You said he creeped you out, right?"

"He did!" Sandra complained, grasping her empty coffee cup between tensed fingers. "My intuition rarely leads me astray. This person raised my hackles every interaction I had with him. The tallest person I have ever seen in a wheelchair. I'll bet if he could stand he would be close to 7 feet tall. He had this funny little square beard that bobbed when he talked."

"That's too bad to have that happen on your first official IAF outing in weeks. What rubbed you the wrong way about him?"

"One, he never identified himself, just kept handing me folders, trying to get me to read his articles, saying they were so important. Every time I turned a corner there he was again."

"I think I know his name," Cita said, smoothing her skirt to take a seat. She leaned forward as if guarding a precious secret. "We received a box of his publications in the mail this morning," Cita said in a hushed voice. "He is on staff at the British Museum of London and is a full professor at UCL. His book jacket photo shows him in a wheelchair, so it has to be the same guy."

"UCL?"

"University College of London. They offer a very extensive listing of majors, including Archaeology, Physics, Astronomy. By the way, Rebekah loves Haddad's articles. She said she can't wait to read them."

Sandra looked at Cita quizzically.

"Makes sense, since they are written on her favorite topic," Cita added.

"Not Stonehenge?" Sandra asked, her eyes a notch wider as she looked up. "Please tell me it's not more material on Stonehenge."

"You guessed it," Cita laughed.

"That girl just can't seem to get enough of Stonehenge," Sandra commented. "It's an obsession with her."

"Speaking of Rebekah, I see she is wearing her new tough-girl jacket today."

"An entire new *outfit*," Sandra complained. "And did you see that tiny mini-skirt? At least she's wearing it with tights. You would not believe what she spent on it. I've never spent that much on *five* outfits."

"Real leather *is* expensive," Cita remarked, standing to her feet. She leaned out into the hall to make sure no one was approaching. "Where did she shop?"

"The Harley store!" Sandra responded in complete exasperation. "It's part of her new persona. No more nice girl look for Rebekah, I am afraid."

"How is she doing?" Cita asked, raising her eyebrows. "Overall."

"Rebekah seems to be doing well. She reached the age to access her trust fund, bought a little red Mini Cooper. She stays out too late to suit me, though. I worry about who she is hanging out with. She has taken up cooking as a hobby, although the way she goes about it you would think she is a professionally-trained chef, has to have all the right utensils and equipment. And you would not believe how much she has spent on gourmet ingredients! She has completely taken over my kitchen at the condo."

"What about that haircut? That's a bold step for her, isn't it?"

"Oh yes, very much so. Had her hair cut in an emo wedge, dark red highlights, does the whole black eyeliner thing when she goes out. She spends a lot of time writing dark poetry whenever she is home."

"But think of all she's been through," Cita responded. "You might understand her wanting to look a little more…what is the word…mature?"

"Tough is the word Jack used, just before he left for Costa Rica. I don't know what else to call it. Jack told her she looks like a punk rocker, that she is the toughest governess he has ever seen. She seemed to like that, to be labelled as tough."

"What do you think, Sandra? Has Rebekah changed that much?"

Sandra thought for a minute.

"After what she went through at Chichenitza, I am surprised she speaks at all, so for her to come to life like she has is a real miracle. I wish I could do as well."

"Self-expression is said to be the opposite of depression," Cita commented. "I am glad she feels better. So does Rebekah have a boyfriend, is that why she's out so much at night?"

"You know, I think it's too early in the day for all this heavy conversation," Sandra remarked, shaking her head and avoiding the topic at the same time. "I need wine to go into that one, but that's for later. Right now I need some coffee," she said, looking at her watch. "Then we need to get to the library for that meeting."

Cita leaned over Sandra's desk and punched up the receptionist.

"Amanda, be a love and bring Sandra a latte, two Stevia, light cream, ok? We'll be meeting in the research library."

"You got it," Amanda responded cheerily.

Sandra stared at Cita.

"You get a much better response out of Amanda than I do," she noted. "What's your secret?"

"Maybe barista is Amanda's calling more than receptionist," Cita laughed.

"Maybe you're right," Sandra commented. "As long as she is still here, can you please get her to dress for a professional office instead of the nightclub? That cleavage concerns me the most. At least before Chartwell returns?"

Cita smiled.

"He is back in town, I've heard."

"I wouldn't know," Sandra fussed. "He does not keep me informed of his goings and comings."

"You haven't met him before, have you?" Sandra asked.

"Oh, I know him," Cita answered. "We met in Peru. I make it a point to steer clear of him, and you should too."

Cita started to leave, then stopped mid-way through the office doorway.

"Sandra, have you heard anything about Martin, anything at all?"

"Not yet," Sandra said as she locked her office door. "I don't really feel like talking about it right now." She felt her back muscles stiffen as she drew in a deep, audible breath and released it. They took a few steps together before Sandra stopped.

"Cita, how would you feel about leading the IAF?"

30

"Are you talking permanently?" Cita asked, her eyes wide with surprise.

"Temporarily at first, to see if you want to go permanent," Sandra replied. She drew another calming breath.

"Cita, I am almost at the point of giving up. That's why I agreed to send the twins to Costa Rica with Jack. It's why I have papers drawn to donate the foundation to one of the Virginia universities. The IAF was Martin's idea, his dream, not mine. I barely feel capable of caring for myself. There is so much going on right now...Martin's gone, the IAF, I am a mess. It's just too much. I plan to be done with all this and be with my kids in Costa Rica by Christmas."

"Can I let you know, Sandra, you know, have some time to think about it?" Cita asked.

"Take all the time you need," Sandra said. "I am interviewing potential universities at the Archaeology Conference I am headed to this afternoon."

Cita and Sandra walked quietly down the corridor toward the research library. The building seemed to buzz with activity as staffers exited the elevator, rushing into the library with stacks of maps and reports.

The library was standing room only by the time Cita and Sandra entered. Sandra gave Rebekah a quick hug, then moved to the head of the long conference table. Conversations ceased as Sandra entered the room. Cita remained near the door, standing with Rebekah. The staffers were already seated, tablets and neat stacks of reports in front of them. Sandra paused, noticing a dark-haired young man slip through the library door and into the small space left between Cita and Rebekah.

"Good morning, everyone," Sandra began. "I appreciate your patience this morning. My thanks to all of you for your hard work in recent weeks and months."

Amanda pecked on the library's glass door, then half-danced her way through the crowded room, excusing herself along the way. Dramatically placing a very full coffee mug on the conference table in front of Sandra, Amanda smiled, then noticed where Sandra's eyes had landed. She backed away, clasping the neckline of her blouse together with one hand. Cita caught Sandra's glance and bit down on her lip to keep from smiling.

31

"Good morning again," Sandra continued. "I am glad to be back with you. Since we have so much going on, let's get right down to business. As you know, due to unforeseen events, I am Acting President of the International Antiquities Foundation. Cita has been doing a remarkable job keeping things running smoothly. The IAF is experiencing unprecedented growth in every area, from funding received to international recognition and awards to an uptick in requests for repatriation assistance."

"I appreciate those of you who have helped to keep things going in my absence. As many of you know, we have entered into a new partnership with Virginia universities that provides the IAF with research staff working on their archaeology degrees, while earning credit toward their studies. This partially explains the crowded conditions around here, and why we are bursting at the seams. I apologize for the tight working conditions. I appreciate your efforts to work together as a team."

Sandra paused, noticing that Rebekah and the young man were obviously avoiding eye contact. She tried to get Cita's attention, but Cita was focused on her phone.

"Before we begin, I would like to remind us all why we are here, our purpose if you will. As you all know, the International Antiquities Foundation motto is "Identification, Preservation, Repatriation". We identify artifacts and archaeological areas that need to be preserved, as well as work towards repatriation of artifacts to their source countries worldwide. Any questions?"

"To begin our meeting, I have a quote from Dr. Zahi Hawass, the Secretary-General of Egypt's Supreme Council of Antiquities that I'd like to read. I think we all know who he is in the world of archaeology."

"In 2006, at the Field Museum in Chicago, Dr. Hawass was present at the opening of the year-long USA exhibit of the treasures of King Tutankhamun, on loan from Egypt for the first time since 1977. At this event, Dr. Hawass became aware that the CEO of the show's corporate sponsor, the billion-dollar electricity giant Exelon, was an avid antiquities collector who kept the sarcophagus of an Egyptian mummy *in his office*."

Several hushed whispers could be heard around the room.

"Here is the quote from Dr. Hawass:

"No one has a right to have an artifact like that in their office or in their home. How can he (the CEO) sponsor an exhibit like King Tut and keep an artifact like this in his office? This man should surrender the sarcophagus to a museum, or send it back to Egypt. If he doesn't, there should be consequences."

"Sources?" the dark-haired young man standing by Rebekah asked.

"Your name, please?" Sandra inquired.

"Hamid," came the response.

"This quote was found in the book "Loot", by Sarah Waxman. It details the struggle that we address every day at the IAF. "

Hamid scribbled notes as Sandra spoke.

"Credentials?" he pressed further.

"Sarah Waxman is a former cultural correspondent with The New York Times and holds a master's degree in Middle East studies from Oxford University. Is there any problem?"

"No," Hamid responded. "Sorry to interrupt. I like this quote very much. I would like to investigate further. I hope to speak to Ms. Waxman. Thank you, sorry."

"Then that is your assignment, Hamid," Sandra instructed. "Please interview Ms. Waxman, research for our next reporting session what consequences Dr. Hawass is in favor of, and what consequences if any, are being meted out in these situations."

"Just Egypt, ma'am?" Hamid asked.

"For a start," Sandra responded.

"I want to go around the table to my right," she continued. "Let's have each of you tell us what you are working on and what resources you need to proceed. If we have not met, which will be most of you, please help me by telling me your name. I'm sorry I have not been here to meet everyone. Let's set aside formalities, so please call me Sandra."

"Good morning, Mrs. Culver, umm…Sandra. My name is Brianna. I have the reports of the ISIS destruction of the temples at Palmyra and Bosra as part of the Syrian conflict, including satellite image comparisons before and after."

"Thank you Brianna. Next?"

"Jason Parson, Sandra. I have the latest status of the Gold Museum of Peru repatriation project."

"Thank you, next?"

"Madison West. Sandra, I have an updated report on the status of the Greek complaint against the British Museum on the Elgin Marbles."

Sandra looked down as she carefully sipped her coffee.

"What a boring meeting this seems to be!" a man's voice boomed from the library doorway. Sandra looked up to see a familiar figure.

The man had made his way unannounced to the second floor. Sandra reminded herself to have another talk with Amanda.

"Is everyone quite all right?" he offered. "I've seen happier faces at a wake."

"Mr. Chartwell, welcome!" Sandra said. "We've been hoping to have you back. What time do we come to work, everyone?"

"Before Mrs. Culver!" the staffers intoned in unison.

Chartwell did not respond. He simply pointed his finger at her, smiled and leaned back against the wall near the door.

"For some it's whenever you damn well please, *apparently,*" she grumbled before turning back to the research team gathered in front of her. "Do not follow Mr. Chartwell's example, please. Mr. Chartwell, we'll discuss this after the meeting."

A hush came over the room.

"We have work to do," Sandra stated. "Let's continue. I have to leave in one hour for the Archaeology Conference in Northern Virginia."

Chapter 5

Approaching her office for the first time in weeks, CIA Director Carter Hall slowed her pace, drawing in as much air as her aching ribs would allow. Punching up an app on her phone, Hall hooked her cane over one arm and scanned the electronic door lock. She then passed her phone along the entire door frame bottom to top, across and then to the bottom. The device made no sound.

Noting the uniformed Marine eyeing her from the far end of the corridor, Hall positioned her body between the door and the new overhead corridor cameras. Shielding the keypad from view, Hall keyed in the new code she had been provided and opened the reinforced steel office door. Once inside, she closed it securely behind her.

Entering the darkened room, Hall stopped again, blinking back the light as the curtains opened and overhead lamps came on automatically. She was not surprised to find the conference table nearest her desk loaded with a two foot high mountain of situation reports. Only a government agency like the IRS could create more unnecessary paperwork than the CIA. At first glance it was difficult to discern if she had been out of the office a month or a year. She had a lot of catching up to do. While multiple crises clamoring for the CIA Director's attention were the norm, the world conflict most on Hall's mind was the one recently uncovered in Panama. No doubt her preliminary report was one of the ones cluttering up her table.

Scanning the expansive room from just inside the doorway, as was her habit, Hall was surprised to see a wall of newly installed television monitors opposite her desk that blinked on seconds after the lights. A barrage of video feeds immediately assaulted her senses. Worldwide news channels, security camera views of U.S Embassy compounds and international airports all competed at once for her attention. The recent election was the news story repeated most often. The news reports reminded her of "The Two Minutes Hate", the iconic propaganda broadcasts from Orwell's novel "1984", where enemies were crucified daily by the media.

Hall gritted her teeth, twirling the head of the cane round in her hand. She had not been apprised of these changes. As the CIA Director, she realized that she held no special privilege or expectation of privacy. Still, courtesy would indicate some warning of such functional alterations to her office.

Suppressing rising anger, Hall realized that her free hand had formed a tight, hard fist. She consciously tried to relax as she quickly surveyed the rest of the room. All of the furniture had been changed round except her desk and chair: the conference table, the sitting area, everything. The arrangement was obviously the work of a powerbroker, seating visitors to the office facing directly into the bright, reinforced glass window. A distant horizon view of the Washington monument was the most prominent visible landmark.

Whoever had access to her office for these changes would also have had time and opportunity to undertake other unwanted modifications as well, Hall reasoned, unauthorized changes such as audio bugs or video surveillance devices. Hall leaned her cane against a nearby chair and quickly punched up another app on her phone, checking the room for electronic listening devices from where she stood. Finding none, she let the device scan and select a frequency blocking tone, a low intensity sound designed to interfere with any undiscovered devices.

To have her office invaded like this was a slap in the face, a wake-up call made worse by it having happened while she was on mission-related medical leave. Suspicion formed in her mind as to how such a violation could have occurred, analyzing who could have authorized such changes. As quickly as the question entered her mind, Hall saw the person's image clearly in her mind. Homeland Security was no doubt involved. She knew all too well who approved their budget these days. Her old adversary had called her just an hour earlier, as she was on her way to Langley.

"I will be over later for your wrap-up on Panama," he had told her. "I hope your report will be ready. I may be a few hours yet. Will you still be there? We'll have a drink."

"No drink. I have some work to catch up on," Hall had abruptly replied, tapping her phone until the screen went dark, just as her driver had entered the Langley garage complex.

Hall gripped the wooden cane tightly in her left hand, locking the office door behind her. Her weak leg dragged across the thick carpet, reminding her to raise it higher. She stopped at the entrance her private, secret closet. Entering her long-standing personal code, she tugged open the heavy door built into the paneled wooden wall. The lights clicked on, sensing her presence. Smiling a crooked, one-sided smile, she realized that her midnight renovators had apparently not been able to crack this passcode. She wondered if they had found the secret room at all. Still, she ran the same electronic checks, to be certain.

The room appeared to be clean and intact. Once more Hall breathed deeply enough to feel her broken ribs click, taking in the scent of Australian redwood from her father's heavy wooden table. She ran her hand along its undulating, live edge, following the grain. This room was her secret place, her safe room, her retreat. She always thought of her father here, of the things he taught her about the tilted world of espionage. She wondered if the private contractor she had hired to build the room was still in business. She had personally paid him enough to retire, just for this one room.

Her clothes and mission essential equipment were all in their familiar spots. Sliding open the arsenal cabinet, she checked several of her weapons at random to make sure they were loaded, then slipped her second favorite pistol into the rear waistband of her slacks. The spot for her favorite pistol was vacant. Since returning from Panama, she had not replaced it. Hall limped out into her office and closed the closet door, watching until the lights went dim inside her sanctuary.

Reaching her desk, Hall sat down slowly, wincing in pain as her hip contacted the arm of her office chair. For a moment her head spun, reality hitting her like a truck. She was so far from being duty ready.

"The ISIS Crisis has grown to unmanageable proportions," the international news reporter excitedly pronounced, volume blaring on the main video feed monitor. "Two more ancient archaeological sites in Syria were destroyed by ISIS militants today, bringing the total to seven devastating demolitions this week alone. More portable treasures were trucked away for sale on the antiquities black market, while larger statues and building facades that could not be easily moved were destroyed with automatic weapons, jackhammers and even dynamite."

Hall grabbed a remote control from her desk, pushing buttons until she reduced the sound from deafening to merely annoying.

"Breaking news from the Associated Press reveals that as many as 400 ISIS militants have been dispatched to Europe armed with suicide bombs in the same manner of the recent Paris and Brussels attacks."

Of the dozen separate monitors that flickered simultaneously, Hall's attention was drawn, then riveted to one singularly sad screen. A UN archaeology expert knelt in the hot desert sand, facing the camera, his glasses slightly askew across his sunburned face. His pleading eyes seemed to no longer be capable of tears. As the masked ISIS combatant standing beside the prisoner drew back a curved, shining sword, Hall clicked the control to blacken the screen. She had no desire to witness yet another senseless beheading. There had already been too many.

Hall thought of the man still missing who was to have been her access to the world of archaeology and black market antiquities trade. She wondered if she would ever see him again.

Hall slid open the desk drawer to her left and removed a full bottle of Jameson's and a glass. At least her midnight renovators had left that in its place.

Hall's new desk phone rang, causing her to catch her breath. The tone was low and melodic, but grating to her ears. She immediately despised the sound, then hated it worse when she glanced at the caller ID.

"Go ahead," she responded, punching up the speakerphone while turning to look away from the phone.

"Do you like the changes to your office?" the voice on the line asked, smug, almost mocking.

"*Bastard!*" she thought. "*I knew it was you.*"

"We need to talk, Senator. Get over here now."

"As soon as the vote on this security bill is over," the Senator replied. "I'm expecting some challenges. You know the drill when it comes to the Agency's budget, especially in an election year. Of course you could always come over to my office."

Hall held her tongue, waiting for the Senator to finish. The last thing she wanted was to get pulled into a budget discussion, or worse yet, be called to testify at some dragged in front of some committee.

"Or not. So what's the latest, Hall? Give me a quick update."
Hall had no doubt which situation he was referring to.

"Do you mean Panama? I still have one asset missing."

"Messy business, this whole Panama operation," the Senator drawled. "Listen to me, Hall. Call off the search. Settle down to that Director's office and run it, instead of being out it the field so much. Your field days are over. As far as Panama, it's over and you are out of funds. With everything that has happened down there, I can't get you approved for another dollar. Besides, you can't consider someone an asset if they aren't one of us. And he *isn't* one of us, Hall."

"When it comes to my people, I will decide who is one of us, *and* when it is over!" Hall replied calmly.

"One of your people?" the Senator ranted. "Hall, he's nothing more than a *missing person*. A meddling citizen. And *if he is* found, he serves no purpose that we can't accomplish on our own. Either way, you need to cut him loose."

"That's my decision!" Hall barked back, digging in her heels. "I'm in charge. I refuse to take orders from you. Especially not about this. I am the Director of this Agency."

The line went briefly silent.

"*Make* the damned phone call," the Senator warned, his voice devoid of emotion. "Let me know when you have wrapped this up."

"We'll talk when you get here," Hall replied, dropping the phone into its charging cradle. "And I'm not waiting all night."

A world away, low fluorescent lamps on the table illuminated the thin, intricately carved *medwakh* pipe loosely cradled between the twisted index and middle fingers of the man's left hand. With the same hand, he deftly opened a jar of pungent *dohka* tobacco, filling the tiny pipe bowl and tamping it full with a single practiced movement.

Bringing the pipe to his crooked mouth, the man wiped away a line of drool. He bit down on the pipe stem, then clicked a battered Zippo lighter to life with one hand, slowly bringing the flame closer. Shadows stretched across the dark landscape of his badly scarred face as a ventilation fan whirred to life overhead.

The man's expression did not soften with his ritual relaxation. After so many years, the burned skin hidden beneath his black-checked *keffiyeh* scarf had stiffened into a frightening mask.

The upside was that his face only ached when exposed to direct sunlight. Wise enough to avoid such a powerful, blazing enemy, he now chose to do battle from within the confines of his underground retreat, rather than directly engage in a losing battle with the sun. He had become accustomed, though not accepting of, living out his days indoors.

Soothing his mind with the first deep draft of scented smoke, the man's wide, staring eyes adjusted to the soft bluish glow of hundreds of wall-mounted monitors as he systematically surveyed of the multiple screens in front of him, exhaling from the one functional side of his mouth.

Every screen confirmed that all was well with his world-wide initiative. Targets were toppling; his emissaries making their deadly, appointed rounds, the reports coming out of the cities he had strategically mapped were growing worse by the day. It was going exactly according to plan. He had not felt more alive in years.

His sharp eyes landed on an American news broadcast. The scarred man found the news particularly gratifying, a report card of sorts on the specific progress of his plan.

"Including the recent Paris and Brussels attacks, 26 major world cities have been devastated by 39 separate ISIS bombings in the last year alone, resulting in over 1,100 persons dead. All sites are considered soft targets, places no one would have considered to be under siege, such as airports, community centers, nightclubs. U.S. authorities are warning that the public should..."

The flat, trim phone sitting on his massive Lebanon cedar desk rang lightly. Silencing the monitor speakers, the man gripped the pipe between his remaining teeth and answered the phone by pushing a single button that sent the call to speaker.

"Talk to me," he responded in perfect English.

"I have filled your order, my friend," the accented voice on the phone intoned. "It will ship this evening from London."

"You have done well, old friend. I will look for delivery soon. Were there any challenges?"

"No challenges. It will complete your collection."

"And my suit? Is there word on my suit?"

"It has been returned from the tailor. I will send it shortly for your final approval. At your word, your tailor is prepared for the next order for five hundred suits."

"Very well then, make sure that every detail is taken care of. I want no slip-ups this time."

Before the caller could answer, the scarred man punched the speaker phone to silent and removed the pipe from his mouth, still using his left hand. He wiped away another trail of drool.

One screen caught his attention above the rest. The unique scene on this screen was a familiar setting, a person known to him long ago, in another life. He was looking right into her private office, yet she was totally unaware of the intrusion. As he watched, she pulled a bottle out of her desk along with a short glass tumbler. A man entered her office, a former adversary.

His anger burned, to see them now, to be reminded once again of their utter ignorance of his very existence, if it could be called that. That oblivious state would change soon, he promised himself. Her complete unawareness of him, of his intentions and of his mission, would not last long.

His plans to send a message of unforgettable hell would bring she and her nation to their knees, a hell much hotter than the one she and her kind had provided him so many years ago. He decided to start with the man.

His staring, lidless eyes drifted away from the monitor screen to his motionless, withered right arm, his mind repeating a silent and oft-rehearsed curse that had become firmly etched in the tracks of his tortured mind.

"Punish the unbelievers with garments of fire," he quoted aloud, his voice hoarse, rasping. The Holy Qur'an, his only guide, brimmed with sufficient violence to match any desire for revenge.

Pipe smoke swirled up toward the ceiling of the dimly lit room, pushed high by moist, cool air falling from the vents along the wall. Tilting his head back on stiff, fused vertebra, he looked up, forcing a very crooked smile. What he saw floating to the ceiling was what he hoped to soon see worldwide: the smoky vapor of the world that came before, a world that would be no more.

Chapter 6

The Pearl Islands
Pacific Coast of Panama

Dan Tate twirled his hand, index finger extended skyward, signaling the U.S. Navy helicopter to take off, while shielding his face from the sun-bleached sand whipped up by the rotors.

As soon as the dust had settled, he went to work.

"We'll check the beach 100 yards in each direction. Then meet back here," Dan instructed.

Mark Culver nodded in response. He started off to Dan's right.

Despite weeks of active searching, no sign of life had been found on any island in the Pearl Islands, the dry land nearest to where Martin Culver had gone missing.

Satellite imagery immediately following the crash initially showed two human bodies in the water, so the search had been geared to two bodies, with unmanned aerial observation drones and heat-sensing satellite monitors making nightly passes over a systematic grid of the entire area.

The challenge of gathering infrared imagery in the tropics of Panama was the pervasive heat. Everything, the island beaches, the trees, even the water gained heat from the sun daily, so the best satellite images could only be gathered at night. Once the relative coolness of nighttime set in, the heat of bodies could be seen against the cooler background.

The few potential targets that had shown up so far on these outlying islands turned out to be nothing more than the heat signature of the beach bonfires of overnight fishermen, and in one case, an amorous couple that had left their sailboat, intending to spend a quiet night ashore. The landing of the unannounced rescue party had managed to completely spoil those plans.

A day earlier, in a tense sat-phone exchange, CIA Director Carter Hall had made it reluctantly clear that she could only authorize one more day of searching for Martin Culver using U.S. government assets. She was being pushed to call off the search. Dan knew would be on their own after that. He clearly understood what that meant for Martin's chances of surviving. He knew that every day a person is lost at sea significantly decreases the chances of them ever being found alive. Dan had worn a hole in his hopes that Martin had made it to an island, but he had not given up.

Early in the search, Mark and Dan had settled into a pattern, lifting off from the U.S. Navy vessel assigned to the search every morning, thudding back down to the flight deck every night with little more to show for their efforts than strained eyes, stiff necks and a few coordinate boxes crossed off the search charts.

The change that re-energized the search came when a submersible ROV with video capability, on an entirely unrelated mission, had located the ruined helicopter in which Martin had crashed nearly three miles from this unnamed island. No other body of land was closer. Hopes rose when the ROV camera showed no bodies viewed through the helicopter's shattered windscreen. That fact, combined with recent infrared satellite images showing a single human body heat signature near a large rectangular heat footprint had led them to this specific island.

Scanning down the beach, Dan was struck by the beauty of this spot. Palm trees lined the beach, extending the length of the curved coastline and out of sight in either direction. To the left, palm trees overhung the sand choked with coconut hulls and fallen fronds. Palm trunks had been dragged together, forming the letters HEL. A good sign.

"I didn't see anything that way," Mark said. "The sand beach ends in huge rocks around the bend. There are no trees or beach after that."

"Good," Dan remarked. "I found an attempt to form the word HELP with palm trunks. Let's check things out over here."

About 60 feet from where they stood, Dan had spotted the imposing corner of a rust-streaked grey barge looming high above them. The barge had roughly parted the palm trees calmly swaying above either side of its deck. The top of the deck was not visible, towering above their heads. This apparently was the rectangular shaped heat signature that showed up on the infrared scans. Dan made note of the confirmation.

Dan took the lead, motioning for Mark to follow him across the beach.

"Look here," he said to Mark. "Your name."

On the vertical side of the boxy barge, chipped out of a patch of white barnacles, the word CULVER stood out dark against the lighter background of barnacle shells.

"My brother did that," Mark stated. He pulled out his phone and took pictures from several angles.

"So we know he made it this far," Dan said. Around the base of the barge, a recent fire smoked lazily, down to embers only. A smoke-smudged can with bits of shell lay beside the barge. It was still warm, though it was resting in the shade.

"Hello, is anyone here?" Mark shouted anxiously. A dry stream bed ran around the end of the barge leading across the sand into the lagoon.

Dan looked skyward. "Anyone up there?" he called.

The rattle and movement of hermit crab shells drew Dan's attention. Congregated at the base of a graceful, curved palm, Dan could see hundreds of crabs moving, their shells merging into a clicking, surging mass. He took one step toward the chaotic scene, stepping one boot into the moving carpet of crabs. Curious as to why so many crabs had gathered, Dan took one step before he realized the worst. He turned to warn Mark. The look on Mark's face told Dan he was too late.

Dan shielded his face from the sand Mark's boots kicked up as he rushed past. Dan managed to catch Mark's arm, stopping him from touching the bones as both of them bent down for a closer look. The stench of death was thicker than the cloud of flies that hovered over the remains.

Most evident was the fact that the body was more bone than flesh, so evidently some time had passed. The skeleton appeared to be human, but only the torso remained. The lower half of the skeleton was nonexistent, the vertebrae cleanly severed below the ribs. Dan knew that these crabs could not have devoured such large bones.

Both arms were present, lying on either side near the ribs. One hand was missing from the wrist down. The flesh had been eaten away from the neck, leaving the skull attached to the spine by a few leathery ligaments. The jawbone hung away from the head at an odd, open angle.

Dan grabbed a palm branch, wielding it to scatter the hermit crabs, then paused for a moment as he scanned further along the beach for the lower half of the bone set. Mark did not turn away.

"Is it him?" Mark said, his face flushed with emotion. He looked desperately at Dan. "Is it Martin? I think I'm gonna be sick."

Dan poked at the skull with the palm branch. The bleached flesh-free temples rotated slightly, mouth agape as if it were shouting in pain. Then Dan breathed a sigh of relief.

"No it's definitely not Martin," he said, a grim smile flattening his lips. "This is not Martin's body."

"How do you know?" Mark said, turning to face the skeleton again.

"Watch this," Dan said, rapping the stick against the skull. From one eye socket, a staring glass eye hung briefly, then plopped down into the sand. It glared at them both.

"Director Hall's briefing stated Morgan had a glass eye," Dan said with finality. "That's Morgan, the Panamanian smuggler Hall told us about. Or half of him, anyway."

"Are you sure?"

"Sure enough to bet money," Dan said.

Mark turned away, breathing a sigh of relief.

"That's too bad for him, but I'm glad it's not Martin. So where is Martin?" he asked.

"Oh, he's here," Dan said. "I'm sure of it."

"Let's hope," Mark replied. "If Martin is here, let's find him and get back to the ship."

Chapter 7

CIA Headquarters
Langley, Virginia

Within the hour, the Senator had made good on his threat. He arrived outside Hall's office door unannounced. Entering her office after she coded him through, the Senator moved with the presence of an undertaker. He wore an expression to match.

"How did you get past my sentry?" Hall asked, dispensing with all formalities.

"There are many ways into this building," the Senator responded.

"Really?" Hall replied. "Thought I knew them all."

"Many ways into this building, but only one way out, when it's all said and done. Your father taught me that when he was with the Agency."

Hall hesitated, eyebrows raised in expectation of an answer.

"I used the rural silo entrance," the Senator stated without emotion. "The ex-Director showed me after your father showed him."

"They never showed me," Hall shot back in response.

"Perhaps they never expected you to sit in that chair," the Senator replied, smiling grimly. "May I sit?"

Sliding his lanky frame into a wing chair facing her desk, the Senator moved his hand in an ominously slow manner, pointing his bony index finger toward the phone without speaking, his eyes posing the question.

Hall considered her words carefully, picking up the conversation where they left off earlier.

"Senator, you have *always* been a cold-hearted SOB, but to call off the search for Culver is a new low, even for you. How does it feel to be completely dead inside?"

"What is it to you if I am dead inside? We all are, after everything we have done. Just pick up the phone and call it off."

Director Hall intensified her glare, then stood up too suddenly. She shielded an expression of pain as she turned away. It was not clear, even to Hall, which hurt worse, the pain in her hip or being trapped in this office, in this situation, with no apparent escape.

46

"I won't do it," she responded after a moment, swirling the whiskey in her glass. "I can't. I have never once abandoned an asset in the field."

"So you insist that he's an asset? *Damn it Hall!* He is an untrained non-professional who can't even find his way home. I just don't understand what you see in him."

"I, we… need him more than ever," Hall stated. "I need his connections. His foundation represents open doors that we desperately need. The International Antiquities Foundation can get us into places and situations where the CIA has lost access, especially in the Middle East. In a complicated world, he brings so much to the table that we lack within the Agency."

"You like this guy or something?" the Senator snarled, leaning back in his chair. He unbuttoned his grey suit jacket and straightened his tie. "Might sound to some people like you're compromised."

Hall weighed her words as she set her glass down on the corner of the desk.

"I've told you. He was vital in Panama. He saved my life *and* he neutralized a Class IV threat. He did our work for us. If not for him, you would be interviewing director candidates right now instead of harassing me. I still believe Culver is alive. We owe it to him and to his family, to find him and bring him home."

Looking at the ceiling, the Senator stifled a grimace.

"So my real question, Director Hall, is this. *Why* does the CIA really need Martin Culver as much as you say? Is this search CIA business or is it personal on your part? Some misplaced sense of loyalty or obligation perhaps? You have searched weeks with no sign of him. Nothing."

"I assure you that this is strictly business," Hall replied calmly. "We owe him this. I have too much invested in Culver to drop the search. I've trained him, developed his value to us. We have an on-going need for someone like him. Someone from outside the Beltway. He is quick and resourceful, and he needs the Agency too. I made a deal, a mutual arrangement that helps this office accomplish its goals. I could send him anywhere in the world with confidence."

"Assuming you locate him, you mean. Is he manageable?"

"How do you mean?" Hall fired back. "Like you tried to manage me?

"Don't play games with me, Hall. Is he controllable?"

"I have some cards to play," she lied. "He is controllable."

Pausing to review her options, Hall continued.

"I do hold a sense of obligation to Culver for what he has accomplished. He is deeply involved with us at the international level. We can't go back to doing business like we did before."

"I have a deal with Culver. In exchange for his access through the International Antiquities Foundation to every country in the world, I protect him to the degree possible and help him when there is no one else to depend on. I cannot, at the present time, duplicate what he offers to this agency."

The Senator closed his eyes, tapping his index finger on the leather chair arm.

"I could get any janitor from the Smithsonian to do the same thing," he speculated.

"I'm not calling off the search, I still have leads to follow up," Hall said before turning her back to him. Even in the security of her office she pondered the wisdom of doing so. Taking her eyes off of the Senator was like looking away from a snake about to strike. She simply could not abide his cold stare a moment longer.

"So that's final?" the Senator asked, his eyes popping open and glaring. "You are risking your career over a single, simple phone call?"

"Don't threaten me. *You* make the damned call!" Hall shot back, tiring of the back and forth game. "Your decision, your responsibility. Be a man, for once."

The Senator stood up, visibly agitated. He ambled around her desk, quietly dragging his long, wrinkled finger along the smooth mahogany edge from front to back, before finally sitting in her personal desk chair.

"Director Hall, I realize," the Senator said in a forced tone, without looking at her directly. "This being your first day back following extended medical leave, that you may not be yourself just yet. Perhaps Bethesda turned you loose a bit too soon."

He turned in the chair to face her. "In consideration of that, I will leave your insults to the side and move on. But do not question my resolve, or my manhood."

48

Hall realized she had crossed a line, a line he had expertly provoked her to cross. She cursed her anger, attempting to wrestle it back into the box yet again.

"This is not *my* decision, Director Hall," the Senator said. "You know that. This is about budgets, about your budget, about what the citizens trust us to do with their money. I have a big responsibility. The Appropriations Committee took a hatchet to our budget this afternoon. As an agency, we have had too many screw-ups and not enough results to show for it. I cannot afford to have these frivolous pursuits of yours become the impetus for more budget cuts. The citizens trust us to not squander their money."

"I disagree that anything about Panama was frivolous," Hall responded calmly. "We eliminated the worst international criminal we have dealt with in years. We uncovered evidence of a world-wide plot to slaughter one third of Earth's population, a threat that may not yet be contained. I have crunched the data. My Panama operation was a bargain. And in case you have forgotten, I nearly died down there."

The Senator paused as he once more pointed his finger to her desktop, pushing folders aside to reveal one folder marked "Confidential Summary - Provisional - PANAMA."

"One could make the case," the Senator droned on, "that further budget cuts to your program, including mission-essential personnel, might be necessary should excessive expenditures continue."

The Senator looked directly at her, leaving little doubt as to his meaning. "The people are not on your side. You work for me, and I represent the people. Of course, you could end up with *all* your assets left out in the cold. Your choice of course."

Hall took a step toward her desk. Everything inside her screamed not to do it, but she had stood her ground with the Senator before. Hall remembered all too well how that had turned out. Her hand trembled as she reached for her desk phone, reflecting an intense mixture of anger, of fear, of the anxiety generated by betrayal: the Senator's betrayal of her, her own betrayal of Martin Culver. She winced visibly as she punched each key of Sandra Culver's number.

"You have never once considered the citizens of the United States in *anything*!" she muttered. "I hope you roast in hell for this."

The Senator smiled a flat, emotionless smile as she dialed. He turned away from her desk.

"I will save you a seat," he responded as he ambled toward the door. "And one for your father, too."

"For the last time, leave my father out of this," Hall snarled toward the closed door. "He should have killed you when he had the chance."

"If that is how you really feel, then you should not have stopped him."

The door closed without the usual slamming sound. Hall considered her words, remembering Sandra's reaction at the news that Martin had gone missing.

Hall slumped into her office chair, exhausted, then immediately stood up, almost falling as she did so. The chair still held the Senator's body warmth, a sensation she had sworn to never experience again. The ringing phone, hanging loosely in her hand, finally connected.

"International Antiquities Foundation, Amanda speaking, may I help you?"

"I need to speak to Sandra Culver, please. "

"She is in a meeting. May I take a message?"

"This is very important. Interrupt her." Hall demanded. "It can't wait."

"Yes, I understand. Let me get her. May I tell her who's calling?" Amanda inquired hesitantly.

"Tell her you have Carter on the line."

"One moment please."

No more despised words were ever spoken to a person of action. Hall hated to be on hold almost as much as she hated to be the one to deliver bad news.

Amanda paged the library conference room by speakerphone.

"Excuse me, Mrs. Culver. . .Sandra. I have a call for you. She says it can't wait. She said to tell you it's Carter on the line."

Sandra looked at Cita and held her hands in the air, palms skyward. Her face told a story of bewilderment and panic.

50

"Amanda, I will take the call in my office. Give me 60 seconds to get there," Sandra replied, weaving between staffers toward the door.

"Yes, Sandra, I will let her know."

Sandra eyed Cita once more as she bolted from the room.

"Cita, please take over and continue the meeting. Someone record the session so I can review it later."

"Will do," Cita responded. "All right everyone, who's next?"

Sandra reached her office in record time, designer heels notwithstanding. She grabbed the phone receiver before the office lights had a chance to come on.

"This is Sandra Culver speaking."

"Sandra, this is Director Hall. Are we still on speakerphone?"

"No, it's just us. I'm alone in my office."

"Sandra, I'll make this brief. I regret having to make this call."

"Oh God..." Sandra said aloud. *"Don't say it,"* she thought.

"Sandra, I'm calling off the search. We have not found Martin. I have overstepped my authority to keep it going this long. I'm sorry."

Sandra was stunned beyond words. She could not speak, think or respond.

"I will continue to keep an ear to the ground, Sandra. But I have to pull back the search."

Fresh out of words, Hall stopped talking.

After a long pause, Sandra regained her composure and her ability to speak.

"I have been afraid of this," she said quietly. "I appreciate your call."

"Are you okay, Sandra?" Hall ventured. "I know this isn't easy."

After another moment's thought, Sandra responded.

"I have to be," she replied. "I have no other choice."

Hall could think of little else to say.

"Please call me if there is anything..." Hall began, before realizing she was talking to a dial tone.

Chapter 8

The British Museum
London, England

Ornate cast-iron lions charged each other in the night to the sound of immense metal gates clanging shut, the impact shattering the pervading quiet. A shower of sparks armed the electrified fence enclosing the museum grounds, briefly illuminating the rear of a speeding armored car before the vehicle disappeared into impenetrable fog. The high metal enclosure hissed, burning off accumulated mist.

Beyond the armored car, London lay quiet, save for the headlamps of the occasional taxi car. Behind, suspended between midnight moisture and pre-dawn dampness, the immense British Museum loomed dark, the multiple buildings of its galleries dissolving skyward under clouds of vapor that obscured the rooftops. Along the way, blurred street lamp shadows cast peculiar angles across every intersection. The fog lay heaviest along the Thames River near Kingsway, obscuring the other vehicles entering the Holborn Circus roundabout, a challenging intersection known to be dangerous under the best of conditions.

"Twenty-Six to dispatch. Come in dispatch, over." Porter replaced the radio mouthpiece into its cradle.

"Bloody ridiculous to be up at such an ungodly hour," the armored car driver mentally muttered, glancing at his watch. *"Don't know why this couldn't have waited for the light of day."*

Charlie Porter reviewed the delivery plan in his mind. It was a simple one. Load the cargo, drive to Heathrow, check in with dispatch office every ten minutes until they had safely put the cargo on a plane, be done with it and home again before breakfast. But Porter knew well enough that plans could go astray. He had seen it happen. Moreover, the three ravens congregated on his garden fence before he left home had served as a warning. His wife had made note of it, although she believed in such omens more readily than he. In any event, he would be glad when this one was put to bed.

Porter was considered trustworthy, dependable, discrete. In the middle of the night. Museum to airport, no questions asked. He was not even a regular driver. They probably chose Charlie because he kept his mouth shut, unlike some. He glanced at the manifest, which read simply "Granite Tablet". The final destination: Larnaca International Airport in Cyprus.

Porter downshifted the transmission to merge with the few vehicles out at such an hour. The armored car rolled into the circular intersection at a reduced rate of speed. He grabbed the radio as he steered round and continued on, trying once more to report in.

"Dispatch, this is armored transport Twenty-Six, come in dispatch."

The radio replied with sharp, crackling static. A faint pulse rose and fell within the staccato tone, like the low hum of a motor. No reply was received.

The driver negotiated the roundabout safely, then glanced up, checking the tiny window into the armored valuables compartment, verifying that his two partners were wide awake.

"Dispatch, this is armored car Twenty-Six, come in. I'm nearly to Aldwych. Request reply."

Static wafted over the handheld radio speaker, the sole reply. A steady hum overpowered the static and increased in volume.

Through the fog, flashing yellow lights indicating a detour could be seen. Traffic was being directed onto Wild Street. Porter slowed the armored truck. No other traffic was heading his way exiting the detour street.

"Damned Public Works Ministry," he fumed. "Haven't the time for this!"

"C'mon dispatch," the frustrated driver sputtered into the mike. "Fine time for a trip to the loo! Get off your lazy bum and answer!"

Porter reluctantly took the detour. Unnerved by the lack of response to his continued hailing of his base, he nervously pressed the petrol pedal harder. At that same moment, Porter watched as his world decelerated into a slow-motion nightmare.

Ahead and to the left, streams of light unexpectedly burst through the brick wall of a warehouse, piercing the night and illuminating the street in front of the armored car like a swirling searchlight. The brilliant light shafts intensified, bursting forth in hot streaks, a series of pulsing blue lightning bolts that cut a dizzying pattern through the foggy darkness.

Mortar melted into glass, then shattered, appearing to litter the sidewalk with molten glitter. The entire warehouse wall swelled out across the sidewalk and burst into a shower of glowing-red brick fragments.

The radio flared with a high-pitched squeal that descended into an ear-splitting treble blast, causing Porter to drop the mike.

Momentarily blinded as though from the flash of a camera, ears numb from the low-pitched percussion, Porter instinctively stomped the brakes. The heavy vehicle dropped to half-speed before going into a skid, tires sliding sideways across the wet pavement. The driver thought twice, released the brakes, his beefy arms yanking the steering wheel in the direction of the skid. He tapped the petrol pedal to control the swerve, crossing the fingers of his right hand.

Porter's mind raced. Nothing mattered more to him at this moment than getting past the intense explosive scene with its increasingly bright flood of light. The heavy vehicle fell into line and surged forward toward the rotating light display.

"Hey Porter, what's goin' on up there?" called one of the guards from the back of the truck. "You've made me spill me friggin' coffee."

The guard's voice was drowned out by a percussive boom from within the ruined brick wall that reverberated through the narrow, quiet streets.

As Porter watched, eyes squinted against the light, the shadowy figure of a man dashed through the smoke and out into the street, directly into his path. All black turban and dark, loose clothes, this overly tall man flowed across the pavement as would a spectre.

In his right hand the turbaned ghost raised the longest sword Porter had ever seen. The sword was refined, ornately made and heavy. This sword pulsed bluish white light that dispelled the surrounding fog with an insistent crackle.

Flooring the pedal, the driver dodged debris and goosed the armored truck to pick up speed.

"Hang on, Harvey!" Porter called to the guards in the back. "We've got a bit of trouble up here."

Unable to avoid the menacing figure who now stood directly in the middle of the street, Porter leaned on the horn. Warning the defiant man, Porter made no attempt to swerve around him.

Raising the electric-blue sword, the dark phantom brought the weapon over his head, slicing cleanly down and into the front grill of the heavily reinforced truck. Electricity crackled and jumped across the hood of the vehicle as the sword split it cleanly in half. The lights in the dashboard flickered, flared and died. The vehicle continued to roll, although its speed slowed considerably.

A tremendous burst of steam had erupted from the damaged engine, obscuring the windshield as the armored truck lost power. Stepping lightly onto the front bumper of the oncoming truck, the turbaned man turned a somersault and landed sure-footed on the roof of the still-moving vehicle. The vehicle crashed to a stop against the nearest lamppost.

Porter watched as the man dropped to the ruptured bonnet, then to the street before running past his door toward the rear of the armored vehicle. Hitting the automatic lockout bar, Porter grabbed the radio as the man approached. A dark cloth obscured the madman's face, but for a moment Porter came eye to eye with him. The look Porter saw in the man's eyes chilled him deep inside.

"Dispatch, come in dispatch!" Porter shouted frantically as me moved away from the thick bullet-proof glass. "I've got a problem here, where in hell are you? I'm disabled near Kingsway and Aldwych! Come in dispatch!"

The ear-splitting sound of torn metal screamed in the night, overpowering Porter's plea for help. Hearing the cries of the guards locked in the rear of the armored car, Porter turned round. He tried to open the door of the secure compartment, only to be overcome by heat and the odor of burning flesh. The guards stopped screaming. Porter covered his mouth, recoiling from the smell.

The screech of tires of a powerful, fast vehicle approached from the rear. Hoping to catch a glimpse or collect a tag number, Porter yanked on the door handle to little avail. The heat in the driver compartment became stifling. The now familiar electric pulse faded in volume as streetlamps flickered and died. As he heard the vehicle drive away, Porter watched helplessly as flames began licking up from under the hood of the vehicle's damaged carburetor. Fire found its way into the driver's compartment just before the fuel tank burst beneath the truck, creating an explosive inferno that lifted the armored vehicle off the pavement, throwing the flaming hulk onto its side in the center of the darkened street.

Chapter 9

Dan looked through the overhanging palms toward the west. In another half hour the sun would drop into the Pacific. A brisk breeze was building from the east. He pulled his sat phone from its waterproof case to verify signal.

"Mark, we need to get settled in for the night. Probably best to stay right here by the barge," Dan said as he dialed. "I have to call in. I will schedule the helicopter to pick us up tomorrow morning. The barge will block the wind. Let's gather as much material as we can for a fire before it gets dark."

After reporting in to the ship, Dan went back and took pictures of the skeleton from several angles, then picked up the glass eye. He was surprised how heavy and cold it felt, not to mention how creepy it looked. It was as if the eye were watching him.

Wiping the eye through the sand to clean it, Dan dropped it into his one empty cargo pants pocket. Directing Mark to gather wood for a fire, Dan began walking around the barge in an expanding circle. By the time he had made his third round, he needed a flashlight to see well enough to light their fire.

The first thing that struck him was how devoid the area was of burnable material. It was as if the ground and vegetation had been stripped of all dry tinder, kindling and wood. He took that as a good sign.

Rounding the corner of the barge furthest from the beach, beneath the shady palms, Dan found several encouraging signs of life. First, he found rotting cargo straps made into crude hammock. Apparently the weathered straps had collapsed. He also found two separate locations that had recently been used as latrines. Then he spotted a built-in set of ladder rungs rising up to the deck of the barge.

"Mark, come over here," he called out in a low voice. "Bring your flashlight."

"Did you see something?" Mark asked.

"No, just a hunch," Dan replied. "Even if it's nothing, we can see from up there if any fires are lit."

Dan began to climb up the rusty rungs. They were sturdy, welded into the hull of the barge. His heart beat faster. He reached the deck of the barge and glanced back to see that Mark made it to the top. Dan crouched low, running across the deck to the small pilot house. His flashlight illuminated a series of scratches, like a prison calendar Dan had once maintained in the Havana jail. A quick count gave 39 marks, including one fresh scratch. Another good sign. He moved to the open doorway of the pilot house. Dan halted, holding one hand up to Mark, a signal to stop.

Dan remembered what happened at Martin and Sandra's house. He also remembered thinking such a thing could never happen. Immediately he slowed to a crawl. He checked the door for a trip wire, looked for a motion sensor, anything out of the ordinary. Seeing nothing, he proceeded, but more cautiously than before. Mark caught up with him before he moved inside the pilot house.

"What did you find?" Mark asked anxiously.

Both their lights played along the outside of the small pilot house. On the deck lay a neat arrangement of coconut shells sawed in half that had been set out to gather rainwater. The hulls with water remaining were festering mosquito pools, the larvae wriggling in the sudden light.

Peering through the open door of the pilot house, Dan saw a tattered vinyl bench inside, its surface smeared and speckled with dried blood. Jack had told Dan what happened on the barge, but there was too much lost blood for one person. A crumpled ace of spades, with what appeared to be a bullet hole, lay in the center of the floor. Dan pocketed the ace for luck.

In the far corner, Dan saw a tattered white shirt with faded blood stains. He first mistook the pile to be nothing more than a pile of rags. On closer inspection, Dan saw ragged black pants.

An emaciated, still body lay on its side facing away from them. Dan sniffed and looked around. No flies, so he took it as a good sign, but there was a distinctive aroma in the still night air, the smell of putrid flesh. The body did not move, did not even appear to be breathing.

Dan motioned Mark forward, then bent down while Mark focused his light on the body. Kneeling, Dan prodded the figure, then leapt back from the person that was suddenly, explosively alive. Scrambling away crab-like, Dan slammed heavily against the console, striking his head on a metal cabinet.

"I knew you were coming!" The man shrieked in a deep, raspy voice as he tried to stand. "I've been waiting for you! You'll be sorry you came back."

Though dazed, all Dan could see was a skinny, bearded madman with eyes yellow from fever and apparently in tremendous pain. The man tried to speak again and erupted in a howl that seemed to energize every fiber of his being. He moved toward Dan, ignoring Mark.

"I knew you were coming!" he screeched. "I know you're here to kill me!"

The man appeared to be delirious. His calloused feet made a coarse scratching sound as they scraped across the deck. His face contorted horribly as he moved toward Dan, holding the bloody saw out in front of him as one would a sword.

Although one hand was heavily bandaged, that same wrist bore a fresh cut across the outside, still bloody and dripping. A rusty saw blade was clenched tightly in the other hand. Blood and flesh clogged the jagged teeth of the blade. It was obvious they had interrupted the man in the process of amputating his own injured hand.

Mark watched in disbelief as this injured wretch approached Dan, who was still trying to stand back to his feet. The wild man did not seem to notice him at all. Standing perfectly still, Mark did not speak until the man stood over Dan, uttering unintelligible threats and nearly growling in his anguish. Mark was close enough to smell a horrific odor, when suddenly he recognized the man standing inches away from him.

Mark yelled out, trying to create a distraction and stay out of reach of the rusty blade. "Martin, it's me, your brother!"

Martin turned to Mark, swinging the rusty saw toward Mark's head, pinning him against the bulkhead as he half-pushed, half-fell against his younger brother. Mark dropped his flashlight, grabbing Martin's good hand with both of his own, trying desperately to fend off the threatening blade. He was surprised how strong Martin was, considering how weak he appeared.

"Dan, he doesn't know it's me! " Mark yelled. "Martin, look at me! I'm your brother Mark!"

"What are you saying?" Martin shouted in a deafening tone, dropping the saw to the deck with a clatter. He stepped to one side, grabbed Mark around the neck, pulling a .45 caliber pistol from inside his belt. "You'll regret following me here!"

Dan made it to his feet, crouching, looking for an opening. *"Where did Martin get a pistol?"* he wondered. *"And why is he shouting?"*

Mark felt the crusty bundle of Martin's bandaged hand scrape tightly alongside his ear, the blood oozing from his brother's wrist warm and nauseating against his own neck. The barrel of the pistol against his opposite temple was cold, intensely pressing into his skin, but trembling at the same time.

Mark could not believe that his own brother was holding a pistol to his head. Martin seemed strong, even in his emaciated state, impossible to defeat. Mark had always been stronger than Martin, winning all but a handful of their boyhood fights. Now Martin's arms were as tight and strong as cables.

Mark felt Martin stumble slightly. He tried relaxing his legs to throw Martin off balance, to make him fall. Martin did not budge, but groaned in pain as he held Mark up off the floor. Mark's eyes focused on the bandage. He looked toward Dan and saw Dan nod slightly.

"Martin, put down the gun," Dan ordered, his voice forced, quiet. "We are here to rescue you, just like you did for us in Havana, remember?"

Martin did not acknowledge Dan's comment. His eyes glanced toward the pilot house door.

"Martin, you rescued us. This time we are rescuing you. Sandra is waiting to hear from you. She loves you and wants to see you."

Dan watched Martin's mouth. He seemed to be trying to repeat Dan's words, to form them in his own mouth, as if he were lip-reading.

"Sandra loves you, Martin! She wants us to bring you home!" Dan shouted in his loudest voice.

Martin's face contorted, a shriek from hell erupting from deep within him.

"NO, NO, YOU LIE! Sandra is dead. They killed her! *You* killed her!" Martin shouted. He turned his attention from Mark to

Dan, jamming the pistol toward his friend's face, shaking the barrel with every syllable he spoke.

Mark took what he thought might be their best opportunity, twisting and smashing his brother's bandaged hand into the pilot house wall.

Martin's expression changed to one of stark realization before his left leg collapsed. He pulled the trigger before dropping the pistol, then fell hard, grasping his leg and taking Mark to the deck with him. He reached down with both hands, clutching his leg and rolling on the deck.

Mark looked at Dan. "I didn't mean to hurt him, Dan. I didn't know what else to do!"

"You did fine," Dan said. He kicked the pistol out of Martin's reach, then picked the weapon up.

Dan ejected the pistol clip, confirming what he had hoped to be true. The clip was empty. He checked the pistol and confirmed the chamber was empty, too.

"At least you didn't get shot. Next time make sure the gun is empty before you try a trick like that." He stuffed the pistol in his belt and knelt down to help Martin.

Dan evaluated Martin's condition as his longtime friend rocked back and forth on the deck. Dan pulled out his sat phone. "We have to get a medic here pronto, or Martin's going to lose that hand."

"How do you know?" Mark asked, raising an eyebrow.

"That's what stinks in here. Look at the color. It's gone septic."

"Do you think he is going to be all right?" Mark asked. "What happened to his leg?"

"Leg cramp is my guess, probably from dehydration," Dan responded. "He has lost a lot of blood and he looks really sick, maybe malaria."

Martin stirred and tried to speak.

"It's ok, Martin, you're going to be okay."

Dan pulled out a water bottle, holding it to Martin's lips, but Martin pushed it away and tried to speak again. His voice could be barely heard, a coarse whisper scraping past his lips.

"Why can't I hear what you're saying?"

Chapter 10

The Pearl Islands
Pacific Coast of Panama

First light dawned as the last of the flight crew piled into the crowded helicopter. On the eastern horizon mountains hung in the air above a shimmering sea.

The medic on board tried to fit an oxygen mask across Martin's face.

"Leave me alone," Martin whispered, his faint voice hoarse but insistent as he pushed aside the corpsman's hand. Falling back against the hard mat lining the rescue basket, Martin gripped the corpsman's wrist with a surprising strength and strained to speak.

"Martin, relax and let the man help you," Dan said from Martin's side. "He's here to help you. There will be time to tell your story."

Martin's sunburned eyelids fluttered, then eased slowly closed.

"The way I hear it you saved a lot of people," the corpsman said to Martin. "Sounds like you're a brave man. Ready to lift off, Captain!"

"Roger that, lifting off! Secure that door!"

The helicopter door slammed shut. It was the last thing Martin felt before losing consciousness. Giant rotors whined and whirred to life. The blades engaged with a bump and a series of low vibrations that made it difficult to focus one's eyes.

The Captain brought the rescue copter straight up into the air before correcting course to make a beeline for Panama. The white sand beach exploded into a sandstorm, then began to fall away as Dan watched through the small window in the cargo door. He felt weighted down as he reached to steady the rescue basket where Martin lay. He tried in vain not to think about all that his friend had been through.

Dan could hear the captain's mike active over the headset in his flight helmet.

"This is the Rescue aircraft designation Triple Tango, hailing host vessel USS New Orleans. We have a priority one rescue onboard, near coordinates 8.124758 North, 79.342157 West. We need to refuel before continuing to a mainland hospital."

"Who is he?" the young medic asked Dan. "Someone important I bet."

Dan smiled but did not answer.

"Is he some kind of secret agent?" the medic pressed.

"Why would you think that?" Dan replied.

"Hey, I watch movies," the corpsman stated brightly. "I have never seen this kind of effort made to save anyone, civilian or military. We have this bet going back on the ship. Come on, mister, help me improve my odds. You can tell me."

Dan thought a long time before answering. He could not reveal all that he knew, that CIA Director Hall had authorized this search and rescue, including its many extensions. He also knew that she would not do that for just any John Doe. Dan knew just enough from what Jack Culver had told him to understand that Martin, Jack and Director Hall had been involved in something important, something international in scope.

Dan remembered his own days of betting on any and every thing to pass a boring day aboard ship. In addition, he remembered how those bets had started out small, eventually becoming a losing lifestyle instead of a mere pastime. He remembered how much it had truly cost him to gamble on any and every thing.

"Save your money," Dan said. "Martin's just a regular guy. He is a U.S. citizen, and he's my good friend. That's all. Now do what you can for him until we can get to a hospital."

The medic smiled a grim smile and went back to work on Martin.

"What if we don't meet the vessel in time to refuel?" Mark asked.

"Then we may be the ones stranded in the Pearl Islands," the corpsman joked. He stopped smiling when he saw the expression on Mark's face. "Just kidding," he said. "The captain will find us a vessel."

As Dan listened, he watched through the small window in the cargo door as the grounded military barge where Martin had taken refuge dropped out of sight. The helicopter bounced uncomfortably as it lifted through thick layers of tropical moisture common to the Pacific coast of Panama.

Dan watched as the medic cut through the old bandages on Martin's injured hand, examining the wound before administering two injections.

"Tetanus and anti-biotic," the corpsman stated, noting Dan's interest. "Bullet wound. Thru and thru."

The corpsman rapidly dressed and re-wrapped the wound.

"I can't say tendons weren't hit, that's for the surgeon to decide. But it's pretty bad," he added, noting the color of Martin's swollen fingers. "He could lose the hand."

Dan nodded, trying not to dwell on all that his friend had been through. Still, he wondered. How had Martin been shot? And how had he survived this long? It was a miracle that he had survived.

Watching the corpsman methodically work to insert an IV into Martin's arm, Dan felt reassured until he realized that ideal IV locations were not to be found, given Martin's emaciated condition. The medic's frustration showed in his knotted eyebrows. Martin's body had reached a state of dehydration that left few options for a viable vein.

The corpsman looked up apologetically at Dan.

"He's gonna hate me, but I have to put this in the back of his good hand," the medic stated. "It's critical that I get this glucose in him ASAP. He's going into hypovolemic shock." Seeing Dan's expression, the medic broke it down further.

"His heart will go into defib if he doesn't get some water in him soon. He has lost way too much body fluid."

"Can't you just give him water by mouth?"

"No, the dehydrated throat dries out. He'll probably just choke on it. That will make things worse right now. I can't sit him up in this rescue basket."

"Got it," Dan nodded in agreement, remembering his efforts to hydrate Martin even before they lowered him down from the barge. The medic thumped the back of Martin's good hand with his middle finger, then squeezed to raise a vein.

"There is one other alternative, if the hand doesn't work," the medic stated as he pulled the needle cap off with his teeth. "It's not a good one."

"What's that?" Dan asked.

"Well, let's put it this way," the medic said as he thumped the back of Martin's hand again, and began to probe for a spot to insert the IV. "If I used that method, he would *really* be mad, and sore in the worst way."

The corpsman looked up at Dan.

"We only use it on patients who have had their arms and legs blown off," he stated. "I have only had to do it once, after the U SS Cole bombing."

"I'm not a murderer!" Martin shouted, trying to sit up and surprising them both. His voice was loud and clear even through the oxygen mask. Dan smiled, thinking this was a good sign.

"His ears have been damaged," the medic stated, not looking up at Dan. He pulled out a small Maglite and passed the light across Martin's left ear, then his right. "I can see crusted blood deep inside. Plus his shouting like that, common to see with hearing damage after an explosion."

"You've seen that before?" Dan asked bluntly. "So he may be deaf?"

"Time will tell, but chances are he will be. It looks like damage we see from an IED. Still, he's lucky. This mission just changed from a recovery to a rescue. At the end of the day, that's always a good thing."

Dan looked past Martin and the medic to the half-filled body bag piled against the aft bulkhead. The odor emanating from the body bag permeated the small cabin despite the thick rubber that enclosed the remains. If Dan had his way, they would have left the body to the crabs.

Dan tried to piece together what had taken place, remembering the fearful, defiant look on his friend's face, his ranting statements. Hall would want to know. Was Morgan the person Martin had referred to about not being a murderer? Had Martin killed him alone, or were there others? Worst of all, Dan could not change the channel in his mind that screamed the obvious question. Martin had survived, while whoever this torso belonged to had not survived. Something other than hermit crabs had robbed that body of its lower half. He knew that from his military survival training, that a person does what they have to do to survive, but could he picture his friend being that desperate? The thought bothered him deeply, but he decided to keep his mouth shut.

"Is he going to be ok?" Dan asked the corpsman, preferring to focus on the present.

"I think he will live. He's made it this far. We will know more when we get him to the mainland and get a triage team working on him. I think we can save him. Like I said, I've seen worse."

"Hey pilot," Dan shouted over the rotor noise. "Can you get any more speed out of this bucket?"

"Not without shaking your fillings out!" she shouted back. "Keep your shirt on, we are 20 minutes from the USS New Orleans. She has exited the Panama Canal heading to San Diego. She has a helicopter pad astern."

"But do you...do we...?" Disordered words tumbled out of Dan's mouth.

"Yes, we have enough fuel to make it. The New Orleans is clearing her landing deck for us now."

Breathing a sigh of relief, Dan whispered a prayer of thanks, then said aloud "The worst is over, Martin, just hang in there."

It occurred to Dan, even as the words escaped his lips, that he was trying to convince himself every bit as he much as he was trying to assure his unconscious friend.

Chapter 11

"Sandra, you'd better take this," Rebekah said, thrusting the phone toward her. "They've found Martin."

Sandra's facial features grew wide with disbelief.

"Is he alive? Did they find Martin alive?" Sandra shouted as she snatched the phone from Rebekah.

"Sandra Culver, with whom am I speaking?"

"Sandra, it's Dan Tate, we've found Martin. He's alive."

Sandra was taken aback. She had so longed to hear these words. Now, after hearing them, she reeled from a wave of dizziness that rocked her entire body. Rebekah recognized the look on Sandra's face and reached for her arm, guiding her toward a chair.

"I just got a call from Director Hall, not 30 minutes ago," Sandra shouted into the phone. "She told me the search was being called off."

"I still have to call her," Dan said. "I called you first. Martin's alive."

"Dan, I'm getting on a plane, I'm coming there now. Is Martin ok?"

"No, Sandra, wait. That's not such a good idea, you'd better wait. Can I talk to Jack?"

"He's on the way to Costa Rica with Eric and Elizabeth. Why?"

Dan hesitated. He had preferred to tell Jack his news about Martin, then let Jack give Sandra the details in a calmer, slower manner. He decided to give her the condensed version.

"Sandra, Martin has been through a lot. He does not remember us. The medic onboard the ship has treated him for now. Martin is being flown to a military hospital near Panama City."

"I am coming down there today," Sandra said. "Which hospital?"

"Sandra, I don't know that yet. Martin has been surviving on an island by himself. He is very sick, with a fever, maybe malaria. Let me call you when I know more details."

"How long will that take?" Sandra insisted. "I need to see him, do you understand!"

"They are refueling the helicopter now. We are leaving in two minutes. It will take a few hours to get to the hospital and get settled."

"Okay, I'll wait. But you have to call me as soon as possible."

"All right," Dan promised. "Sandra, there is something else."

"Oh God, what is it Dan?" Sandra breathed, reaching behind her to find a chair. She sat down gingerly on the edge of the seat. "Dan Tate, don't you dare tell me any bad news. I simply can't take it."

"Sandra, Martin has lost his hearing. We don't know how serious it is, only that his ears have been badly damaged."

"Oh no!" Sandra cried. "Could the loss be permanent?"

"The shipboard medic said that things like this can end up being temporary, but it's too early to tell. It depends on the damage to his ears. He has a fighting chance according to the medic."

"Where did you find him? Was he out on the water?"

"No, we actually found him on an island, off the Panama coast."

"Oh yes, you did say island."

"Sandra, I'm sorry," Dan said. "I'm sorry we did not find him sooner."

Sandra responded. She gripped the phone tightly but spoke calmly.

"It's okay, Dan. Go take care of him, and call me as soon as you know anything new."

Chapter 12

"You have nothing to fear from me, you know."

The words brought Sandra back from the place to which she had drifted, a place far away from hospitals and uncertainty.

"I had no choice but to call off the search," Director Hall stated.

Searching Director Hall's face for any trace of emotion, Sandra noted the furrows etched in Hall's deeply tanned brow. Sandra did not respond to Hall's comment, instead examining her fingernails, then looking away. The ICU visitor's room seemed too small.

"I'm here to help," the Director added. "What can I do?"

"Haven't you done enough already?" Sandra thought.

Sandra opened her mouth to speak, cleared her throat, then deleted everything she was about to say. Instead, she remained civil, straightened her spine, and sat taller in her chair.

"I accused Martin of leaving me to be with you in Costa Rica," Sandra said to Hall. "Was I right?"

"Direct, I like that," Hall replied quietly.

Sandra was silent once more.

"So it wasn't true?" Sandra asked.

Hall turned in the seat to face Sandra.

"Sandra, I had no intentions toward Martin, not like that. He is a fine man and a good husband. He is loyal to you and to your family. No one could ever come between that."

Sandra let her finish, then spoke her mind.

"I don't think you answered my question," she said firmly.

"That is the best answer I have for you," Hall replied, turning toward the door. "I'll have to leave as soon as we get the doctor's update."

"How long before Martin is able to go home?" Sandra asked.

"We'll have to get the doctors' word on that," Hall responded. "There are so many…uncertainties. Where were you when they called you?"

"Actually, I was quite close," Sandra said calmly. She felt as if she were about to tell something that was well-known. "Rebekah and I were at my hotel. We're in Northern Virginia for an Archaeology Conference."

"I wondered how you got here so fast," Hall responded, pretending to remove a stray hair from her dark wool blazer.

"Where is Rebekah now?"

"She flew back."

"Do you have transportation?"

"I have my Range Rover."

"It's late. Where are you staying?"

Sandra felt as if she was sharing fully known information as she was being grilled.

"I'm at the Ritz Carlton at Pentagon City."

"I know that hotel," Hall responded. "I can see if from the conference room that I often am called to in the Pentagon."

Sandra replied, "Yes, I saw the Pentagon out my window."

"Will you call me if there is anything I can do, or if his condition changes?" Hall requested. "I can't wait for the doctor, I have an early meeting."

"Sure," Sandra said, simply wanting the conversation to be over. She noted Hall's peculiar limp as the Director headed to the elevators.

Sandra stood up, leaving the small visitor's room, stepping out into quiet hospital hallway.

Her back pressed against the painted pastel wall, Sandra Culver shook off the chilly air conditioning as she tried to blend into the background. The sterile corridor seemed hollow, abandoned. Standing beneath the dim hallway lighting felt appropriate somehow, her every feeling and emotion highlighted and on display.

Separated by a broad expanse of glass from the intensive care unit humming and beeping before her, Sandra felt helpless, useless in spite of her gnawing desire for things to be better.

In the time it had taken to have Martin moved to a stateside hospital, Sandra felt herself slipping a little more each day, edging once more down the dark slope that she knew ended in black despair. The updates from Dan had not been enough. She wanted to be where Martin was, to touch him, to hold his hand, to make sure that he was real and alive. She had been through enough nightmares following his disappearance to make every glimmer of hope suspect, devoid of joy. She shivered and pulled her dark sweater together across her thin blouse.

Now she could see Martin, but could not go to him. His chest and arms, covered with bandages and intravenous lines, were tan, his muscular upper body exposed by a sheet folded to his waist. One hand was raised on a traction right and heavily bandaged. He seemed taller than she remembered, one brown foot hanging off the bed. His long hair and slight beard reminded her of their surfing days when she and Martin had first met at Croatan Beach.

Sandra could do little more than stand there and watch, spellbound as nursing personnel entered and left Martin's room at a frantic pace, masked and outfitted in accordance with the quarantine protocol spelled out in giant red letters on the door of the hospital room. She tried to pray, but was afraid to close her eyes, lest she fall asleep standing up. In another hour dawn would come.

The nurses seemed to be avoiding her, shunning eye contact in order to evade any possibility of engaging her in conversation. Although three of five ICU units were currently occupied with critically ill patients, all three floor nurses were all working in the room across from her, the room where her husband struggled to live.

Despite all the people and activity, Sandra realized that she still felt as starkly alone as when she had first entered the hospital. She found the darkened hall adjacent to the ICU nurse's station, comforting, almost womb-like, in contrast to the rest of the hospital, so brightly lit even at this late hour.

Sandra finally closed her eyes, taking mental inventory of everything that had happened over the last three months, rolling the images through her mind in fast forward. From the time Dan had called to say that Martin had been found until she heard he would be brought to Bethesda, her hopes had climbed despite the voice of reason that cautioned her thoughts. What she faced now was not at all what she had expected.

After an eternity, the lead nurse approached, stepping quickly and silently towards Sandra, stopping at a respectful distance, but still close enough to converse personally.

"Mrs. Culver, I'm Lt. Simmons, RN. You have been here all night. You should try to get some rest."

Sandra withdrew her extended hand, realizing that the nurse would not be returning her greeting.

"I cannot leave," Sandra stated quietly. Although the hallway clock read 5:45AM, she truly did not feel tired. She did not feel anything.

"How is he?" Sandra inquired. "Please tell me as much as you can."

"Mr. Culver has had a rough go, but we are hoping the worst is over," the nurse responded after a moment. Her face revealed that she did not find her own words very believable. "We'll know the full story soon," she added. "All the tests have been run, we are just waiting on results."

"It's been a long few months," Sandra replied. "I really don't want to wait, but a few more minutes won't kill me."

"I appreciate your understanding, Mrs. Culver," the nurse said soothingly.

"When can I go in to see him?" Sandra inquired.

"Not just yet," the nurse replied, tugging her face mask back into place. "He still has not gained consciousness following the transfer. I would say, once the test results are back and he has regained consciousness," she promised, turning back toward the patient's room. "He has had potential malaria exposure, plus his early bloodwork showed some unexpected results. Let's ask the doctor when he comes by."

Seeing these were not the answers Sandra was hoping for, the nurse added, "Hopefully things will take a turn for the better."

Sandra breathed in deeply. "They really couldn't get any worse," she sighed.

With sudden urgency, a bell sounded, a monitor alarm beeping in quick succession. The nurse held up one index finger to Sandra, then turned and hurried away.

Sandra's eyes followed the nurse as the uniformed woman quickly re-entered Martin's hospital room. Searching the ICU window through reflected hall lamps, the riot of blinking lights and digital readouts surrounding Martin's the single, central hospital bed, Sandra blinked away tears in an attempt to stem what would surely be an unstoppable flow once started.

Crossing the corridor, she stood as close as she could, touching her fingers to the glass where the heart monitor glowed, its halting, erratic pattern etched across the small screen. The signal from Martin's heart was weak to the point of being nearly flat.

"It was easier to think you were gone forever than to lose you like this, so close to home," she whispered, her fingers running down the glass. *"Don't take him away now, God, please."*

The RN suddenly exited Martin's ICU unit and grabbed the nearest phone. As soon as she cleared the room's doorway, she removed her face mask and gloves. In a methodical flurry of conversation, she spoke in hushed, professional tones, ending the conversation almost before it began.

"What is it?" Sandra asked, approaching the nurse. "What is happening? Has something changed? Please, I have to know."

The nurse looked up, thumbed quickly through the small stack of files at her station, then placed the files in a metal basket. Looking up, the nurse took both of Sandra's hands into her own comforting hands.

"Mr. Culver was awake, dear, for just a moment. He asked me something, and I understood him quite clearly. He made a request, so I made a call for him."

"What did he say?" Sandra said frantically. "What did he ask for?"

The nurse squeezed Sandra's hand a little tighter.

"Mr. Culver asked for a chaplain."

Although Sandra's voice did not respond, her face revealed her thoughts. Her mouth opened in horror at the thought that her worst nightmare was about to come true.

"How long will that take?" she asked the nurse. "Can I see him?"

"The chaplain is on his way up right now. His doctor should be here shortly."

"Lt. Simmons, how is he? Please tell me the truth."

"His signs have stabilized. Let's wait for the doctor to tell us. He's on his way."

Sandra waited, watching through the glass as all the nurses returned to Martin's heavily bandaged body lying tall in the center of the short hospital bed, switching on bright overhead lights that contrasted Martin's sun-bronzed arms dark against stark white sheets. She turned her gaze to the doctor who arrived at the ICU nurses station, watching as he promptly took Martin's chart aside for review.

"Doctor Holmes, Mrs. Culver was just asking for an update," Lt. Simmons said loud enough for Sandra to hear.

The agonizing pause from the doctor spoke louder than any words he might have said to her.

"Of course we will know more once all the test results are complete," the doctor replied in well-rehearsed tones. He slowly closed the medical chart he had been reviewing and removed his glasses.

"He has been through a lot, Mrs. Culver, but he seems tough. That gives him a fighting chance."

"Culver men," she replied. "A family trait of hard-headedness and determination. That's where that toughness comes from."

"Is the name Irish?"

"No, I think he told me Anglo-Saxon, first appearing in 1273. It means "dove". Why do you ask?"

"No one fights harder than the Irish," the doctor said, flashing his college ring her way. "Notre Dame, 1974."

"Doctor, about Martin?"

"Yes, yes, forgive me. The question is, Mrs. Culver..." the doctor began.

"Please call me Sandra," she replied.

"Sandra. Martin has suffered significant untreated infections, including his hand injury, which appears to be a bullet wound, deep lacerations to his back and the gash on his head. We are treating Martin with massive doses of antibiotics. The hospital in Panama started him on chloramphenicol, an antibiotic commonly used on horses. The infections have responded to intense treatment, so I believe we can save Martin's hand. There will be some therapy required. The million dollar question is whether he will be able to hear again. That is our greatest concern."

"What do you mean *whether* he will be able to hear?" Sandra asked, finding it hard to hide her surprise. "I thought Martin's hearing damage was just temporary."

"Martin has suffered severe damage to his eardrums. We believe he survived an extreme explosion. That part may take a while, and some surgery, to resolve. He may also require hearing devices."

74

"They told me he was ok when they found him," Sandra argued. "His friend told me that Martin was fighting back. They said he fought like ten men."

"That is true, Mrs. Culver," the doctor replied. "He fought like that because he did not recognize his friend or even his own brother. He did not realize who they were, or that they were there to help him. It remains to be seen how long it will take for him to recognize you."

"One of the first Navy doctors to examine Mr. Culver made an initial diagnosis of retrograde amnesia. "

Sandra turned away, feeling an uncertain, familiar paleness overtake her. Her hands shook uncontrollably.

"Among his more serious injuries," the doctor explained, re-opening the medical file, "the MRI revealed concussion. But perforated eardrums are at the top of the list. The eardrums were both infected, as is the hand wound. Simply surviving those challenges, combined with blood loss and dehydration makes him strong. He's lucky to be alive. His main battle up to now has been survival. If he makes it through the next 48 hours, then his prospects are very good."

Sandra felt unable to breathe. All these months waiting to learn whether Martin was alive had been so hard. Hearing that he had been found brought a fleeting sense of relief. Now, to realize that Martin might be left with hearing impairment, was almost too much to take. She bit her tongue, then asked her most pressing question.

"You said he may not know me? When will that improve, when will he know who I am?"

"Loved ones are the first to be recognized after significant head trauma," the doctor replied. "I will consult with the neurosurgeon regarding the full extent of his brain injury. There is swelling of the brain tissues. Recognition can be take weeks, or a few days. Time will tell us what we need to know."

"What about the chaplain? The nurse said Martin had requested a chaplain."

The doctor smiled a practiced smile, placed the medical file in a bin to be updated and turned to face Sandra directly. Behind him, she saw the chaplain arrive, don a mask and gown, and enter the hospital room, escorted by the nurse.

"I did not want to be the one to tell you this, but a body was found on the island with Mr. Culver. The body was badly decomposed with significant portions missing, below the waist, one arm. Mr. Culver is convinced that he is responsible for the murder of this person. He has maintained his guilt since he was first found."

"Well is he responsible?" she asked. "Who was the person, the body?"

"I would have no way of knowing, Mrs. Culver," he replied, glancing over her shoulder and behind her.

"So why did he ask for a chaplain?"

"I've just spoken to him," the chaplain said, exiting the room and disposing of the protective gear he had been given. "We prayed together. He asked to be forgiven."

"For what?" Sandra asked.

"For murder," the chaplain replied solemnly. "Apparently Mr. Culver's sense of faith runs deep. He believes he needs to be forgiven, in case he were to die."

Sandra did not remember wandering dizzily away from the nurses' station toward the hospital room where Martin lay. The tubes, wires, and blinking monitors were stark clarification of the worst. It was worse than if Martin were dead. He might live, and if he did, he might not ever know her. If he did know her, he was likely to be have permanent hearing loss. All the medical talk about tests, wait and see, waiting for confirmation, it was all too much.

Sandra turned away crying, and started running. She heard the chaplain calling, but continued to run, her heels barely making contact with the polished floor. She did not stop running until she reached the elevator doors, where one elevator miraculously opened before she pressed the button, mercifully shutting her in and away from the news she had just heard. Her sobs echoed inside the elevator, magnifying the sound of her emotional outpouring.

Reaching ground level, Sandra ran outside, slipping undetected through the southern exit of the hospital. Sunlight broke through the early morning clouds, then closed off again. As the sun as it struggled to show through the clouds, an early morning call from Cita drew her attention away.

"Hi Sandra, I came in early to get a jump on the day. Everyone wants to know how Martin is doing." Cita said. "They are asking about you too!"

Sandra bit her lip in an effort to stop crying. Holding her phone at arm's length, she sniffed away a few last tears.

"Martin is very touch and go, but they are trying to be positive. So I am trying to be positive too," she said, wiping her eyes on the sleeves of her sweater. "It's not easy!"

"You sound so tired Sandra, are you okay?"

"I've been up all night. I just spoke to the first doctor since he was brought here."

"You need some rest. Do you still plan to come back to the office this week?"

"Now that the Archaeology conference is over, I need to get back, I know you must be going crazy."

"Did Rebekah make it back ok?"

"Yes, she's fine. I've been checking with her now and then. How's Bethesda?"

"It's a hospital, Cita. I hate this whole area, DC, Northern Virginia. I hate everything about it, the traffic, the busyness. And you know how I hate hospitals."

Cita did not say anything, waiting for Sandra to finish and take a breath.

"Cita, Martin is not doing so well. I got my hopes up when Dan called to say that Martin had been found and again when I found out they were bringing him home. Now I don't know…"

Sandra's eyes dropped to her shoes, where a reflected light seemed to highlight a slight imperfection in the slick finish of one shoe compared to the other. Focusing her thoughts, she continued.

"I just talked to Martin's doctor. His test results are still pending. There's a lot to do and he may not know me yet. As soon as I am done here day, I will be heading back to Norfolk. There won't be anything I can do for a day or two, then I will come back up here for the weekend. Set up a meeting with Chartwell for mid-morning tomorrow and keep my schedule clear until at least after lunch, in case we go that long."

"Ok Sandra, will do. Are you still thinking about asking Chartwell to represent the IAF on the U.N. repatriation panel?"

"If it will get him out of my hair, then yes, I am thinking about it. I just don't know if he can handle it properly. We'll talk tomorrow. UNESCO is too important to hand off to just anyone."

Sandra paused and realized that talking about work was helping, by taking her mind off of the issues at the hospital.

"Anything of critical importance happening there?" Sandra asked, changing the subject.

"Everyone is working hard to mobilize on the requests to intervene across the Middle East. I have five teams working on this and they all are ready to report."

"Set that for tomorrow afternoon, ok?"

Cita waited to respond.

"You're doing it again, Sandra. The over-scheduling, I mean. You asked me to remind you."

"Yes, of course, Cita. Thank you. Set the report session for day after tomorrow, but not too early. I am starting back to the gym that morning. If I can still walk I will be in to meet with them."

Chapter 13

Sandra walked up the stairs to the second floor, ignoring Chartwell, and walked straight into her office. Cita arrived moments later.

"What, no elevator today?" Chartwell remarked.

"I need to get back into shape," Sandra commented, putting down her briefcase. "You can set that mail on my desk, Cita," Sandra instructed.

"So who is the one late to work today?" Chartwell asked, squeezing between Sandra and Cita, his brusque manager irritating Cita in the process.

He extended his hand toward Cita, whose hands were still grasping the overly full mail tray.

"Peru, if I'm not mistaken? You favored me with the bride's second dance."

"I remember you, and you are correct, it was Peru." Cita replied in a cool monotone. "You grabbed my ass during that dance, moments after I said my wedding vows."

"I'm so glad you remembered me," Chartwell grinned.

Cita rolled her eyes, excused herself and left, muttering a phrase unintelligible to most.

"That was Gaelic," he laughed. "I'm a bit rusty, but thank you for the suggestion."

Cita continued walking.

"I'm surprised she didn't deck you," Sandra remarked. "She could, you know. She works out. She can whip your butt in ancient languages or in the gym. How is it you two have not run into each other yet?"

"She just wasn't here whenever I came by," Chartwell offered.

"That tells me you have not been here much," Sandra countered. "John, Cita is *always* here, if the doors are open. Sometimes later."

"I'll try to do better," he said, sitting in front of her desk. "You don't look like you've gained weight."

"Stop trying to change the subject," she laughed.

Suddenly Sandra felt uncomfortable alone with Chartwell. She turned toward the window.

"So where were you all this time?" she asked.

"What, you missed me?"

"Where have you been!" Sandra said, turning and raising her voice. "I have been through hell. I needed you here. I have had a terrible time, the house explosion, running from hit squads, losing Martin. It has been a long, terrible summer."

"I noticed the perimeter hardening steps taken you've taken outside the building."

"Oh, the IAF was bombed too."

Sandra sat in her chair and glared at him, still waiting for his reply.

"Well, after I got out of the Merida jail I stayed at the beach for a few days to recuperate. Met some nice Brits with a place called Casa Rosa. I figured my chances with the IAF were screwed after everything that had happened. I made a few contacts and started getting job offers. I went to Costa Rica for a job interview then took a few days off in Panama with Mary. The client was a nut case who abruptly cancelled the contract and returned to Europe after a death in the family. I kept my retainer, though. Then Cita contacted me and told me to get my ass back here."

"In so many words," Sandra said, smiling just a little.

"In Gaelic, no less," he responded. "Mary wanted to come back to Norfolk, too. So there we are, all up to date."

"Slow down. You are dating Mary Power? I thought that was a rumor."

"Don't know if dating is the correct term," he responded. "It's not against the law you know."

"So how are things with Mary?" she asked him cynically.

"Pastimes," he responded simply. "We agreed to be each other's pastimes. We'll see what happens. We are adults, Sandra."

It was Sandra's turn to roll her eyes.

"I know, I just have to make sure we keep potential issues the IAF might face to a minimum as we move forward. And move forward is what we must do, which is why I need you. We have so much to do. There are dozens of repatriation issues coming up every week. The IAF has carved out a very good platform for assisting countries on how to achieve their goals. From the

Parthenon Marbles to Incan mummies and Egyptian statues we are swamped."

"Who is the biggest contributor to the problems we face?"

"Your friends at The British Museum, of course. They are making life hell for us. Every effort we make at repatriation of their antiquities gets blocked."

"Of course. Any suspects in particular?"

"We think the problems are coming from an educator inside the museum. "

"That is interesting. When I arrived downstairs, I had a message waiting for me from London, someone I know at the British Museum.

As an afterthought, Chartwell interrupted Sandra's next statement.

"By the way, Amanda is perfect," he interjected. "She is everything I've ever dreamed of in a secretary. Could not have done better myself."

"Down boy, Amanda is not here for you. I'm sure we have a personnel policy about dating employees, but if we don't, I will write one on the spot," Sandra declared, pointing her finger at him.

"Relax, Sandra, I'm with Mary. I'm just commenting on your taste in employees."

Desperate to change the subject, Sandra walked out of her office with Chartwell in tow. They met Cita in the corridor.

"Cita, I will catch up with you in a half hour, ok?"

"Sure, I have a bunch of things to do. Is this guy bothering you?"

"No, I can handle him. Come on Chartwell, let me buy you coffee."

"I would prefer tea," he responded.

"I'll drop in several teabags at once if it will make you feel any better," Sandra offered.

"Now you're talking."

They entered the second floor breakroom, gravitating to the employee lounge coffee bar by the window overlooking the Little Creek marinas.

"Chartwell, who called you from London?" Sandra asked as she prepared their drinks.

"Professor M.A. Haddad, PhD. I'm sure you've never heard of him. He's a terrific bore, fascinated with all the flaky stuff, trying to add academic weight to studies of Merlin, Arthur, the literature and that whole Camelot mythology, which by the way he believes was all real."

"So you know him?"

"All too well. He was a colleague. I did not admire his work. I thought he was rushed and amateurish in his documentation, therefore his conclusions. It has cost him, in credibility and in his health. He suffered an injury during a temple cave-in in Egypt. Left him paralyzed in a wheelchair."

"A wheelchair?"

"Yes, why the surprise?"

"I may have run into him recently. In fact, if it is the same man, I talked to him on the phone."

"That is fascinating. What did he want?"

"I don't know. He wouldn't say. Haddad keeps calling and asking for you or for Martin."

"Well, he left me an interesting phone message. Wants me to meet him in London. Do you want to hear it?"

"Do I have a choice?"

Chartwell fished his hand deep into his cargo pants pocket to retrieve the paper message Amanda had given him. Along with a ragged batch of baggage tags, air transfer coupons and receipts, he fished out the wrinkled paper.

"I hope those receipts will be neater before you submit them for reimbursement."

"Funny", he laughed. "The message reads:"

'Think of me as friend or foe,
The world advances, as you well know.
I obtained a sword,
I give you my word,
A sword of legend and lore.
Tell a soul, and I shall withhold.
(I've told you the story before).' "

"He left his message for you as a poem? How touching!"

"Amanda said he dictated it exactly, down to the punctuation. Like I told you, boring, right?"

"Weird is more like it. What is his deal?"

"He's just like that. Although early British history and a great many legends were recorded in poetic form. A bit on the dramatic end, I would say."

"Or off the deep end. So are you going to London to meet him?"

"Planning to in a few days. I have other business there too. Want to go?"

"No, I will need to stay here until Martin is fully recovered and back in the office. I would like for you to meet with Cita and I in the next day or two to review where we stand on everything. "

"Yeah, plus me and Martin still have a few things to talk about, as I recall. When we he feel up to a visit?"

"Don't start trouble, John."

"No intent to start trouble, Sandra. It's not every day your boss leaves you to rot in a Mexican jail. I deserve a few answers."

"John, listen to me," Sandra pleaded. "Don't push him. He paid your attorney. He made arrangements for your belongings. We held your job. John, Martin needs more time. You will see what I mean. Take it easy, ok?"

"All right, I'll go along with that. For now."

"So what is all this busy activity downstairs about? I must have seen thirty people working all through the building."

"I told you there is a lot going on at the IAF right now. This is why we need to meet. Repatriation of antiquities is in the news every day. Some of the situations are getting hot politically. One of those topics is the Parthenon Marbles."

"The Elgin Marbles, you mean, for Lord Elgin of Britain, who took them," Chartwell responded, correcting her error.

"Okay, the Elgin Marbles." Sandra replied, exasperated. "They have been sent to Russia without Greece's permission or even its knowledge. Now there is concern that Russia will not return the sculpture."

"Surely Putin won't keep them?" Chartwell ventured.

"The current thinking is that Russia may return the statues directly to Greece in exchange for a warm-water port for Moscow."

"Because theirs all have to use icebreakers ten months a year," Chartwell realized.

"This is why I need you, to stay on top of these situations."

"Okay, well. Before I get started, I should like to see my office."

"That's right," Sandra said. "You have not yet seen your office, have you?"

"No I haven't. You may recall that I have been unavoidably detained. You also took the key when you left for the conference last week, and since then you have been at Bethesda."

Sandra took him by the hand.

"I'm so sorry for all you have been through, John. Let me show you what you've been missing," she said.

"I'm ready," Chartwell said, putting down his tea.

Sandra stopped short as she tried to exit the break room, to keep from bumping into Cita, whose arm was stretched across the doorway.

"Yes, I'd like to know, too," Cita announced. "Just what has Mr. Chartwell been missing?"

Neither Sandra nor the archaeologist spoke, each too stunned at Cita's sudden appearance to string a decent sentence together.

"Chartwell, this is a new low, even for you," Cita said. "Your office is down the corridor, last door on the left. It's unlocked. Sandra, you're coming with me."

"What about me?" Chartwell asked.

Cita pointed her finger at him, mouthing a few choice words.

"I know," he responded. "Gaelic. Once again, thanks for the suggestion, as improbable as it may be."

Chapter 14

Across the Atlantic Ocean, a black phone handset was carefully returned to its cradle, the neatly coiled cord laid to one side of the otherwise cluttered desk. Diffused afternoon sunlight pushed its way into the room through broken clouds, past thick wooden window-frames, illuminating stained glass squares into quadrants of pale color across the far wall.

Staring at the series of black and white photographs strewn across his desk, the Professor brought his fingertips together, peering through them to focus his attention. He then reached down, drawing his right index finger across the photograph of Martin Culver.

Shifting uncomfortably in his chair, Professor Haddad began to drum the fingers of his right hand at the edge of the desk. Lifting the photo of Culver out of the way, the Professor revealed the next photo, scowled, and punched his fist down onto the table, figuratively smashing the face of John Robert Chartwell.

Rubbing the knuckles of his right hand across his bearded chin, the Professor reached out, this time touching his finger to the worn corner of a photograph nearly hidden at the center of the pile.

Sliding the photo out of the stack, his eyes widened, then narrowed behind thin-framed spectacles. The familiar female face that stared back at him, almost completely swathed in multiple linen strips, had no idea of his true thought or intent.

For a moment, the Professor pretended to be unaware of the dark-haired woman who had entered his study unannounced. He watched her from a peripheral perspective as he returned the photos to their folders.

"Professor Haddad," the woman's voice chimed, "I know you're busy, but it's time for your afternoon tea."

Turning sharply, the professor smiled a sincerely artificial smile. Everything about his assistant, her American accent, her lack of manners, her very presence grated his nerves. It had taken far less time for him to feel this way than with the others.

Tugging his tailored shirt sleeve down to hide an exposed band of black elastic fabric, the Professor slowly surveyed his assistant from head to toe, pausing at intervals to dwell upon her generous curves.

"Is it that late, Miss Hopewell?" he inquired, licking his lips. "The afternoon is half gone and I have accomplished nothing today."

Grasping the edges of her sweater, his assistant doubled the garment across her chest, looked away, then walked behind him and reached for the Professor's wheelchair. She hated his gaze, knowing full well he was scrutinizing her body in the most minute detail. These lecherous gazes, his unwelcome advances, the continuous off-color comments and innuendo had everything to do with why she had decided to end her association with him, to say nothing of the social isolation she had experienced living an hour from London with no internet and no friends.

Today absolutely had to be the last day. Her bag was already packed and tucked into the boot of her tiny British convertible. Miss Hopewell had made her up mind to simply advise the Professor of her plans once afternoon tea was served, and then promptly leave.

The Professor made no sound as he spun away from his desk, his cane tucked between useless legs. As he turned, the Professor searched Miss Hopewell's face for something lost, for something familiar, a sign of hope. The clenched knot in his chest drove home the realization that he had already come as close to Miss Hopewell as he would ever hope to be, at least in this life.

"Perhaps a warm cup of tea in the sunroom will provide you a new perspective," Miss Hopewell offered. As she gripped the steering handles of his chair, she felt tension tighten her shoulders. "That has always helped relax you."

"Perhaps you are correct," the Professor agreed as she wheeled him through the paneled double doors of his study, down the short, dark hallway towards the light streaming in from the sunroom. "You always know what is best for me."

Miss Hopewell did not reply. She hated his double meanings. She also hated the sunroom, with its multiple mummies lining the walls like so many morbid, unresponsive guests.

As they entered the pyramid-shaped sun room, with its soaring glass roof, the Professor glanced toward the 20-foot tall statue of Anubis standing near the center of the room, amid four inscribed obelisks of equal height. A native Egyptian, the Professor knew the story of Anubis from his youth. But Anubis was so much more to him than a story. As the lead Egyptologist on Staff at UCL, the Professor worshiped Anubis, the Egyptian god of embalming, as his one true God. Anubis spoke to him directly, Haddad believed, speaking daily, giving him instructions, advice, and the esteem that a god offers freely to a devoted follower. In return, he was subservient to Anubis' every desire and appetite.

Nodding his head in mute acknowledgement to Anubis' latest demand, the Professor glanced up, then to one side. He knew exactly what was to become of Miss Hopewell. He knew that the time had come. He felt obligated to make conversation, but his mind was occupied by concerns that hung heavy on the horizon, concerns that reached far beyond the walls of this estate. He knew his place in those events as certainly and as inescapably as he knew Miss Hopewell's destiny.

Pressing a button on his left inner sleeve, the Professor felt a surge of energy flash through his torso and lower limbs.

Miss Hopewell poured hot water into her own teacup, pausing to take a long sip, as was her custom. Her action stood in stark contrast to British custom, where the host is always the last to consume. He had come to expect her error.

"Damned Americans," the Professor thought. *"It's time to finish this."*

Miss Hopewell wavered slightly as she leaned forward to fill his tea cup, her eyes showing white as they rolled lazily up into her head. The Professor stood to his feet, tall and strong in front of his wheelchair. Watching her eyes flutter before she went limp, the Professor reached for the nape of her neck with his left hand, and the back of her belted skirt with the other, holding her body upright. With a quiet crackle of electricity, her body jerked stiffly, her eyes opening wide. Stunned, Miss Hopewell dropped the teapot, splattering its steaming contents across the sun-patterned marble floor amid shattered Wedgewood china. A low, slurred moan escaped her lips, her arms dangling at her sides like a puppet.

Finding she could still think, Miss Hopewell fought through the mist to understand what was taking place. Wild thoughts flashed through her mind, then flickered away. *"How is it possible he is standing to his feet? How has he escaped the wheelchair?"*

She felt helpless as the Professor lifted and draped the upper half of her body across the great stone table at the center of the sunroom. She felt it cold against her face, felt his grip tighten on her neck. Feeling the Professor standing over her, Miss Hopewell registered the sound of his silver-tipped cane hissing through the air. With one motion the Professor whipped the head of the cane down with lethal force, striking at the base of her skull. The sickening crunch of the cane against bone was muffled by the girl's long black hair, but the impact of the blow was in no sense diminished. Miss Hopewell ceased to exist in the conscious world, her immobilized body at once folding to the floor in undignified silence.

Unable to move, but conscient to the minimal possible degree, the research assistant knew she had been struck, but felt no pain. She remembered her studies. This was how King Tut had died. Drugged and struck at the base of the skull before being mummified. She thought of the tea.

She felt the Professor lift her body lightly, felt him place her fully on the cold stone table in the center of the sun room, positioning her on her back. Through unmoving, half-open eyes she registered multiple pointed obelisks looming above her, covered with Egyptian hieroglyphics.

Paralyzed, she was unable to so much as blink. Yet Miss Hopewell could still feel lurid sensations bombarding her from all sides. The cool stone tabletop, the chill of the room, the faint tingling in her limbs, the dull pain at the base of her skull.

She could not move, yet she felt movement; slight, unwelcome movement, a tugging at her clothes, a new chill across her entire body, followed by a certain painless pull stirring in her belly before falling into that most permanent of all sleeps.

For the Professor, the glass atrium roof provided all the light he needed. The crescent moon depression carved into the cool stone table top provided a useful repository for the residues of the task at hand. By the rays of the late afternoon sun the professor went to work, unrolling a papyrus sheaf of long thin knives, uncorking ceramic jars of balms and rolls of infused linen strips. He worked steadily, methodically, carefully, until it was time to begin wrapping the shapely body.

Stopping to answer the phone, the Professor apologized to his subject for leaving her in such a revealed state, and peeled off one bloody glove. He punched up the speakerphone, openly leering at his work in progress splayed horribly across the table as he spoke.

"Hello? Yes, this is Professor Haddad. Yes, in fact I am running an advertisement for a research assistant. I should be most happy to meet you soon. Yes. I prefer to meet at the British Museum, in London. Be prompt at 11:00 AM, a week from today, would you?"

Hanging up the phone, the Professor went back to work, swiftly, and with precision. Within the hour, he stood back to admire his creation.

His former assistant's clothing lay to one side, neatly slit from her body, placed with her shoes and undergarments. White linen strips soaked in pungent ointment that bound her limbs, torso and head, were already drying into a stiff, tight bundle. The Professor gently wound the final turn of linen around the top of Miss Hopewell's head and tucked the loose end beneath the nearest band. Beneath the table, in place of canopic jars, a cryogenic container labelled for Ankara, Turkey rested, sealed and neat.

Tilting his face upward, the Professor faced the towering jackal statue and stretched his hands out over his horrifying handiwork. Thus did he dedicate his creation to Anubis, intoning an ancient chant, reciting the ancient Sumerian embalming ritual from the original Ebla cuneiform tablets.

"O Anubis, Wisdom eternal,
I bring to you my offering, my Lord
In the time of your Light and your Fullness,
Do not deny your servant thy strength and power
May your temple rise once more to the heights,
to the heavens, O Lord of the gods."

As the sun steadily dropped, his droning prayer continued until the room was blanketed in occult darkness. The Professor looked up through the skylight to see the crescent moon advancing into the night sky directly over the stone table.

89

Dropping exhausted back into his wheelchair, the only sounds in the room were the Professor's intense respiration, and a slight, infrequent drip from beneath the massive table.

"Miss Hopewell, Anubis is pleased at your sacrifice," he breathed. Pulling aside his priestly linen robes, the Professor unsnapped the collar contacts leading from the nerve-like electric cables that ran through the fabric of the form-fitting suit that he was wearing.

Feeling the one piece garment relax, Professor breathed an instant sigh of relief. He was still learning to manage the suit, the pressure, the tension, the heat of it. The power and strength that it provided, including replacing his lost ability to walk, came at the expense of complete exhaustion afterward. The suit sleeve blinked, already beginning to regenerate power from his body heat while he rested.

Chapter 15

"You've been very quiet this morning," Cita remarked. "Want to talk about anything?"

Sandra stared at Cita over dark-framed glasses and rolled her eyes.

"I haven't asked you in several days," Cita said, apologizing. "I just hope everything is ok. You have so much on you right now."

Only the whirring of the printer on Sandra's desk broke the overhanging silence, spitting out an agenda for the IAF morning meeting.

"Norfolk, Virginia is a long way from Costa Rica, that's all I know," Sandra responded. "Is that what you wanted me to say? Because until one month ago, that is where I planned to be."

Cita chose her words carefully.

"I meant about Martin."

Sandra put down the papers she hand in her hands and removed her glasses.

"Martin has made an amazing recovery. His doctors all agree, he's getting better every day," Sandra said, frowning as she spoke. She focused on the printer output, avoiding Cita's straightforward gaze. "He even has some hearing returning."

"Then what's wrong?" Cita asked. "I'm worried about you."

"Cita, it has been a crazy few weeks. I'm exhausted. I just hope Martin gets back to normal soon."

"Why are you so tired?"

Sandra seemed visibly wounded, but it was unclear if her reaction came from Cita's question, or the information Sandra felt compelled to divulge. Sandra motioned for Cita to push the door closed. Obliging, Cita closed the door and tip-toed back to her seat.

"Because, Cita, if you must know, Martin keeps me up every night. He has the energy of a man half his age. I don't understand it. One week he is on death's door and the next he is the guy I married, *when we were first married*! From the time I get home until past midnight…"

Sandra's voice trailed off as she sipped the last of her coffee. A hint of a smile crossed her face before she turned back to the printer. She tried her best to avoid Cita's gaze.

"Ooh, I see," Cita said. "So that's it."

"And then sometimes he wakes me up again," Sandra added without turning around.

"Oh my," Cita giggled. "So… just think of it as a second honeymoon. He's glad to see you, Sandra. Martin was gone a long time. How many weeks in all?"

"Almost twelve weeks. Part of spring and the whole summer."

"See, that makes sense. He missed you. He is just making up for lost time with you."

"Cita!" Sandra blurted out. "Martin was not gone on a cruise or something. I was never expecting to see him again. I am so grateful he is alive, but I was not expecting his recovery to be like this. I am sure glad the twins are in Costa Rica. I can hardly get a meal or get dressed for work. And where he gets these ideas…"

Cita tried to not press, realizing she had touched a nerve.

"No roller coaster I have ever ridden matches this for ups and downs. There is a huge gap between feeling that you have lost someone forever to being newlyweds again."

She took a deep breath.

"Anyway, the doctor believes Martin's hearing will fully return, but she's not certain when. He has to wear these hearing devices that attach with magnets and enhance what he hears. He hates those."

Sandra placed her empty coffee cup directly on the desk, no coaster, no paper beneath. It was so out of character, something that Cita had never seen her do. Obviously, Sandra was distracted.

"Martin seems strong physically. Even his hand is better. He finished therapy, his hand has a good grip and a hell of a scar."

Sandra collected her thoughts before continuing.

"Inside Martin's not completely back yet, like a part of him is still out there somewhere. And even when we are close, I wonder if he really is there, you know?"

"You mean like when a guy seems to be thinking about something else, even when he's with you?"

92

"Yes, that's it exactly. More than once I wondered. At least he does remember my name."

"So he remembers you now, right? That must have been hard."

"The challenge is that since his memory fully returned, it seems like Martin has been trying to make up for lost time, if you know what I mean."

"Trust me, I understand more than you know," Cita affirmed. "Since the baby, I have to hold Dan at arm's length just to get a decent night's sleep."

Cita blushed, realizing that they had both potentially crossed TMI boundaries. She quickly changed the subject.

"Sorry, Sandra, you were telling me about Martin's doctor."

"The doctor says he has is a form of post-traumatic stress disorder."

"I don't know much about it, but I have heard that people who have PTSD exhibit behavior that really isn't normal for them," Cita offered. "They are trying to cope. Little things throw them off, bring back bad memories. I have met a couple of Dan's friends who have been to Afghanistan. Even the toughest soldiers are fragile when they first come home."

The room went silent but for the plink of heavy raindrops on the glass of her office window. Sandra glanced at a picture of she and Martin from happier times, then laid the picture face down on her bookcase. She stared out the window toward the Chesapeake Bay.

"All I know is, I need a break. Martin seems to be either on high speed or low, nothing in between," she said, looking out across the Chesapeake Bay. "He has a wild amount of energy most nights, then at times he is asleep before Rebekah and I finish cooking dinner."

"Are you going to stay at the condo for now?"

"Yes, until Martin gets better. We don't really have enough room for the three of us. The walls are thin with Rebekah there. Martin wants to build another house, but his doctors say for him not to attempt too many changes right now. I will give him credit, Martin keeps trying to move ahead with life. Nothing, even this, ever seems to hold him down. He has ordered a new Jeep, that ugly military tan, keeps going on about our safety. He bought a small armory of weapons last week."

"Is that a good idea?"

"I don't know, I wonder sometimes." Sandra's mind went to the pistol that Martin brought back with him. He never let it out of his sight, except to have it professionally cleaned and restored. She did not know where he got it or why he carried it.

"So has he told you what happened yet, Sandra?"

"He hasn't told me much of anything. I don't know how he ended up on that island, how he lost his hearing, got shot, any of it. What little I do know comes second hand from his doctor, plus the few things CIA Director Hall has told me. Everyone says Martin will tell me when he is ready, that he will wake up and snap out of it at some point. He is so stoic, though, it's hard to talk about this, plus his hearing gets in the way."

"The thing is, Martin still has not once told me that he loves me, or that he missed me or our family. I can kind of tell, but it would be nice to hear, especially with him chasing me around the house until all hours."

"Is *that* why you agreed to let the twins go with Jack?"

"I think this was the motivation behind Jack's idea to take them with him to Costa Rica, so that Martin and I could kind of adjust to each other again, in the event he was found alive. Jack said Martin would be like a sailor that had been at sea too long."

"Jack probably remembers exactly what that is like, being ex-Navy," Cita smiled, putting her arms around Sandra's shoulders and pulling her close.

"Give it time," Cita said. "At least he's here, at least he survived."

"I keep trying to tell myself that," Sandra said, burying her face in Cita's sweater. She bit her lip and told herself to not cry. "He can't hear me well, and he hasn't talked much. We are all out of sync. He is up until all hours, sleeps four hours max and is up again. Every morning, he goes outside and lights up the patio fire pit before dawn. I never hear him when he gets up."

"So you're saying Martin's energy runs in cycles?"

Sandra grabbed a tissue from her desk and dabbed at her make-up.

"Cita, did I ever tell you that you ask too many questions?"

Sandra opened her desk and pulled out a small mirror.

"I wish there were cycles I could identify," she said, noticing the tired lines in her own face. "Martin has so much energy, but he's on no schedule. I keep hoping things will smooth out, but I haven't found the courage to tell him no."

"Hoping what will smooth out?" the female peeking in through Sandra's office door inquired. Sandra and Cita looked up to see a short, trim blonde with a store-bought coffee and a yellow legal pad standing with the door half opened.

"Umm, have we met?" Sandra asked.

"Sandra Culver, allow me to introduce Mary Power, PhD. She is the new curator for the IAF. She will be handling our University Public Relations, directly interacting with museums and archaeology departments around the country."

No one spoke for what seemed like an eternity. A phone rang unanswered in the library down the hall.

"I am…pleased to meet you Mary. I'll see you at the meeting," Sandra said, gathering up the printed outlines. "Cita, I'll meet you in the library. Have Amanda bring up coffee, ok?"

"Sure," Cita said quizzically as Mary turned to leave.

"Why did we hire her?" Sandra asked bluntly as soon as Mary left.

"Sandra, my plate is too full - being your assistant and sometimes CEO here. If you want me to take on more, I need some help."

"Cita, do you realize who Mary Power is?"

"No, do you know her?"

"She and Martin worked together on a Spanish treasure recovery near Cuba. She made a play for Martin the night they found the site where the ship went down."

"Did anything happen?"

"No, Martin told me about it after he got back. He turned her down."

"Sandra, I had no idea! I will give her the boot on your say-so. I have other potential candidates. Mary has her doctorate. She was prior faculty at Old Dominion University. She seemed like the right person for university relations for the IAF."

"Why did she take the job, did she say?"

"She said she took the job to be back near Old Dominion. I also suspect it was to be near Chartwell. They seem to have a thing."

"I knew about that, just not that she was working here." Sandra stated without emotion. "This place is full of surprises."

Chapter 16

"What have you done, Uncle?" the woman's voice inquired, directly confronting her father's only brother.

The Professor hesitated, taking a deep, measured breath. There was no hiding from her on the video conference screen in his UCL office.

"It is so good to see you, too! As always, my precious niece, I have taken great care to achieve the wishes and the instructions of the Jackal, nothing added, nothing taken away," the Professor stated without hesitation. "You look marvelous, may I add?"

"And of your own agenda, Uncle? Have you taken similar care to achieve your own goals as well?"

Melinda Medina waited for a reply, pushing a strand of damp hair from her forehead. She gently applied a plush towel to her face and neck, using a patting motion.

The Professor looked away from the camera as he responded.

"Melinda, my child, unlike you, I have no burning goals of personal status or achievement. I am a peaceful man who seeks peace. We are not to judge, or to point out the shortcomings of another as long as we have improvements to make in our own lives. Did your mother and father not teach you this?"

Melinda left the conversation silent, but only for a moment.

"Do not speak of my mother. After you labelled her a witch, I have never forgiven you. As for my father, he was nothing like you, and neither am I, Allah be praised. My father did not possess *your* flawed delusions, and he never worked on his own account, always working under the guidance of the Jackal. *Everything* he did was for the good of his own family, the Jackal and the Kingdom of Allah, blessed be his name. Can you say the same?"

"I can only say what I know to be true," the Professor stated. "I have been loyal to the Jackal longer than anyone. No matter what the appearance, neither my personal beliefs nor my life goals will ever cross paths with my allegiance to the Jackal."

Melinda cleared her throat and spoke back sharply to her blood relative, glaring into the video screen at close range.

"Uncle, do you realize what we are up against?"

"No, my dear, educate me."

"From the time the Jackal conceived the plan to revive the Islamic State, our organization has never faced stronger opposition. The murderer of my parents has returned from the dead, this Martin Culver. He has picked the bones of *mis parientes y mi prometido,* my parents and my fiancé, while our efforts to eliminate *his family* have failed. And he has once again joined forces with your old nemesis, Chartwell."

"Now I fear that Culver's CIA sponsor has picked up your ther end of the smuggling pipeline operating through the British Museum to Istanbul. This Director Hall believes that you are the link, but she does not know how it all connects to me. She has been snooping and she is good. She does not know, at this time, that you are my blood relative."

"How does Martin Culver link to Chartwell the archaeologist?"

"I found out Chartwell is on Martin Culver's payroll. From appearances, Martin Culver is an assassin working for the CIA. He has killed our people in Peru, in Mexico, and now in Panama."

Pausing to allow her words to crystallize, Medina waited.

"Then we have no time to waste. We must redeem the time, to bring our plans to pass," the Professor stated mechanically.

"I am glad you are clear on where we stand. Prepare for a visit from me within the week. I must see your progress on the historical pieces the Jackal has ordered and be apprised of your plans and progress. I wish to personally deliver to him the sword you have spoken of. I also want to receive an update on the EXO project to give him. Your status report is overdue. While I will extend the respect and courtesy you deserve as my uncle, I will not go empty-handed when I go to the Jackal the following week."

"You do not trust me to deliver the sword?"

"I have been in this business long enough to despise the word trust. My own father was not trustworthy to my standards. My own actions will I trust."

"Where will you be meeting the Jackal?"

"I do not know when or where that might happen. I never know until the day prior. If I did know, I would not tell you. He makes the travel arrangements, I show up to the airport and go where the ticket takes me."

"That implies a tremendous confidence on your part. I commend you for your bravery."

"Do not flatter me, uncle. I am merely doing my duty. The Jackal has never threatened my personal safety or well-being, which is more than I can say for you."

The Professor's frustration showed in the color of his face.

"Must you always bring that up? I thought we had settled those matters between us long ago."

Melinda draped her hand across her perspiring neckline without thinking, unconsciously hiding her bosom from his sight.

"You are lucky that I did not bring your perversions to my father's attention when he was alive. If I had he would have surely killed you himself."

"So when are you coming to visit?" the Professor asked uncomfortably. "I have some tidying up to do before your arrival."

"Spare me the sordid details, please," Melinda said, cutting him off. "I have no desire to hear it. I will call you from Heathrow when I arrive. I prefer to meet at the museum."

The Professor was taken aback.

"You prefer not to meet at my estate? But Melinda, I cannot receive you properly at the museum. As the daughter of my only brother, my favorite niece, do you not wish to be in the hospitality of my home? Honor me, stay with me on this visit."

The Professor's persistent unwelcome pleading managed to insert into Melinda's mind images of the atrocities she had witnessed at his hands while still a young teenager, of the many attempts he had made to involve her in his depravity, images that had taken years of time and hours of therapy to forget. Melinda shivered, her skin crawling with disgust. She wrapped the towel around her shoulders, rubbing her hands lightly across her forearms, smoothing dark, fine hair that literally stood on end. Melinda composed her thoughts before speaking.

"If I have failed to speak clearly on this matter in the past, Uncle, allow me to do so now. If I am made to come to your home, under any circumstances, it will be uniquely on the orders of the Jackal. The results will not be pleasant for you. Do you understand my meaning?"

The Professor did not reply.

99

"I did not ask for the role of enforcer to the Jackal's interests," Melinda said, apologetic in words but not in tone. "But I *will* do my job."

"Then the museum it is," the Professor relented. "I will await your call when you arrive."

"Is there anything else that you wish to tell me, uncle? The headlines from London are tragic. They always lead me to think of you."

"To which headlines might you be referring?" he inquired.

"I will read them to you," Melinda stated in a sing-song manner, holding up each London Times headline as she did so. "'Tragic Dual Death at Stonehenge'," she began. " 'Armored Car Heist of Museum Shipment' should ring a bell. Oh and let us not forget 'Disappearance of Young UCL Research Assistant'. Second in as many months that worked directly with you at the college and lived at your home. Still beyond your recollection?"

"Coincidence, speculation, innuendo," the Professor retorted. "I have spoken to the authorities and I am not linked to any of those unfortunate incidents, either directly or indirectly."

"If that is what you maintain, then who am I to disagree?" Melinda replied. "But you have been busy, and if any one of these things did involve you, then our operation is exposed and therefore vulnerable. In that case my duty is clear."

Changing the subject, the Professor took an offensive, rather than defensive tone.

"Speaking of exposed and vulnerable, my child, I can see from here how little you are wearing."

"I returned this instant from fencing practice. Hotter than a burqa inside that fencing suit."

Melinda lifted the straps to her tank top away from her shoulders and fanned herself generously.

"I hope you put a cooling fan in the exo-suit, as I requested."

"The exo-suit will fulfill your every desire, I swear to it."

"Are we finished, then?" she asked, sensing an oncoming lecture. "My shower and massage are waiting."

"When will you abandon your devotion to Western fashion?" the Professor asked. "Or shall we have another discussion with you about the exposure of your legs or the depth of your décolleté?

Your father was growing more concerned in the months before he died. Your body is meant for your husband's eyes only."

"I would prefer that you not look at me at all," Melinda replied. "I have no husband, thank you for reminding me. I will remind you of your earlier words, dear uncle. We are not to judge, nor to point out the shortcomings of another as long as we have improvements to make in our own lives."

"*Touché*, my dear," the professor replied. "Of course you are correct."

"Until next week, then," Melinda stated with an air of finality.

The Professor heard a clicking sound, then watched the video image of his niece diminish and fade as she walked away from her computer. He began to methodically roll his wheelchair back and forth using one hand along the Egyptian marble floor of his study.

"Your time is coming, precious niece," he said to no one in particular. "Soon you will see things from my point of view. What a fine queen you will make."

Chapter 17

Martin Culver gazed into the intense, blazing fire, its warmth welcome in the late-fall darkness. He surveyed the patio around him, confirming his surroundings. He was not dreaming.

He was at the condo Sandra had rented during his extended absence, an alternative that made perfect sense after outgrowing the temporary living arrangement with Cita and Dan. The stars told him it was nearly midnight.

Compared to how he had lived while stranded on the island, the scene was surreal. Instead of a few sticks nursing a smoky fire on a mosquito-infested beach, he had a neat circle of fire brick, a tidy fire blazing next to a stack of dried oak. Instead of the oppressive humidity of the tropical Pacific, he was facing Pretty Lake at the mouth of the Chesapeake Bay, with a cool, clean breeze.

Martin stood motionless, gazing deeper into the flames. Dry logs burned with a distinct fury, radiating intense heat that reddened his face. He backed away from the flames, moving a step deeper into the crisp evening. Although it was late, he had no desire to go inside, much less try to sleep. The hissing in his ears was keeping him awake again, a constant distracting background to his scattered thoughts. Glancing up and to his right, Martin watched a shooting star glow its path across the sky and then fade away. He pondered what message the fiery messenger brought. In ages past, such signs were a portent of trouble to come.

Closing his eyes, Martin unconsciously flexed his muscles and stretched, progressing through a range of martial arts moves.

Returning to the only outlet that had calmed and motivated him while awaiting rescue on the island, Martin knew what he needed to do. The only thing he had found to dispel the deadness and the darkness that had overwhelmed him would have to sustain him now.

Now that his mind was catching up to everything that had happened, he relived his most vivid, horrific memory from the time he went missing, of choking the same man to death, over and over again. Martin watched the man's eyes bulge, watched his face go purple.

Martin's hands moved independently, making the motions his thoughts dictated, as if they were disembodied spirits. The adrenaline rush, the endorphins coursing through his veins was pleasant, restorative. Knowing that he had personally rid the world of a citizen evil and most vile pleased him.

Still, he felt strangely disconnected, observing a frightening side of himself struggling for control, a side he did not actually recognize, but knew he must contain, lest he become all that he hated.

The intense anger Martin felt rehearsing this ugly scene burned away anything resembling remorse, just as the heat from the fire pit pushed back against the night air. After remembering that his family had been victims of a revenge killing, that anger would not, under any circumstances, leave him.

Martin knew this emotion had to be channeled. He felt guilty, but he enjoyed the feeling of having killed someone who deserved it, of ending a life dedicated to bringing pain and misery to others.

Martin's heart told him that he should be paying more attention to the Gideon's Bible he had found onboard the barge, and less to the Military Close Quarters Training Manual he had found alongside it. The Bible instructed him to forgive, while the Training Manual taught him to exact a physical penalty, an eye for an eye, as it were. Two sources of guidance, in conflict.

Martin had sought forgiveness from the hospital chaplain for the men he had killed. He felt certain that it would take a spiritual component, in some form, to lead to his restoration. For now, that spiritual component came mixed with physical revenge in the form of self-taught martial arts.

Martin kept his eyes closed, then began to recite the Lord's Prayer silently as he stepped through the training moves he had memorized from the hand-to-hand combat manual, practicing deadly defensive motions in front of the firepit. He defended himself from imaginary weapons - swords, spears, firearms.

Struggling to strike a balance in his mind, Martin felt torn. The Close Quarters Training manual, dated December 1944, had been printed at the beginning of WWII to give captured sailors a fighting chance if they became Japanese prisoners of war. Using these defensive techniques, a soldier stood a chance to wrest a battle sword away from a Japanese guard, to gain the upper hand. The Bible had been written centuries before, to give men an opportunity to live better lives.

As he moved, Martin caught sight of his own shadow on the brick wall behind him. Looming dark and tall to the second story, his long-haired image did imaginary battle in the flickering firelight, challenging the same unseen enemies as he had done on the island beach before he had become too weak.

Martin stopped and stretched. He appreciated the muscular firmness that had built in his arms, his abdomen and his shoulders, especially from the sword exercises. He carried scarcely an ounce of body fat. Moving left to right, he worked through the series of motions as would a martial arts expert. He closed his eyes and continued doing battle with ghosts.

The vibrating force of a slammed car door jerked his eyes open. He did not so much hear the door as felt the shock wave pass through the air surrounding the condo patio. Martin took a deep breath, shook off a chill and leaned in toward the fire, wishing somehow that the flames might purify his mind, sear away his most condemning thoughts. Closing his eyes again, Martin then stood tall and continued to put himself through the paces until he was nearly out of breath.

Chapter 18

Near Pretty Lake
Norfolk, VA

Sandra watched from the dark kitchen through wide wooden blinds, nervously biting the same fingernail again and again. She had not chewed her nails since she was eleven.

Watching Martin standing in front of the fire pit, gazing into the darkness, she felt weak, trembling from constant physical activity and a lack of sleep.

Pulling a strand of hair away from her face, Sandra twisted it with her left hand, her right arm absently pulling her robe closed. Her hair, still damp from the shower, was loosely wrapped in a towel.

Martin had become almost unrecognizable to Sandra. The mop of longish, sun-bleached hair topping his tall, muscular frame reminded her more of the young surfer who had first caught her eye at Croatan Beach than the tired man she left in Costa Rica. Martin's broad, scarred upper back reminded her of just how much he had changed, how much he had been through since then.

Martin stood only a few yards beyond the window glass, yet he seemed so far away that he may as well have still been stranded on that forsaken Pacific island. The on-again, off-again pattern of his behavior was to be expected, she had been warned, but still, it had been hard to take. She touched the glass, as if that alone would bring him closer.

As she watched the repetitive scene taking place on the patio. Sandra wanted so badly to rush outside. She was dying to tell Martin how much she had missed him, but the awkward silence between them had been too great. There had been so little unoccupied time since he had returned. His hearing difficulties complicated their communication. She wanted so much to pull him into her arms and weep - for time lost, for words wasted, for opportunities missed. She opened her eyes again and saw the reflection of her wedding rings in the window glass in front of her. It felt odd to wear them again, so unfamiliar.

Sandra tied her robe securely closed and looked away from the window. At that moment, she heard Rebekah's key in the front door. The interruption was welcome. She had hoped for some sort

105

of break in Martin's activity so that she could talk to him, but the opportunity did not present itself. At least now she would have someone to talk to.

"What are you doing up so late?" Rebekah asked as she cruised into the kitchen.

"I could ask you the same thing," Sandra responded, shielding her eyes as Rebekah flipped on a light. Sandra blinked back the brightness, but did not complain. She was too exhausted, her mind adrift on waves of confusion.

"So, you are out till all hours again tonight?" Sandra asked. She had hoped that Cita had been wrong about Rebekah having a boyfriend. "That's three nights this week, young lady."

Before Rebekah had a chance to respond, Sandra heard an answer pop into her mind. She felt she knew what Rebekah was going to say. She stood up and walked to where Rebekah was hanging up her leather jacket.

"I've just been out, been talking with my friends," Rebekah said brightly. "Everything is fine, really."

"What's his name, Rebekah? You can tell me."

Sandra followed Rebekah into the kitchen, where her young house guest started pulling out ingredients for a late dinner.

"You're going to cook at this hour?" Sandra asked.

"We met after the movie for a late coffee, but we were so busy talking I simply forgot about the time. I'm truly starved. We can talk while I cook if you like," Rebekah offered, continuing her preparations.

"I worry about you when you are out so late," Sandra acknowledged. She reached to plug in Rebekah's new electric wok, recognizing from the ingredients which dish Rebekah planned to whip up.

"I know, Mrs. Culver, but when I tell you why I'm so late, I believe you'll understand. Just let me get everything into the wok, I'm *so hungry*. Then I'll explain all about my plans."

"Did you just call me *Mrs. Culver*?" Sandra asked, gingerly taking a seat on the edge of a stool at the kitchen island. "I thought we were first name friends," she said nervously.

"Um…we are. Just hear me out, Sandra. I want to tell you about my plans." Rebekah pulled an apron over her tinted wedge cut and tied the strings loosely behind her tight black t-shirt.

"What plans are you referring to, Rebekah?"

Rebekah rapidly chopped *bok choi* and broccoli, blending the ingredients into the wok along with several ounces of cooked rice and sesame oil. She cracked an egg on the edge of the rapidly heating pan, expertly looping her hand over the mixture to extract all of the egg from both halves of the shell.

"I want to go home," Rebekah calmly stated, without looking up. She added a dash of soy sauce, then a capful.

"You want to do what?" Sandra asked, her voice wavering in pitch from low to high. She found herself edging closer to Rebekah as she finished her question.

"I want to go home," Rebekah stated flatly as she stirred the mixture. "I believe it is long past time, don't you agree?" The sizzle and crackle from frying vegetables filled the awkward pause in conversation.

This was a moment that Sandra had long feared. Though she had known for some time that Rebekah would eventually feel emotionally strong enough to live on her own again, from the time she had taken Rebekah into their home she had dreaded hearing these words.

"And by home I assume you mean Florida?" Sandra calmly asked.

"England, of course," Rebekah said, her glance unwavering. "I've thought it over. I want to go home. To England."

"Rebekah darling, has something happened?" Sandra asked, standing up. She felt her strength draining away. "Have we offended you in some way, dear? I know things haven't been normal lately, with Martin back and all."

"Oh no, it's not that..." Rebekah said, smiling behind the red-tinted wedge of dark hair that dangled near her chin. "I don't mind that you are renewing acquaintance with Mr. Culver. It's proper that you should. But when I look at my friends here, only wanting to hang around coffee shops and complain about things, it makes me want to accomplish something. I need to finish my studies and I want to do so at home, in Britain."

Although Rebekah never looked her in the eyes, this was the first hint of a smile Sandra had seen cross the young woman's face since bringing her back from Mexico. "You have been so kind to me, Sandra, I can never forget that. And don't think I'm not grateful. You have been better to me than family."

Sandra paused, almost smiling but weak.

"Really," Rebekah said. "You *have been* my *only* family."

Sandra turned toward the window, dabbing away a tear as she stood up. "Are you sure you're ready?"

"Come here, let me hug you," Rebekah said. "Of course I am, I'm perfectly fine, really."

As Sandra reached toward Rebekah, she noticed a difference in her young friend's face, a new confidence as she moved and talked. Rebekah took Sandra's tear-stained hands and kissed them both lightly.

"Yes, Sandra, I am ready to go," Rebekah assured her. "And I want you to go with me, so you'll know where I am and feel comfortable to come visit. The thing that worries me is whether you are ready for that."

Sandra hugged Rebekah tightly, clinging desperately to her, no longer able to hold back the tears. She sobbed openly as they stood by the window.

Sandra had opened her home to Rebekah after their ordeal in Mexico, guiding the young woman to regain her bearings. Now Rebekah was concerned for Sandra's fragility. The entire time Martin had been missing Sandra had occupied herself with her own children and with Rebekah to keep her mind busy. To lose Rebekah at this juncture seemed to be a crippling loss.

"My food, my food," she heard Rebekah softly say, wrinkling her nose.

"Of course, go ahead," Sandra agreed. "Don't burn your dinner."

After they had finished their late-night stir fry, Sandra reached across the table to take Rebekah's hand.

"Rebekah, what is the real reason you want to go back to England? I thought there was nothing for you there but bad memories."

"Well, I want to go back and finish my graduate degree. But actually, I've met someone online."

Sandra leaned back in her chair, putting one hand over her eyes.

108

"That's what I was afraid of," Sandra replied. "The 'met someone' part. Are you sure about this?"

Rebekah laughed, covering her mouth as she tried to eat.

"Sandra, it's not what you think. This man is a Professor at University College in London. He's old enough to be my bloody father."

This was worse than she had imagined.

"And just what is his interest in a young woman like yourself?"

"That's just the thing, no special interest on his part. It's a job. He needs a research assistant. I would have a respectable position, a place to live, *and* be able to further my studies. UCL has an excellent Physics and Astronomy program, as well as being among the leaders in British Archaeology. The Professor has direct connections with the British Museum and best of all, *an exclusive research grant at Stonehenge*. Can you imagine? I'm over the moon! I have been reading all his papers. I think his theories make a lot of sense. I talked to him this afternoon. I have an interview a week from today."

"An interview? You mean online, like Skype?"

"Yes. If that goes well, which I believe it shall, I will have another interview the following week."

"Online, another Skype interview?"

"No Sandra, a real in person interview - in London."

Sandra tried to take it all in, but bells were going off in her mind.

"What is his name, Rebekah? This professor of yours."

"You may have heard of him," Rebekah gushed. "He is famous you know."

"Oh, here it comes," Sandra thought. "It's that man who keeps calling the IAF, am I right?"

"Yes, that's him. Professor M.A. Haddad."

Sandra's heart plummeted. She gripped the island counter for support.

"First he found me online, based on my previous work in Paleolithic Astronomy. Then we started talking, then after the archaeology conference, he sent all his papers on Stonehenge to the IAF office. His theories are some of the best I have ever read. He initiated the Stonehenge Hidden Landscape Project!"

"I don't know what that is," Sandra admitted.

"It's ok, Sandra, I wouldn't expect you to know. You're more of an administrator at the IAF."

"What are you saying, Rebekah?"

"Nothing, only that Chartwell might know more..." her vocal volume decreasing to a whisper. "Oh Sandra, I'm so sorry. Always going 'round with my foot in my mouth."

"Rebekah, it's ok, I just need to know. Chartwell might what?"

"Chartwell might know that every day new and more exciting discoveries are being made around Stonehenge. Ground penetrating radar or GPR is the main tool, although they are using aerial drone cameras too. Neolithic monuments have recently been found that dwarf Stonehenge in size, serious paradigm-changing discoveries. Professor Haddad is the archaeologist leading all of this."

"Okay, enough, enough! I am tired of hearing that name!" Sandra said, her tone of voice causing Rebekah's eyebrows to rise higher than the frame of her dark glasses.

"Sandra, what are you talking about?" she asked, seeing Sandra was angry.

"That name, that Professor Haddad. His name keeps coming up."

Sandra snatched up the phone from the counter and dialed hurriedly.

"Hello, yes, I need to talk to you. Tonight, now. Yes, I know it's late. Well, plans can wait for another night."

"Who do you need to talk to right now?" Martin asked, closing the patio door behind him. He toweled his skin dry, preparing to clip his hearing devices behind each ear.

Sandra shivered nervously, setting the phone quickly on the counter. She pulled the towel down from her hair and tried to fluff it drier.

Martin was shirtless and sweaty. His muscles rippled like cables from his jeans upward. He strode bare-footed to the fridge and brought out a bottle of orange juice, closing the fridge before taking a deep swig from the bottle.

"Who were you talking to?" he asked Sandra again.

"Your hearing is improving, that's great, honey," Sandra replied, fumbling with the neckline of her robe.

Martin stopped and looked directly at her. "Sandra, I asked who do you need to talk to so much that you would call at this hour. It's 2:30 in the morning."

Rebekah caught Sandra's eye, managing a weak wave of her hand as she placed her dirty dishes into the sink.

"I'll just get those dishes in the morning, ok?" Rebekah murmured, scooting from the room.

"Were you calling Chartwell?" Martin asked Sandra.

"Martin, it's not what you think, let me explain," Sandra relented.

"Were you calling him?"

"Yes," Sandra replied, her eyes pleading with him. "Martin, don't jump to conclusions. Let me tell you why."

"I don't have to jump to conclusions. I *know* why you called him. You think of him before you think of me now. When you need someone, he's first on your list. You gave up on me ever coming back. I get that."

Sandra gasped and reached for Martin's hand. "It's not like that," she said. "Don't even think things like that."

"How do I know what to think anymore?" Martin said abruptly, walking to the front door and grabbing his keys. He reached for his sweatshirt hanging on a coathook by the door.

"Where are you going?"

"Don't worry about me," he said. "I'm going over to Mark's house. He and I have some planning to do."

"At this hour? What are you talking about?" Sandra asked.

"I'm looking at building us a new house, somewhere safer. I put a deposit on a piece of property through my brother's bank two weeks ago. We need a house of our own, some land, not this crowded condo. I need to be further away from the city."

Sandra felt like she had been hit in the gut.

"Martin, we did not talk about this. You said nothing to me about this."

"You're pretty busy these days, talking to Rebekah, or to Chartwell, or someone," he said, closing the door. "I didn't have a chance."

Chapter 19

Hearing a knock at the door, Sandra ran through the living room. She had nearly fallen asleep, given the late hour.

"Sandra, it's me. Open up!" Chartwell called as he continued knocking.

Hurrying to the door, Sandra realized she was still in her robe and towel. She crossed the towel around her neck, concealing as much skin as possible before opening the door.

"Hello, John, come in," Sandra said sheepishly, standing behind the door as he entered. "I'm sorry for bothering you at this hour."

"No bother," Chartwell lied, eyeing Sandra's outfit with curiosity. He watched as she hurried to the living room, drawing the robe closer around her body.

"So what's up Sandra, why the frantic call?"

"John, everything is going wrong," Sandra said plaintively. "I just got bad news from Rebekah and then I had a misunderstanding with Martin because I called you. He left just now. He was angry."

"I just passed him at the end of your street. He was driving pretty fast. I wondered where he was headed."

"He's going to spend the night at his brother's house."

"What? I thought you two were getting along famously since his return."

Sandra stared at him over her empty coffee cup.

Chartwell raised one eyebrow, then winked.

"Oh God, has it been that obvious?"

"Not obvious, just expected," Chartwell replied, smiling. "Why don't you put some clothes on while I make coffee? Then we'll talk?"

Sandra looked down, embarrassed to still be in her robe, embarrassed that the whole world seemed to know her business, embarrassed that she might have over-reacted to Rebekah's announcement, and especially that she had blown it with Martin.

"John, Rebekah wants to go back to Britain," she said in a low voice as she started up the stairs. "I need your advice."

Chartwell's expression changed to one of concern. "London can be a dangerous place these days."

Sandra stopped climbing the stairs, weighing his words.

"No more questions. Clothes, then coffee, then conversation," he directed. "I have a rule about talking to married women who are not fully dressed."

"You do? What rule is that?" Sandra asked.

"Clothes, then coffee, then conversation. Now scoot!"

By the time Sandra had returned to the kitchen, Chartwell had coffee brewed, with warm toast, marmalade and butter at hand.

"Pull up a stool, the bartender is in," he laughed.

"I wondered who was rummaging about in the cabinets," she responded. "I could hear you from upstairs."

"You wouldn't have heard the racket had you closed the bedroom door," he remarked, pouring a big mug of black coffee.

Sandra stopped short, wondering how he knew about the door.

"I could hear every sad note of that song you were trying to sing," he laughed. "Sound travels through open doorways."

Sandra added cream to her coffee and lifted a triangle of toast to her lips.

"So what did you and Martin fight about?" he asked.

"Because I called you," she replied.

"He feels left out, since he hasn't been your main support system, I'll wager," Chartwell said. "He has been through quite a lot, Sandra."

"Everyone keeps telling me that," she said between nibbles.

"None of my business, but perhaps you would do well to listen to them. Let's get back to the subject now. Why did you call me?"

"To get your advice about Rebekah."

"Sounds like we're back to where we started."

"John, she wants to go back to London. Says she met a Professor online who needs a research assistant at the University College of London. He works with the British Museum on a Stonehenge project?"

"Ok, UCL. I know the school. Good credentials. They offer a quality degree program."

"John, the Professor is named Haddad. Do you know anything about him?"

"Haddad? As in Professor M.A. Haddad? Weren't we just talking about him?"

Chartwell's entire manner and presence changed. He stood up from the kitchen bar and walked toward the sliding glass door, his coffee in hand. He faced the patio, but actually he was watching Sandra's reflection in the glass. He decided not to tell her everything he knew, at least not yet. Perhaps it would not be necessary.

"Haddad is a name I know. I have worked with him in the past. I would have some concerns about Rebekah working for him, for her sake. He's the chap sending his term papers to the IAF, am I right?"

"Formal papers, John. Professional journals. What do you know John? What do I need to know?"

"What's the rush?"

"She has an interview with him in a week, in London."

Chartwell again chose his words carefully.

"Haddad is best approached with caution. I have trust issues regarding him. I would think that for all the good that might come of Rebekah being his assistant, there is the equal possibility of it not working out well for her."

"I was afraid you would say that, John. What do I do, how can I check this situation out to help her?"

"My suggestion is, that someone close to her, you Sandra, go with Rebekah. While he is interviewing her, you interview him. You are very good at that. Do you recall interviewing me in Peru?"

"I do," Sandra blushed. "I drank too much that night. It ended up being one of the worst nights of my life."

"The point is that everything worked out well in the end because you grilled me so thoroughly. You have to go with Rebekah to check this out. I could tell you more, but I think it would be best to form your own opinion."

"Why John? Why won't you just tell me?"

"I tell you what. I'll do you one better. I'll go with you. I have been invited to London myself. A lecture ten days from today. Why don't we all go, the four of us? I will be there while you guide the discussion. It will be like old times."

"Would you do that, John? I would feel so much better."

"What about Martin? Can he go along with us?"

"Oh, that could be a problem. He has not been cleared to fly," Sandra replied. "His ears haven't healed enough to take the cabin pressure. He will be so angry if you and I go without him."

"I see," Chartwell said. "Well, I can swing it if you can get permission. I can be persuaded in a variety of ways, all of them involving money. Now, if you will excuse me, I need to get back to some unattended business."

Sandra handed Chartwell his coat, as he made a point of audibly clearing his throat.

"You called at the worst possible moment, you know."

"Oh John, do you mean…I am so sorry. You should go. I did not even think before calling. Was it …?"

"Mary… ," he replied. "I'll let myself out now."

"John, I am so sorry. But before you go, your rule?"

"Pardon?"

"Your rule about married women? I'm just curious, that's all."

"That, my dear, is a story best left for another time," Chartwell replied. "Perhaps there'll be time on that long New York to London flight."

Chapter 20

"I should tell him goodbye." Sandra remarked. "I can't just leave."

Chartwell shrugged as he helped Rebekah with her coat. He nodded toward Mark to finish helping Sandra.

"He'll be okay," Mark said, wrinkling his brow. "He knows you're leaving today. It's almost 6:00AM. We have to get you to the airport. Besides, you'll be back in a week. Martin will be worlds better by then. I promise I will come by and check on him every day."

Sandra looked doubtful.

"He seems so angry," she said. "I've never seen him like this. It's worse since the doctor would not clear him to travel with us."

"This is how Culver men handle things," Mark continued, checking his watch. "I've seen Martin like this before. He's not angry."

"You have?" Sandra asked, turning toward Mark. "When?"

"When our mom died, when she drowned…" Mark started, pausing to maintain his composure. "Martin was very stoic and quiet for weeks. He took the loss very hard, hardly eating or talking. And then he got better. He just needs time to process."

Sandra took Mark by the jacket sleeve.

"How will I know, Mark? How will I know when Martin is getting better?"

Mark picked up his coffee cup, watching as Chartwell donned his coat. Chartwell checked the inside pocket to make sure he had their boarding passes.

"Has he started writing again?" Mark related, sipping the last of his coffee. "He will start writing again. As he comes back to reality, he will have to write it out. That's his outlet. That's how you will know. But when he starts writing, look out, because he will write for days and days and not even come up for air."

"He asked me for notebooks last night," Sandra confirmed. "I took him to buy a new laptop yesterday. His did not come back from Costa Rica."

"How did that go?" Chartwell asked, "At the stores, I mean?"

116

"It was frustrating," Sandra said, hanging her keys on the hook by the door. "For the notebooks we went to the bookstore at the mall. It is as quiet as a library there. Martin talks so loud, the whole loss-of-hearing thing."

"I'd call that a good sign," Chartwell commented. "He's gearing up to write. Martin has had a major setback, Sandra. He's a fighter. He'll pull out of this, you just watch."

"Like I said," Mark responded. "He'll be fine, just be patient. He talks loud because of the hearing damage. Be glad he is here to talk at all. I was there when we found him. He was in bad shape. He thought he had nothing to live for. He thought you were dead."

Sandra stood silent and turned toward the window just as the sun spilled the first rays of daylight over the horizon. She put her purse down and started to take off her coat.

"That's it, I'm staying. I can't go. Not right now."

"Sandra stop, Martin just needs time to process it all," Chartwell advised. "He's been through a lot. I've seen this in men back from battle. It can't be rushed. If it is rushed, the resulting consequences aren't lovely. We have a plan, Rebekah needs our guidance, and Martin needs some space. He'll be okay."

"I know you're right," she said. "Dan said the same thing."

Sandra took one more look at Martin standing beside the fire pit on the patio, facing the rising sun. He did not move. The lower the coals burned, the brighter the streaks of sun appeared across Pretty Lake.

She tapped the window, but he did not turn around.

"Sandra dear, he can't hear you, his hearing devices are here by the coffee pot," Chartwell said.

Rebekah slid her arm around Sandra's waist.

"Come on now, we have to leave to make our plane," she said gently. "By the time you get back Uncle Martin will be fine."

Sandra took one more longing look, kissed her own palm before blowing a kiss toward her man, then turned and walked toward the condo entry door. Chartwell grabbed her suitcase and followed, closing the door behind them.

Once they were through the Customs and TSA checks for the first leg of their flight to London, Sandra sat silently at the ticket gate, staring at her phone.

Rebekah returned with two airport-priced frappucinos, all smiles with a friend in tow. Sandra sat up straighter in her seat. Chartwell was nowhere to be found.

"Sandra, you will never guess what! Look who I found. Hamid! Hamid is at Old Dominion University. He has been working with us at the IAF."

"Hello, Hamid," Sandra said, without extending her hand in greeting. She waited for the other shoe to drop, as Rebekah offered her one of the high-dollar frappucinos.

"Are you traveling to London, Hamid?"

"Yes I am, fortunately. We will be traveling on the same flight, according to Rebekah."

"Are you on semester break, Hamid?"

"No, I have business to attend to in London."

"Oh, what type of business?"

"Family business, in London."

"I see," Sandra replied, understanding that she had received as complete an answer as she was going to get.

Rebekah sat down beside Sandra, but Hamid remained standing.

"Sandra, you are quite the inquisitor," she chided, smiling past the awkwardness of the moment.

"Let's sit over by the window, Rebekah," Hamid suggested. "We can watch for the plane to arrive."

"Our plane is not here yet?" Chartwell asked, walking into the gate waiting area. He sipped a large paper cup of steaming tea, the Twining's tags fluttering alongside the cup as he walked.

"Not yet," Hamid replied. "I have been tracking it since it arrived in Atlanta. There has been no progress, so I assume it has not left Atlanta yet."

He and Rebekah moved to take seats looking out onto the tarmac, as Chartwell walked over to the gate counter, smiling broadly as he spoke to the young lady staffing the counter. He leaned across the counter, nearly spilling his tea in feigned surprise at the answer he received from the gate agent. He threaded his way through a growing knot of people and sat down by Sandra.

"At this point it looks as though our flight may have returned to Atlanta, if in fact it ever left."

Sandra did not reply, craning her neck to see Rebekah through the crowd.

"So who is Rebekah's young man?" Chartwell inquired. He seemed amused.

"He is not her young man," Sandra replied tersely.

"Okay, don't get testy with me," Chartwell replied, taking a long sip of his hot tea.

"Hamid is just someone she knows who happens to be on our flight."

"Who also happens to work with her at the IAF. I saw him that first day back at the office."

"He is an international student at Old Dominion, and yes, he works at the Foundation."

"Is he traveling on to London?"

"That's the thing. He is, but he was being very evasive about it all."

"Are you worried because he is a boy or because he is Muslim?"

"Yes," Sandra replied. "I worry about everything."

"But there is no indication that he is radical, is there?" Chartwell asked.

"No, but you can't be too careful. No one on TV ever says, "Yes I saw this coming!" after a tragedy. It's always, "He was such a good boy, I never would have expected this from him."

"Sandra, you can't be her mom."

"Someone needs to be. I'm worried about her falling in with the wrong people. That has happened to her before. In spite of all that has happened, she still is overly trusting."

"It is her nature. Do you want her to change?"

"No, I want her to be safe."

"You have kept her safe, Sandra. Now it's time to let go."

"Exactly, but the world chews up people who are too trusting. I want her to be more like, more like…"

"Like who Sandra?"

"More like you. More wise, less likely to be swayed."

"That takes time Sandra. Time will help with that. New topic, ok?"

"All right," Sandra replied. "But if that plane does not come soon we will be here another night."

"So have you ever been to London, Sandra?"

"Never been to Europe, period," she responded. "I always wanted to go though."

"What did you imagine it would be like?"

Sandra realized what he was doing. Chartwell was leading her away from her worst thoughts and fears. She liked that about him. Sandra remembered Cita's wise advice. She leaned back in her chair, keeping some distance away from Chartwell. Whenever a person felt herself being drawn in, Cita had told her, physically reset the barriers to keep an even keel.

"I grew up watching Princess Di, imagining life in a castle, going to the Tower of London, Big Ben, riding a double decker bus. I always wanted to go to Madame Tussaud's Wax Museum, but then I saw the scariest movie about that. No desire to go there now. So what's it like growing up in England?"

"Well, it's different than you think. For starters, we usually say Britain instead of England. But try to imagine a culture with knights and swords, and castles too, a few Druids thrown in, headed by the world's leading explorers, flavored with Indian curry and peppered with rock stars. That's what I saw growing up. Oh and add to that the Muslim influence, where Mohammed is the most popular name for new baby boys now, and the mayor of London is now a Muslim."

"And yet you determined to become an archaeologist? How did that happen?"

"I met a woman at university…" he started.

"Oh, here we go," she said.

"If you please…," he continued. "She was very involved in fieldwork. I followed her everywhere. Eventually I followed her right off campus to Egypt. I liked archaeology as much as I liked her. I knew I could never settle down to instructing for very long. She and I got along famously. The rest, as they say, is history."

"And where is this famous love interest now?" Sandra inquired.

Chartwell paused.

"A gentleman always maintains a hint of mystery."

Sandra laughed.

"There's nothing mysterious about you. Two minutes after meeting you, most people know exactly what you're all about."

Chartwell laughed too.

"But on a serious note, I want to talk to you about this Professor of Rebekah's."

"Oh, ok, what about him?"

"So I have been thinking. I decided I should tell you what I know. He is not that well regarded in most archaeological circles."

"Is that the reason you don't like him?"

"No. I can find a million reasons not to like Haddad, starting with the fact that he does not recognize my doctorate, always calling me Mr. Chartwell instead of Dr. Chartwell. But the worst of it is that the people who do consider him vital are not good for archaeology. We would consider his supporters to be the more nefarious ones, the shadow players. "

"Tell me about him John. I need a complete picture."

"Haddad is Egyptian by birth, Muslim by religion, but in name only. He is unlike any Muslim I have ever met."

"How do you mean?"

"Haddad loves everything about ancient Egypt. I always pictured him having a houseful of Egyptian artifacts. I think it's a power trip for him. Most Egyptian Muslims do not hold their Pharaonic ancestors in high regard. The Pharoahs are a part of Egyptian history that the true Muslim considers a travesty."

"Why?"

"They don't like the pantheon of gods in Ancient Egyptian history, its obsession with polytheism. They see Egypt's artifacts as a sacrilege, useful only to be sold and traded as worship objects of the infidel."

"Another reason to hate non-Muslims?"

"You said that, not me," Chartwell replied.

"Is that why ISIS feels free to trade in Middle Eastern antiquities? We have received reports at the IAF that ISIS actually licenses looters for a percentage of their haul."

"That much is true, but that is only the fundraising arm of ISIS. They have a much darker agenda. But let me finish telling you about Haddad."

"Okay, go ahead," Sandra responded, leaning forward to get a better view of Rebekah and Hamid sitting a few rows away.

"Haddad is obsessed with the darker side of Ancient Egypt. Osiris, specifically, god of the underworld and Anubis, the god of embalming represent his worldview. Accordingly, his tastes run to the eclectic, if not downright perverted."

"What are you talking about?" Sandra asked, squinting her eyes as if she did not really want to hear the answer.

"He likes to tie people up. Specifically, he likes to tie women up. More importantly, he gets his kicks tying up young girls."

"What?" Sandra exclaimed, her voice a little louder than she intended. She laid her phone to one side, shifted in her seat and leaned closer to Chartwell. "What did you say?" she asked in her most disbelieving tone.

"You heard me right," he responded. "He gets his kicks tying up young women."

"You mean tying them up, like bondage?" Sandra asked.

"No," Chartwell replied. "Like mummies."

"And then what?"

"The only person I knew to be directly involved said he let her go after taking a few pictures."

"That's terrible. What did she do?"

"When she convinced him to free her, she made him promise to delete the photos and get some help."

"So did he?"

"I don't know. I stayed away from him after that. I heard rumors that he had kidnapped his niece from her father's home and tied her up too."

"Mummified her?"

"Not completely, just wrapped her up a bit."

"Who was the person you knew, John, the one that told you all this?"

"My second wife," Chartwell stated matter-of-factly. He stood to stretch, draining his tea and tossing the cup away. "She thought he was kidding around, until it became obvious the bloke has a problem."

Chartwell pointed to the window.

"Looks like our plane pulling up to the gate now," he said.

Chapter 21

"Now I feel better," Sandra said plainly, looking from Chartwell on her right to Rebekah on her left. Their three seats together on the entry side of the plane were not roomy, but at least they were all together. Sandra hated middle seat, but Chartwell needed the aisle for leg room.

"Now that we have taken off? Chartwell asked.

"Now that Rebekah is with us," Sandra whispered.

"Where did Hamid end up?" he questioned.

"He is in the front, in first class," Rebekah chimed in. "I wish he and I were sitting together. We have so much in common. "

Sandra turned back to Chartwell, rolling her eyes. She patted Rebekah on the arm as if she were a child.

"He will be fine up there. They will take good care of him."

"I'm going to watch a movie," Rebekah replied, plugging her headphones into her iPad.

"So is that why you feel better?" Chartwell whispered. "Because Rebekah is with us?"

Sandra nodded without saying anything.

"Tell me about the documents that Professor Haddad sent you."

"Well," Sandra replied, hesitantly, "I have not actually viewed them myself. I do have them scanned onto my iPad to read on the way over. Would you want to have a look?"

Before Chartwell could reply, Sandra brought out her iPad and handed it to him, showing him how to power it on.

"I expect it will be boring," she added.

"I want to see how he might have changed over the years," Chartwell said. "Maybe I am wrong about him. I have misjudged people a time or two in my life."

"That one, read that one first. That is one of the documents Cita insisted that I read. She said it sounded very far-fetched."

Chartwell scanned the title before flipping a few pages into the document. He came back to the beginning.

"This is not the Professor's presentation to the Royal Society, that's for sure. At least I hope not, for his sake."

"Why what's wrong with it?"

"It appears to be an attempt at a novel, with historical facts connected by, *how should we say*, history-related fiction. It says the historical facts have been translated from the original Viking Ogham text. Want to have a read first?"

"No. Wait, what is Viking Ogham text?"

"Viking Ogham is a system of writing found in many Norse settlements. Interesting because there was also Ogham text found in the Book of Ballymote, written in 1390, along with a drawing of the layout of Stonehenge. The Book of Ballymote may be a type of Rosetta Stone, since it contains both Ogham and Gaelic."

"What does that have to do with anything?" Sandra asked.

"Ogham was also a Scythian writing system. The Ogham of the Scythian kings lists the descendants of the wise men of the Bible as the keepers of Stonehenge."

"The ones who visited Baby Jesus?"

"Fennius Farsaid was a legendary Scythian king related to Balthazar the Wise, one of the three wise men. Balthazar's descendants were named in records found there."

"Bo-ring!" Sandra replied. "I would rather look at the inflight magazine."

"Well, this should keep me busy," he said, noting the last rays of sunset fading behind them. "If nothing else for Haddad's fictional take on the facts."

"How long is our flight?" she asked.

"We will be to London by about 10:00AM in the morning. And we cross 5 time zones to do it."

"Ok, well let me know what you think. I may take a nap instead."

Chartwell reached to turn on the reading lamp. He viewed the electronic title page.

The Epic Battle at Stone Henge
Presented by
Professor Moammar Ahmed Haddad, PhD.

(Historical content translated from
the original Viking Ogham text)

The defenders of the temple stood rooted to their ancient and hallowed ground. Their robes, the color of tree-bark, hung damper and darker from the knees down, soaked by blood and water that oozed through the tall grass of the Henge Plains near Amesbury, the site of the Temple of the Sacred Stone. Beneath the mounded, thatched roof rising high above, each intoned a separate note as they collectively made an effort to control their breath, forcing more oxygen into their rapidly beating hearts. The resulting hymn became a mournful baritone moan that unnerved their fierce opponents. They peered through gathering dusk and fog, the type of obscuring mist that on these flat, grassy plains always signaled an impending rainstorm. Watchers of the weather, and of the earth, the robed defenders were also united in the hope that their hero would arrive and turn the tide from defeat to victory. So they watched and they waited.

The enormous domed roof rising high above the stone temple had always protected them from the weather, but its beam and thatch construction would not long protect them from the relentless onslaught of the fierce aggressors they now faced. One fiery arrow well placed, or a hell-bucket of flaming pitch hurled their way, and the temple would surely burn.

The central opening of the dome, surrounded by massive arched timbers resting heavily the ancient standing stones like cathedral buttresses, allowed a single beam of moonlight from a split in the clouds to shine down upon the Sacred Stone, the ancient one given to them by the heavens. Black and sharp in places, smooth and concave-glassy in others, the Sacred Stone reflected light from every inch of its massive surface.

The Sacred Stone was the center of their crumbling world. It had always been so since ancient days. The defenders would in no wise abandon it. To the man they had taken the oath to guard the Sacred Stone till their last life-breath.

The Stone was believed to have the power to wring the truth from a liar, repentance from the guilty. Sparks flew from it when struck with iron, yet it did not rust. It gathered warmth when the sun went overhead, then radiated the heat back beneath the dome during evening sky-watch. This stone had become their sacred altar, ensconced within a pit central to the temple as deep as a man is tall.

The portion of the stone visible above the pit floor was itself huge as an *auroch*. No one knew just how deep its craggy roots ran below the plain, or how massive the Sacred Stone actually was, only that it had been last touched by the Deity himself before it fell from the heavens in a streak of flame. A gift, yet it was also a burden of responsibility. The robed ones remembered The Falling, retelling the story reverently at their nightly fire ritual.

The invaders, terrible Norsemen from the Sea to the North could now be seen in the distance, smoke-breathing silhouettes, re-grouping in front of a massive bonfire. Some stood immoveable, on guard, while the others retrieved fallen warrior comrades and their weapons, dispatching their fatally wounded ones to Valhalla atop the flaming pyre, as was their custom. Their blue and yellow standard fluttered from a tall wooden cross upended high above the smoke and fog, a blue and yellow banner of fear. Their conquest march across the British Isles had advanced with punishing swiftness.

Separated by two *akrlengds* of grassy plain, the blood-soaked battleground between the two groups that had screamed in the night with the rattling din of death now groaned, hoarse whispers drifting across the fields in the scant light of a foggy morning, the final words of men breathing their last. Keeping the Druid custom of the wake, watching their dead enter the sleep from which one would never awaken, did not compel them to leave the safety of the Great Temple to retrieve their fallen, but to instead leave their kith and kin to return to the earth in the natural order of things. The rain, which had now begun in earnest, would wash away the blood, chill the flesh, beginning the process of the earth reclaiming its own. This was enough, for the present.

The first wave of Viking invaders had butchered scores of Druid defenders all across this holy plain as easily as one might slaughter children, first ripping apart hundreds of conical thatched Druid cottages as though they were but cobwebs and sticks, putting the torch to every last one. The Druids, priests and caretakers of the land and all its holy places, had offered up no significant resistance, defending themselves with little more than sticks and farm implements. Still, they had fought bravely, inflicting more than their share of death and destruction on their attackers.

With no hope of reinforcements from the nearby villages, which had all likewise been pillaged and destroyed, the defenders had dispatched a runner to the coast, a runner with but one mission. Return with the hero.

Hours of intense, drawn-out battle had ensued, despite the steep odds in the invader's favor. Hours stretched into days, but Druid staffs and clubs naturally stood little chance against the rugged steel swords and iron-bound shields of the Vikings. The Druids knew steel. Indeed their altar bristled with the swords of kings past, but the Druids revered swords as testaments to valor, not to use for fighting.

Fifteen Druid men now remained, tired, somber, but standing. Their noble efforts in confronting these savages had been no match for the sheer ferocity of the Norsemen. The invaders had decimated the faithful of this place. Now there remained these few, the devoted ones, the survivors. Their valiant effort to defend these rolling plains and the holy temples scattered across the countryside appeared to be a lost cause. All seemed lost. Their understanding of the stars, the heavens, of nature itself, had not been enough to save them. The timeless concepts that the Druids had brought to this place from across the inland sea to the South would now perish with them, short of the intervention of the Deity. The Deity, whose name was too holy to be invoked, had come to be known through their history of the study of nature, and of the certainty of a creator of the entire natural world surrounding them. This was why they had come to this faraway place, to be free, to worship and believe as they pleased, to investigate the mysteries of the universe that the creator had established, to conduct the ceremonies of life and of afterlife.

What goal the marauding Norsemen had in mind was anyone's guess. They obviously intended to possess the Great Temple and the ground it stood on. Perhaps they intended to have the Sacred Stone for their own. Perhaps the swords collected as tribute from the hundreds of kings they had buried was their goal. Rumored to have their own religion, a cross-symbol and a thirst for blood, the Vikings had besieged the region for days, subduing one templetown after another. The invaders had now had gained the upper hand.

Rain became more intense, a wall, a downpour that threatened to douse the Viking bonfire and collapse the roof of the Great Temple as well. No gods were smiling on this terrible, bloody encounter. Perhaps they were all meant to die.

Then, from the small clutch of remaining Druid defenders, a murmur arose. A shadow trotted across the plain and into the Great Temple itself, first at a great distance, then growing, at once larger and taller as it neared. The Viking camp grew restless as the Druids stirred to life. The man approached at a rapid rate, a single column of steam escaping from his lips every four paces.

When the runner had reached the Druid position near the Great Stone Temple, they all watched as he paused to catch his breath. Thick hides drenched in rain were cast aside at the entrance. Into the midst of the faithful stepped the most intimidating of warriors. To these remaining Druids, this was the miracle they had yearned for. Their hero had arrived, just as the last round of battle was about to begin, just as their strength and numbers were waning. The hero's mighty chest heaved for breath, yet he stepped forward, ready.

This imposing figure of a man stood a full head taller than those around him, his mane of long, yellow hair nearly reaching the thatched roof overhang when he entered the temple. Attired in armor modified to fit his commanding stature, this Druid defender bore physical witness to his conception, having been forcefully sired by a Viking raider some thirty years prior. His mother had been unfortunate, a local maiden who committed no more grave an error than choosing the wrong day to search the rocky shoreline for seabird eggs. Her son an unaccepted half-breed, she found no quarter in her former Saxon village, and had taken to cooking for the Druid elders at this, the Great Temple. She had christened her son Ulfberht, a name with meaning in both Saxon and Viking, to reflect the circumstances of his birth, the son of Ulfhedin.

After a subsequent Viking band had killed his mother in a raid four years now gone, Ulfberht had taken his leave, to find peace, and to find purpose. Having already learned the ways of a Druid, Ulfberht altered course, giving in to anger at those who had mistreated his mother to the point of death. His quest to become a warrior had begun that same year.

Ulfberht had carried little with him, other than his particular gift chiseled from the Sacred Stone altar itself, a woven bag of precious metal flakes weighing nearly a *stone*. For four long years he studied his enemy, their battle techniques, their weaponry, forging his own sword from the metal of the Sacred Stone. Surviving as a mercenary, he traveled wide and far to listen to the story of Viking conquests, to learn their methods, to gauge their madness. They had an insatiable thirst for iron, the iron that came from heaven. He watched their dragon-ships sail along the coasts and prepared daily for the battle that he knew would one day come.

This day he had run half the night to meet his enemy, his own half-blood kin. He had heard of this Ulfhedin, this Viking savage, had seen the results of his raids. Ulfberht's heart ached for a fight, for a chance to even the score, for the memory of his mother. In fact, this battle was in his heart as he forged his sword under the tutelage of the Damascus sword makers. He felt awake for the first time that he could remember, his purpose about to be realized, his strength at its peak.

The remaining Druids reverently stepped aside, exhausted physically by the fighting, depleted mentally by the act of killing, their robes irreversibly stained by intense, bloody battle. Giving way to this giant among them, the Druids spoke in hushed tones, invoking the blessing of the Deity as the intimidating warrior lowered his linen hood, revealing a defiant face defined by chiseled cheekbones, a full yellow beard, and sky-blue eyes. His over-sized robe hung from his body, reaching to his feet loosely gathered in the middle by an armored belt. His shoulders were twice as wide as his waist. He took several strides forward and stopped.

Ulfberht's formidable appearance took on a dark and terrible tone as he unsheathed the massive sword he had brought back from his travels. He hefted the long, heavy blade with two hands, brought it around in front of him, and planted the broad, sharp tip several inches into the soft earth. Easily twice the length of any sword on this gentle plain, this sword was exceptional, its metal reverently removed from the Sacred Stone of heaven itself. Its blade was said to have been forged in the mouth of a dragon in the native homeland of the Druids. Designs hammered into the hilt combined golden runes and sacred circles into intricate patterns that spoke of magick and protection. Runic characters revealed his name chiseled into the sword above the tang that ran nearly half the weapon's length.

Placing both heavily armored gloves against the sword hilt, Ulfberht rested, inhaling deeply. Now he regulated his breathing to control his racing heart, to load his blood with the air-energy as those around him had done. The sheer weight of his muscular arms drove the mighty sword deeper into the damp ground.

Ulfberht knelt and prayed the prayer on the lips of every Saxon in this age, his open eyes staring at the ground beneath.

"*Från nordmännens raseri bevare oss*," he uttered. "Save us from the wrath of the Norsemen." Little did he know that his words would become the nightly prayer across the British Isles and the continent to the Blue Sea for generations to come.

Standing to his feet, the giant half-breed held a hand gloved in heavy chain mail to his broad forehead, shielding his eyes from the unyielding downpour, peering across the groaning scarlet landscape toward the still-dark western sky. The enemy funeral pyre still blazed brightly, but their bristling line had begun to advance, slowly, methodically, more subtly than anyone was willing to acknowledge. They clanked their swords and shields together, steadily, a rhythm of death known to clear whole villages, able to make strong men weak at heart.

Ulfberht lifted his sword from the ground and stood at the ready. He rightly perceived that these Viking invaders were no mere savages, but trained, hardened warriors, highly successful in every respect of battle. Knowing that he shared Viking blood and Viking instincts gave him confidence, but he had been raised among the Druids, so he also knew their strengths and their strategies, the strategy to step aside, to defend oneself while avoiding battle, the ability to bend and flex, to dodge and to strike.

Ulfberht looked to his right and then his left in this small crowd, not surprised to see among the remaining faithful Myrddin, the one who had urged him to withdraw iron for his sword from the Sacred Stone, the one who had hidden this secret from the others. In this sense his sword had been drawn from that sacred stone. Myrddin, skilled in all science and magick of the age, had been the first among the Druids to recognize Ulfberht's strength, his potential.

Perhaps this was because Myrddin was himself a half-breed, unaccepted, but also because he was gifted with foresight, and with knowing. Myrddin also knew that Ulfberht had been the only one among them strong enough to remove the metal from the Sacred Stone, to chisel it free.

"It has been too long, my friend," Myrddin said, leaning forward slightly. "I see you have changed in many ways."

"I was at the shore, biding my time."

"Your time has come," Myrddin replied solemnly.

The remaining Druid defenders, following Myrddin's lead, dipped their pitch-tipped wooden staffs into the fires on either side of the entrance to the Great Temple, then stepped several paces toward the advancing enemy. They raised their staffs in a circle, surrounding Ulfberht with smoke and with flame both holy and sacred, a sight designed to generate fear and mystery in the very souls of their enemies. Facing the advancing enemy line in the distance, the tallest Druid scanned the jagged line of wooden shields, swords and iron ax-heads beside him, surrounded by a corona of flame and smoke.

As Ulfberht watched, the line of Viking invaders stopped, then parted, making way for a Norse warrior easily his equal in terms of size and strength to step forward from among them. The large man sported bands of iron on his wrists, around his shaved head, and around his ankles, areas known to be easy targets in close combat. The man's posture, indeed his very manner was familiar, his swagger somehow reminiscent, a man confident of his abilities on the field of battle.

In one hand the Norse invader wielded a keen, rugged sword, short and heavy, a sword that by sight alone spoke danger and hammered perfection across the flat, bloody spanse that separated the two men. On his other arm, a banded wooden shield edged with iron spikes was held loosely at his side. Intimidation flared from his every action. He was at once daunting, his eyes taunting, his muscles flinching beneath his belted tunic. His beard was tied up in multiple short knots, giving his face a spiked, unholy appearance.

"I am not afraid of your petty fire-tricks," the Viking's voice shouted, booming rough and hostile in its resolve. "You will abandon this place, and deliver to me what I came for, or by Odin and by my sword I will leave you neither legs to run nor arms to drag your own worthless bodies away!"

"What is it you seek, miserable cur?" Ulfberht shouted back. "Have you lost your way? There are no children's bones here for you to gnaw upon. Are you in need of directions homeward? Allow *my sword* to point the way for you!"

With that the half-Druid defender planted his sword in the ground in defiance, yanked aside his tunic, and let loose a mighty piss, arcing high and forceful toward the Viking line.

The Viking captain laughed, then grunted. He turned momentarily to one side, then spun back towards the domed Druid temple, flinging his heavy shield at shoulder level and straight as an arrow. The spiked iron disk traveled at unbelievable speed, hissing through the rain, closing the distance between the two ragged battle lines in half a blink.

Ulfberht uttered an oath, stepped to one side and leaned sharply back, rather than be instantly decapitated. As he moved aside, the spinning shield tore open the necks of the two Druid defenders standing directly behind him, cleaving the head of their fiery staffs to fall to the blood-soaked earth as well.

Jugular veins shredded, the two priests croaked in agony as life-force spurted from their severed necks. Their bodies fell away from each other and to the ground, joining their fallen comrades already resting on the field of battle. The men's heads, connected by little more than spinal ligaments and a few tenacious tendons, rolled to face one another, their eyes still wide in frightened surprise.

Ulfberht did all he could do for the two fallen defenders, using both hands to raise his sword high before plunging it deep into the heart of each man, putting a rapid end to their twitching and suffering, to send them speedily on to the next realm.

Ulfberht turned back to the Norse challenger, watching as the Viking began to twirl his sword with the shrill sound of the wind, slowly at first, then more quickly, steadily increasing both the pace and the volume of the weapon moving expertly in his hands.

"I will have your Sacred Stone altar and all that lies at its feet!" Ulfhedin announced, pointing his sword toward the stone temple. "I have come for it. I will not be denied."

"Continue your blasphemy, and you will be next to be laid at the feet of the Sacred altar," Ulfberht replied, raising his sword.

"Get back inside the temple!" Ulfberht shouted, directing his fellow Druids to step back within the upright temple stones. They immediately moved, robes flowing across the ground, encircling the pit at the open center of the structure. The sacred altar stone was to be protected at all costs, to the last man.

"The Sacred Stone will remain here where it belongs!" Ulfberht responded calmly, his loud voice booming across that stormy plain. "From this altar stone was my sword drawn, and by my sword this altar stone must remain."

"Then you will die, and I will possess your sword as well as your pathetic heathen stone!" the Viking challenger shouted.

Ulfberht stood defiantly. He began to spin his own blade in rapid, tight circles. The sword practically sang as it passed through the air.

The Druids at last understood. They realized why the Vikings had come, what they sought. The Vikings intended to take their altar stone, the heart and soul of their society, of their worship. This massive sacred stone, the stone altar the gods had sent them, would no longer be theirs. When it left, they would be no more.

They trusted that the sword Ulfberht wielded would protect them, knowing now the source of its strength, that this sword had been taken from the altar's essence of heaven-forged metal that had fallen from the sky, the hardest metal known on earth. The Vikings desired the metal bestowed to men by the gods, to be counted as gods themselves. They desired the heavenly iron more than gold, since it could be fashioned into nearly indestructible weapons.

"Such things cannot be permitted!" Ulfberht shouted. He mimicked his Viking opponent, continuing to twirl his unique sword in a menacing, manner, easily matching Ulfhedin's defiant display. Myrddin was not the only one among the onlookers to raise an eyebrow, noting the striking similarities between the two warriors as they prepared to fight. He thought to advise his young friend, but looked skyward, then retreated upon consulting the fates.

The Druid defender took a step towards his challenger; the Viking advanced another stride toward him. Ulfberht recalled an image of his mother's face, the face that motivated him to good.

This time he saw her face as she lay dying after the Viking raid. The sound of the spinning swords grew piercingly intense, the blades of the swords now only a faint blur. The two men advanced towards each other steadily, the only sound the constant whir of blades, low throb to high-pitched whine, spinning to the side, overhead and in front of the two men. Soon their blades would meet. Then the matter would be decided.

When they did meet, the two blades generated a mighty clash of sparks that lit up the battle-field. The sound wrought by the collision of these two swords, wielded by these two mighty combatants, had never been heard in the history of the occupation of these plains. The horrible metallic clash shook men's teeth and made them squint their eyes. What happened next was completely unheard of, the stuff of drunken tavern tales spoken in hoarse whispers.

Ulfberht stepped forward, the image of his mother's sweet face fading as a blood-thirsty rage overtook him, his whirling blade forcing his Viking opponent to stumble and drop to one knee. Ulfberht drew his arms back, bringing his sword over his head with a mighty shout. Victory would come easily. He aimed for the right shoulder of the menacing Norseman, aiming to separate his opponent's sword-arm from his body, He brought his blade down straight and true as an axe.

Rotating his own sword around in front of him, the Viking blocked the Druid defender's unrestrained lunge and stepped to one side. Viking and Druid alike, flanking their heroes on either side, covered their ringing ears at the sound of it.

The Viking invader now advanced upon the Druid warrior, forcing him to haltingly retreat with each resounding blow. The onslaught continued to increase unabated until Ulfberht had been forced backward between the two upright temple entrance stones Though he defended well, Ulfberht was no match for this battle-hardened Viking. He remained on the defensive to preserve his life.

Sword now rang against sword inside the Great Temple. In the distance, lightning flashed, momentarily lighting the open center of the roof structure, accenting the rain that continued to fall. Ulfberht held his heavy sword high as the Viking hammered his own weapon harshly down across it. Connecting metal to metal at a weak point, the cold-forged Viking sword blade shattered like glass. The failure of his blade, combined with the momentum of his powerful strike caused the Viking challenger to fall forward, landing on all fours at the feed of the Druid hero.

Metal fragments rained down around them both, as the Druid drew himself to full height, his sword now over his own head.

"I can think of no better place to end this than here!" Ulfberht shouted as he prepared to remove his opponent's head. Fate had other plans. Before he could advance another step, Ulfberht's sword attracted lightning out of the sky, arches of unique, blazing light trailing sparks like those from a blacksmith's anvil. Throwing away the ruined hilt of his own shattered sword, the Viking leapt to his feet and reached for Ulfberht's sword.

Both men grasped hold of the sword hilt as the lightning grew brighter. The energy burst overpowered both the Druid and the Norseman in a blinding illumination that cast shadows trailing across the sacred temple ground as they struggled, edging ever nearer the altar stone with each violent crackle of heavenly fire.

The sparking sword passed powerful bolts of unmeasurable intensity through the bodies of the struggling duo. The Druid's sword changed to a glowing blue.

With the crackling roll of thunder, the lightning retreated. The two men fell backward into the pit containing the Sacred Altar Stone, plunging the superheated sword blade as deeply into the stone of heaven as if the altar were a melon. The sword imbedded itself deeply in the stone, attempting to return to its heavenly source.

Both men's hands clenched tightly to the hilt of the Druid hero's sword, unable to release their grip.

Grimacing in agony, the Viking at last managed to let go of the weapon, his burned skin peeling away from his hand.

The intense heat had ruined the Druid's fingers as well, fusing them inside his metal glove into a permanent curl. Ulfberht gritted his clenched teeth, still gripping the sword hilt where the sword had become imbedded in the altar. Smoke emanated from his nostrils as he tried to breathe.

"How are you called, Druid hero?" Ulfhedin managed to rasp.

"I am called Ulfberht," he replied from the ground beside him.

"You fight well, but you have lost all. Whose son are you, that I may make songs to his name?"

"I never knew my father," the Druid hero gasped. "But I do now."

"Whose son are you, I say?"

"I am, though you do not know it, your son."

Ulfberht's body collapsed, his face pressed against the sacred altar stone, his knees on the ground, but he did still not release the sword.

Stunned by the revelation, and by the truth, Ulfhedin crawled closer.

"This magnificent sword of yours, my son, does it have a name?"

"*Ish-kalabar* is its name, but you shall never possess it."

"But that is where you are in error, for indeed, I will possess it now. Give it to me."

"I will not. I give it back to the Sacred Stone where it belongs. A curse upon he who removes it!"

Ulfhedin's words had barely been uttered when another bolt flashed from the sky, this time directly striking the Sacred Stone, illuminating the inside of the Great Temple like daylight.

The stone first, then the sword, glowed from within, an unseen fire welling from deep inside the Sacred Stone of Heaven, extending up the sword and into Ulfberht's arm.

Ulfberht's last earth act was to extract his gloved hand from the sword, whereupon he fell to the ground and died. His glove remained, bonded to the sword hilt until he breathed his ragged last, then it too fell back to the ground, as all earthly things do. A single bolt of lightning had entered his body through the sword Ish-kalabar, returning through the sacred altar stone into the sky.

The remaining Druids, save Myrddin the Wise, stared and gasped collectively at the sight of their conquered hero before scattering and turning to run. They poured from the rear entrance to the Great Temple. The field was still slick with blood and rain as they slipped and fell in their haste. The bloodthirsty Norsemen advanced as one fearsome body toward the temple defenders, chasing them through the temple and across the plains through rising wisps of fog. The stragglers were dismembered first. One by one, the Viking raiders eventually overtook the entire group of remaining priests, ending their lives in the most violent manner possible. All across the field of battle, shrouded vapors of expended breath and ebbing body heat rose in the morning sunlight like souls toward heaven, souls that now slept the sleep of the ages. Myrddin simply walked away, unnoticed by anyone.

The victorious Norsemen strode boldly into the temple to join their leader, standing over the body of the lifeless Druid warrior. They gazed in awe at the tremendous stones that made up the foundation of the great wooden roof, and wondered how such stones had been moved.

Ulfhedin prodded Ulfberht's burnt body with his foot.

"I regret it has come to this, my son," the Viking intoned. "You were brave in battle. People far and wide will speak your name, and the name of your sword with reverence and awe."

"For my people and for my king, I must possess this place, I must possess this great stone, and most of all, I must possess this powerful sword of yours."

The elder Viking stepped closer, viewing the sword imbedded deep in the still-smoking altar stone.

"Ish-kalabar," he repeated reverently.

Turning to the Viking on his right, Ulfhedin struck him with his meaty hand and pointed.

"I will have that sword now, if you please!" he shouted.

Turning toward the metallic altar stone, still hot from the lightning strike, the Viking guard removed a heavy hide from his belt and cautiously gripped the sword's handle, trying to free it.

Pulling with all his might, this Viking endured the derisive laughter of his comrades. He sought a better grip realized that this was going to be no easy task. Gathering all his strength, the warrior tried again, anxious to remove the sword from the altar stone and please his leader. His fur boots, planted against the sacred stone, began to smoke.

Ulfhedin struck the frustrated man with his fist, pushing him away. He turned to his followers and raised his arms.

"Remove the sword, if you can," Ulfhedin called to his men. "The man who can do so I shall leave to become the King of this pagan land."

Chapter 22

New York to London
Somewhere over the Atlantic Ocean

Chartwell finished reading, having read the manuscript before the first layover. He turned off the overhead reading light and powered down Sandra's iPad. An amused look crossed his face. "That is some story," he said under his breath.

Turning to his left, he found Sandra sleeping under a light blanket, her mouth open slightly. Beyond Sandra, Rebekah had finished her movie and lay curled in her window seat amid a pile of jackets and pillows. Through the open window curtain, Chartwell could see that she was missing a magnificent display of the northern lights. He prepared himself for an uncomfortable sleep and closed his eyes.

Waking up beside Sandra Culver and Rebekah, Chartwell shook his head to get his bearings.

Sandra's blanket and hip were pressed against his leg, while her head leaned against his shoulder. Rebekah yawned as she woke up.

The flight attendant stopped at their row.

"Hot towels to refresh your face? This is a lovely family scene, sir. I reminding passengers that your flight will be ending in the 90 minutes, in case anyone needs to use the facilities. There will likely be a rush."

"We're not a family...," Chartwell tried to explain.

"He's my uncle," Rebekah said, smiling.

The flight attendant raised one eyebrow, as Chartwell found himself speechless for one of the few times in his life.

"It's not like that," he said in a quiet voice.

"No need to explain," she said cheerily. "Hot towel for the lady?"

Chartwell folded down his tray table, accepting a hot towel for Sandra. He tapped her on the hip to wake her up.

"What, are we there?" she asked. "How long did I sleep?"

"They said we have about 90 minutes left," Rebekah said. "Do you fancy a visit to the loo?"

"Yes I probably should," Sandra replied, washing her face, wrists and hands.

Rebekah scooted closer, taking the middle seat.

"Know what I think, Mr. Chartwell?" Rebekah asked.

"Do tell," he responded, "unless it has to do with me being your uncle."

Rebekah fairly ignored him as she continued.

"I think that the megalith circles around the world were sacred places where meteors struck. I think the ancients took the meteor landing as a sign to occupy that place."

"We know that the megaliths were built with astronomical considerations, normally the constellations from which the meteors fell. To remember this, the location of the sun and moon had to be marked accurately."

Chartwell did not respond.

"At the center of each aligned circle, a magnetic anomaly exists consistent with a meteor impact."

"You don't believe any of this, do you?" Rebekah asked, raising her voice. "You think it's all just rubbish."

"Early peoples learned to use meteor iron to make farm implements, weapons, everything metal. The metal was considered to be holy, heavenly provision, protected by the spirit of the gods," Chartwell said cautiously.

"The Professor has surveyed Stonehenge with drones, with Ground Penetrating Radar, analyzing all the data on computer. He stands convinced, as do I. He believes he knows where the sword of Stonehenge is, he just wants to confirm his theory."

"The best scientist is an excellent skeptic," Chartwell said. "You as an astronomer, myself as an archaeologist, we are scientists. While I agree that a sword made of meteorite iron is nearly indestructible," Chartwell said. "This translated story is a little much for me, the part about Excalibur being made using meteorite iron from Stonehenge."

"From a scientific standpoint, we know that there were meteor strikes on earth long before there were iron mines. There are stories associated that talk about unusual quantities of iron, more than was being produced by any known method. The iron pillar of India that never rusts, the superior iron that bound Hercules, chains across entire harbors, cannons and cannon balls. It is even speculated that the hammers the Vikings were so famous for were merely the tools by which they obtained the meteoric iron and formed swords from it. There are also many examples of swords being made from meteorites. "

"Do you believe it, Mr. Chartwell?"

"It's the story your Professor has translated from the Ogham texts. He has done his research, I'll give him that."

"So if it's true, why do you think they haven't found the meteor at Stonehenge?"

"Well, they could have taken it away a bit at a time making all those swords," he said. "A little at a time adds up."

"Then what about the power of Stonehenge, strange lights, vaporized visitors, the magnetic anomalies?"

"If at the center of each aligned circle a magnetic anomaly occurs, consistent with a meteor impact, then there is some potential in his theory, even if the original meteorite has been removed. According to his papers, the Professor has surveyed Stonehenge thoroughly. He seems convinced. He thinks the sword of Stonehenge will yet be found."

"What is it that a man likes so much about a sword?" Rebekah asked. "I heard Sandra say you were off looking for one."

"It's used as a figure of speech," Chartwell replied. "For me, the idea of swords is the concept of valor. Of all the Arthurian concepts, valor was the one proved by the sword."

"So it's an extension of one's manhood, is that it?"

Chartwell cleared his throat, just as Sandra returned. They made room for her to scoot into the window seat.

"Don't ask," he said once he saw the look on her face.

"No harm intended," Rebekah said. "Just a bit of a joke."

"All I know about swords is "Live by the sword, die by the sword," Sandra said. "Martin used to quote that."

"Uncle Martin also said the pen is mightier than the sword," Rebekah replied. "I'm going up to see if Hamid is awake," she said. "May I take my leave, please?"

Sandra watched Rebekah until she passed through the curtain to first class.

"I am worried about her," Sandra said, putting her arm on his. "I'm glad you are here to help me."

Chartwell hesitated.

"Sandra, I am here on a work assignment. I am along to help you get Rebekah safely settled. We will find her a proper flat, a small auto perhaps. As soon as that's over, I've someone to return to."

"I understand," Sandra said, "I didn't mean, oh never mind. Rebekah said the Professor offered her an apartment and a small convertible to use."

"In case you can't tell, that bloke concerns me. He's not to be trusted. We'll see how that pans out, but it might be better for her to have her own separate space. It's not like she can't afford it."

"I just worry that she isn't ready," Sandra responded, gently withdrawing her hand. "Maybe I worry too much."

"She is growing up," Chartwell replied.

"I mean about her friends. Her Muslim friends."

"All Muslims are not bad," Chartwell said. "There is good and bad everywhere. The bad ones want to hurt the Western world in retaliation for how the Arab world has been treated. Muslim radicals have sworn to avenge this history by violence against the West," he continued.

"How do you know so much about Muslims?" Sandra asked.

"I grew up around them in the U.K.," Chartwell replied. "I also worked around them a lot in the Middle East, on various digs for private and military purposes."

"How did you find Haddad's paper?" Sandra asked, locating her iPad before placing it inside her bag.

"It's pretty fantastic, but it is apparently written as history, not in the mythical style. I wonder what the Royal Society would say if they ever saw it?"

"I heard that after they read it they withdrew his permission to work at Stonehenge," she replied. "They were afraid of what he might do to prove his theory correct. Plus two people died on the last day the project was worked."

The trio arrived at Heathrow Airport with varied reactions. While Rebekah experienced a true welcome home sensation, Chartwell found the sounds, the announcements, the entire airport experience an unfamiliar adjustment.

Sandra choked back an overwhelming homesickness as the three of them worked their way through the London airport, which seemed to be on high alert. Military men and women were everywhere.

As they exited the baggage claim together, Chartwell was surprised to see a limousine driver waiting with a card flashing his name.

"Mr. Chartwell, sir? Professor Haddad has dispatched me to collect you to your hotel."

"Has he now?" Chartwell inquired, impressed at the courtesy, but suspicious at the same time. "Trying to make up for old wounds is he? Well, which hotel are you taking us to?"

"I would not know sir, only that you will be directing me."

"Very well, then. I can't see any harm in accepting a kindness. Ladies, we have a limousine, courtesy of Professor Haddad."

Chapter 23

The Professor parked his van in the large garage adjacent to his estate house. Pushing the button to close the automatic garage door behind him, he spun his wheelchair and rolled out of the van. Having driven directly from the museum at the maximum speed possible without attracting unnecessary attention, he now let his excitement flow, moving more quickly.

Once inside, he locked the entry door and flung aside his coat. Wheeling down the adjacent corridor, he mentally checked off a long list of the things he needed to do before his niece arrived in three days, before his new assistant made her appearance in two.

Anxious to reach the cellar of his main estate house, the Professor headed for the peculiar lift he had designed himself. No one would ever suspect that this small pantry off the kitchen would disguise an elevator, he had assured himself. Locking the door, the Professor wheeled into the space between the shelves, toggled off the light switch and felt the entire room start its descent.

Reaching the lower floor, the Professor wheeled out of the lift and to the left, entering a well-lit room, unfurnished and futuristic, where two lightweight fabric suits hung on charging hangers against the far wall.

He had named the suits *Nabi* and *Haway*, Arabic for Adam and Eve. One suit, dark as night, hung taller than the other. The smaller suit, a more obvious feminine shape, was the same dark color.

More subtle, built in differences were not evident. The Eve suit had been programmed differently. It could be controlled by the Adam suit, offering restraint or relief as needed. The control resided in the thoughts and actions of the wearer of the male exo-suit. If the world were to begin again, as plans called for, there would be no mistake this time that the male would be in control.

Passing his hand over a sensor beside the door, the Professor watched as the first suit, the larger of the two lowered automatically from the ceiling. He removed his street clothes, working in a practiced and efficient manner. He inserted his feet into the exo-suit, pulled across his shoulders before zipping up the front. Only then did he begin to breathe easy.

Feeling the flexible fabric mold to his body, feeling it warm to his body temperature and begin to buzz slightly, a sensation to which he was now accustomed, the Professor strapped the cuffs of the suit tightly around his wrists as he stood up, leaving his wheelchair behind.

The experience of walking on his own was exhilarating, no matter how many times he donned the suit. His atrophied muscles gained new strength, stimulated by the electrical charge that the suit itself generated. The nerves of his back and spine received increased signal and control at the same time.

Haddad had essentially modified the exo-skeleton suits made for medical and industrial use to a militarized form per the Jackal's orders. Insulated contacts in the neck, wrists and belt of the exo-suit powered headphones, lights, and communications gear. By virtue of a special glove of the Professor's own design, anything a person might hold, such as a flashlight, even a sword could receive electrical current.

Walking with ease, he headed down a dim hallway and descended stone steps down to darkness. Now that he could walk, he strode confidently, the joint- lights from his suit piercing the dark with glaring illumination, slicing through the shadows ahead of him.

Reaching the lowest level, he stopped and listened before flipping the breaker switch on, lighting a seemingly endless row of LED light bulbs stretching into the distance.

Turning left into a stone-lined alcove, the Professor grasped the handlebar of the nearest Segway transporter, stepped aboard and turned in the direction of the endless overhead lights. He ducked under the first and each succeeding bulb, presenting the appearance of an awkward, stooping stork.

 Passing through stone arches, past multiple side tunnels laid out in rings, the Professor came to a large room with a high ceiling supported by immense wooden beams. Lit by a ring of lights, a round table replica of the Knights of the Round Table fame sat imposing, open in the center, much like the design of Stonehenge itself was a round structure, open in the middle. At each of a dozen seats sat a mummy, each one a former research assistant or worker at the estate, the Professor's personal handiwork.

The Professor barely paused, passing by this morbid display to continue until he was directly beneath Stonehenge itself. Here, lit by more lights, he stepped off the Segway and entered a ring of stone columns, themselves the bases for the sarsen uprights that Stonehenge visitors gazed at daily. Perhaps they were doing so at this moment, not thirty feet above his head.

Stepping off the Segway, walking between the great uprights, the Professor stopped to gaze at the Sacred Stone of the Druids, their reason for erecting this Great Stone Henge around it. He walked reverently to its massive flank, reached his hand to the pommel of the Great Sword, sliding it from the Stone with ease to the sound of whistling, grating metal.

"Ish-kalabar," he breathed. "Excalibur!"

Unmarked by the ages, Ish-kalabar, the sword of legends, appeared as it always had. Light concentrated in its surface, leapt out at the viewer's eye. Even as Haddad held it, the sword trembled from the electrical power building in the exo-suit at that moment. His own body heat powered the suit, recharging it while any excess power fed into the sword. His limbs tingled as he walked, a side effect of the flow of current through the suit. The sensation was one of strength, of power, of manhood.

Chapter 24

CIA Headquarters
Langley, VA

With the buzz and click of a secure door, CIA Director Carter Hall's office moved from Martin Culver's imagination into stark reality. Surprised at Hall's invitation, Martin had wondered what he might find on today's visit.

"Come on in," Hall barked, sipping from a short glass. "No one's going to bite you."

Martin entered the room escorted by a female Marine sentry.

Hall hobbled to the window, facing the Washington Monument in the afternoon light. She turned and waited for the female Marine sentry escorting Martin to complete her introduction of him. The Marine kept her eye on him, waited for Hall to confirm that everything was okay, then left.

"You're late," she said as the door closed.

"I lost my phone. No phone, no calendar."

"No excuse," Hall said as she turned toward him. Her mouth wore a twisted look that managed to turn into a smile. She gave Martin a long but stilted, hug, as if she had thought a long time before deciding it was okay to do so.

"The doctor told you I called?" Hall asked.

"She did," Martin replied. "I was just wrapping up my last appointment at Bethesda Naval."

"Your Marine sentry seems efficient. Do you need a guard?

"I had the male guard replaced, my gut, something wasn't right. You can't be too careful. The ex-Director's secretary was a double agent. The one you met just now, that's Lt. Stoner, soon-to-be ex-Marine. She is ending her term of service and starting here next month."

"Lt. Stoner?" he asked, smiling. "I thought there were no ex-Marines. Too many jokes about her name?"

"Stop it," Hall replied. "Her full name is Lieutenant Candace Stoner. Candy for short. Following her separation from service, she will be working directly with me as an Inspector. You may see her around."

Martin wandered the perimeter of the room, taking everything in. Hall's office was larger than Martin expected.

Noticing Martin taking stock of his surroundings, Hall engaged in more small talk. Conversation was not her strong point.

"Not what you had in mind, Culver?" she asked.

"I had pictured a smaller space, windowless, more of a war room with a wall arsenal of knives and pistols, a dark cave of spy gear and disguises waiting to be deployed at a moment's notice."

"You pictured the Batcave," Hall laughed. "Sorry. This was my father's office, you know. When he was with the CIA. It was offered to me, and until this recent midnight renovation, I could find something every day that reminded me of him."

"This is a first for us, the first time we ever met anywhere official," Martin noted as he sat down. "We have always met in the field, on the run, in the middle of some crisis, always in some foreign location."

"I thought about that too," Hall agreed. "That's why I thought it might be useful to catch up with each other a little, to iron out the details of our working relationship while there is not actually a full-blown crisis going off around us."

"You could have just called," he remarked. "Except I have no phone."

"Oh, that reminds me," Hall said. She walked slowly to the library wall and pulled out a Gideon Bible. Opening the book, she removed a smartphone from a hidden compartment and handed it to him.

"I know you haven't been using a phone because of your ears. How about a phone that cooperates with your hearing devices? I had a replacement set up for you. You can you keep an agenda on that, or at least use it to call if you're running late."

"Sounds reasonable," Martin responded without looking up. "I've missed having a phone."

"So how are you doing?" Hall inquired. "The doctor released you yet?"

"I'm doing ok," he lied, straining to hear her words. "Can you speak up?"

"Still getting used to the wireless hearing devices?"

"Yes." Martin focused on the phone. "I'll get used to them. I may not have to wear them long. That was my last appointment for a month."

Martin still did not look up. Hall began to drum her fingers on the desk.

"I was amazed to see what Bethesda is doing for our soldiers coming home injured from the battlefield."

"What impressed you the most there?" Hall asked, hoping to engage Martin in some form of conversation.

"There was a guy in an exo-suit that looked like nothing more than a wetsuit," Martin replied, maintaining eye contact with the new phone. "He was learning to walk again using it."

"It was nothing like the old-style industrial exterior skeleton suits that I have seen used for lifting. This fit the guy wearing it almost like a second skin. He had been declared a paraplegic a month ago. This morning he was walking on his own."

"I have seen those, "Hall commented. "We have had a CIA prototype for about two years. Do you know how they work?"

"Not all the details," he mumbled.

"The suit is powered by very fine lithium battery fibers woven into the fabric that converts body heat in excess of 20 degrees Celsius to charging current. Our design seems to have a problem common to exo-suits, in that they tend to overheat too quickly. That actually is related to something that I wanted to talk to you about."

Martin still did not look up.

Hall had enough of being ignored.

"Culver! What fascinates you so much on that damned phone? I wish I had waited to give it to you."

"I'm sorry," he replied. "I am searching for an app for my hearing devices. At Bethesda they said I would be able to download an app to be able to control volume and sound quality."

"It's already loaded," she said. "Check the apps again."

Martin looked up. "I found it. How did you know the app was already loaded?"

"We have been over this," she sighed. "As long as we are working together I will know more about you most days than you know about yourself. Where you have been, what you have done."

"What did I have for breakfast four days ago?" he challenged.

Hall glared at him.

"Are you talking about what you ate at 4:00 AM or what you ate after you nearly made Sandra late for work?"

Martin stopped smiling. Hall was accurate.

"OK, point taken. But how did you know?"

"I didn't. But sometimes I go fishing. And that time the bait worked. By the way, you might want to give Sandra an occasional rest break. She's only human."

Martin laughed uncomfortably, shifting in his chair.

"Well, Sandy has gone to London for a week, so hopefully she will get her rest."

He searched for a way to change the subject.

"Nice office, by the way. You could keep an eye on the world from here."

"I hate it. Someone has been re-arranging while I have been away. But I will see very little field work from here on out, so this is my little corner of the world now."

"I can't picture you behind a desk all the time," Martin replied.

"Time is catching up with me. Responsibilities of being Director, not to mention my injuries."

Hall sat down in the second guest chair beside him. "I would rather be anywhere than be stuck in this office."

"Anywhere?" Martin asked, his eyes narrowing a notch.

Hall reconsidered her words.

"No, not anywhere," she responded. "There are places I never want to go back to."

"I'll bet," Martin said. "How are you getting along?"

"I still don't feel strong. My leg has healed, but I still have trouble with my shoulders and wrists. The surgery on my hip is taking the longest, although some of the ribs I cracked still haven't knit."

"Was that the reason for that awkward hug?" Martin asked.

Hall reached to her desk for the short glass she had been sipping from and drained the glass.

"*That* was because you are the only man who has seen me that naked in a very long time. When I went to hug you, that whole awful experience came rushing back."

"I'm sorry," he said. "Next time I rescue you, I expect you to be fully dressed."

"There won't be a next time, mister," Hall joked. "I do the rescuing around here."

"So why am I here today?" Martin asked. "You mentioned something that you wanted to talk about?"

"Yes, I have a lot to go over. What I mentioned earlier is that it appears we, meaning CIA, we have a significant problem. ISIS has obtained a design for an exo-suit that was made to rob tombs, to make the wearer faster and stronger. One of the contractors they licensed to loot antiquities in Syria brought it in. They have modified it and are close to mass production. If their soldiers ever got these in their hands, our efforts to stop them would receive a significant setback. "

"Is there any way to stop it?"

"Only if we can find out who is having them made."

"Any leads on who that is?"

"Yes, remember what the Ex-Director said just before he died?"

"Yes, I believe I will always remember that. He lay dying in my arms, remember? "Find the daughter" he said, as if it were the clue to end *all* artifact smuggling. "

"Well I have been working on that. I am tracing a smuggling connection through Spain to London, then to the Middle East."

"Where in the Middle East?"

"Right now the trail goes cold in Istanbul," she said.

"Why Istanbul?"

"It's the city most notorious in the world for fencing smuggled archaeological treasures. ISIS has agents there, and it is home to hundreds of small shipping firms."

"The ancient crossroads of the world," Martin commented.

"But what are the ISIS agents doing in Istanbul?"

"ISIS, the Islamic State, has been fencing stolen goods for months to finance their militant campaign. All of the money appears to flow through Istanbul. The government there is not friendly to us, so it has not been easy to get their cooperation. We thought we had made a contact at Arabic educational conference there, but before we negotiated a deal, he was killed in an explosion."

"Like the one that killed your father?" Martin asked.

"Very similar," Hall responded. "In any event, with our source killed, we had to start over."

"Do you need the International Antiquities Foundation to look into it? I've never been to Istanbul."

"You've never been anywhere but south of here," she said. "Don't forget, I've seen your passport."

"Speaking of that…"

"Yes," Hall said, turning to her desk. "Here."

Hall handed him a new U.S. passport. And a yellow card.

"The passport shows all your stamps including one for Miami to account for your recent return to the U.S."

"It also has my current picture, with the goatee and all."

"Just not the long hair," she reminded him. "Get a haircut, would you?"

"I left it long to hide the hearing devices. I wanted to wait until I don't need them to cut it shorter."

"That may not happen as soon as you think, Culver."

"What's with this yellow card?" he asked.

"After you get medically cleared to fly, this will let you take the pistol onboard. It says you are attached to diplomatic staff. You still have to unload the weapon before flying though."

"You know about the pistol?" Martin asked, looking up briefly.

"This is getting to be a tiresome game. When will you just accept that I know almost everything that you have done. I have my sources."

"Ok, so I have the pistol. I have had it cleaned and serviced. I intend to keep it."

"It's a clean gun, no serial numbers, so there should be no problem," she said. "I'm glad the weapon is still in use. I'm still curious. It surprised me when you brought that pistol out in Panama. How did you get it out of Mexico?"

"I smuggled it in a box of meteor chunks. Can we get on with our meeting? I have to hit the road."

"Not yet," Hall hesitated. "I want to have all my ducks in a row first. Are you even listening to me, Culver?"

"Sorry, I'm listening. I was just thinking."

"About me nearly naked again, I'll bet? Forget it, just get that out of your mind."

"You are the who keeps bringing that up. No, I *was* thinking about rescuing you, though. I was trying to remember what happened. I still have a lot of gaps."

"You and I both," Hall said. She cleared her throat, then lit up a cigarette from the wooden box on her desk.

He watched her visibly calm down as she inhaled the second time, the tip of the cigarette glowing briefly.

"I'll tell you mine if you tell me yours," she offered.

"Deal."

"You go first."

"Okay," Martin said. "All I am really sure of is that God got me through it. It's weird, what I can remember and what I can't. After I rescued you, I took you to Morgan's warehouse. Jack and Morgan's sister found us there. "

"Do you always call your father by his first name?"

"I always have. Why?"

"It's just funny. I always called my dad by his first name, too. So what else do you recall?" she asked.

"I left you with Jack while I went to find Morgan. I killed several of their men, shut down power to the island. I was forced into Morgan's helicopter, but we fought. I dropped the sonic device into the Pacific. That is about all I remember until I reached the island. I woke up with half of Morgan washed up on the beach not ten feet from me."

Hall shifted in her chair, then leaned back, obviously in deep thought. She seemed stunned but relieved at the same time.

"But not the other half was not there," she inquired further. "That's what you woke up to, half a person?"

"Don't know what happened," Martin said. "No earthly idea."

"I don't remember much," she started. "I was in and out. Your father kept me alive until help arrived. He was amazing. I see where you get it. We were rescued by a Navy helicopter. Then, I gave the order to have Smuggler's Island destroyed."

It became Martin's turn to be stunned.

"How did you know I wasn't still there?"

"I had no way of knowing if you were still there or not," she said flatly. "I did what I had to do. I hope you understand."

"I'm not sure I do," Martin replied, leaning forward in the chair.

"My mission is *always* my priority," Hall said, rolling her eyes. "I had to make sure those sonic weapons were not replicated. I had to be sure that Morgan was dead."

"Even if it meant ending my life? If that is how you treat friends, remind me to stay out of your way if revenge is ever on your agenda," Martin said curtly. He stood up and paced the floor.

"Sit down, Culver. It had to be done. Ask your father. He was ready to give the order for me. I could hardly speak. But I made him give me the microphone. I made the call."

"I can't believe it, Jack knew about this?"

"You had not signaled us, Culver. We had no way of communicating, and no way to know you were alive."

Martin turned away and looked out the highest window at CIA Langley toward the pinnacle of the Washington Monument standing like a tall, sunlit exclamation point in the distance.

"I get it," Martin said. "Morgan was evil, the whole situation was evil. So do you know how I got to the island?"

"Not every detail," Hall said slowly. "We were looking for you when the MINR IV submersible working on a separate mission found Morgan's helicopter over 100 feet down. The forward windscreen of the helo was shattered. Somehow you got out of the helicopter and onto the island."

"We suspect the barge beached itself on the island due to the sonic device detonation. The explosion made a monster wave that reached Hawaii. That happened a short time after Jack and I were rescued. That old Navy barge of Morgan's helped save my life, your father life, and eventually your life. Think of it as a positive."

Martin breathed deeply, then looked at the floor.

"So that is how I will think of it, then."

"That's the right attitude," Hall said. "Speaking of attitude, have you seen a counselor yet?"

"If by counselor you mean shrink, then no, I haven't," Martin replied, offering no further explanation.

"You actually should, Culver. Here's why. People who have survived like you did tend to have overreactions to surviving. Their lives are never the same after."

"You mean like being depressed?"

"Some people, go inside, get depressed. Others have the opposite reaction, they go wild, almost a delusion, taking risks, driving faster, as if nothing can harm them."

"Have you noticed anything else unusual since you have been back?"

"Odd sleep patterns, every noise bothers me, can't get enough time alone with Sandy, other than that, nothing unusual."

"Like I said. Have you dealt with your 'body count'?"

"The body count. What the heck is that?"

"It's what I call it, the baggage we carry from killing people. By all accounts, Culver, you killed at least five people on Smuggler's Island, not counting Morgan. Counting the deaths you were responsible for in Mexico, I'd say that's a lot to process. I have removed people from duty for less."

Martin turned away from the window.

"I have not dealt with any of that, other than to talk to the Bethesda chaplain," he responded. "Since then, I haven't thought about it. I think I am afraid of going to sleep, like I need to be ready for something."

"Sandra said you were wide awake, 24/7," Hall said.

"That's our personal business."

"And now? How do you feel now?"

"I feel like I am coming back to life, screeching tires around the corners in a big race. It's as if things are improving, but at the same time falling apart, especially for Sandy and I."

"Have you talked to her about any of this?"

"Again, no. We don't talk, or haven't."

"So you and she just…basically just…"

"Yeah, that's it in a nutshell…that's where our communication starts and ends."

"Martin, Sandy, um, Sandra…talked to me in the hospital, about you, about us, about things on her mind."

Letting her words linger in the air, Hall came to the point.

"She wanted to know if you and I were involved. She seemed to think we are, or were."

"What did you tell her?" Martin asked.

"Of course I told her the truth, that we were not and are not involved. But I'm not sure she believed me."

"Sandy is in a weird place right now," Martin acknowledged. "The re-entry phase has not been good for us."

"Martin, she loves you. I saw her reaction when you went missing. She thought she had lost you forever, then found out you were alive. That's not an easy road."

"I wanted to talk to her about it before she left, but it didn't work out."

"I'm sorry about how all this went down," Hall offered. "What do you mean before she left?"

"Sandy left for London yesterday with Chartwell to take Rebekah back to London."

"Why London?"

"That's where Rebekah is from. She has a chance to finish up her studies and work as a research assistant for a London professor who's doing cutting edge work on Stonehenge, two dreams she has had for a long time." Martin explained.

"And Chartwell?" Hall asked, eyebrows raised. "Why did he go along?"

"They needed someone with them, someone who knows London. I was ok with Chartwell going, until after they all left."

"I think Sandra needed a break from me," Martin added. "I know she hasn't been getting enough sleep."

"Why is that Culver?"

"I don't know," he admitted. "I thought I had lost her, too."

Neither of them said anything for a long time until Hall broke the silence.

"You'll figure it out," Hall reassured him. "Can we get down to business?" she asked. "I have another meeting and you want to be on your way. "

"Sure," Martin said, walking to where she stood. "But don't take all day. I am hoping to hit the road before 1:00 PM to get back to Norfolk. You know how crowded I-95 gets after lunch."

"First let's go over my investigation into the bombing of the IAF and the explosion of your house. This stack of reports details what I have discovered," handing him a four inch thick ream of reports. "A hired gang out of Morocco, came into Norfolk through the port. They have been charged with terrorism on both counts, but there is something that you should know, Culver. These attacks occurred on a different level than we are used to seeing."

"Different level?"

"More personal," Hall responded. Her eyes scanned Martin's face for any reaction.

"This means I have bad news for you," she continued.

"What is it? What could be worse than anything that has already happened?"

"Your name popped up on an ISIS hit list."

She waited for Martin to respond.

"I did not think this was possible for any certain individual, especially non-military, but ISIS has identified over 500 civilian targets that are non-military and non-governmental."

"How did I earn such an honor?" Martin muttered flatly.

"You are being personally held responsible for the death of individuals important to ISIS, including those who trafficked their stolen artifacts."

"Señor Medina," Martin said quietly.

"Plus the death of individuals such as Morgan. These have brought you to their attention. Morgan was one of their favorite smugglers. Not counting that his fiancé is Muslim, of Moorish descent. You take away her *prometido*, you make the list."

"What should I watch out for?"

"Nothing in particular and everything at the same time. Anything unusual, out of the ordinary. We have had attempted bombings, poisoning made to look like accidents, reports of drone training to go against individuals, like a kind of poor man's cruise missile. Intelligence sources have intercepted numerous credible drone threats against U.S. Citizens."

"How are the drones targeting?"

"Key data specified sophisticated trigger mechanisms, including individual facial and schematic profile targeting of buildings."

"What can they do?"

"The drones? They can video and give away your position, they can fire bullets or small missiles, or they can deliver an explosive payload such as C-4."

Hall closed the report folder.

Martin's thoughts strayed from the conversation. He drew a deep breath, thinking about Sandy in London and his kids in Costa Rica.

"How do I protect my family in the face of such a challenge?"

"Culver, don't obsess over it. I am on their list too. I have been for some time. In fact, all Americans are, at some level, given their declaration of *jihad* against the United States."

"Someone is going to have to do something about these bastards," Martin blurted out. "I don't even know where to even start."

"Culver, you can't take ISIS out on your own," Hall counseled. "I am bringing our resources in to protect your family and your foundation."

"This is what we are doing, why we are doing it," she said, counting off the known factors on the fingers of one hand.

"We know there is a master antiquities smuggling ring funding war and insurrection around the world. ISIS is the best, most obvious example we have. We know that ISIS is financing their war and their weapons with stolen and smuggled artifacts. We need to know who runs this operation. Who is behind it? Then we cut the head off of the snake."

Martin scanned the conference table laden with thick report binders, then glanced up to the silenced video screens on the wall in front of him.

"This brings me to my next report," Hall began. "London is showing up more frequently for the anomalous customs and shipping entries that indicate an antiquities trader or ring of traders. We have had several events recently, including a missing antiquities shipment from an armored car that was attacked, its cargo stolen on the way to the airport. I am tracking the money on several players there, as well as a museum."

Martin considered what she was saying.

"You might never find out who it is, unless it turns up in the IAF audits of museum shipments to stop artifact trafficking. I agree, if we follow the flow of money, that might do it. I would start with which museums receive significant donations, then lose items in shipment, have the shipments stolen or go missing altogether."

"Exactly!" Hall interjected. "That's how we'll nail them. While you were…away, I started working on this. Since then I have been on it day and night."

Hall pointed to the conference table.

157

"This stack of reports show the links that I have been able to pull together. It covers an extensive network of museums."

"So where does it lead?"

"Remember the single biggest clue, the greatest unsolved mystery, since you and I have been working together?"

"Our trust issues?"

"Besides that," she smirked, pointing a finger at him. "Do you remember what the ex-Director told you? "Find the daughter," he said."

"A simple statement from a dying man," Martin countered.

"I don't think so. I believe I know who the daughter is. I think she has a direct link to who is behind all of this. I have it figured out. "

Chapter 25

Martin pulled his new Jeep Wrangler through the coded gate of his condo community just after 4:00PM, managing to make good time on the drive back from CIA Headquarters in Northern Virginia. He returned the gate guard's greeting and continued on.

Parking across both parking spots assigned to the Culver condo, Martin paused to think where Sandy's Range Rover was parked, remembering that she had left it at the IAF after being driven to the Norfolk Airport. Technically the Range Rover was an IAF registered company vehicle.

He grabbed his overnight bag from the passenger seat and looked in both directions before approaching and entering the condo. His impaired hearing had taught him to become more alert, more dependent on what he could see or smell.

Once inside the house, Martin coded the alarm to occupied, dropping his overnight bag on the bench nearest the door. He removed his jacket, but not his pistol. His keys and hearing devices were laid with care on the entry table.

The house felt cool and quiet, the fall sun not having warmed it excessively. Entering the kitchen, Martin searched the cabinet, bringing out a can of black-eye peas and an unopened jar of pickle relish. He placed his phone on the island counter, dumped the beans into a pan to warm, then cracked open the relish jar lid.

This ritual meal connected Martin to his father's rural Virginia roots. After dumping the hot beans into a bowl, he plopped a thick spoonful of relish, or chow-chow as his aunt had called it, into the center of the bowl, then added a generous amount of sea salt over the exposed beans at the edge of the bowl. He had seen Jack prepare this same dish many times. Martin worked methodically, symbolically. His memory was returning. Family traditions and memories were once again within his reach. Checking his phone as he ate, Martin saw no messages since leaving Alexandria.

Stepping outside, Martin relaxed in a metal mesh chair warmed by the sun and surveyed the view of Pretty Lake as if he had never seen it before. Calm waters provided a mirror reflection of blue skies that gave way to lighter blue where high clouds attempted to form, lit from beneath by the fading afternoon light.

To the east, seabirds gliding past a circular sun halo briefly drew Martin's attention, enhancing the relaxing scene, until he remembered how often he wanted to catch and roast a passing seabird when stranded on the island.

Martin stepped back inside. Seeing the lights lit on their home phone answering machine, Martin casually pushed the button to see if there were anything other than telemarketers.

"Mrs. Culver, this Stephanie with your attorney's office. Sorry it has taken us so long to get back to you. You are definitely within your rights to pursue having Mr. Culver declared deceased, based on the amount of time and the circumstances of his disappearance. Please call our office to provide details to complete the paperwork. You have our number. Thank you."

Martin was floored. Sandra had been in the process of declaring him deceased. She had given up on him ever returning. He started to push call back to the attorney's office, when his cell phone rang.

Martin considered not picking up the phone. With Sandy in London, his kids in Costa Rica and the IAF on autopilot with Cita since two days ago, he felt compelled to check, just in case anyone had run into trouble.

The number showed on his phone as the International Antiquities Foundation.

"Hello, Martin Culver speaking."

He could hardly make out the words, the crying, pained voice barely intelligible without his hearing devices.

"Hold on, hold on, I can't hear you," Martin stammered, dashing to the front door with the phone. He snapped on a hearing device, then held the phone to that ear.

"I was having interference. Who is this? What is happening?"

"Martin, please come to the IAF immediately. There has been a terrible tragedy! Come quickly!"

"Who is this?" he asked again.

"Martin, it's Cita. Martin something terrible has happened! There has been an explosion in the parking lot! Come to the IAF now!"

"I'm on the way!" Martin shouted, grabbing his coat and his keys. He pocketed the second hearing device, hit the door running and did not slow his pace until he jumped into his Jeep and sped away. Driving out of the condo community, Martin could hear emergency vehicles approaching through the one hearing device he had attached.

"What happened here?" Martin asked as he pulled into the IAF parking lot. At least one burning vehicle could be seen past the half dozen fire trucks and countless emergency responders. Finding no one to answer his question, Martin sought out the Fire Battalion Chief.

"Who is in charge here?" he demanded. "What has happened?"

"Better stay back, sir," the young fire captain advised. "There has been a vehicle explosion. We are trying to get the fire out."

"This is my property," Martin fired back, looking over the head of the fireman to get a better view. "Who was in that vehicle?"

"We have restricted all employees from the building to this location sir. I'll ask that you stand back for your own safety."

"Martin, Martin, I'm over here."

Realizing Cita was calling him, Martin took a step right as if he were heading toward the burning vehicle. The closest fire engine to the flaming wreck was actively dumping its tanks on the vehicle without any result. The fire captain turned to cut Martin off, but Martin simply reversed his movement, side-stepped the younger man and slipped under the crowd control tape. Martin heard booted footsteps trying to catch up to him, but he did not look back.

"Martin!" Cita called, beginning to cry again once she saw him. "Martin there was an explosion! Mary was in the vehicle."

Martin reached for Cita just as her knees buckled. Holding the shaking girl to keep her from falling, Martin looked again toward the smoking vehicle shell. No glass endured intact, no paint remained unscorched. The glass in both headlight assemblies had melted, as if the very eyes of the vehicle had dissolved. Every tire was flattened, adhered to the pavement by the intense heat. Even the license plates were melted. The intense hissing of hot metal and rivers of rainbow colored water escaped the melted hulk into the air and the parking lot, polluting both with the acrid smell of burned rubber.

The vehicle appeared to have been an SUV, Martin noted, but now resembled nothing so much as an overheated meteor crashed to earth in the first row of the IAF parking lot, closest to the building. Without asking, Martin knew that no one could survive such an event.

"Cita, what happened here?" Martin asked, his suspicions aroused.

Between sobs, Cita tried to respond.

"Mary was leaving on an errand. She heard you were coming back to work tomorrow, so she said we should have a cake."

Cita stopped to regain her composure before continuing.

"Mary was leaving for the bakery when the SUV just went up in flames."

Martin hugged her tighter in the cool afternoon air.

"Don't cry," he said to her.

Martin had a sudden flash to his conversation earlier in the day with Director Hall.

"Was she in her own personal car?" Martin asked, looking around the crowd.

"No. We've kept her so busy since she came on staff that she hasn't registered her vehicle in Virginia yet. We gave her the keys to Sandra's Range Rover, since it was for company business."

"Mr. Culver, are you in charge for the IAF?" a voice asked from behind him.

Martin turned to see a younger woman with a Norfolk Fire Department investigator's badge.

"I am," Martin replied.

"Katelyn O'Keefe with Virginia ME," she said by way of introduction.

She was attractive, with glasses and the wrong haircut for a breezy afternoon beside the Chesapeake Bay. Her badge read, "Medical Examiner."

"Please come with me, sir," she said, pointing toward the destroyed vehicle.

"For what?"

"Sir, I need you to make tentative identification. It appears that one of your employees has died in the vehicle explosion."

"As an investigator, do you believe this was an accidental explosion?" Martin asked, looking away through the crowd.

"Sir, judging by the blast and the ferocity of the flames, my first judgement would be non-accidental in nature. Fire investigators would have to make the final determination."

"Do you know the history of this building, of my home?"

"No sir, I don't know any of that personally."

Martin let go of Cita's arm and stepped up on one of the concrete barriers along the sidewalk leading to the building.

"What are you looking for, Martin?" Cita asked, sounding nervous. She realized she had seen this look on his face before, a long time ago, a continent away.

"Ms. O'Keefe, this building has been bombed before, my home has been destroyed, my family threatened," Martin said in a low voice. "What happened to this vehicle may not be the end of it."

The fire captain approached.

"What's going on here?" he demanded.

"Had a refresher on your Soft Target Awareness training lately, Captain?" Martin asked, before ignoring the official as he continued to survey the gathered crowd.

"Cita, what is the rendezvous point for an IAF building emergency?"

Cita wiped her fingers across her cheeks to catch runaway eye makeup.

"We always gather right here," she said. "We're in the right spot. All the employees know. We drill on this monthly."

"Then we are in the *wrong* spot," Martin said. "Captain, have your crew pull everyone away from here. Take them to the other side of the fire engines!"

The fire captain did not budge.

"Do it now! This is just the first stage, move the people and sweep this area with your bomb squad."

Martin did not descend from his vantage point above the crowd, instead pulling out his phone and turning to video the scene as the IAF employees retreated to safer ground. He spotted one person moving contrary to the flow of people.

The medical examiner did not move, a strained look crossing her face.

"Mr. Culver, don't move," she said cautiously before stepping back several paces.

Martin stood still, leaving the video running in case there was any data to be gained from what happened next. He looked down at O'Keefe.

"What is it? What do you see?"

"Sir, there is a package beneath the concrete bench where you are standing. It has a red LED that I can see from here."

Martin thought fast. He knew this bomb was meant for secondary damage once everyone had gathered. Not only that, Martin knew the clock was ticking.

He aimed his phone under the bench to video the bomb, then slipped the phone inside his jacket to protect the device while leaving it on record.

"I took a video but I can't see it in the afternoon light, Lieutenant. Any wires or switches on that thing that you can see?"

"None that I can see, sir," she replied.

"Any suggestions?" he asked, a tone of finality in his voice.

"There is a large concrete planter to your right," she said. "It appears to be a vehicle mitigation barrier. If you could get to the other side of that, you might be safe."

With few choices, Martin decided a plan of action.

"Keep backing away," he instructed O'Keefe, "When I say run, you run as far and as you can as fast as you can. We are out of time." He watched as she kicked off her shoes and turned to run.

Martin leaned from the waist to his right, raised his right hand, then motioned for the medical examiner to run. At the same time he pushed off forcefully against the bench, launching himself over a low block wall toward the concrete planter.

In slow motion Martin watched as O'Keefe sprinted away, wrapped in a protective silver blanket by one of the attending firemen before being pulled to the ground for safety. The fireman positioned himself between her body and the blast.

As the bomb went off, Martin rode the force wave of the explosion over the planter barrier, falling clumsily to the ground, striking his shoulder on the corner of the concrete barrier. He felt the heat sear the air above him, heard metal shards bouncing off of every hard surface. A billow of smoke expanded rapidly, enveloping him in a thick, dark cloud.

Martin scrambled to his feet, in case the vapor was toxic. There was no odor, no stinging in his eyes. Thankfully, the bomb had not been chemically armed. His ears rang like whistling chimes. He was missing one hearing device, but found it once he stood up.

"Mr. Culver, are you all right sir?" the fire captain called.

Martin reattached the hearing device and stepped out of the cloud of smoke, each footstep marked by the crunch of metal on pavement as he stepped on shrapnel.

"I'm ok," Martin said quietly, stifling a cough. "Was anyone else hurt?

"Your jacket and shirt are torn," the medical examiner noted. "Your shoulder is bleeding and look at your hair in the back. It's all singed. Let's have a medic take a look."

"Not necessary," Martin said, craning his neck to the side to see the shoulder wound. He winced as he turned, then caught wind of his own scorched hair.

"I needed a haircut anyway," he tried to joke.

O'Keefe was not about to surrender.

"You have been injured," she insisted. "Injuries must be attended to." She took him by the arm and led him to a waiting ambulance.

Martin relented. As he walked toward the ambulance, his phone rang.

"Martin Culver," he answered.

"Are you all right?"

"Who is this?"

"Who else would know your office had been targeted and that you had nearly been killed?"

"Hall," he said. "What just happened down here? My parking lot looks like Beirut on a bad day. I've had a company vehicle go up in flames, one of my employees is dead, and then a bomb went off under my feet."

"Whose vehicle was blown up?"

"The one Sandra normally drives, her Range Rover, why?"

The line went silent for longer than he expected.

"Was anyone inside it?"

"Mary Power. She is a recent hire, former IAF contractor."

"Then it's worse than I thought. We intercepted a video feed on a drone frequency that we have been monitoring. Since this was Sandra's work vehicle, it sounds like someone tried to take her out. Culver, are you in a secure location?"

"I think so," he responded, scanning the horizon. "Yes."

"Get to shelter, somewhere out of the open. Get the bomb squad to check your building and all the cars before anyone drives home, starting with your Jeep. Then you need to get away from there, move indoors."

"Hall, what are we facing here? Level with me."

"Best case scenario, lone wolf actor. Worst case, there may be multiple actors planning secondary assaults, as you have seen. I'm not certain," she said, "but it doesn't look good. I'll have someone there shortly."

"I will call you back," Martin said. "I need to call to check on Sandra, to warn her. "

"Do that and you may as well kill her yourself," Hall said without emotion. "If you do that your call can be traced."

"Then I have to go to London to warn her."

"What about your ears?"

"They want to do electric impulse treatment, like a TENS unit. I can't wait though. I'll just have to take my chances."

"I will send you the name of someone I want you to contact in London," Hall said. "Let me know what you find out."

Martin slid his bandaged hand across the screen, closing the conversation.

"Who was that?" Cita asked.

"A concerned friend," Martin replied.

"Cita, I am going to London to warn Sandra. Do not let her know I am coming, ok."

"Sure, Martin, but someone has to tell Chartwell about Mary."

"Why is that?" he asked.

"They were an item. They had been seeing each other for a couple of months," she said.

Martin grabbed Cita's arm, steering she and the Medical Examiner away from the crowd.

"O'Keefe, I need for you to do me a big favor. I'm going with you to identify the remains now, as you requested. But I want your report to read only the facts: the vehicle was owned by the IAF, the primary user was Sandra Culver, the body of an adult female will be taken to the M.E.'s office for positive identification. Keep it simple, can you do that?"

"That's actually all we have right now. The full report will take days to complete," she said. "It looks like I will have to use dental records. I can do that for you, but why?"

"Because I believe it will buy us all some time," he replied.

Afterward making the identification, Martin solemnly returned to his Jeep. The vehicle had been examined top to bottom by the bomb squad and given the all clear.

He had just settled into the driver seat and reached for the ignition when his phone signaled a text. Martin put his keys on the passenger seat and reached into his jacket pocket.

It was a text message from Chartwell.

"If you get cleared to travel, join us in London. We're at the Ambassadors Hotel in London. See you soon, old man."

Chapter 26

Four hours later, Martin settled into his first class seat, amazed at the generous leg room compared to coach. He found the luxurious leather seat to be much wider than standard coach, with nearly enough space for two. The leather was as soft as fine silk.

Finally able to catch his breath, Martin had made it to the airport in record time, leaving his Jeep in the Long Term Parking garage. Having decided to fly to London, he booked a ticket on the 10:30PM British Airways direct flight from Dulles. The cost of a same day flight, at almost $10,000 US, had caused him to think twice. He booked it anyway, before deciding taking a quick shower and scissor-cutting his singed hair, leaving enough length to cover his neck and ears. He hoped these steps would rid him of any explosive residue from the bomb going off. To be sure, he did not bring any of the same shoes or clothes for the international flight.

Martin re-packed while holding for the young audiologist handling his case. Waiting for her, he realized that she would not agree to him flying this soon. Hanging up, Martin left the doctor wondering. Only just now had his phone stopped ringing, all calls from the concerned audiologist. He turned his phone off while he was still thinking about it.

Once inside the Dulles terminal, the only hitch had been as Martin made his way through TSA check. The officer took note of his passport, hesitating before marking his boarding pass. The officer studied the yellow weapons permit at length.

"Martin Culver, no middle name. Mr. Culver, your passport raises some flags," he remarked. "It is, as we say, attention-worthy."

"What concerns you, sir?" Martin respectfully asked.

"Your passport shows recent entry stamps for Miami, Peru, Mexico, Costa Rica, Panama, back to Miami, now off to London. What type of work do you do?" the CBP officer inquired, lowering his wire-framed glasses to the end of their tether.

"I'm in antiques," Martin replied. "Mostly I advise collectors and museums, a sort of diplomatic outreach."

"Ah yes, diplomatic outreach. What takes you to London today?"

"I am joining my wife and colleague there for a meeting," he responded.

"And this work requires a pistol?"

"I arrange repatriation of stolen antiquities to the source countries," Martin responded simply. "Not everyone is on board with that."

The CBP officer looked Martin in the eye, folded the passport with his boarding pass and handed it to him. He handed the yellow weapons permit back to Martin separately.

"Made certain it is unloaded, I trust?"

Martin raised his carryon to show the yellow tag attached at the ticker counter confirming his pistol's status.

"Enjoy your flight sir," the agent remarked, already looking past him to the next person in line.

Seated in first class, Martin absently watched the rest of the passengers file past. He noticed two brunette girls pointing at him and whispering the moment they stepped onboard the plane. These were the same young women who had been chatting and staring at him while they stood on queue at the boarding gate.

One smiled and nodded toward him as she inched down the aisle, then giggled to her friend as Martin smiled back. He self-consciously checked his hearing device to make sure that they was properly attached, then looked up when the second brunette slid beside him into the remaining seat space.

"Hi, I'm Madelyn," the young woman said, pushing her eyeglasses higher on her nose. "You probably noticed us giving you the once-over." She presented her hand. "Forgive me for being forward, but aren't you a famous author?"

Martin smiled as Madelyn's excitedly shook his hand. The second thing he noticed was her clipped British accent.

"I don' t know about famous," he replied. "But you're correct, I am a published author."

"I knew it!" she said excitedly, before shushing herself. "You certainly look the part in that blazer and black t-shirt! My friend and I have been on a fabulous holiday to Cuba. On the way down, we bought a book to share. To read on the way, you know, for the adventure of it all, pirates and Spanish treasure and Havana. When we saw you we just knew you were the same man on the cover."

Martin smiled again, more at the animated, continuous way that the young woman spoke than at anything in particular that she said.

"Pirates, eh? That sounds like my first novel," he responded. "Where are you flying?" he asked.

"We are headed back to London. University starts in less than a fortnight and we simply must return, you know, register for classes, get our bearings, plus we don't want to miss the pre-semester parties."

"Madelyn, would you like for me to sign your copy of my novel? If you have it handy, I would be pleased."

"Oh, would you?" she exclaimed, holding her own finger to her lips, realizing that she had responded in too loud a voice for the setting. The female flight attendant greeting passengers as they boarded the plane smiled curtly and made a shooing motion for Madelyn to move to her assigned seat.

"My friend Brittany has it just now. I'll get it from her straightaway," Madelyn said breathlessly. "Don't go anywhere, I'll be right back!"

"I'll be right here," Martin said, amused. *"Where would I go?"* he thought.

Martin glanced over his shoulder as Madelyn slipped into the steady stream of passengers crowding into coach. He quickly lost sight of her.

Settling into his seat, Martin smiled. Being recognized for his writing did not happen often. He was ready to get back to writing. He checked his jacket pocket for the notebook that held the outline of his next novel.

Martin took a deep breath and tried to relax, unable to shake the image of her smoking SUV. He hoped to be able to warn Sandy in time. He liked her preference of the name Sandra, but she would always be Sandy to him. On the way to the airport he thought about all she meant to him, how much he missed her, even for a day. He did not look forward to the grim task of informing her about Mary's untimely demise.

Martin realized he was noting the exits, sizing up fellow passengers, calculating the path of least resistance if needed. He was not expecting trouble, but awareness was better than an ugly surprise any day.

The dark-haired female flight attendant stopped at his seat.

"Mineral water while we are waiting, sir...a drink perhaps?" She offered a glass of ice and an opened bottle of chilled Perrier wrapped in a cloth napkin. He was certain that he had not seen her open the bottle. He remembered his training.

"No thanks," Martin responded. "A can of ginger ale, please? Unopened, and a glass with no ice."

The attendant managed a tight-lipped smile.

"Will there be anything else, sir?" she asked.

"Yes, do you have anything for equalizing cabin pressure in one's ears? I've had some trouble with my eardrums lately."

"You mean other than a stiff drink?" she asked.

"I don't drink," he responded.

"Of course sir. I have just the thing, pressure equalizing earplugs. I will bring you a pair." The attendant then turned away. Martin smiled until she left.

Surprised by a second young Brit who slipped into the half-seat beside him. Martin found himself amused. The two girls were practically twins except for the eyeglasses.

"Mr. Culver, I'm so pleased to make your acquaintance! I..., that is we, the two of us appreciate this so much," she gushed, clutching the hardback of Martin's first novel to her chest. "I'm Brittany. I just love your novel."

Martin smiled again. He pulled out a black Zebra pen and clicked it open.

"Good to meet you, Brittany. So glad to sign this for you," Martin said, reaching to take the book from her.

"You look so much younger than your photo inside the book jacket! You've got a true Branson look going on with that goatee. We simply must take a selfie!" she insisted, raising her phone. Before Martin could reply Brittany had leaned in toward him and snapped several shots of her face pressed extremely close to his. As Brittany moved further into the crowded seat, she dropped the book to the floor.

The novel hit Martin's shoe, landing beneath the seat in front of him. The young woman immediately leaned down to retrieve the it.

"I'm so sorry, Mr. Culver," Brittany said, her voice muffled, her head nearly buried. "I'm so clumsy. I've almost got it."

"Excuse me, Miss?" the female flight attendant interrupted, tapping Brittany on her upturned hip. "Have we misplaced something?"

"Only my sense of dignity, I'm afraid," Brittany replied, laughing nervously as she stuffed the recovered novel into Martin's hands. The hair framing her flushed face strayed aloft from static. "This isn't how it appears…"

"No one made *any* assumptions, my dear," the flight attendant re-assured her, sending a knowing wink Martin's way. "It is, however, high time we all returned to our seats. We will be departing soon."

Nodding with finality, the flight attendant moved quickly down the aisle, slamming overhead bins shut as she moved.

"Please, quickly, sign it to Brittany and Madelyn, BFF's forever!" Brittany blurted out. "Brittany with two T's, Madelyn with a Y. Hurry, before the attendant returns."

Brittany watched every move of Martin's pen as he scrawled the inscription, cradling the book in his still-bandaged left hand.

"Whatever happened to your hand?" the girl inquired. "That's quite a large bandage."

"Work accident," Martin replied as he finished signing. "There you go, Brittany."

Brittany took a quick glance at what Martin had written.

"To Brittany and Madelyn, BFF's Forever, May you always find the treasure you seek. Martin Culver".

"Oh, thank you, Mr. Culver, this means so much! We had *so hoped* to meet someone famous on our holiday."

"Thank you Brittany. It's always good to meet a fan of my novels, so this means a lot to me also."

" 'Bye then," the young woman chirped, standing up and then leaning back over to hug him. Martin felt her plant a kiss on his cheek before she took off down the aisle, holding the book in both her hands to show her friend.

"This means *so much*, Mr. Culver!" the female flight attendant mocked as she stepped into the space vacated by Brittany. She handed Martin a cold can of unopened ginger ale, wrapped in a cloth napkin. She immediately took the napkin back and dabbed at his cheek, folding the napkin over the bright lipstick smudge she removed from his cheek. She handed the napkin back to him.

"A souvenir from one of your fans," she said, smiling. "More discrete this way, I think you will agree."

"I agree," Martin answered, wiping his cheek a second time. He checked his face for any remaining lipstick before returning the cloth.

"That was more than a little embarrassing," he admitted.

"We see things like it all the time, especially on the flight to London," she said. "Famous people meet impressionable youth. Everyone wants someone to look up to."

"Thanks for your help," Martin said. "I'm Martin Culver. "

"I heard," the flight attendant replied. "I'm Lynette."

"I notice your accent, Lynette. Are you Spanish?"

"I was once," she replied. "Now I live in the sky. I only return to Spain for short visits. Do you know Spain?"

"Regrettably, only through the travels of a few friends," Martin said.

"I could show you a side of Madrid few people know," she replied, her eyebrows hinting at her meaning.

Before Martin could reply, a grating electronic tone sounded over the intercom. Lynette spun immediately away, moving quickly to the front of the first class section just as the flight safety video started.

The attendant looked directly at Martin through the entire video. He noticed and then realized why she was looking his way. When the video played directions about leaning forward into crash position, she winked at him again, certainly referencing Brittany's fumbling attempts to retrieve the errant novel. Lynette completed the safety presentation, smiled, then disappeared down the aisle.

Standing to one side in the plane's tiny galley, Lynette cupped her phone in both hands, talking in hushed tones.

"Yes, he is on the plane. No. He is traveling alone."

"Good work," the thick voice on the other end of the line replied. "Keep your eye on him and call me if anything changes. You know our plan."

"Okay, amor, love you too!" Lynette said a bit too loudly as another flight attendant walked by. "Gotta run, we're taking off now!"

Chapter 27

"What time is it?" Martin thought as he opened his eyes.

Martin checked his watch, amazed at how long he had slept. The flight was only three hours from London. Had he slept through the entire overnight flight, including their layover in Iceland? He felt confused and a bit groggy. Martin did not remember requesting a pillow or a blanket.

Rubbing his eyes, Martin viewed a silhouette that he recognized approaching in the darkened cabin. Pushing aside the light blanket, Martin removed the equalizing earplugs, attaching his wireless hearing devices to the electrodes behind each ear. Adjusting the volume, he waited for Lynette to speak first, in order to judge the incoming volume, to prevent shouting.

"Mr. Culver," Lynette whispered, leaning in close to him. "Do you need anything?"

"I seem to have misplaced my carry-on bag," Martin inquired warily. "Have you seen it by chance?"

"It was on the seat beside you when I brought your blanket," Lynette said. "You were out like a light. Regulations require that it all bags be stowed. Your carry-on is in the first class luggage compartment forward of the galley."

"I'll have it back now, thanks," Martin said tersely.

"Right away, Mr. Culver," she said, bringing her palms together in the ubiquitous, prayer-like gesture that always rankled Martin, no matter where he saw it. He seemed to see everywhere he went. Sandra referred to it once as the Namaste greeting. As Lynette backed away, she did something with her hands that irritated him even further. She unfolded her hands as if opening a book, leaving the palms extended and facing up, then turned and walked away. He had seen that hand motion before, but from only one person, a person no longer alive.

Señor Medina, the former antiquities smuggler that Martin had met in Mexico used that same gesture multiple times in the short time Martin had known him, usually whenever Martin took the upper hand in a heated discussion. Martin knew the gesture to be a

Muslim prayer motion. To see it again, here and now, did not make for pleasant memories.

Martin lifted the blanket to his nose. It had a faint mint-like odor, not unpleasant and very relaxing.

Lynette returned with Martin's bag, placing it on the seat beside him. Martin waited until she moved away, then did a quick inspection, checking the zips and pockets to confirm everything was in its place. He did not find anything amiss and took a deep breath. The prayer gesture still bothered him.

Heathrow Airport was at once smaller and busier than Martin had anticipated. The landing was uneventful, leaving him anxious to deplane, gather his bags and get to the hotel. Once Martin had retrieved his bags, he hurried to the car hire stands.

"Quite a queue, what?" a familiar voice inquired.

Martin turned to find Madelyn and Brittany standing behind him, both equally bleary-eyed but smiling ear to ear.

"We tried to make the lift with you up from baggage claim, but it was too full, "Madelyn pouted.

"Are you waiting for a taxi, too?" Martin asked. "I thought you lived here in London."

"We haven't a *car*," Brittany said, rolling her eyes and laughing. "We're just poor students at *University*, remember?"

Madelyn smiled. "How *did you* manage to clear international customs so quickly?"

Martin had been thinking the same thing. The officer had simply scanned his passport, raised an eyebrow, then waved him through.

"Just lucky, I suppose. No family coming to pick you up?"

"No, ours are all working at this time of day."

"Or still asleep. Besides, our families don't live in London proper."

"So where are you headed?"

"The UCL. We already have dorm space assigned, and then tomorrow we register for classes."

"I am headed to a hotel near the UCL, as you call it," Martin said. "The Ambassador, I think it's called? It's in Bloomsbury."

"The Ambassadors? You're staying there?" Madelyn asked, looking at Brittany in open-mouthed surprise. "I hope you booked in advance. Hotels in the Bloomsbury district go very full this time of year."

"I also hope you brought a full wallet, that place costs!" Brittany said. "Must be there's more money in books than I fancied."

"Would you care to share a car, then?" Madelyn asked. "We're practically going the same place."

"Sure," Martin agreed. "We can do that. I think this next car is ours."

"Where to?" the cabbie called through the open window.

"His hotel is the Ambassadors in Bloomsbury," Brittany stated. "After that, the UCL at Gower."

Gathering their luggage in a line, Martin waited while the driver piled their bags into what seemed to be a bottomless trunk.

"Everything in the boot, so we're off then." the cabbie said.

Martin held the door for the young women. Madelyn entered first, while Brittany insisted on waiting until after Martin. She slid in and closed the door, sandwiching Martin in the middle. There was not a centimeter to spare.

"His hotel, huh?" the driver muttered as he pulled out into traffic. He leered in the rearview mirror at the three of them. "Where are you two duckies sleeping then, the bloody street? That would be a shame."

"Mind your manners, chum," Brittany said in a low voice, leaning close to the cabbie's head. "I'll have your license yanked."

The driver scowled but said little.

"My father's the police commissioner," she smiled.

Before many minutes had passed the small taxi wheeled to a stop in front of the Ambassadors Hotel. The driver jumped out at the curb and opened the door behind him. Brittany stepped out of the car first. While the driver unloaded Martin's bags, Madelyn opened her own door into traffic and scurried behind the cab to where Martin stood.

Martin pulled out his wallet to pay the driver.

"Dollars okay?" Martin inquired. "I haven't been to an exchange yet."

"Better than nothing," the driver growled. "Is the USA still afloat?"

Martin smiled and nodded, counting out the bills. "Will this be enough to cover the girls to UCL?"

"More than enough, guv'nor. It's only just 'round the corner."

"See to it that they get there safely," Martin insisted as he handed the driver the cash. "Keep the rest."

"C'mon duckies, let's roll!" the driver said impatiently.

Both girls both hugged Martin at once, then jumped back into the taxi. They waved, Brittany lowering the window and shouting "G'bye!" as the taxi pulled away from the curb.

Martin immediately sensed someone watching him. He turned quickly to see Chartwell and Sandra descending the steps of the hotel with Rebekah.

"Uncle Martin, you're here!" Rebekah shouted, running toward him. "I've missed you so!"

Martin tried to wave to Sandra before Rebekah practically tackled him. Sandra seemed frozen, staring, her mouth slightly agape.

"How in the world…?" Sandra blurted out.

Chartwell reached the bottom of the short staircase, turning to find Sandra stopped midway, still not believing what she had just witnessed.

"Sandra, look who's here," Chartwell said in a cheery voice. "So, how was the flight, old man? No ear trouble I hope."

"I'm so glad you came, Uncle Martin!" Rebekah said, still hugging him.

Sandra found her voice after the rest.

"Martin Culver, you have some nerve," she said. "How did you find us? Don't tell me that CIA witch tracked us down for you."

Chapter 28

Watching Sandra turn on one heel and march back into their London hotel, Martin set his jaw and followed, taking the steps two at a time. One doorman pulled the door open for Sandra while the other gathered Martin's luggage. They obviously knew her.

"Sandra, it's not what you think. Let me explain," Martin pleaded. "There's something important I came to tell you."

"Let's all go inside," Chartwell said, "No need in creating a scene on the street. We can talk while Martin is getting settled."

Rebekah held onto Martin's right arm as they walked inside the hotel. The front desk was at the far end of the long lobby, past a steep, open staircase.

Sandra stood by a sleek, modern couch, the only furniture in the bare, stylish hotel lobby. Martin reached to hug Sandra, only to find her turning away.

"Sandra, we really need to talk."

"Check in first," she said, pointing.

He walked to the front desk.

"Good morning, I'm Martin Culver. I have a reservation."

"Good morning, Mr. Culver. Your room is not quite ready yet. May we offer you tea in our restaurant while you wait?"

"No, that won't be necessary," Martin replied. He turned to find Sandra standing beside him.

"You had time to make a *reservation*, but not to call me?"

Martin waited for her to finish.

"Then you have the nerve show up here in a cabful of cute girls, without the courtesy to call and let me know?" she continued. "What about the doctor? Two days ago you were at the doctor's office."

"I thought you would be happier," Martin stated. "I made it to Dulles last night for the overnight flight. I wanted to surprise you."

"Well, I am surprised. Surprised that you are here. How were you cleared to travel?"

"I am feeling much better, just since you left."

Sandra's eyes narrowed.

"How did you know where we were staying?"

"That would be me," Chartwell offered, holding up the morning Times-Herald as a shield. "Guilty as charged."

"Ooh, you two drive me crazy!" Sandra exclaimed. "Well here is how it is going to be. I am staying with Rebekah, Martin, so don't expect me to stay with you in whatever suite you have reserved."

Sandra stormed off, heels clicking across the polished lobby floor.

"Come on Rebekah," she called.

"Martin, I'm glad you are here, old chum," Chartwell said. "Glad to see you're on the mend. Had us worried for a bit. You and I have a lot of catching up to do. Fancy a drink?"

"This early in the day? Think I'll pass. Is there a decent cup of coffee around?"

"I seriously doubt it."

They watched until Sandra and Rebekah entered the lift.

"Let's walk down to the café," Chartwell suggested. "I'll buy you that coffee."

They were seated without waiting at a table near the center of the café. Chartwell signaled the barkeep and ordered their drinks.

"Just coffee for my friend, and Twining's for me, if you please."

"Chartwell, before we get on to anything else, I have bad news," Martin said.

"Yeah, what?" Chartwell asked.

"Mary Power," Martin said simply.

"Did something happen?" Chartwell inquired.

"Mary Power was killed in the IAF parking lot yesterday afternoon. The vehicle she was using exploded. She was inside."

Chartwell did not speak. He hunched his shoulders forward, shoving his hands deep into the pockets of his coat.

"The bomb was meant for Sandra, we think. It was her car."

Chartwell leaned back in the chair, visibly shaken.

"So unlike me," Chartwell said.

"To get involved?" Martin asked.

"To have no response," Chartwell replied. "I am, for once, speechless. I hope she didn't suffer."

"She was gone instantly, according to the authorities. Had you known her long?" Martin asked.

"Long enough," Chartwell replied. "Fun girl."

Martin did not respond. He saw Sandra standing in the café doorway. She walked slowly to their table, then perched on the very edge of the seat next to Martin.

"I just talked to Cita. She told me what happened."

"I was trying to tell you," Martin said. "Did Cita call you?"

"I called her," Sandra replied. "I was checking to see if I had any messages. She was surprised to find that you were here."

Martin placed his hand over Sandra's. He felt her shaking when he squeezed her hand slightly.

"Director Hall suspects foul play targeted at you and I. She told me that to call you would endanger your life. So I came to London instead, to find you, to tell you."

Sandra looked at his hand covering hers.

"That must have cost a bundle," she said. "John, I am sorry about this, for your sake. I did not like Mary Power, but I would not wish this on anyone."

Sandra pulled back her hand, fiddling with her wedding band nervously.

"It was me they were trying to kill, wasn't it?" Sandra asked. "I'm going back upstairs."

"All right," Martin said.

"What is your room number?" Sandra asked Martin.

"Two twelve," Martin replied. "It should be ready soon."

"It will be our room now," she responded quietly. "I will have my things moved to your room when it is ready,"

Sandra slid out of the booth and stood up.

"Martin Culver, I have always said that trouble follows you wherever you go. I just hope that does not include London."

Chapter 29

Salisbury Plain
Amesbury, Wiltshire

"John, I'm sure glad you're driving," Martin commented from the back seat of the rented minivan. "This wrong side of the road takes some getting used to."

"No worries, old man, we'll be there soon enough. I must object to the wrong side aspect, though," Chartwell laughed. "We were first, Mother Britain and all that, so it's you Yanks that decided to go the contrary way. "

"Oh, here we go," Sandra said smiling, turning around to look at Rebekah. "The old rivalry surfaces."

Rebekah responded straight away.

"He's definitely right, you know. Left hand drive has been a part of Britain since sword carrying days. "

"Really? Why is that?"

"Right handed swordsmen, the majority, could more easily engage an enemy from horseback with this lane arrangement. "

"So John," Sandra interjected, changing the subject. "Tell us something about Stonehenge that we may not know."

"Why don't you ask Rebekah?" Chartwell replied, smiling. "Stonehenge is *her* favorite topic, not mine. She's your expert. I'm just the driver today."

"Among the hundreds of megalithic monuments in the British Isles, Stonehenge is neither the largest nor the most impressive, but it is the most studied, the most visited. Yet, it is the least understood," Rebekah stated.

"You can see it ahead on the horizon," Chartwell pointed out.

Martin leaned forward from the rear seat to look ahead. The windscreen was covered in raindrops, but even so he could make out the massive stone lintels, then the upright columns as they drew closer.

"Stonehenge sits in the middle of the expansive Salisbury Plain, a wide green area with little in the vicinity to impede the view," Chartwell added.

"Right out in the open. What are those trees over to the right?" Martin asked.

182

"To the northeast there are a few estates," Chartwell responded. "Mostly large landholders with stables and such, a few smaller residences. A good distance separates them from Stonehenge proper. Always makes me wonder, what there might be of historical value on those properties. Professor Haddad lives out this way, in the neighboring parish if I remember correctly. We'll drop by there after."

"Unannounced, John?" Sandra asked. "Is that proper?"

"It'll have to be. I have his address but no phone details."

"Who built Stonehenge, John?" Sandra asked.

"So many opinions," Chartwell responded as he turned toward the modern visitor's exhibition centre. "Too many really. Everything from Merlin building it by magic to Irish giants. The only real evidence, and that is limited to burials, are a group called the Beaker people."

"Why the name?"

"The people were buried with ceramic jars resembling beakers from a science lab, narrow necks with wide bases. Evidence shows the jars contained the ingredients for embalming compounds."

"Who do you think built Stonehenge, Rebekah?" Martin asked.

"I know it's fallen out of favor, but I have always believed the Druids were involved with building Stonehenge," she replied.

"Tree-huggers?" Martin asked. "Hardly seems like they would put in the work necessary."

"Old thinking my friend," Chartwell interjected. "The Druids were much more than nature worshippers. Outstanding astronomers, mathematicians, engineers. There is evidence they came from Babylon. They knew how to work stone, how to follow the stars. "Philosophers, mystics, priests," Sir Norman Lockyer wrote of the founders of Stonehenge, in his 1906 treatise. They were of the same class of people as the Wise Men, the ones who followed the star of Bethlehem to find Jesus. It is known that they came to England from across the continents, from the Blue Sea to the south."

"I agree with Mr. Chartwell," Rebekah said. "The Druids established Stonehenge as an astronomical observatory. The great stones once supported a framework of timbers that left the roof open in the center. This is the way modern observatories work, darken most of the sky, then remain open to the area you choose to study."

"The way a camera shutter works?" Sandra asked.

"If you had a camera set for long term exposure, then yes, you are exactly right," Rebekah affirmed. "The lens stays open while the sky rotates overhead, making observation consistent."

"Geoffrey of Monmouth recorded in his *'Choreo Gigantum'*, or Dance of the Giants, written in 1136 AD, that Stonehenge was built during the days of Uther Pendragon, the father of King Arthur," Chartwell said. "The *legendary* King Arthur," Chartwell added, correcting himself. "The stuff of legends always has a basis in truth, but is not always what it seems. And it was Lockyer who also reported mysterious forces emanating from the ground at Stonehenge."

As they drove closer to the visitor centre grounds, Sandra voiced a question.

"Have there ever been any great treasures found here at Stonehenge?"

"If by treasure you mean gold, the answer is yes," Chartwell replied. "Many gold artifacts have been found here, smaller, inscribed gold jewelry. There were, at one time, thousands of them, more than have been recorded. Today they have only have 250 gold items on display at the Stonehenge exhibition centre. Ceramics too, as well as Beaker-era skeletons. One skeleton has been dated by the items found around it at 5,500 years old."

Martin simply replied. "3,500 B.C. "

"It is my opinion that Stonehenge, in addition to being well-studied, has also been plundered every time the land changed hands, Druids, Saxons, Vikings, Romans, - dozens of times over the centuries since it was built. A Mr. Colt Hoare was one of the most notorious plunderers of the site, a pre-1900's "antiquarian", as they called him. Took more things from Stonehenge than exist in museums today."

"I guess that's always the million dollar question, isn't it?" Martin commented as they exited the rental caravan. "Where have the missing artifacts gone?"

When they got out of the van, Martin looked across the fields to see Stonehenge standing out starkly, like a sentinel, against the darker clouds.

"How old is Stonehenge really? Does anyone know?"

"We rely on the carbon dating that has been done with the artifacts found on the grounds. Most opinion believes that Stonehenge was constructed in stages starting around 3,000 B.C."

"So why would the Druids, or anyone else for that matter, go to the trouble to build on this particular spot?"

"Rebekah?"

After clearing her throat, Rebekah began in a small voice that seemed to grow in volume as she spoke. Her enthusiasm was obvious, as was her effort to contain herself.

"If you remember my theory of the megalithic monuments, nearly all, on every continent, are astronomically aligned," she began. "For Stonehenge, the question is, why build here? I further think the question is, why were they built anywhere? The truth is, most of these megaliths worldwide were built as centers of observation and reverence in locations where meteors landed."

Her voice fading near the end, Rebekah punched her glasses back up on her nose and waited for someone to comment.

"Meteors," Chartwell laughed. "It's always meteors."

"There are meteors at Stonehenge?" Martin asked.

"There apparently are meteors beneath every stone circle and barrow in Britain, it would appear. Some of the barrows, the low rock-pile hills, are man-made. It's as if there was an attempt to cover up the meteor stones. In other places the meteors dug in below the surface of the earth, pushing up the soil like a cosmic plow."

"Wow," Sandra said simply.

Martin thought a long time before he spoke.

"Rebekah, do you have proof of your theory?" he asked.

"I am here to hopefully prove some of this," Rebekah replied confidently. "I plan to focus my study efforts in this area."

"What gave you the idea?" Martin asked.

"When we were in Mexico, when the meteors fell, I looked around. I took into account that by knowing where meteors fall, we can plan for the future. This fact is recent knowledge for science, but must have been known by the ancients. From these spots, not always conveniently located, they looked at the skies intently, spending much blood and treasure to build the great observatories.

They knew the meteors had fallen before. By studious observation, they could plan ahead to be ready for when the meteors returned."

"Are you saying that every megalithic observatory has a meteor at the center?" Martin asked.

"Yes. Interesting example," Rebekah confirmed. "Did you know that in Mecca, every year at the annual *hajj*, tens of thousands of Muslim men crowd into the pilgrimage site annually to walk in circles around the Kaaba, which contains a meteorite?"

"I saw a photo of the Hoba meteorite," Sandra added ."It's one of the largest on earth. It sits in the center of an amphitheater. It has marks that look like pieces were scraped off."

Martin stood at the car, his hands in his coat pockets, looking at Sandra, then Chartwell.

"Can anyone tell me why we are letting Rebekah leave the IAF to work for Professor Haddad?" Martin asked. "We need a mind like this on our team at IAF."

"I've always thought so," Sandra agreed. "She has always had my vote, but she also has her own mind. Who am I to change that?"

Rebekah hugged Sandra as they walked toward the visitor centre.

"By being here, I can learn," Rebekah said. "By working with the Professor, I can confirm my theories as well as his."

Martin looked at Chartwell, who shrugged his shoulders, lifting his hands palms up.

"Don't look at me," he said joking. "I've always considered her a great catch. For the IAF, I mean."

"John, you always have an ulterior motive when it comes to women."

Rebekah gathered the neckline of her raincoat and looked across the plain toward Stonehenge.

"He doesn't bother me," she said, smiling. "Let's go!"

After paying their entry fee, the foursome wasted no time with the museum, since the rain had stopped. A chill breeze welcomed them onto the paved walkway leading toward the great stone uprights of Stonehenge. Too irregular to be called columns, and too large to be called anything else.

"These stones mark a crossroads of history, Martin."

"I was just thinking about that," Martin responded as they approached the site. He pulled his coat collar up against the wind.

"Chilly?" Chartwell asked. "Fall will become winter before we can blink."

"Stuck on a more temperate climate," Martin replied. "Ladies is it too chilly out here for you?"

"Not for me!" Rebekah replied.

"I can take it for a little while," Sandra answered, shrugging her shoulders and pointing at Rebekah, who eagerly led the way.

"So you say the Saxons, the Druids, the Vikings, the Romans, all possessed this land at one time or another?" Martin asked.

"Also the French, if you believe them. Appearances are that Muslims also controlled it briefly. That's an intense level activity for one archaeological site," Chartwell answered. "It's not clear why."

As the four of them approached the stone sentinels of Stonehenge, Rebekah exuberantly ran from the designated path onto the wet, green grass.

"I have wanted to see this since I was a child," she announced, her voice returning in echoes from among the great stones. "Sandra take my picture won't you?"

Sandra and Rebekah snapped pics together, while Martin and Chartwell stopped at every explanatory posting, reading every word.

"Here Sandra, take some on my phone as well."

"Wait up," Martin called. "You're getting ahead."

"No Uncle Martin, you're falling behind!" Rebekah laughed.

"I am here for the experience of it, not the words. Words I can read in a brochure," Sandra stated. "Plus look. We have the whole place to ourselves."

The closer they walked, the more massive the stones appeared. As Martin drew close, he noticed that some of the stones had short swords carved into the blocks.

"What is this?" he asked Chartwell.

"Apparently someone thought of swords when they came to Stonehenge," Chartwell replied. "It's difficult to know. As we discussed, the primary human remains that have been found here are from the Beaker people."

"I remember you saying that earlier."

"The beaker shaped crockery found with their burial …," Chartwell said, his words coming more slowly as he seemed lost in thought. "…contained traces of…"

"Are you ok, Chartwell?" Martin asked.

"Just thinking, reviewing," he said. "I recently read a translation of an ancient story about Stonehenge. I just realized that you and I were discussing two pieces of evidence in favor of that story being true."

"What are you talking about?" Martin asked

"The beakers contained evidence of embalming spices. The Stonehenge columns have swords carved into them. It may add up."

"Let's get more photos!" Rebekah said. "We have to have proof that we were here! My friends in the U.S. are going to be *so jealous.*"

"Let's hurry, I think it is getting ready to pour," Sandra said.

After taking pictures will all of them together, Martin stood back to take it all in.

"I wish there were a vantage point to look down on all this," Martin said. "I would like to see it from above."

"Good point," Chartwell noted.

"So walk me through this, John. What are we looking at here?"

"We are standing near the South Barrow, a raised feature southmost in the outer henge. Directly to the North and through the great stones is the North Barrow, another man-made, raised feature."

"I'm with you so far."

"The outer ring of stones are the bluestones, the inner horseshoe shape are the sarsen stones. All of the bluestones were capped at one time. The sarsen stones within represented five doorways, three of which are still capped. Center of the sarsen stone horseshoe is the Altar Stone, the one thought to be a meteor, which runs quite deep into the ground. The next stones to our right, at the outer bank are called the Slaughter Stones. Following that, to the Northeast, are the three Heel Stones, each one getting progressively taller as they move away from the center."

"Interesting," Martin commented. "And interesting names."

"Can you hear the echo as we speak?" Chartwell asked.

"I notice a very unusual echo," Martin replied. "I thought it was my ears."

"No, that's natural to the formation," Chartwell confirmed.

As they looked around for the others, Rebekah and Sandra were see dashing for the rental van.

"Come on," Sandra called. "You're both about to get soaked!"

Martin looked to his left and saw a great white wall of rain proceeding directly toward them. The sound of it was like a muted waterfall, but the sound grew in intensity as he and Chartwell picked up their pace and made it to the van.

"Get in, get in," Rebekah called as she slid open the passenger door.

No sooner had the men boarded the vehicle til the bottom completely dropped out of the sky. The wall of rain hit the small van, shaking it, bringing visibility to zero.

"Well, I'm happy," Rebekah announced. "I've been to Stonehenge. Now I plan to see it all the time. I will get to study it and everything! Simply smashing!"

Martin glanced at Sandra.

"I had a good time too," she ventured. "Although I think Rebekah enjoyed it more."

Chartwell started the van and set the heater to high.

"I will drive as soon as it's clear," he said. "These roads and this entire plain is so flat, it tends to flood in a downpour like this. We'll wait a moment to leave."

"I'm very impressed with what we saw today," Martin said. "We should take in the museum another time."

"I'm starting to get hungry," Sandra replied. "Didn't you say we still had to stop at the Professor's home?"

"Yes, we can ride by there. We won't actually visit but we can see where it is located."

Chartwell looked up to see the sky clearing. The heaviest rain had passed. He began backing out of the parking space.

"We're just around the corner," he stated. "I think that's his house on the other side of that wide field."

Martin peered through the raindrops across the field.
"I can barely make it out," he said. "I do see houses there."
"I'll show you," Chartwell said, turning on the signal flasher.

Chapter 30

Kentworth Manor
Amesbury, Wiltshire

"Don't you think we should have called before barging in on the Professor at his home?" Rebekah asked.

"All I know is that if Chartwell is going to drive like a maniac, I should have visited the restroom before we left the Stonehenge visitors center," Sandra said. "I just hope the Professor's home."

Chartwell pulled into the driveway and shut the engine down. He reminded himself why he was here. The Professor's potential hiring of Rebekah and his questionable past history were simply lead-off topics.

"There is no one home, but the front door is open," Chartwell said.

He got out of the van, looked inside the open front door, then wandered around to the side of the house. No other cars were present, and no one working in the gardens. Noticing the GPR tractor parked around the side, Chartwell walked closer to check out the machine.

As he approached, Chartwell noticed something stuck in the grill of the tractor. Reaching down, he plucked a student ID from the grill. Brooke Burnside, UCL, the ID read. He wrapped the lanyard around the ID and placed it in his pocket.

"Let's go," Sandra called. "I really have to go."

"No one's home, you could come round the hedge on this side," Chartwell laughed.

Martin smiled too, but then corrected himself. "That won't do, Chartwell. Unless there is a better alternative, let's just leave."

"Run inside and go," Chartwell said. "I will watch the door. Then we'll run back to town."

Sandra scooted past Chartwell, needing no second invitation. In a definite hurry, she had to check three doors before finding the bathroom, tucked under a stairwell. Before long, she had reappeared.

"That house gave me the jitters," Sandra said as she rushed back to the van. "It smells odd, like a hospital. Pictures of tombs and mummies everywhere. I don't like his decorator."

191

"He's his own decorator, I'll wager," Chartwell said. "Where were the pictures?"

"Some were on the wall in the bathroom, but most were on a table inside the library door."

"I'll be right back," Chartwell said, disappearing inside the house.

"We should wait…" Martin said, throwing up his hands. "He's bold, I'll give him that," he said to Sandra.

Before long, Chartwell came back to the van, a worried look on his face.

"Everything okay in there?" Martin asked.

"Just poking around a bit. Doesn't hurt to check out Rebekah's future host," he said.

"Chartwell, I have an idea how about we return to town. You can take us to your favorite London pub?"

"They're all his favorite," Sandra said, laughing. "Pick one with food, John. By the time we get to London I will be hungry."

"Then can we go shopping?" Rebekah asked. "I've promised Sandra to take her some cool places."

"I don't see why not. Martin, do you want to drive? Give you a chance to drive on the right side of the road for once," Chartwell smiled, holding up the keys.

Settling down to a second pint of Guinness after dinner, Martin took in the heavy, dark atmosphere of the pub.

The waitress came back by their table to check on them. Leaning overly far, Charlene was friendly, plucking empty glasses and dishes from their table as she talked. Chartwell's eyes never strayed from her.

"So you went to Stonehenge today, did you? In the rain? Cool place, my parents met there. But it's haunted or something, did you know?"

"There's no such thing as haunting," Rebekah said in her matter-of-fact manner.

"Oh, I am pretty sure," Charlene assured her. "Strange things happen there. A friend of mine from school disappeared out there less than a month ago. She was working on a research project out of UCL and the British Museum."

"What type of work was she doing?" Chartwell asked.

Charlene swung round to directly face Chartwell. "John Robert Chartwell, at your service," he said, extending his hand.

"A fellow Brit, that's great," she said, shaking his hand vigorously. "Brookie was working on a GPS crew, I think she said..., Ground Penetrating...oh, I don't remember. She and Pete from the college used to come in here after working out there all day."

"GPR, maybe?" Rebekah offered. "Ground Penetrating *Radar*?"

"Yes, that's it, that's what I meant to say. Come to think of it, I haven't seen Brooke or Pete either. I wonder if they ran off to France or something? Except Brooke was engaged. Oh well, for Mr. Right, being engaged wouldn't stop me! Pete had money!"

"You said Brooke, with an 'e', correct?" Chartwell asked, struggling to bring his eyes up to hers.

"Yes that's it," Charlene replied. "Brooke Burnside. Me and Brookie were set to rent a flat together, 'til she got engaged. Kind of weird how she disappeared, though."

"Very strange indeed," Chartwell commented. He slipped the ID lanyard he had found out of his shirt pocket and into Martin's hand.

"Got to run, folks, I'll be around to check on you," Charlene said, hefting the heavy bus tray carelessly enough to make everyone at table cringe, fearing a colossal spill.

"That was interesting," Rebekah said. "What a bubblehead."

"Rebekah," Sandra reminded. "Not so loud."

Chartwell smirked.

"Rebekah, ask John what color her eyes were?" Sandra said, smiling. "I'll bet he doesn't know."

"Of course I do," Chartwell countered. "They were a hazel green."

"Lucky guess," Sandra said, throwing her napkin at him.

"John, where did you get this UCL ID?" Martin asked.

"Stuck in the front of the tractor sitting in the Professor's side yard," he replied. "It was like someone stuck it in the grill to keep from losing it."

"Or to make sure someone saw it," Martin said. He kept his voice low. "We should put this back."

Chartwell pulled Martin aside.

193

"Not tonight, Martin. When we take Rebekah to the Museum to meet him, I will buttonhole him about the ID."

"What do you think it means, that this was found in his garden?" Martin asked. "Other than shoddy investigative work?"

"Between you and me, it means that he knows something about what happened to Brooke Burnside of the UCL, something that he isn't telling."

Chapter 31

The British Museum
London, England

Rising high above the street side courtyard along Great Russel Street, occupying an entire city block on the ground level alone, the British Museum stood awe-inspiring and formidable to visitors from around the world. With over eight million items in its catalog, the British Museum truly offered a world of history under one roof.

To some visitors, though, the British Museum was more intimidating than impressive. The real issue was not the Museum itself, but what it represented. The stealing of ancient treasures from other lands revealed a phase of colonialism and conquest now far out of favor.

Behind the impressive Greek Revival styling, beyond the storied reputation and unmatched treasures found inside, the outward appearance belied the dark and ominous secrets contained within its walls. Like so many disappointments in life, the secrets of discovery, of hidden history, and of infamy were unmatched in the modern world.

Below the museum's colonnaded facade, Martin Culver stood back to admire the frieze relief.

"The frieze is called 'The Progress of Civilization'," Chartwell said. Sandra watched nervously as Martin nearly stepped backward into the motorway as he positioned to take a photo. He did not hear the cars.

"Have a look, old man!" Chartwell called to him from the museum steps. "You'll be mincemeat if you're not more alert!"

Martin snapped a quick photo with his phone, then walked to where Chartwell stood with Sandra and Rebekah on the museum steps. He stopped nose to nose with Chartwell and looked him right in the eye.

"Call me old man again!" Martin challenged, then laughed.

"Hurry up, Uncle Martin," Rebekah urged, taking Martin's arm as he approached. "We don't want to be late!"

"Some of us don't want to be here at all," Chartwell commented, turning his collar up against the morning fog. He looked away to avoid Sandra's wilting stare.

A garish printed poster greeted them inside the grand entrance lobby of the Museum, announcing Professor Haddad's lecture.

"Look, "The History of the Sword at Stone Henge". That's Professor Haddad's lecture title. This is why we're here," Rebekah said. "I'm so excited!"

Her enthusiasm reverberated through the hallowed halls of world history looming above them.

"Come on," Rebekah called, using a quieter tone. "The lecture hall is this way."

A velvet rope closing off the corridor was removed by a museum attendant. The three of them followed Rebekah in the direction that the flow of visitors now moved.

Sandra smiled at Martin. "Do you notice the difference in Rebekah?" she asked.

"She's more grown up. She truly seems to have come to life," Martin responded. "So much more alive than I remembered."

"She seems to have found her motivation," Chartwell commented in a snide tone, "while I seem to have misplaced mine completely." He stopped walking at the theatre doorway.

"What are you doing?" Sandra asked.

"I'm not going in," Chartwell said without explanation.

"Go on in, Martin," Sandra instructed. "Find Rebekah and save us some seats."

"I see her," said Martin. "She's all the way at the front."

Sandra nodded and lifted her hand in a slight wave before turning to Chartwell with a scowl. She practically pushed him around the corner.

"What is with you?" Sandra snapped at Chartwell. "The only thing more dreary than you today is this crummy weather."

"I'm just not motivated to hear this pompous windbag spin his tales," Chartwell stated. "He's just a quack trying to sell some books."

Sandra took him by the arm.

"What is it John? What is bothering you? You said you know Haddad. Do you have something more against Professor Haddad that we all need to know?"

"I do, but it can wait," Chartwell replied. "Go on in to the lecture. I'm going to look around the exhibits. I will catch up with you all afterwards, when we meet with the Professor."

Sandra could not hide her displeasure, nor did she try.

"John, I know this isn't your idea of having fun, but I need for you to be more mature. Do you hear me?"

"More mature about what?"

"Everything. About Rebekah. About Martin. Stop provoking him, for God's sake. I invited you to London to help me."

"You did? Because I am feeling very much like the fourth wheel on a two-wheeled bicycle."

"John, you agreed to come along. You knew what to expect."

"It's okay, I understand. I'll meet you after the lecture," he replied, turning to walk away.

"John, please," Sandra begged, practically stamping her foot.

"We'll be closing the doors, madam," the museum attendant urged. "The lecture is about to begin."

"The real lecture will begin when this one is over," Sandra muttered under her breath. She turned and stalked into the lecture hall just as the doors were being closed.

The lights in the room dimmed to half power as Sandra took her seat between Martin and Rebekah. She found them down front as Martin had indicated, but only was able to locate them by the light of Martin's raised phone.

"Chartwell isn't attending the lecture?" Martin asked as Sandra settled in.

"No, he won't be joining us. I'm not sure what got into John," she said.

Rebekah leaned across Sandra to quiet them both.

"You're being too loud," she admonished. "Read your program. It's fascinating."

Martin looked at Rebekah and nodded, then at Sandra, lifting one eyebrow.

"The program says that Professor Haddad is one of the leading voices for the repatriation of antiquities to their source countries," Sandra read. "It says he has a big announcement today."

A single spotlight was illuminated, casting a brilliant oval on the finished mahogany planks, as the lecture hall went dark. The stage was expansive, making the lit-up area appear to be a drop in a very large bucket. In short order, a manual wheelchair began to roll slowly out from behind the curtain at stage left.

Approaching a short table with single folder and a glass of water, the Professor rolled to the center of the stage and slowly positioned himself to address the crowd.

The Professor took his lecture position not fully in the spotlight, but in such a way as to illuminate his body and chair from the chin down. Martin assumed that the positioning was to prevent the spotlight from shining directly into the Professor's eyes.

"As we begin today, allow me to thank the Royal Archaeological Society for permitting me the great honor of presenting an outline of my research entitled 'The History of Swords at Stone Henge'. I say outline, because this barely scratches the surface of my work."

"I want to talk to you today about the history of swords at Stone Henge, which in a sense, is the history of weapons trade itself. Most times we do not think of weapons and arms dealing as being involved with archaeology, but I will show you today how closely connected the two topics really are."

"Swords have been found at Stonehenge since man's oldest memory. For reasons we do not fully understand, Stonehenge has attracted people to this area even *before* the Great Stone Temple, as the Druids called it, was ever conceived."

"Of the many swords found at Stonehenge, the greatest quantity of swords found are Saxon swords. Swords of the highest quality found are Viking swords. Daggers of an unknown style and culture have been found to be engraved upon certain of the stone uprights at Stonehenge. All weapons found seem to have retained a magnetic charge and orientation, unusual for the average ancient site. Swords have been found here with deep gashes, indicating battle. Swords have been found so decorated as to be useless in battle. Celts, Druids, Saxons, Vikings, Romans, the list goes on of the types and origins of the swords found here. Swords are found in graves and in streams, rivers, lakes. So many swords have been found in and round Stonehenge to make it appear that this was a place where people came to renounce swordsmanship, or to battle to the death for this land, to have and to hold it for whatever reason."

"Professor S. Nilsson, in his report to the Ethnological Institute of Britain in 1866, reported that at the wondrous monument at Stonehenge the most beautiful swords could be found, with short hilts, of the oldest date, and were consequently those swords which were first introduced amongst the people of the west of Europe, who were certainly not advanced sufficiently to entertain the possibility of their having fabricated these splendid weapons. The question remains, who made these swords?"

"In short, ladies and gentlemen, the earliest swords found at Stonehenge are no doubt swords which had been traded, bought and sold. What was used to pay for such weapons? No doubt, the Phoenician articles of fine jewelry with intricate spiral designs found everywhere around the Stonehenge megalithic circle. Stolen cultural antiquities were traded for the weapons required for war and defense."

"Moving forward centuries in time, today we look at ISIS. The fledgling Islamic State is but one example of the greatest risk to archaeology today, that of groups and causes that seek recognition and power to propel forward their specific agendum or agenda as the case may be. In so doing, they seek to rob the great archaeological treasures of the world and destroy what they cannot carry away. All the while these groups profit on peddling items of history as if they were wicker baskets on market day, to achieve the purposes of war, of weapons and arms purchases, of destruction."

Sandra leaned closer to Martin.

"He's right about ISIS being a major problem," Sandra whispered.

"With the inherent risk of ISIS, and groups like it, to the archaeological history, artifacts and resources throughout the world, we in archaeological circles must waste no time in protecting the world's great archaeological treasures."

"Egypt in particular, my home country, has much to fear from the current world situation, for as the Muslim world has destabilized, as Syria has both declined and been depleted of artifacts, the greatest resources remaining untouched are those of Egypt. Believe me, such treasures have not gone unnoticed."

Martin glanced at Sandy, who nodded in cautious approval.

"As we are all aware," the Professor continued, "the ancient artifacts of Iraq and Afghanistan have long since been destroyed or looted, either by the Taliban leading up to the Iraq conflict, or through outright theft by the Americans and their military contractors who have been brought in since the war began."

"One question we must ask ourselves is whether UNESCO Heritage Sites here in the United Kingdom are any safer than those of the Middle East, for Britain too, may be under attack."

The change in the Professor's tone was marked, an attitude that could scarcely be contained by word or tenor.

"British history is said to be about the sword, the knight, and the castle, or so it would seem. But what if I told you that British history is also the burqa, Damascus steel, and the influence of Allah as well."

"In a weapon as simple as a sword, in a location as simple as Stone Henge, which I spell as two words because there were and are various henges, a henge simply being another name for a holy place. How many of you knew of the history of the Stone Henge as it relates to the sword? How many of you knew about the dagger engravings in the upright stones? How many of you knew of the many hundreds of swords, knives and daggers found on this sacred historical ground, which have been squirreled away in private collections, government treasuries, and even the odd museum?"

"The era of the sword brought Stone Henge to a turning point, ending the history of peace and harmony that the British Isles had been known for. At one time, the British Isles had become a retreat from madness, from sickness, a place to rest, and to be laid to rest."

"With the sword came war. The Vikings came to Stone Henge and violently ended the age of Druids. Other cultures clashed here. The face of Stone Henge changed with the sword. With war came the need raise funds, to finance campaigns to fight more wars. Enemies had to be pushed back. Fund-raising efforts have come to be called campaigns in our day, from the time when the purpose of most fund-raising was to wage war campaigns."

"To discuss the history and impact of the sword at Stonehenge, we must take into account that this very museum where we sit today holds items of questionable provenance, items of great artistic and cultural value have been obtained with raised and donated funds, and at times, with violence. The end result of violence is to perpetuate more violence."

"The history of archaeology is a history of obtaining what is not ours, through means that are other than ethical."

"I submit to you today, that without careful planning, immediate action, and a methodical dismantling of the worldwide networks that provide a black market for the world treasury of artifacts and antiquities, we shall, in our lifetimes, see the complete and total loss of such treasures, in much the same way as an endangered species meets its end, without fanfare or attention, as the public at large tires of hearing the story."

"Undiscovered treasures present perhaps the greatest risk of all. Imagine for a moment the Ark of the Covenant, the Emerald Tablets, the Lydian Horde, the great sword Excalibur. All represent unrecovered opportunities for discovery and learning that will likely change everything we know about the age from whence they originate. But these objects are prime targets for those in the notorious black market."

"In fact, for all we know, some of these treasures have *already* been discovered, have *already* found a home in some baron's estate or millionaire's gallery. For this reason, such treasures may *never* reach the public eye."

"I caution you, members of the Royal Archaeological Society, to not think there is safety when it comes to the immovable, unchangeable sites treasured through the eons, such as Stonehenge, or even the Tower of London, as an example," he cautioned. "Remember what happened within the last year in Syria, at Palmyra. After taking whatever could be moved, presumably to be sold, ISIS attached dynamite to the ancient columns and structures of Palmyra. In an instant, these sites were destroyed."

"In conclusion, it is unreasonable to assume that any one or two, or a few of us hold sway over these lesser elements of our world. All we can do, indeed all we should do, is to guard the existing treasures to the best of our ability, and remove the markets for their exchange, be these markets legitimate-seeming, such as museums and auction houses, or the black market, which is, believe me, more insidious and pervasive than any of us in the field of archaeology dare admit."

"At this juncture I would entertain questions or comments by those in attendance. In this manner, I get to see if you are paying attention, and I get to take a drink of water. Please introduce yourself and speak up so others can hear you."

A murmur of laughter passed through the audience.

Martin popped to his feet.

"Good day. My name is Martin Culver. I've been listening closely. I propose that payment be made to source countries by those who hold ownership of its antiquities as a matter of principle, a cultural lease if you will, as part of a negotiated repatriation agreement to eventually have the items returned to the source country."

"It is my belief that museum patrons who can afford to donate millions to their favorite gallery, resulting in historic objects of antiquity being stolen, looted and delivered to the museum's door in the dead of night, can afford to pay this form of reparation to those original source countries. These countries have suffered an indignity, from a monetary, cultural and legal standpoint. I propose that the United Nations administer these fees in the form of a tax."

"With United Nations help, I further propose a network of neutral zone facilities where antiquities with questionable provenance can be guarded, held, catalogued and secured until such time as their rightful status can be determined and safe repatriation can be accomplished. I propose, if necessary, to confiscate any museums found guilty of repeated offenses, to use those facilities as these secure and safe locations, under U.N. control. I would be pleased to participate on any level that you might find helpful in order to accomplish these goals, either personally or through my foundation. Thank you."

"Thank you, Mr. Culver. Let us give Mr. Culver a round of applause."

"In conclusion, we must take as a personal affront the efforts by ISIS to obtain and traffic in the antiquities of Egypt as much as I do the fact that the British Museum holds, in its galleries and its vaults, more Egyptian treasures than exist in all of Egypt today, with the sole exception of the pyramids themselves. While not given to radical thoughts or actions, I will do everything in my power, as we move forward, to right this wrong, and to restore the balance of Egypt's cultural and historical heritage to its rightful place in the world. Thank you."

The audience seemed stunned as the spotlight dimmed and the Professor left the stage. After an awkward hush, those in attendance began to applaud, albeit reservedly, but politely.

Martin looked at Sandra, leaned back in the cramped theater seat and tapped the folded speech program against his knee.

"So now you have heard him," Sandra said. "And he has heard you."

"He said all the right things," Martin replied.

"I have a feeling he can't be trusted," Sandra stated.

Chapter 32

Following the lecture, Martin, Sandra and Rebekah waited for the crowd to thin out, watching for the Professor to move from the stage down to the floor of the lecture hall.

"There was not a lot of applause for his lecture, did you think?"

"No, not much," Sandra said distractedly. "The audience seemed a bit on the reserved side."

"I found a lot I could agree with," Martin stated. "Haddad's statement that some priceless artifacts may already have fallen into the hands of private collectors, instead of being held by the original countries was disturbing."

"I picked up on that as well," Sandra stated. "The idea of a neutral zone is great. As long as those locations would be adequately policed and guarded."

"Here comes your guy now," Martin noted.

"Mrs. Culver, we meet again," the Professor said as he rolled to where they stood.

"Yes sir, Professor Haddad. So nice to meet you again."

The Professor turned to face Martin.

"Mr. Culver, I presume," he said, with little emotion. "I trust you are well now sir. Well enough to travel is an improvement, is it not?"

Martin looked quizzically at Sandy, who shrugged.

"Forgive me," the Professor stated. "Word travels fast in archaeological circles, the good and the bad. I had attempted to contact you several times. You are an important figure on the archaeological scene, so there is an interest."

"Well, thank you for your concern, Professor Haddad. It is an honor to meet you. Yes, it is good to be able to travel again."

"Is Mr. Chartwell with you on this trip?" the Professor ventured, retrieving his cane like a scepter from a narrow cylindrical sleeve on the side of his wheelchair. He laid the cane across his lap.

"He is indeed, sir," Martin replied. "He will be meeting us in the Egypt gallery."

"I shall look forward to re-acquainting myself with him. So how do you find London?"

"Different than I expected," Martin related. "More modern, more traffic, and more Muslims."

"Interesting comment. Those of us who live here pay no mind. You know how they say things go in cycles? All this has been seen before, the Muslim part I mean."

"How so?"

"At one point in history most of Europe was under Muslim control. Overrun by zealous fighters who stopped at nothing for control. It all began innocently enough, with a few shopkeepers and merchants, mostly traders. It was not long before they started taking over."

Rebekah stepped forward boldly.

"Hi, I'm Rebekah. I notice your cane sir," Rebekah asked. "Are you able to walk with it?"

"No child, I unfortunately lost the use of my legs doing field work in Egypt, the unheralded collapse of a tunnel. Ten years in this bloody chair, and that's ten years too many, I assure you."

"Then the cane, sir?" she persisted. "How does it help you?"

"That, dear Rebekah, I use to open doors, push elevator buttons, move aside the slower moving museum visitors," he replied with a wink.

"So nice to hear your talk today," Rebekah oozed. "I have a great interest in Stonehenge, its astronomical significance, and its history. I hope it can be protected."

"You are quite advanced in your thinking, Rebekah," the Professor said, looking at her over his glasses. "I have read with interest your *curriculum vitae*, especially your thoughts on the astronomically aligned megaliths. Your education and credentials make you an excellent candidate for the research associate post."

"Oh thank you," Rebekah said excitedly.

"Of course it helps that you are British from the go," the Professor encouraged. "You could start as early as tomorrow if we agree. The research assistant position is very practical experience for whatever your future brings, very hands on."

"With whose hands on whom?" Sandra found herself wondering. She felt creeped out, to the pit of her stomach. Her original gut reaction to the Professor seemed to be confirmed.

"Tomorrow morning we have tickets booked for the double-decker bus tour, we could come to your home after that," Sandra interrupted.

"We drove by your house, yesterday," Rebekah said straight out. "Were you not home?"

The Professor seemed surprised. "I must have had errands," he managed to reply. He continued talking to Rebekah, appearing to take quite an interest in her.

"I would like to show you something, Rebekah, since you have an interest in all things astronomical."

The Professor turned away with Rebekah walking at his side, ignoring Martin and Sandra for all practical purposes.

"There is a treasure in the Egyptian collection that combines the best in Egyptology with the best in Astronomy," Haddad said. "You will never guess it, I would wager unless you are very, very sharp."

"I can't imagine what it could be," Rebekah stated.

Martin watched as the Professor leaned to the far left in his chair, watching someone or something at the far end of the gallery corridor.

"Can you meet me within the quarter-hour?" the Professor asked, suddenly seeming quite anxious. "Come to the Egyptian gallery, ground level. I will meet you near the Osiris twin guardians to the gallery."

"We can go there now if you like," Martin offered.

"I have one stop to make, if you please," the Professor countered. "The issues one faces in my condition are, unusual," he said apologetically.

"In 15 minutes, then," Martin agreed.

Chapter 33

The British Museum
London, England

The Egyptian gallery statues stared coldly into space, holding court over the relics of history that surrounded them. The tallest and most ominous of the exhibits found there reached high into the vaulted ceilings, where special indirect uplighting glowed above them, like a sunrise on a winter's day. The lights were designed to illuminate but not deteriorate the ancient items.

"How long has it been?" Sandra asked.

"About twenty minutes," Martin replied, looking at his watch. "He will be here soon."

"Uncle Martin, no one wears a watch anymore," Rebekah told him. "They use their phone."

"I like a watch," Martin replied. He tucked his pen under the watchband, notebook going into his inner left pocket, as always.

"Here's Chartwell now," he told Sandra.

"Where have you been?" Sandra asked impatiently.

"I've been wondering the same thing about you," Chartwell replied. "Browsing the naughty artwork and statues, you two?"

"John Robert Chartwell, don't be crude. You are such an impossible man. We've been right here, as we agreed," Sandra replied.

"Professor Haddad has not joined us yet, so by that measure, you're early," Martin offered. "What caught your interest?"

"Every time I set foot in a museum my fraud radar goes off," Chartwell began. "I started in religious artifacts, Bible times, early Levant and Middle East. But I really enjoyed the Egyptian gallery. That's where the fun was."

"Did you find everything in order I hope?" Martin asked. "I know you have a good eye for artifact fraud."

Martin stepped closer to Chartwell. His lip-reading skills were improving, but the echo in the museum was playing havoc with his hearing devices.

"As a matter of fact, things are a mess," Chartwell stated. "Horrible frauds in the Mesopotamian collection," he added. "But the worst fraud I found was right here in Egyptian pieces. To top that, the piece in question is one of the most contested pieces in the British Museum's Egyptian collection."

"This ought to be good," Martin said. "Show me."

"What is it?" Sandra asked. "What did you find?"

Rebekah looked on with growing interest.

Chartwell paused for dramatic effect, looked to either side, then leaned in to deliver his pronouncement in a hoarse whisper.

"Only the most visited object in the British Museum, the Rosetta Stone," he laughed. "It's a fake, a fraudulent copy. Of course, only a trained eye could determine that. Come on, I'll show you."

"Professor Haddad promised he would meet us," Rebekah objected. "I am waiting right here."

"Wait," Martin said. "*The* Rosetta Stone? It is still here in the British Museum? Sandra, I thought the IAF received a report that Egypt had asked for it to be returned more than a year ago."

"You are correct," Chartwell interrupted. "Egypt did formally request repatriation of the Rosetta Stone along with other priceless artifacts. Zahi Hawass got a lot of media attention from the request. He asked for it fourteen years ago, in 2003 at the 250th anniversary of the British Museum."

"I love that guy," Sandra said as they walked. "He's bold."

"Britain has never agreed to return it," Chartwell continued. "Britain always cites precedent in these cases."

"Precedent?"

"The greedy concept that if they ever started giving back antiquities to their source countries, there would be no end to the demand for repatriation. The museum would be emptied within a month."

Chartwell stopped in front of the display case purported to hold the Rosetta Stone.

"This impressive, irregular black granite tablet contains three columns of language engraved into its surface, hieroglyphic, demotic, and Greek," he said, his voice mimicking the Museum tour guides perfectly. Discovered in the Nile Delta by Napoleon, the Stone fell into British hands after Napoleon's defeat."

"How do you know it's false?" Sandra asked.

"Elementary, my dear. The actual weight of the true Rosetta Stone is 760 kilograms. That's over 1500 lbs., three quarters of a ton! This is a relatively new display case, but there is no way this case was built to support that much weight."

Sandra leaned forward to have a closer look.

"The granite does not have the right gloss to it, although the color is close," he explained. "The black granite the Egyptians used was not this dull. It had more of a shine."

"What do you think happened?"

"I would venture that someone with questionable morals and unbridled greed has a different idea of what to do with it," Chartwell surmised. "Beyond that would be pure speculation."

Martin looked at his watch.

"Speaking of questionable individuals, where is our Professor?" Chartwell quipped. "Rolled off in a corner to take a nap, has he?"

"John, there is no call to be mean," Sandra admonished.

"Well, he did say he would meet us in the Egyptian gallery a good thirty minutes ago," Martin mused. "I wonder where he could be?"

"Did he say exactly where? That gallery is extensive."

"He told Rebekah to meet near the King Tut artifacts, which is where you found us, but I can see from here that he is still not there."

"Let's wander back up that way," Chartwell said. "Not too late for him to yet show. The museum will close in an hour."

Chartwell strode down the wide center walkway, Martin and Sandra a few steps behind, watching Rebekah as they approached.

"The professor was going to show me something unique," Rebekah said disappointedly. "He said it would combine the best of Egyptology with the best in Astronomy."

"I know exactly what he was referring to," Chartwell offered.

"You do?" Rebekah exclaimed, immediately becoming more animated.

"I do. You are standing in front of it. Turn round."

Rebekah and Sandra took a step toward the glass display case. Looking at the varied displays, Rebekah saw the jagged blade first. The handle was ornate Egyptian gold work.

"King Tut's dagger," Chartwell explained. "The iron blade of that dagger is made of meteorite. The best of Egyptology and Astronomy in one."

Rebekah leaned forward for a closer look.

"The Kharga meteorite that fell in Egypt," Chartwell continued, "was determined to be the source of that iron in 2015."

"Notice that the dagger has never rusted. It was unearthed in 1925. It is over 3,000 years old."

"Meteors were the leading source of iron prior to the Iron Age, when mining began in earnest. Many swords and daggers from around the world have been found to be made from meteorite."

Overhead, a small camera blinked once, hidden inside a mirrored, semi-circular enclosure. Professor Haddad controlled the camera from one of two security offices within the Museum complex. He checked his watch for what seemed like the hundredth time, as the museum visitor he sought to track eluded his view once again.

He was perplexed. It was happening too soon. He pondered his predicament, puzzled at the preponderance of evidence that he had gathered. Here she was, Melinda Medina, his unpredictable and worldly niece looking for him in every corner of the museum. He caught another brief glance of her. She seemed to know where every camera was located, and how to avoid them.

Why had she come without calling? What the meaning of her arrival in London a day early? This was all very suspect. Perhaps the Jackal had sent her. He knew what that could mean.

Seeing Melinda round the corner and enter the final unsearched gallery, the Professor's anxiety increased. He watched her test each service staff door. Finding one unlocked, she stepped through the door and into the service hallways and the network of tunnels that ran below the British Museum. The time had come for him to take his leave.

Chapter 34

Martin watched the crowds of visitors dwindle as the afternoon wore on. There was little else to do. The museum was scheduled to close in 15 minutes. Still no word from Professor Haddad.

"Martin, I'm tired," Sandra pleaded. "Can't we catch up with Haddad tomorrow?"

"We'll go to dinner soon," Martin promised. He reached for Sandra's hand to reassure her.

"Does Professor Haddad keep an office here at the Museum?" he asked.

"I inquired earlier," Chartwell replied. "He does not. Perhaps he had to leave unexpectedly."

"If so, he did not tell us, so that's kind of lame," Rebekah said.

"Not for him," Chartwell muttered. "It's more of a *modus operandi* with him, disappearing at the worst time, mysterious and unexplained."

Rebekah glared at Chartwell, then wandered toward the gift shop.

"What is it that you have against the Professor?" Martin asked. "Why not just come right out and say it, instead of all this innuendo?"

"Sandra thinks I should tread lightly for Rebekah's sake," Chartwell answered. "But if you must know, I have worked with this Haddad character in the past. Other than the fact I see him as a bit of a pervert, he and I worked together on a dig in Luxor, excavating a tomb in the Valley of the Kings. We thought it might be the tomb of Nefertiti, or at least he did."

"But why do you hate him so much?" Sandra asked.

"Let him finish," Martin cautioned. "Go ahead, John."

"He and I had a complete falling out," Chartwell explained. "I had gone for supplies, I thought Haddad had stopped digging for the day. After I left, he pushed ahead to get to a particular wall of hieroglyphics on his favorite topic, embalming. Without me being there, of course. I was planning to tell him that I was done working with him, because of things just like this."

Rebekah walked by, handed Chartwell a one page flyer on Stonehenge, then walked away again.

"Anyway, I was delayed due to a bit of banditry in the area. The Valley of the Kings near Luxor is notorious for that. When I got back I found that he had committed a double atrocity."

Sandra leaned in, all ears.

"An archaeological atrocity," Chartwell explained. "As well as a human tragedy. Haddad had set explosive charges to free the section of wall that he planned to remove. He had to possess it."

"Explosives? He blew out a section of the wall?"

"It is done far more often than one would suppose," Chartwell answered, frowning. "I could write a book about it."

"I arrived just as the tunnel imploded in a cloud of dust. We could not get into the area for over an hour. When I finally got inside, Haddad was crushed by huge stone blocks. Our partner on the dig was dead."

"Oh, John, that's horrible. Who was the partner?"

Chartwell folded the museum flyer that he had been playing with two more times before responding. He pulled his hand back and launched the paper airplane that he had made the full length of the main gallery.

"That partner was my second wife," he said simply.

"Oh John, I am *so* sorry," Sandra said.

"I worked all night to dig them out. She died. He ended up in a wheelchair after months of surgery and unsuccessful rehab. Last I heard he had checked out of the hospital with no warning, poof."

"Does he have a spinal injury?"

"It appeared that he maintained a neural pathway, but never regained the strength in his lower body required to move about."

"John, how terrible that must have been for you to lose her like that."

"No wonder you don't like him," Martin added.

Following the flight path of the paper airplane, Martin noticed movement at the far end of the gallery. All the museum patrons had departed, with mere minutes left until closing time. To his surprise, Martin saw what appeared to be a hooded ninja, a figure dressed in black, tight clothing, including a face covering that exposed only the eyes. He found himself drawn toward the sight.

"Martin, where are you going?" Sandra asked. "I'm ready to leave."

Martin held up his hand as if to indicate silence, then pointed to Chartwell and to the far end of the main gallery.

Both men started down the wide center walkway.

"I see it too," Chartwell whispered. "To the right, up ahead."

"Looked like a ninja," Martin said incredulously.

"Not ninja, *hashashin*," Chartwell corrected. "Similar black clothing, but ninja is looser. *Hashashin* is the Arabian origin for the word assassin. They got high on hashish before going on their deadly missions. Be very careful."

"The museum will close in 5 minutes," the intercom announced. "Please collect the members of your party and move toward the museum entrance at this time."

The dark figure tried to blend into the shadows not one hundred feet from where the two men stood.

"There, to the left, in the corner by the doorway," Martin said.

"I see him," Chartwell whispered.

"Or her," Rebekah interrupted. "What man wears tight clothes like that?"

"I'm calling for help," Sandra stated, lifting a phone at the front counter. "I'll ring security, then I'll be right here."

"Chartwell, you go left along that wall, I will head straight to the doorway. This person could be trying to hide until the museum closes, then take advantage of whatever they choose to steal."

"What can I do?" Rebekah asked.

"Make as much noise as possible so the intruder does not come back this way," Chartwell answered.

"Got it," she said, glancing to either side.

"Go," Martin instructed.

Chartwell moved as directed, keeping an eye peeled on the corner where he had last spotted the intruder. As he and Martin moved into the next exhibit gallery, Rebekah made her move.

Leaning her full weight against a suit of armor labelled 1221A.D., Rebekah sent the display crashing to the polished stone marble floor. The deafening sound of metal on stone reverberated through the museum as sections of ancient armament scattered across the floor in every direction. The sound echo found its way to Martin's hearing devices, momentarily rendering his ears useless before falling silent.

Martin caught sight of the shadowy figure, then watched as it disappeared again. He waved to Chartwell to get his attention, but then the intruder was nowhere to be seen.

"He disappeared into the wall!" Martin said in frustration.

"Why do you insist it's a he?" Rebekah asked, finally catching up to them. "A high percentage of professional burglars are women, especially in the area of fine art and antiquities."

"Is that true?" Martin asked.

"She's right," Chartwell admitted.

"Well, whoever we're dealing with, where did they disappear to?"

"The British Museum has a million secret doors and passages, I'll bet," Rebekah commented.

"She's right again. Everyone who studies in archaeology in London has heard about it. Hidden passages for the employees to move around, like Disney does in their parks. Some passages lead into the London Underground, the subway system dating back to World War II. "

They stopped at the wall where the person disappeared.

Martin tapped the plaster to listen for hollows. Nothing appeared to conceal a door. No knobs, latches or hardware, only a single fire-alarm box and a dark painted panel broke the plainness of the wall facing them.

"Not thinking of pulling that, are you?" Chartwell asked, halfway hoping Martin would say yes.

"I think that's how the wall opens," Martin replied. "It's the only way I see in."

"Pull it if you dare," Chartwell replied.

"Hold up there, what are you doing?" A voice boomed behind them.

Martin turned to find the museum security guard with Sandra in tow. She shrugged as if to deny responsibility for the interruption.

"You could pull it, Martin," Chartwell said. "Either you're right or centuries of history gets ruined by the sprinkler system."

"Don't touch anything," the guard warned.

"Is this a legitimate firebox?" Martin asked.

"I can check," the guard responded. "If it is, it will respond to my scanner. All of the doors and alarms are scan-coded, so as we make our rounds, the scanner proves we were there. "

"Well check it, man, we don't have all day," Chartwell barked.

The guard passed his QR code reader over the fire alarm. Although there was a printed code on the box, his reader did not pick it up.

Before asking, Martin pulled the handle. Immediately the dark wall panel to their right slid open.

"That's it, let's go," Chartwell said, ducking through the opening. Martin followed, with Rebekah and the museum guard close on his heels.

The small, windowless room they had entered was without a door. Their entry point hissed shut, blocking their escape.

"Uncle Martin, do something. I can't see," Rebekah urged.

The guard lit his torch the same moment Martin turned his cell phone on. Chartwell began methodically tapping the walls of the roughly square, featureless room. They took a good look around, including above them. The ceiling in the room was at least 3 meters high. They were at a dead end.

Suddenly the panel they had entered by slid open.

Sandra peeked in as they shielded their eyes from the museum lights.

"What are you doing in there?" she asked. "I've been waiting. Someone promised me dinner."

Chapter 35

Kentworth Estate
Amesbury, Wiltshire

As darkness fell across the Salisbury Plains, an unwelcome draft of chill air passed over the Professor's shoulders, as would a portent of death.

"As salaamu alaikum," the feminine voice said from behind.

"Wa alaikumu èl salaamu," he responded. "And may Peace be with you, my child."

"Uncle Ahmed," Melinda cooed from the shadows. "It has been such a long time."

"Let me look at you, my child," the Professor said evenly. "Come into the light."

Melinda stepped into the light of the Professor's reading lamp, moving as a model might strut onto the catwalk in Milan. She performed a perfect spin on expensive black stilt-heels, then tried to curtsey as best she could in skin-tight leather pants. Her bosom practically spilled from her black zippered jacket.

"My daughter, Allah would not be pleased. Your appearance is very much that of the world, not that of a devout woman. What would your father say, may Allah have mercy on his soul?"

"What did he always say when he sent me to stay with you?" Melinda asked. She tilted forward to hear his answer, her partially gloved hand cupping her ear.

Keeping his hands under his lap blanket, the Professor replied in his best monotone. "He always said, 'Give Melinda what she wants, and make her happy'. So that is what I seek to do."

"That is exactly what you should do. And do put the safety on that pistol before you hurt yourself," she admonished.

An audible click confirmed that he had followed her advice. He pulled the pistol from beneath the blanket, placing it on the table adjacent to his chair. He did not give up the dagger, wondering if she knew about that too.

Melinda noticed the files bulging with photos and documents on the table to his left.

"Who is the girl? She's *pretty*," she said, thumbing through the file. "Is she your new assistant?"

"No one, just another child, she starts tomorrow."

216

"Whyever would she want to work with you?"

"She admires my work. Does there have to be another reason?"

"No, there does not. I hope she pleases you."

"Then why have you come to me, my niece? I am responsible now, as your male guardian, this I understand. Is your honor at stake?"

Melinda giggled, her cleavage jiggling above the opening in her jacket.

"A little late for that, Uncle," she laughed, then grew deadly serious. She stepped closer to his wheelchair while remaining just out of reach.

"I missed you at the museum today," she said, looking him straight in the eye.

"Are you here to kill me?" he asked, returning her gaze.

"If I were, you would already be dead," she responded. She took a chair opposite his.

"I am here to try on the suit."

The Professor appeared calm, but his insides immediately knotted up. He was not prepared to reveal this much so soon. He needed time and opportunity to bring Melinda into his plans.

"I will have it for you at noon tomorrow," he lied graciously. "It is safely stored until time for shipment. Let us talk instead of your travels."

"I won't be put off," she cautioned. "No is not an acceptable answer. I will come for the suit tomorrow."

Melinda stood up to leave. "Have you tried the suit on yourself?"

"I have been instructed not to do so," the Professor responded nervously. "I have not defied this order."

"That is well for you. Defy the Jackal and I must take your life!"

"Such bold talk from someone so young," he said. "Sit down, relax. Tomorrow I will have the suits moved here from their secure storage. Do you care for some tea?"

Melinda sat back down, crossed her legs, and bobbed one leather encased lower limb nervously for several seconds.

"Uncle, I believe our operation is being seriously threatened."

"By whom?"

"By Martin Culver, and by his organization," Melinda stated matter-of-factly. "You met him today. His organization is the International Antiquities Foundation."

"What makes you say this?"

"I have researched this organization. When they go into action, someone in our network usually ends up dead."

"Have we tried to eliminate this problem?"

"Yes, we have. We have tried everything. They seem to have deep pockets and tremendous good fortune. They always seem to come out on top. As time goes along, they are making a big dent in our cash flow and the closer they get, the worse my comfort level. After I deliver the sword and the suits to the Jackal, I am thinking about retiring."

"Retiring? What is that? I do not know this word," the Professor said, more than a little perturbed. This was not in his plans. Melinda would be his queen, she would rule from *his* side.

Melinda continued.

"Retired, you know, getting out, stepping away from the game. I have breathed enough ancient dust, hauled enough stone work in the middle of the night. I have defied every curse ever cast by the pharoahs and truthfully, I am tired."

The professor looked down at his hands, at the red marks across the backs of his hands, where the hair was scorched away. His hands were tense, so he rubbed away the pain.

"Melinda Medina, you listen to me. You are not retiring. It is not in your blood to do such a thing. Look at me, I am in this wheelchair, and I am not talking retirement. I insist that you remain with our organization and help to achieve our goals. You cannot abandon us at this point. We have nearly emptied the British Museum of its Egyptian collection. We are so close. And you are in too deep."

"Then listen to me, uncle. I will agree to stay on a little longer, but I want a larger share befitting my contribution. When I choose to get out, I want you to honor that, and not try to convince me differently. Otherwise, I will simply disappear. And you will not be able to find me."

"I will *always* be able to find you," Haddad said sullenly. "There is no place that you can run to hide from me. Do you not remember our game when you were young?"

"I am no longer afraid of you," Melinda stated, pointing a finger at his face. "Your sick game of hide and seek. Binding a helpless girl is not the same as controlling a grown woman. Just as I have changed, the smuggling game has also changed, the changes great enough to bring about a change in our priorities, changes all due to the International Antiquities Foundation. I remain convinced that they could do us great damage."

"Then the threat must be mitigated. What do you suggest?"

"I will deal with it," she responded. "I was only seeking your blessing. Consider it done."

Chapter 36

The Streets of
London, England

"So how was breakfast?" Chartwell asked.

"We ordered room service to save time," Martin replied.

"That was always my excuse," Chartwell replied, not looking up from his newspaper. "Yet you were still late downstairs, hmm?"

"Moving on," Sandra commented drily. "Weather report?"

"So it's our third day in London," Chartwell replied. "Martin's second. Of course it's raining, because in London it rains one-third of every day. Then every third day it pours."

"Can't you just say "It's going to rain?" Would that be too much to ask?" Sandra asked. "So irritating!"

"Plans still on for today?" Martin inquired.

"Well, we have our raincoats," Sandra replied. "If I don't get to ride a double decker bus today, I'm afraid I might miss out. We leave day after tomorrow."

"Then let's get ready," Chartwell said. "Anyone need to run back up to their room?"

"No, I think we're good, unless the ride is going to be extra thrilling," Sandra replied.

"I haven't been on a double decker bus ever," Rebekah said. "I never went even when I lived here with my Gram."

Walking outside, Martin checked the skies and gave a thumbs up. The rain had turned to a light mist. The skies showed signs of clearing. Together they hurried down the steps of the hotel, walking quickly the half-block to the nearest bus stop.

The red double decker bus arrived within minutes. As they boarded the crowded lower deck, Sandra's face showed the promise of a smile, even as she shook the water from her raincoat.

"This is an experience that I have always dreamed of," she said to Martin, kissing him on the cheek as she slid past him to get on the bus. "I am glad I get to see this with you."

"In the rain, even?" he remarked.

"Yes," she replied. "Even in the rain."

"Can we go upstairs?" Rebekah asked as they boarded, looking around for seats. "The rain has all but stopped."

"I'm happy about that. Thank goodness Chartwell took us to the London Fog store last evening," Sandra replied.

"Look how crowded it is. I'm glad we bought tickets for the bus tour in advance," Rebekah said. "Follow me," she told Sandra, scampering up the stairs to the second deck.

Martin averted his eyes to avoid looking up, since Rebekah's raincoat was shorter than her skirt. His eyes met Sandra's smile.

"I've made peace with my concerns over Rebekah's style," Sandra said to him, smiling at his predicament. "You should too. We are not her parents." Sandra then proceeded to follow Rebekah topside.

"No running please!" the bus operator called back after the two women. "Wet deck topside."

Chartwell extended his arm toward Martin and bowed slightly.

"I guess we are riding topside," he laughed. "After you."

Martin and Chartwell joined Rebekah and Sandra on the second deck. They quickly settled into adjacent bench seats as the tall bus started to move.

"This is so fun!" Rebekah shouted. "I love it!"

"The seats are soaking wet," Chartwell said, raising his butt up off the seat.

"You've got a soggy bum, John Robert," Sandra laughed.

"You can see a long ways up here," Martin commented. "Breezy though."

"Martin, you should see your hair," Chartwell laughed. "It's blowing around in your face. You look like George Harrison."

The bus continued to rumble along, thankfully veering clear of wet, overhanging trees. The bus driver's assistant announced upcoming stops, as well as points of interest along the way, but the raucous crew on the upper deck was having too much fun to pay attention. Around the corner, the Big Ben clock tower could be heard sounding the hour. It was 9:00AM.

As the tall bus cruised along, Chartwell decided to sit as close as he could to the edge of his seat, which still felt wet. As he leaned forward, he caught the glint of moisture drops hanging from wet monofilament line stretched across the roadway not thirty meters in front of them, running from one street lamp to another. Having worked in Syria and Afghanistan, Chartwell knew what was coming. He tried to alert the others, but there was no time to even speak.

Chartwell's reflexes took over as he went into action, standing and spreading his raincoat as wide as possible. He leapt toward Rebekah, taking her down to the deck. Martin followed suit in an attempt to shield Sandra, spreading his raincoat over her, attempting to cover them both.

"Get dow…" Chartwell attempted to shout as he hit the deck. The explosion from both sides of the bus drowned out his voice. The IED explosives, mounted high in the light poles, were triggered by the trip wire, ripping holes in the forward metal plate railing and seats with hundreds of nails. The sound of the pinging shrapnel was as if bullets were riddling the metal structures surrounding them.

Sandra cried out, gripping her leg. Martin felt stings across his back as if bees were attacking, dozens of impacts pounding like being caught in a hailstorm. Acrid smoke burned his eyes and his ears rang like chimes.

The bus slowed to a rolling crawl before veering left and slamming into a delivery truck. Hearing another crash, Martin lifted his head enough to see the tops of both streetlamps shatter down into the roadway.

He heard groaning from Chartwell before he heard Rebekah's muffled moans. Sandra cried great tears as Martin lifted his body from hers and examined her injuries.

Two nails that had pierced the plate metal railing surrounding the upper deck were now protruding from Sandra's left shinbone below the knee. Her face was an expression of pure pain. Martin helped her up to a nearby seat with the fewest imbedded nails. As Martin stood, he could feel his back muscles being pricked by sharp, hot points poking through his raincoat. Nails were sticking out of the soles and heels of his shoes, making it difficult to walk. He stayed low, crawling to reach Chartwell and Rebekah.

"Are you okay?" Martin asked urgently. "Chartwell, talk to me!"

Martin reached for Chartwell to help him, but could not find any area of his coat free of imbedded nails. Chartwell's entire back and arm looked like a pin cushion. Some nails already showed wet, bloody circles where the metal points had pierced his skin.

He finally heard a groan and realized Chartwell was still alive.

"John, are you able to move?" Martin asked. "We need to check on Rebekah."

Chartwell got one knee beneath him, pushing himself to a kneeling position. He leaned against one of the seats for support.

"See if she's ok, Martin. I can't hear her breathing," he whispered hoarsely. Martin could not hear him, but understood the pleading look on his face.

Martin turned to Rebekah, took one long look, then looked back at Sandra. Seeing his expression, she turned her head away.

"Someone call an ambulance!" he shouted desperately. "We need help up here!"

Rebekah coughed, her shattered glasses falling away from her face. The unique wee-ooh sounds of British ambulance sirens rose and fell, echoing against the buildings as they drew closer.

Blasting past Chartwell's protective efforts, multiple nails had pierced Rebekah's neck, face and temple in a ragged line, a dozen nails in all, driven deep by the explosives. Slight trails of blood trickled from each entry wound, gathering in dark puddles on the rainy topside deck. She stirred, and tried to swallow, unable to speak.

Martin smoothed Rebekah's hair away from her face, avoiding the nails. She reacted with a partial smile. The nail at her temple had imbedded itself deepest, her eye on that side open and staring. A single tear rolled from the corner of her eye before the pupil went wide. Rebekah exhaled one last time, the same smile still gracing her peaceful face.

Martin passed his hand over Rebekah's eyes, gently bringing her eyelids closed. He had no words, but the Psalm that he had memorized on the island came to mind. He repeated it under his breath as he straightened her limbs to a more modest position. He stood up, yanking off his raincoat, dislodging the few nails that had lodged in his back. He covered Rebekah's face and body, then stumbled his way back to Sandra.

Martin felt a hot wave of anger wash over him. He began to tremble from the adrenalin coursing through his body. Martin looked up to see Chartwell openly sobbing as he knelt beside Rebekah, his body racked with emotion and pain.

Martin felt Sandra squeeze his left hand in an attempt to tolerate the pain in her knee. Rain drops randomly pelted the three of them, but no one moved.

The heavy footsteps of rescue workers made their way to the top deck of the bus. Viewing the scene, the medics stopped in their tracks.

"Bring more medics, and hurry," the first responder called on his radio. "Notify the hospital we have another casualty and multiple injuries."

Chapter 37

"I have seen enough of hospitals this year to last the rest of my life," Martin commented from his seat on the gurney. Circular bandages adhered to his back in a half dozen locations. He stood to his feet, pulling his shirt on one sleeve at a time.

"Sir, I have your pain injection," the nurse said to Martin.

"Save it for the next person," came his terse reply. "I'm fine." Restricting the anger rising inside, Martin unclenched his fists, flexing his fingers to restore feeling and circulation. Putting his fist through a door was not an option, at least not at the moment.

"Sandra, how are you doing?" Martin asked, his voice calm and caring.

Sandra adjusted in her wheelchair, moving her heavily bandaged leg to one side. Her slacks, expertly slit at the seam by the head nurse, were neatly pinned aside above thick bandages.

"I'll be willing to go to one more hospital," Chartwell said angrily. "When I kill the bastard that did this, I'll visit the hospital to identify his sorry ass."

"How about identify him in the morgue?" Martin wondered.

"Now you're talking," Chartwell replied from a prone position on the next gurney. He gritted his teeth once more as the last of the nails was removed from his back.

"Forty-seven," the nurse counted, dropping the nail into a glass jar with a clinking sound. "Now to get you disinfected."

"You two always think it's a guy, like at the Museum. I see this more as something that a vindictive woman would do," Sandra said. "A woman bent on revenge."

"If this bombing were aimed at us, we were targeted," Chartwell explained. "If it was random, then it could have been anyone."

"Who do you think did this Chartwell?"

"London has some mean ways," he commented. "It's not always a nice town. You've got the jihadists, the lone wolves, the copycats. But this was intended to do some damage. I believe it was aimed at us, either one, or all of us."

225

"What about the driver and driver assistant that were killed? What about all those other people?"

"Collateral damage. They were incidental to a goal."

"How could they have known we would be on that bus?"

"We bought tickets at the hotel front desk. They knew we were on the tour this morning."

"But why?" asked Sandra, eyes filling with tears all over again. "Why Rebekah?"

"When lions fight, the lambs get hurt the worst," Chartwell said. "I did the best I could for her, though I wish it had been more." His tone was saddening, so unlike his usual bravado.

Martin took a deep breath.

"Director Hall warned me to expect things like this. Before Mary Power's death she warned me again. That is why I came to London, Sandra, to look after you. I'm glad you were not hurt worse."

"I'm glad you did. If you had not been here, there might have been two dead women topside on that bus."

"I can't stop thinking about Rebekah," Martin said. "Her face looked so peaceful."

"She wanted to come home," Sandra said. "And she got to see Stonehenge. At least she had that."

"Excuse me, all, might I have a word?"

The police detective entered around the thin curtain separating the emergency ward from the rest of the trauma center. An MPS officer came with him, standing silent a few feet away at the entry of the trauma area.

"Condolences regarding the passing your friend, Rebekah Jayne Osgood, I believe," the detective stated, reviewing his notes. "I want to give you an update on the situation, then need to ask a few questions, if you don't mind?" he inquired.

"Of course," Martin agreed. "Thank you for your kindness."

"Not at all, Mr. Culver," the detective said. "So then, we have taken the evidence to New Scotland Yard, where it will be analyzed. We've no suspects at this time, but we do suspect terrorism was at the root of the attack."

He paused as if rethinking his words before proceeding.

"Fourteen people were killed, including your friend. We wish to be more certain before declaring this a terrorist act. I'm sure you understand."

"We understand," Martin said, not understanding in the least.

"I don't understand!" Chartwell said, sitting up and yanking on his bloody shirt over multiple torso bandages and wrappings. His face showed the pain of every movement. "I don't understand the mindset of people who would kill innocents to settle a score, or why it can't be declared terrorism when it was clearly an ISIS-style IED attack, as if we were in Syria or Iraq. Someone should be held responsible."

Taking a deep breath, Chartwell motioned to the nurse.

"I need a little help with my shirt," he said. "I'll take Martin's pain shot *and* mine both."

The nurse practically ran to prepare the pain injection.

"Perhaps we are taking this a little too personally," Martin said to the detective. "Although I don't think so. Up to this point, my home has been bombed, my foundation has been bombed twice, and I have been informed that I am on an ISIS hit list."

"You're on what?" Chartwell shouted. "When were you going to share that little gem?"

The detective waited to be sure that Chartwell was finished.

"Your anger is understandable, sir. Perhaps it is not as serious as all that. Do any of you know who would do such a thing as this? Did young Rebekah have any enemies? Any run-ins with any locals during the time you've been in London?"

"No," Martin replied simply. "No idea who would do this, no enemies. No issues with the locals. This was totally out of the blue."

"Pardon?"

"Totally unexpected," Chartwell translated. "Like this ISIS hit list bit."

Chartwell stared right at Martin, then looked away.

"Where are you staying, in the event we should have further questions or information?" the detective inquired.

"We are at the Ambassadors Hotel," Sandra replied. "The address is on our hospital forms. When will we be able to retrieve Rebekah's body? We will take responsibility for her final arrangements."

The detective raised one eyebrow slightly.

"But she is a Brit, according to her passport. No family, then?"

"All her family has passed," Sandra said without elaboration.

"Shall I list that you will take the body back to the U.S.?"

Sandra looked at Martin.

"No, we will handle all that here. Rebekah is home now. It was her wish."

"I will check with the coroner and let you know as soon as there is word on her release," the detective promised before leaving.

Chartwell finished buttoning his shirt. The nurse came to help Sandra with her wheelchair.

Before they could talk about what had just taken place, the doctor handling their cases came to talk to them.

"Gentlemen, you are both lucky to have no nerve damage. Your coats and sweaters helped in that respect. Mrs. Culver, the best news is that you are able to go home. The bad news is that one of the nails chipped a bone in your leg and you may have on-going pain from that until it is surgically corrected. This is something I would recommend once you are back in the U.S."

Martin squeezed Sandra's hand.

"Let's get out of here," Martin said. "The bill will go to the IAF. I've already made the arrangements."

Chapter 38

"Are you heading up to your room?" Chartwell asked as they entered the hotel lobby together.

"Yes," Martin said. "Sandra is tired, I want to help her get comfortable. I want to clean up a bit. I think we will rest. This afternoon we have arrangements to make for Rebekah."

"Sounds good," Chartwell said. "I'll have the desk send up a bottle of wine for you. I think I'm going to hit the pub next door."

"Thank you, John. But it's early for the pub, don't you think? "

"By my clock, it's way too late. Anyway, it's two in the afternoon. I expect a pint will take the edge off whatever the pain shot couldn't. "

"Still hurting?" Martin asked as the elevator doors slid open.

"This is going to hurt for a long time," Chartwell said. He maintained eye contact with Martin until the lift doors slid shut.

Turning, Chartwell headed to the front desk.

"Send up a bottle of Chardonnay to the Culver's room, if you will. Thanks so much. Put that on my room tab would you?"

The front desk clerk scrambled to make notes, then repeated everything back.

"Thanks, that's perfect," Chartwell said. "Now could I speak to your manager?"

"Certainly sir, he's just through that door."

Chartwell smiled the best he could manage, turned and walked into the adjacent office without knocking. He closed the door behind him.

Surprising the hotel manager at his desk, Chartwell walked directly to where the man sat and stood beside his desk chair. The manager leaned away, adjusting his ragged comb-over with nervous fingers.

"Through which agency do you book your double-decker bus tour tickets? " Chartwell asked. "The agency name, if you please."

"Is there a problem, sir?" the manager asked nervously .

"There will be unless you tell me what I want to know."

The manager cleared his throat.

"I heard what happened on your tour this AM. So sorry. Bad news, that."

"You don't know the half of it, chum. We booked that tour through your front desk. Someone knew we were on that bus and had time to plant a bomb. I am sick of standing by and seeing people I care about picked off like sitting ducks. The agency name please, or we may have to notify MPS of another related casualty."

The manager grabbed a sheet of paper and began to scribble.

"Here it is," he said. "It's a student organization. All I have is the sponsoring department phone number. They set up tours online as a side project regarding tourism promotion. They are connected with the university."

"Which university?" Chartwell asked, stepping closer.

"The UCL," the manager responded. "Don't hurt me!"

Chartwell stepped back.

"No intention of it, old man. The hurt I'm saving for someone who deserves it. I know someone connected with that university, I wonder."

Snatching up the phone from the manager's desk, Chartwell turned the sheet of paper so he could read it, then dialed the number rapidly.

"Professor Haddad's office."

"Professor Haddad, please."

"The Professor has no classes scheduled today," the receptionist said. "His agenda indicates he is working from home."

"Thank you," Chartwell said. He returned the phone to its cradle, then turned to leave the manager's office. The bloody holes in the back of his coat were visible.

"Sir!" the manager asked, standing up. "Are you quite all right? You appear to have been shot!"

"No, but thank you for reminding me," Chartwell said. He struggled out of his coat, sizing up the manager.

Throwing a handful of pound notes on the manager's desk, Chartwell hung his coat on the corner rack, taking down the managers raincoat. As he did so, the multiple wound marks across his back and arm could be seen across the back of his shirt.

"Buy yourself a new coat," Chartwell said cheerily. "That should cover it."

He walked out of the manager's office without another word.

"Hail me a cab, would you?" he asked the front desk clerk.

"We have two standing by at this time," the clerk responded. "We have fulfilled your earlier request by the way."

"Thanks so much," he said, heading for the street door.

Wincing as he pushed open the hotel door, Chartwell walked down the steps and directly to one of the two waiting cabs.

"Kentworth Estate in Amesbury, Wiltshire, please."

"That's about an hour, guvnor. It'll cost you."

"I've got it covered," Chartwell replied as he gingerly leaned back in the seat. "I'll double it if you stop so I can pick up a pint or two for the trip."

"If you're buying for two, no need to pay extra," the cabbie smiled.

Chapter 39

CIA Headquarters
Langley, VA

Hall flipped through the folders on her desk, trying to calm her frayed nerves without a cigarette. The information summary she held, a single sheet of paper, connected almost every international situation she was currently keeping tabs on, weapons smuggling, artifact shipments, currency laundering, illicit transport. Her hand trembled at the thought that she might finally hold the key.

When Hall's father was at the Agency, he used to tell her that bad guys focus so much on their mission that they make mistakes on their paperwork: banking, shipping, insurance documentation. Those mistakes, under the correct light, stand out, leave a trail.

Her father, a 40 year veteran, called it running the table, those few times when one piece of long-sought intel links all the current cases. Considering how much her father loved to shoot pool, the reference to how an 8-ball sinks every ball on the billiard table was appropriate.

The document Hall held in her hand told the tale with a minimum of words. A shipping audit had disclosed that the weight of the Rosetta Stone's recent shipment from the British Museum had been declared at 76 kilos, one-tenth of its actual weight. That shipment had ended in tragedy, with the artifact missing. Hall's intelligence team at Customs and Border Protection connected the dots, discovering the errors on the shipping manifest.

Professor Haddad, of the UCL in London, had been the one to sign off on the shipping documents for the Rosetta Stone the night it was stolen. He represented the university but actually lacked sufficient authority to direct the work of the British Museum.

But it was not the Professor's fraud that animated her. The key was the name of the shipping company at the top of the form. Hall looked out across the conference table. She was able to count five additional cases where the same issue had occurred. One thing caught her attention about every one of these cases. The shipping company read Medina Shipping.

Her phone rang, startling her as it always did when she was trying to focus.

"Director Hall here. Go ahead."

"Hall, it's Martin."

"Culver, I am glad you called. Are you still in London?"

"Yes, unfortunately. I have some bad news."

"What is it, Culver?"

"Rebekah has been killed in an IED explosion. We were on a double-decker bus. Sandra, Chartwell and I have all been injured to varying degrees."

"What was in the IED? Ball bearings, nails?"

"Nails," he replied.

"Damn, I'm sorry Martin. How badly are you hurt?"

"Just a few scratches on my back. Sandra took two nails to the knee. Chartwell was closest. He took over forty nails through the back of his coat. Miraculously, none did serious damage."

"Do you need assistance? How is Sandra doing? I know she was very attached to Rebekah."

"She's resting right now. I am on the balcony to keep from waking her. We got a break from the rain."

"Go back inside *now*, Culver!" Hall instructed. She moved to the edge of her chair. "Go inside and pull the drapes!"

Martin paused, then headed indoors.

"How do you know we have drapes…oh never mind," Martin said as he closed the balcony door. "Do you like the shirt I'm wearing?"

"Do you think I'm spying on you?" Hall asked. "I simply notice details. And yes, blue is a good color on you."

"So you are spying on us? A heads up would have helped. "

"Looking out for you is what I'm doing, but I'm no mind reader. When you leave a fixed location, it gets trickier to track you. I did not know you were hitting the streets of London so early this morning."

Martin was silent on the other end.

"Was it grim, her passing?"

"It was awful to have her ripped away so suddenly. Sandra is devastated. So is Chartwell, and well, I am too."

"Martin, I'm sorry. I am inches from knowing who the actors are in the London smuggling scene. Have you heard of Medina Shipping? Does anyone you know use them for artifact shipping?"

"Never heard of them."

"Medina Shipping keeps showing up on suspicious antiquities shipments and transfers. I am trying to find out more."

"Are you saying Medina, as in Señor Medina, from Mexico?"

"Spelled the same way. Hold on, Medina Shipping is listed as formed in 1956. Then it shows that it was dissolved, but does not say when. So it might be a dead end."

"Or it might mean that Señor Medina had a London shipping company?"

"I'm bringing up the principal's names now on the tax register," she said. "Give me a second."

"Oh damn," she said a second later.

"What did you find?" Martin asked, trying to keep his voice low.

"The company is still doing business, even in a dissolved status. They have several vessels and mostly run in the Mediterranean. The current head of the company is listed as Melinda Medina."

"Melinda Medina? Isn't she Morgan's fiancée from Panama? The one always wearing leather. She blamed me for the death of her parents."

"Exactly, now is it starting to make sense?"

"Is she the one behind all this violence?" Martin asked.

"It all makes sense," Hall said. "She blames you for her parent's death, no doubt for interfering with her plans and her livelihood. She is trying to send you a message."

"That doesn't explain the ISIS hit list," Martin said. "What's the connection there?"

"I don't know," Hall replied, obviously in deep thought. "I'm trying to piece it all together as we go along. My father was working on this issue his entire CIA career. The whole Palestinian problem, the state of Israel, the European interference, he hated the way it all went down. I heard it plenty when I was small. He advocated peace with the Arab world, certain that the repercussions of war with Muslims would not be pretty. He foresaw the rise of groups like Al-Qaeda and ISIS."

"So what happened? Did anyone listen?"

"Neither U.S. leaders nor the Arab world leaders wanted peace."

"So what happens now?"

"My job is to prove connections between Medina Shipping, and ISIS. If Medina Shipping is moving stolen archaeology pieces for ISIS to support terrorism, and I can prove it, then I can end this."

"Where is she? The last I remember she was in Panama," Martin said.

"I am getting ready to put someone on that detail now."

"Wait," Martin said. "Is Melinda Medina the daughter we have been looking for?"

"I will make it a point to find out," Hall declared. She pressed a button on her phone and patched Lieutenant Stoner in on a three-way conference we call.

"Stoner, get me everything you can on Melinda Medina. I want to know what she had for breakfast this morning, and where she was sitting when she ate it. I also need the itinerary and stops for every shipment by Medina Shipping Company of London, who they bank with, who they ship to."

"How far back?" Stoner asked.

"At least five years," Hall decided. "I think that will tell us what we need to know. The company is listed as dissolved so you may not find much.

"I'm on it, boss." A click on the line said she had left the conversation.

"So what are you looking for, exactly?" Martin asked.

"We will look for patterns," Hall replied. "If I can dig up Medina Shipping's client list, I can find out everything I need."

"Okay, keep me informed. We have to go tomorrow to claim Rebekah's body and make arrangements for her," Martin said. "Sandra and I are taking charge of it."

"Be careful, Culver. I'll let you know what I find out."

Hall punched the phone off speaker and moved a few of the case folders, arranging them on her conference table in order.

"Director Hall?" Lieutenant Stoner interrupted over the speaker phone.

"Go ahead," Hall said.

"I'm already starting to build a pattern on your request. Melinda Medina was in London *this morning*. She has a relative there, a Professor M.A. Haddad."

"Haddad? I just read his name on a shipping manifest."

"NSA intercepted a video chat a week ago from Medina to Haddad. I searched based on key words and phrases. Medina met with Haddad yesterday at his home outside London."

"Okay hold on," Hall stated. "Give me a second to think."

Hall began rehearsing the facts, as she always did just before a breakthrough. She thought of the name of the shipping company. Medina Shipping. Medina was the holy city where the Prophet was buried. Medina was a perfect name to avoid attention in the Muslim world.

"There are no coincidences," she said aloud. "Medina Shipping connects the stolen antiquities manifests. Haddad is Sr. Medina's brother. Haddad's name keeps cropping up. His niece Melinda Medina was in London yesterday. Today Rebekah got killed. Oh my god, she *is* the daughter! Stoner, you just earned your first promotion."

"What? What are you talking about?"

"The daughter. The ex-Director told us to find the daughter. He was talking about Melinda Medina! I've got to contact Culver. What else have you learned?"

"According to intel, Medina Shipping works exclusively for one import export firm, putting in to port only in France, Sicily, Greece and Istanbul on any regular basis. I do not know who the company principals are yet, but my search algorithm revealed some interesting traits. Analysis reveals that the one person most involved in Medina Shipping communications, according to his online profile and preferences, is not Muslim born and was likely educated in the U.S. He may have received intel training."

"A double agent?" Hall asked. "I didn't think we had one."

"Whoever this is, he seems to be the money manager, the architect behind the plan for ISIS to license antiquity looting and the sale of ancient items to the highest bidder."

"Anything else?" Hall asked, weary of juggling details.

"Director, we have tried to investigate this individual before, on some level. He seems to anticipate and thwart our efforts to find him, as well as blocking the strategies that the U.S. initiates to track and stop ISIS activity," Stoner continued. "He anticipates our every move and counters it."

"Chess logic," Hall said under her breath. "Oh my God."

"Excuse me?" Stoner asked.

"No, go ahead," Hall instructed. She brought her hand to her forehead and rubbed, staring down at the carpet between her boots.

"This individual has apparently been in place longer than ISIS. The shipments go back for years, to 1956. This was about the time of the formation of Israel out of British Palestine."

"The British battle for Suez Canal happened in 1956. Was Medina Shipping behind the movement of arms to the battle zone?" Hall asked. "The Soviet Union nearly nuked Britain *and* France over that one."

"Analysis trends suggest the possibility that ISIS has been in formative stages since Israel took Palestine for its homeland." Stoner asked. "Now we are seeing it brought to life."

"Talk about your sleeper cell," Hall commented.

"If so, then our "mystery man" may be the money, the brains and the inspiration behind the Islamic State. Wait, I have found something here," Stoner added. "It's a logo for the import firm."

"What's on the logo?" Hall asked.

"It looks like the Egyptian symbol for Anubis, like a jackal."

Hall looked at her computer again. After Stoner hung up, she knew what she had to do. Finally, she made herself stroke the keys. She went to secured Agency Personnel Files, keyed in her code, and drew up her father's death certificate.

She knew he was dead, she knew where he was buried, but her gut told her there were too many coincidences, in a business where there are no coincidences.

The death certificate spelled it out. Jackson Lee Hall. Death by asphyxiation, burns deep inside the remains of victim's lungs, identification by dental records only. No identification by DNA, she noted, a standard for CIA operatives.

Hall racked her brain to remember what her mother told her about her father wanting to take them to live in London. It was the year she had been due to be born. His personnel file held the record of the rejected transfer. 1956. Another coincidence.

Hall pushed speed dial on her phone.

"Hello," the voice drawled. "State your business."

"Senator this is Director Hall. We need to talk."

"What is it, Hall? I'm getting in my car, I've got more meetings later. Are you calling to complain about your budget?"

"Senator, I have found out some significant details about smuggling weapons out of London to the Middle East...."

Hall jumped as an explosion rang out through the phone before it went dead. No sound, not even static, made it through.

Grabbing the nearest remote, Hall called up the cameras in the parking garage nearest the Senate chambers. Two cameras showed nothing but smoke. Gradually the smoke cleared, giving way to fierce flames enveloping an SUV.

Hall stood up, barely limping now, as she moved spellbound toward the screen displaying the horrific images. She could not make herself look away.

Her desk phone rang. It went immediately to speaker.

"Director, have you heard? Check your Senate garage screens."

"I already know, Stoner. I've already seen it. I was talking to the Senator when it exploded."

"Don't think you saw this, ma'am. A drone was hovering outside the garage just before the explosion. I caught it on a low angle camera near the guard booth. It could have carried the bomb."

"Bring the fight to them," Hall thought to herself. She knew where she had heard that saying so many times before. It was being played out, both as a warning, and as a statement of what she needed to do to respond.

"Stoner, get me a flight to London. I want to leave tonight."

"Ma'am, checking now. We can have a jet ready in two hours, no wait...we are denied clearance. Repeat we did not get clearance."

"Then I will fly commercial. It's less obvious. Book the tickets, please."

"Shall I use your business credit card?"

"Yes," Hall replied. Hall could hear furious keyboard clicks on the other end.

"Ma'am, this card has been denied."

"Are you calling about your budget?" Hall remembered the Senator saying.

"Leave it, Stoner. I'll deal with it."

As soon as Stoner cleared the line, Hall went online with her personal credit card. She booked the commercial flight to London and opened the door to her closet. There was packing to be done, and very little time to do it. The questions would not stop coming.

Chapter 40

"Keep it running," Chartwell told the cabbie. "I shouldn't be very long."

"The meter's running, I'm enjoying the scenery," the cabbie replied, lifting his pint bottle as a toast. "What more could a fellow ask? Take your time, I'll be right here."

Hearing the vehicle in the drive, Professor Haddad wheeled himself into the foyer of his home, where he greeted Chartwell as soon as he activated the bell. Haddad opened the double doors wide, then rolled a few feet back.

"Are you going to invite me in?" Chartwell asked.

"Forgive me, Mr. Chartwell. I assumed you would burst in uninvited, brandishing your usual dusty enthusiasm. Please do come in."

Chartwell took two steps inside the door, then stopped. An odd, astringent smell reached its fingers into the foyer.

"Would you like to sit down, Mr. Chartwell? Something to drink perhaps?"

"I'll stand thank you. This is not a social call."

"Where are your friends?"

"They're a bit shaken up, staying in tonight."

"I'm sorry to hear that," Haddad said in a most insincere tone.

"There are some things you and I need to talk about," Chartwell said.

"Please tell me, but would you mind closing the doors? Can't have people passing out from exhaust gases, you know. Not only that, the breeze bears a chill."

Chartwell stood his ground.

"Haddad, Rebekah won't be coming to work for you."

The Professor raised his eyebrows, but his eyes did not meet Chartwell's eyes.

"Changed her mind, did she? Or did you change it for her?"

"She's dead, Haddad. A bus bombing today. She was a good friend. Someone is going to pay."

"Oh dear, that is so unfortunate. I am sorry to hear of this. So young and full of life. My condolences."

"Here we are again, Haddad, talking about someone I cared who died under suspect circumstances, someone connected with you. You seem to be bad luck."

Professor Haddad did not respond.

"You did not meet us at the museum yesterday," Chartwell challenged. "Why? Rebekah was counting on you, Haddad. She wanted to believe in you."

"I had to leave, unexpectedly. You sound as if you suspect me. That would be a grave mistake," the Professor warned.

"Why is that, Haddad?"

"Because I had nothing to do with it."

"I told her you could not be counted on," Chartwell stated.

"What else did you tell her, Mr. Chartwell? Did you tell her my story, my history, in your own inimitable manner?"

"I told her you're never around when needed, never where you say you'll be."

"I have been here all day," the Professor countered. "I stated so to the University office."

"You seem to spend more time here than at the university."

"Mr. Chartwell, need I remind you that 10,000 years of history lies beneath our feet here on these plains. That alone makes it worth being here. This is sacred archaeological ground, not only for what it yet holds, but for what it represents. Stonehenge is our laboratory, as well as our classroom. Think of our place in the timeline of history, think of what still lies below these floors."

"I have become nothing, Mr. Chartwell, an error that I hope to correct. But why are you really here Mr. Chartwell? Surely not to accuse or harass me, you could do that well enough from a distance."

Chartwell stifled the urge to throttle Haddad's pompous ass.

"I came to ask if you lead any student groups at UCL who are promoting jihadi violence in your so-called work as a professor of whatever it is. Anyone you sponsor or know?"

Professor Haddad rolled his chair back a foot to avoid the late afternoon sunlight.

"I answer to no one for how I make my living or with whom I associate. I operate for my own account and do not take kindly to being pressed for my details in this matter, of all places in my own house by a would-be barrister."

The Professor lowered his voice and changed his tone slightly.

"Violence has never been a path to peace. Violence is a only path to more violence, a path littered with anger and hatred."

"Your god *demands* violence. The God I am familiar with says love your enemies, do good to those who harm you," Chartwell said. "You are the only person we told about that bus tour. Someone targeted us. Does someone you know at UCL espouse the Koran's more violent teachings? Yes or no?"

"You are barking up the wrong proverbial tree," the Professor admonished, backing away another few feet.

"I am Muslim by birth, but not by faith or ideology. I only offer allegiance to Anubis. Your accusations are off base," the Professor said, turning and wheeling himself toward his library.

"I am sorry about your friends, Mr. Chartwell. I also am sorry for your painful loss, but I have more important fish to fry."

"What do you have that's so important?" Chartwell asked.

"I have found a sword, a sword that you and I both have sought in our own way. A career-making discovery."

Haddad suddenly wheeled round to face Chartwell.

"I have found Excalibur!" he claimed, his eyes gleaming.

"Oh, here we go," Chartwell said to himself. He took several steps towards the door. "I've heard it before."

"Ish-kalabar," the Professor whispered in a barely audible voice. "I have it."

Chartwell stopped, his hand on the door latch.

"How did you find it, assuming you are telling the truth?"

"Have a seat, Mr. Chartwell. I have a story to tell you."

Chapter 41

"Before I agree Haddad, are you the only one that knows about this?"

"Only I, Professor M.A. Haddad, know the secret to removing Ish-kalabar, or Excalibur as it has come to be known in its Anglicized from, from its prison deep within the Sacred Stone. For not only have I learned the secret of the sword, I have unlocked the secrets of the stone itself."

"Go on."

"Although the place came to me through translation of the Ogham texts, the key revelation occurred during a lightning storm watched from my home last summer. The lightning seemed to branch out over the center of Stonehenge, flashing along the stone uprights in a spoke-like pattern. That is when I learned where to look. I found the sword, right where history had left it, imbedded in the side of the Sacred Stone of Heaven, thirty feet beneath the Salisbury Plain, beneath Stone Henge itself. Apparently the Viking raiders could not remove it, so they filled in the proscenium surrounding the sword and buried it to ground level."

"After thorough analysis and testing of dozens of samples from the stone, I discovered two things," Haddad said. "I determined that the Sword was fused through electro-molecular bonding into the stone, meaning that only electricity would free the sword."

"And the second discovery?"

"Mr. Chartwell, I discovered that the Sacred Stone buried at the center of the Stonehenge megalith is made of pure meteoric iron, metal forged in heaven. "

"I discovered all of this because of the wonderful, powered exo-suit that I had developed. I was not strong enough. I needed mobility and great strength. I used the resources of the university and whatever I could raise by selling off key pieces from the British Museum."

"The suit did more than give me the strength to walk. It made me whole again. I had sought to develop the right device to remove the sword from the stone. The exo-suit turned out to be that tool, and more. What I found was that not only would the exo-suit technology give me the strength, but that my design would provide unanticipated electrical current to detach the sword from its metallic prison, particle by particle, allowing Excalibur to practically fall out of the stone and into my hands. Ignited ions unlocked agitated ions until release was obtained. By the power flowing through this suit, by enhanced technology, the sword could at last be freed."

The Professor paced the room in his wheelchair, lost in his thoughts.

"Mr. Chartwell, I feel a kinship with the Babylonian astrologers, ancestors of the Druids, who came to the Salisbury Plain looking for the site of a great meteor that had fallen to Earth. They were scholars, bringing with them a knowledge of the stars, the methods of embalming, the secrets of the universe."

"So you think the story you translated from the Ogham text is a valid account?"

"I have no doubt that the story I translated of the Vikings' attempt to take the great sword from the Druids by force is true."

"Think of it Chartwell. The legend of this sword. The lore of history. Of Ulfhedin, father of Ulfberht. Of Ulfberht his son, the half-Viking, half-Saxon hero of the Druids."

"Think of Myrddin the Wise, the perceived magician who daily displayed his unique understanding of chemistry, physics, and electricity to the astonishment of the local heathen tribes. You and I, Mr. Chartwell, would be Kings among them. "

"Why did the Vikings leave?"

"They failed to remove the sword after much heroic effort. The Viking horde took what they could carry of the heavenly iron found in the Sacred Stone, enough for hundreds of swords and hammers, completely burying the meteor stone afterwards, leaving only the uprights of the Great Stone Temple to mark its location. And that is where I found Ish-kalabar."

"It does not exist, Haddad. Excalibur, or *Ish-kalabar* as you call it, is not real. You have always chased the myth of archaeology and not the science."

"And you, my British friend are the purist? You are the one chasing fraud and fortune through every ruin and temple on the planet, yet you do not understand that myth is based in history. You cannot have one without the other."

Professor Haddad took a deep breath, stroking his long rectangular chin-beard.

"Need I tell you the story one more time? That there existed in antiquity a great sword, A'ish-kalabar, a sword of great evil in Mecca, a sword said to be the Prophet's own sword, made from meteorite iron found in the Kabah. Ulfberht the Son forged Ish-kalabar using Stonehenge meteorite iron and Damascus steel forging secrets, after seeing A'ish-kalabar. Then there were two swords, Ish-kalabar and A'ish-kalabar, the good and the evil. Ish-kalabar was forged by Ulfberht to be the good counterpart to its evil twin, to bring balance."

"No need for repetition. I read your translation from the Ogham text," Chartwell said. "At least my feet are planted on solid ground, not in the clouds," Chartwell countered as he prepared to leave.

"So where would one store an object like Excalibur, assuming it were true?" Chartwell asked. "I can see it's not in plain sight, hanging on your wall."

"You know I cannot tell you that," Haddad replied. "But I can tell you that for now it resides in that place where it has been safest, where no one has found it for 1,000 years."

He paused for his words to register.

"I can show it to you, Mr. Chartwell. Bring Mr. Culver tomorrow. You know you want to see it, even if to prove me wrong. It will be hard for you to admit, that I have been right about it all along. When you see it you will find you are wrong about me."

"What difference is it to you what I think?" Chartwell asked.

"I understand that you have moved up in the world, have the weight of an international foundation behind you, have the ear of the leading philanthropist repatriation group in the world. I would need their approval and assistance to be able to hold onto my treasure, to get proper credit for its discovery. The people I work for are not to be trusted. They wish no one well but themselves."

"So are you saying you need my help with this discovery of yours?" Chartwell asked. He gripped the door handle tightly.

"If you were to help me keep it, I should be most grateful."

"I'll talk to Martin," Chartwell promised. "If there is anything to talk about, I will contact you."

"I will not be at the university again tomorrow," Haddad stated. "I plan to be here all day."

"Very well," Chartwell replied, his suspicions raised to high alert. "I will see if he feels up to a visit with you tomorrow."

"You still don't believe me, do you, Mr. Chartwell?"

"I never have," Chartwell stated. "I've never believed a word that came out of your mouth." He closed the door with the click of the heavy iron latch.

Watching through the window as Chartwell's taxi drove away, Professor Haddad reached for his telephone.

"Melinda. Can you hear me? Turn the radio down. Listen for a moment. The trap is set. He took the bait. He is coming back tomorrow. With Martin Culver."

Hanging up the phone, Professor Haddad wheeled his chair to the library table around the corner. He retrieved a single photo from its cluttered surface. The first shot he ever took of Excalibur.

It was his sword. Except that *she* wanted to ruin everything. *She* would have it, to personally present Excalibur to the Jackal as a demonstration of her fealty and devotion to him.

No matter. Soon she would bring the companion to Excalibur for comparison. Soon he would have both swords, both suits, and he would have *her*. She would be completely his. It was only right, that he take his niece to be his own. That was the family way.

This land would become his kingdom now, as had been promised to he who could remove the sword, so many ages past. Stonehenge would be the center of his world, his palace. With the exo-suit, Excalibur by his side, Stonehenge for his throne, and Melinda for his queen, he would be invincible, feared and revered.

Chapter 42

Kentworth Estate
Amesbury, Wiltshire

Leaving the Professor's estate house, Chartwell's taxi rounded the corner leading into Amesbury proper at a reasonable speed, when the cabbie swerved to avoid a small, late-model convertible. The female driver of the car drove into their lane, then corrected her course. Chartwell glanced in the rear-view mirror but could not catch the license plate.

"She almost took my mirror off," the cabbie said.

Chartwell continued to look back.

"Keep your eyes on the road," he reminded the cabbie. "I think I know that woman," he thought. "She looked familiar."

"She's not from around here," the cabbie remarked. "Not with that car, she's not."

Chartwell pondered the wisdom of turning around. Perhaps she was going to see the Professor. There was little else down his road.

"Getting dark soon," the cabbie said, as if reading his mind. "Anywhere else you have to be?"

"No, I'll just head back to the hotel, thanks," Chartwell said, cracking open the last pint of beer. It was slightly warm, as he liked. "Tomorrow's another day."

High above the Atlantic, Director Hall tried to connect on the inflight communications setup to call Martin Culver. She needed to warn him about everything she had found out. From all indications, Culver was walking into a trap. The communications link on the plane was still down.

Hall hailed a passing flight attendant.

"Excuse me, can you tell me when the comm link will come back up?" Hall inquired. "I need to make a call."

"I will be glad to check for you, but normally the link is out when we are in the range of other commercial traffic. It happens again as we near our half way point of the flight. It sometimes depends on the position of the satellites as well."

"Okay, thank you," Hall said, irritated at the delay.

"My name is Lynette, should you need anything else. Would you care for a glass of wine to help you sleep?"

"Scotch," Hall said. "With ginger ale and a glass."

"Right away, ma'am. Any ice?"

"No ice. I love your accent, Lynette. Are you from Spain?"

"I used to be," the attendant replied. "Now I live in the skies."

Chapter 43

Ambassadors Hotel
London, England

Before noon the following day, Martin walked into the cafe to find Chartwell already half-finished with his meal.

"Chilly start this morning," he commented. "Trouble sleeping?"

"Yes, I kept getting blown up. That's terrible for the REM cycles," Chartwell quipped without putting down his paper. "No way to get comfortable wrapped up in all these bandages."

Martin looked for a waiter. "I thought I'd never wake up."

"How's Sandra?" Chartwell asked.

"She slept well, thanks to the pain medication. We went to bed hoping that yesterday was all a collective nightmare. Guess we were wrong."

"Here's your proof," Chartwell said, laying the front page across Martin's empty plate.

The article, complete with stunningly frank photos, showed the double decker bus with the front completely destroyed, the remainder riddled with a thousand nail-holes from a double IED. Passport and ID photos of those killed were shown in a thoroughly non-compassionate line-up.

"The bus driver, the driver assistant, nine passengers, including a honeymooning couple from the U.S., and Rebekah," Chartwell grumbled. "All dead. Everyone else on the bus, twenty persons, all injured to some degree. It's unacceptable."

"You seem tense," Martin observed, noting Chartwell's flushed appearance.

"You are damn right I'm tense. I'm mad as hell. This just isn't right, and I won't feel better until we make it right with whoever killed her. No sleep, no patience, and I hurt like hell. Damn right I'm tense."

"You're keeping check for fever?" Martin asked. "The nurse said infection could be a problem for any of us."

"No fever. Just a lump from the tetanus injection. I'm stiff as a board though. Movement is very limited across my back."

The waiter approached with a bottle of Kahlua.

"Another dose of medicine, Mr. Culver?"

"Not as much this time," Chartwell said, holding one index finger level with the rim of the mug.

Chartwell watched as the waiter poured coffee for Martin. When the waiter offered Kahlua, Martin held his hand over the cup to say no.

"Maybe it's not so good to drink with the medicine," Martin said.

"You're not my mother," Chartwell barked. "Get off my back."

Shifting gears, Martin decided to ease up and listen.

"Martin, I went to see Haddad yesterday. At his estate."

"You did? I thought you were in the pub. We missed you. We claimed Rebekah's body and saw to the proper arrangements for her. Kind of sudden but it all came together."

"Martin, I'm sorry, but I had to do something."

"It's okay. She is at rest, at peace with the world. We found where her Gram was buried. Rebekah was laid to rest with family."

Chartwell shook his head.

"I should have been there, Martin. But the thought that someone knew we were going to be on that bus yesterday and used that against us bothered the hell out of me. The fact that this information was used to kill Rebekah bothered me even worse."

"Sandra said she told Haddad about the bus plans two days ago at the Museum. I found out that the tickets were booked through a student venture connected with UCL, the Professor's university. And Haddad is the only person I know on faculty at UCL. So I went to his house and confronted him."

"What did you find out?"

"He denies it, of course. He felt that he was being unfairly accused, but everything about him seemed so insincere."

"Maybe he knows something, but he didn't actually do it."

"That is my thought too."

"Is there something else?"

"Yes. He says that he has found Excalibur, and that if I bring you, he will show it to us. Could be a deflective move. I doubt he actually has found it, but I read a translation of an old story about Stonehenge recently that jives with his story. The Book of Ballymote, contains three languages, including Old Norse and Ogham text."

"You mentioned that when we were at Stonehenge."

"Yes, he has been dropping teasing hints about this since before we left for London. I don't know what his game is, but I'm thinking there might be something to it."

"Or it might be a trap. You said there was bad blood between you. Now Rebekah has died, seemingly either at Haddad's hand or someone he is associated with. He wants us to walk into his web."

"Yes, you could be right," Chartwell said, pondering Martin's words.

"Then let's go," Martin said. "An element of danger never stopped us before, did it John?"

Chartwell was quiet.

"You know, Martin, I appreciate being back. I hope it means we are on better terms."

"What do you mean?"

"Don't get me wrong, I think you have always appreciated my knowledge. But I appreciate the acceptance into the IAF again."

Now it was Martin's time to reflect.

"John, you are a great asset to the IAF. I appreciate everything you have done. Now get us a cab while I check in with Sandra. I will tell her we are taking in a museum, so she won't worry."

As Martin stood up, he looked at his phone. It was 11:20AM. "That's funny," he said.

"What is it?" Chartwell asked as he signed the restaurant bill.

"It looks like Director Hall tried to call me last night. I had my phone on silent from where we were at the hospital."

Martin checked for a text, but had nothing new. They both walked toward the elevators.

"Better call her now," Chartwell advised. "There was no phone signal when we were at Stonehenge or the Professor's house yesterday."

"Hall said she would call with any updates," he said aloud. "I have to grab something from the room, just in case."

"I'll meet you out front," Chartwell said. "Grab a coat, too! That breeze is cold!"

The roads were quiet as the cab drove into the small town of Amesbury. No one was out of doors. The day had a definite chill, hinted at by the frost on the taxi windows, confirmed by the

251

chimneys of every estate and cottage sending up plumes of light smoke.

"So is all of this area a historical site?" Martin asked.

"For miles around," Chartwell replied. "As far as you can see."

"Taken all together, this entire area forms a UNESCO World Heritage Site called "Stonehenge, Avebury and Associated Sites". It's huge, covering hundreds of stone circles over thousands of hectares."

No more had Chartwell said it until they passed a sign that passed boasted Amesbury's claim to fame. It read:

"Historic Amesbury, Home to Stonehenge.
Britain's oldest continuous settlement."

"So I'm trying to not get confused," Martin admitted. "Amesbury is the parish town where Stonehenge is located, right?" Martin asked. "And Avebury is another stone circle site, like Stonehenge but separate?"

"Exactly," Chartwell replied.

"There's his house, Kentworth Estate. That's where he lives," Chartwell said, pointing to help the cabbie.

"Hopefully Haddad will be home today," Martin commented.

"He told me he would be home all day," Chartwell said.

Hall did not remember the plane landing, but once she was awake, she realized how bad her head hurt. She looked around to find the plane half-empty, blankets and pillows strewn about by her fellow passengers, who appeared to have evacuated due to some emergency.

Hall tried to stand, feeling wobbly at the knees. Her ribs and hip did not hurt for the first time in months. It was then that she knew she had been drugged.

"Hey," she called to the front of the plane, her hands pressed hard into the headrests to steady her movement. "Attendant."

A male flight attendant smiled and walked her way.

"Awake now?" he asked in a sing-song voice. "You're *quite* the sleepy head."

"Where is Lynette? The other flight attendant?"

"Girlfriend, don't tell me you are looking for Lynette too? She is so *popular*."

"What do you mean?"

"Someone was here to pick her up as soon as the wheels touched down. I got the feeling that they were close, if you know what I mean."

"No, I don't know what you mean. Where is my bag?" she asked.

"Here, let me help you," the attendant gushed. "You seem a little out of it, honey."

Hall listened to his lilting voice, realizing the echo of his words came from whatever drug she had been given.

"I need to get off the plane," Hall said, feeling flushed.

"Yeah you don't look so good," the attendant replied. "I just got through cleaning these bathrooms, so let's get you into the terminal, pronto."

Hall looked around as she wobbled towards the plane door. She felt as if the world was tilting to one side. The attendant walked with her as far as the ramp before leaving.

"Sit down for a minute, honey. Take a minute to get your land legs back." Extending his hand at an odd angle, the attendant continued. "I'm Val, if you need anything else. We won't be leaving for another hour." Then he did the smile again.

"Thank you, Val." Hall did a quick check for her phone and wallet. She checked her pistol and its permit. Dialing up, she attempted to call Martin Culver. The call went to voice mail.

Switching to another page of contacts, Hall punched the third number down on her list.

"Stoner, yes it's Hall. Listen, I need some help. I am trying to get to Culver and his team to warn them about Medina and the Professor. Do me a favor and get them some help. No, I'm not ok. I think I've been drugged. I can function but every step is a battle."

"Ok, I'm trusting you to handle this. Get me some coordinates on the Professor's usual locations, his office at UCL, his home. If you can locate him, that would help too. Ok, thanks."

Hall pushed back against a wave of dizziness, then swiped across her screen to close her phone.

"Excuse me," she asked the nearest Heathrow hostess. "Can you direct me to the rental car area?"

"New to the airport?" the hostess asked cheerily. "The car hire stand is just down this corridor, with car rentals immediately past. You can't miss it."

"Thanks," Hall remembered saying, just before she stumbled, her feet uncooperative, seeming to be detached from her body.

Chapter 44

Chartwell exited the taxi as soon as the wheels stopped rolling, leaving Martin to take care of the bill.

"I don't know how long we'll be," Martin told the driver. "Can we call you when we're finished?"

"Sure thing. I will be between here and the next town, to see if I can snag a fare. Give me a buzz, if I'm free I'll come back, if not, I will send out one of my buddies."

"Keep an eye on the sky," the cabbie advised. "They are actually calling for heavy weather, including the possibility of thunder snow tonight. The weather has been crazy, but snow before Thanksgiving is totally bonkers."

"Thanks," Martin said. He turned to find Chartwell pounding on the front door.

"Door chime not working?" Martin asked.

"That's not the half of it. The door was standing wide open when we drove up, just like the other day. That's why I got out so quickly. That's not normal to leave a door wide open on a chilly day like today. Then as I walked up, the door slammed shut and now it's locked."

Martin walked to the side of the house.

"Who do all these cars belong to?"

"That one's a rental, I can tell by the tags," Chartwell said. "The van is the Professors because of the wheelchair lift. Oh and here we have the AMG. It's the latest model, the SL63. This is the car that almost ran my cab off the road yesterday."

"What kind of a car is AMG?" Martin asked. "I've never heard of it."

"AMG is the racing division of Mercedes-Benz," Chartwell answered. "The SL63 is a cool $150,000 US."

"Sweet," Martin commented. "But I thought you said it was a convertible."

"These have a power retractable hardtop. Looks just like a coupe when you have the roof in place."

"So where is everyone? The place seems empty."

At that moment they both heard the sound of breaking glass on the side patio.

"Hey, what gives?" Martin asked. As he rounded the corner of the building, pistol shots rang out, fired at him by a single gunman.

Martin dropped to one knee, brought his pistol around, leveled it at the intruder's head, and pulled the trigger twice. He wasted the second .45 caliber round. The man was dead with the first shot.

"Martin, where did you learn to shoot like that?"

Martin put his index finger to his lips, motioning Chartwell to stay behind him.

"Where did you get a pistol *in Britain*?" Chartwell whispered hoarsely.

"My hotel room," Martin replied, holding the barrel upright as he attempted to peer around the corner.

Stepping over the dead body, Martin retrieved the intruder's pistol and handed it to Chartwell. Chartwell confirmed a nearly full clip. As they reached the back of the house, Martin pointed.

Through a line of trees, a helicopter could be seen. Four men were on their way to it, practically running, carrying what looked like an Egyptian sarcophagus.

Martin raised his pistol, but did not get off a shot before bullets began raining down against the bricks where he was standing. He turned and pushed Chartwell down to get them both out of the way.

Martin waited for the withering fire to slacken.

"We can't go that way," he remarked. The bullets continued to chew away at the brick at the corner of the house.

Chartwell backed up, with Martin crouching behind him. Together they went to the front door. Chartwell walked right to the door and stood at an angle, blasting the door latch from the door.

"Anyone home?" Martin shouted, entering the foyer.

Chartwell moved from room to room, reaching the library, where he examined the suits of armor, the swords, and other artifacts with an expert eye.

"Where is everyone?" Martin asked. "This is creepy."

"Look at this table Martin. I saw this yesterday. Photos of you and I, and apparently of everyone on the Professor's bad list."

"That picture is Melinda Medina, when she was younger."

"Why is she undressed and all tied up with bandages?" Martin asked.

"The Professor is a pervert, like I've been saying," Chartwell said.

"So what is really going on here?"

"We saw those men taking the sarcophagus. Seems we walked in on a robbery," Chartwell said.

Feeling a cold draft of air, Chartwell noticed Egyptian artifacts through an adjoining door. He peered in to see a tall statue of the jackal-god Osiris. Near that, a shapely female mummy stood against the far wall beneath twin beams of recessed lighting. The mummy wrappings showed brilliant white beneath the intense lights. Beyond the other statues were more mummies, eleven in all.

"What are you looking at?" he asked Chartwell.

"That mummy, the well-endowed one."

"What about it?" Martin asked.

"Totally a fake. Nothing authentic about it," Chartwell pronounced, "although great pains have been taken to make it authentic."

"Do you mean that this is a new mummy?"

"Recent," Chartwell said confidently. "I can still smell the spice mixture in the linen."

"Wait," Martin interjected. "If the mummy is recent, where did the body come from?"

"A very good question," Chartwell stated, observing the mummy from a safe distance. "Someone lost their life to make this little decoration. My guess would be the young woman whose vacancy Rebekah was intended to fill."

"Let's find the Professor. He may have some answers."

"I've found the Professor's wheel chair," Chartwell said. "He's not in it."

"I found him," Martin called out. "He's in the doorway between the library and the sun room. He's still breathing, but I think he's in shock."

Chartwell knelt down to check.

"He's been shocked, you mean. Look at the burn marks on both sides of his neck. He has been electrocuted. It looks like systematic torture."

The helicopter still had not lifted off, the rotor throb so familiar to Martin, having recently been rescued in a similar one.

"They're waiting for someone else, or something else," Chartwell said, reading the expression on Martin's face. "Maybe they're waiting for the Professor."

"I'm not getting into another firefight over a sarcophagus," Martin said.

"We should get him some help," Martin said.

"I'd be fine with leaving him to die right here," Chartwell said.

"Stop it, John. Get me a pillow or something."

Martin reached for his phone. A slight buzz made him check the screen.

"Hall tried to call me again."

"What is this he's wearing?" Chartwell asked.

"It looks like an exo-suit, a really refined version," Martin said. "I saw some like it at Bethesda."

"Loosen the collar, can you? I think it unsnaps."

A whirring noise coming from the corridor to the kitchen distracted Martin from what Chartwell was trying to say. The walls shook to the whining rhythm of a freight elevator.

When the noise stopped, Melinda Medina opened the pantry door and walked into the corridor, having no idea anyone else was in the house. She turned to see Martin and Chartwell raise their pistols before leaping back, slamming the pantry door closed.

Martin heard the sound of a different whine, high-pitched, like a dentist drill. He heard a voice over a radio, then the sound of the helicopter lifting into the afternoon air. A light glowed beneath the pantry door shortly before the door burst into splinters to a blinding light.

Martin began blindly firing. He saw Medina move into the corridor with a sword whose honed surface danced with electrical surges. Blue bands of pale light emanated from her partially gloved hands, moving toward the tip of the sword. The bullets he fired hit the walls on either side of her body, encased as it was from the neck down in a female version of the Professor's exo-suit that hugged her every curve, leaving little to the imagination.

Chartwell aimed low, apparently connecting a shot. A howl preceded Melinda abruptly turning and launching herself back into the pantry. A nub of skin with red polish lay against the baseboard.

When the rhythmic motors started to turn again, Martin ran to the pantry door. Looking inside, he saw a gaping hole where an elevator had disappeared.

He walked back into the library.

"You shot off her little toe, Chartwell!" Martin exclaimed. "Now that's good shooting."

"Yeah, but I've been trained," Chartwell said. "Who taught you to shoot?"

"I had a lot of time learning to aim stuck on that island," Martin admitted. "Then Hall set up lessons for me at the local Shooting Academy."

"Help me," they heard a man's voice faintly call. They ran to the Professor.

"He's trying to speak," Chartwell said. "Listen."

Haddad's blackened lips were dry and split. He took a deep breath and closed his eyes. Then his eyes popped wide open again.

"What is it, Professor?" Martin asked.

"Melinda came last night. She knows that the sword can be powered by the exo-suit. She forced me to tell her."

"She tortured you?"

"All night until I gave her the suit. She did not get the sword."

"What sword?"

"The greatest sword of all time, *Ish-kalabar*," the Professor said.

"The girl who just left, the Medina girl, does she have the sword?" Martin said.

The Professor coughed. "No, she has the evil twin to Excalibur. She brought it to compare to Excalibur. Ish-kalabar is still here," the Professor groaned. "Look there, on the display wall. I brought it from its hiding place, but I did not tell her. She must not possess both swords."

Chartwell drifted over to the display wall.

"Melinda has the evil sword, the original, the one the Prophet used to impose Islam on half the known world."

"Melinda killed your friend with a bomb. She admitted it to me. Did you find your other friend?" the Professor gasped. "The one from Washington, DC?"

"Who are you talking about?"

259

"Your CIA friend. She came here. Soon as she walked in, Melinda grabbed her by the neck, stunning her. She fell to the floor so fast. The men carried her out in the sarcophagus."

"Director Hall was here, in this house? Is she dead?"

"They took her away," the Professor said, closing his eyes.

"Why Professor? Where did they take her?"

The Professor did not respond.

"He's gone," Chartwell said. "And I'm out of cartridges."

"So it was more than a robbery," Martin said, checking his pistol. "I'm empty, too." he said, stuffing the pistol into the back of his belt. "The what does Melinda Medina still want here?"

"I don't know, but we have to find her. Melinda Medina may be the only one who knows where Hall is now."

The sound of breaking glass and wood stopped him in mid-sentence.

Chapter 45

"Someone crashed through the Egyptian room, through the window," Chartwell shouted.

A blast of cold air blew across the tile floor from the direction of the sunroom. The Professor's body lay at the entrance to the library.

Martin walked to the door of the sunroom, but saw no one. The room was expansive, filled with Egyptian statues, topped by a high ceiling of glass. There was no door, but one panel of glass was broken out.

"Who's there?" Martin called. He carefully pulled aside the drapes to look outside. It was getting dark outside.

Chartwell looked out the window toward Stonehenge.

"Why are the lights at Stonehenge still on this late?" Martin asked. "I can see them from here. We are at least a mile away. Wait, there's Melinda, running toward Stonehenge."

"With winter solstice in a few weeks, they always test out the Stonehenge lighting to prepare for the annual night show," Chartwell said.

Martin tugged the drapes back to get a better look at the clouds gathering on the horizon. "I am going after her."

"Martin, this sword that she has, A'ish-kalabar. The 'A' " prefix means "not". It is the opposite of Excalibur. It is the ancient Sword of Brokenness, used by the Prophet to rule with an iron hand. Both swords were forged by the same maker. Think of Melinda's sword as Excalibur's evil twin."

He grabbed Martin by the sleeve.

"Take Excalibur. It was forged to counter evil."

"Do you believe it's really Excalibur, John?" Martin asked.

Chartwell reached up, grasped the handle of the sword and reverently removed it from the display rack. He handed the sword to Martin. Chartwell seemed barely able to stretch or move, as he wiped sweat from his forehead.

"You can feel the good in it, can't you?" Chartwell asked. "It can feel the good in you."

Martin wielded the sword, feeling its weight as he twirled it several times in his strong right hand.

"Chartwell, she has to be stopped."

"Excalibur can only be wielded by someone good, someone pure of heart," Chartwell urged. "If ever anyone qualified, Martin, that is you through and through."

"It was your childhood dream, to find Excalibur. You take it, finish her."

"I can't Martin. I can barely move my arms. You have to do this, or she'll get away." Chartwell pushed the sword back to Martin with both hands.

Martin took Excalibur. He closed his eyes, bringing the hilt of the sword in front of his face. He prayed out loud the Psalm that he had read on the island.

Martin opened his eyes and turned, walking out of the house purposefully, into the darkness toward the stormy Salisbury Plain. He tugged the raincoat on over his sweater. His shoes were slick against the damp stones. He turned up his coat collar, greeted by a mix of snow and rain. A bolt of lightning outlined the Stonehenge silhouette in the distance, illuminating a sweeping band of precipitation advancing across the flat terrain in brilliant display. From where he stood, Martin could see Melinda well ahead of him, also striding powerfully across the plain.

Martin ran through the open courtyard past the vehicles. As he cleared the court-yard and rounded the last high hedge, Martin felt his boot catch on a taut string stretched across the end of the driveway. He was surprised to hear the sound of a tractor motor chug to life just beyond one of the garden outbuildings. The headlights of the machine, mounted on top, lit up the area like daylight, momentarily blinding him. Before he could think, the lights came roaring across the lawn in his direction. Martin turned to run, then thought better and ran 90 degrees to the direction of the on-coming tractor. He rounded another hedge, turned and ran along it to put as much distance between himself and the tractor as possible, running in the narrow space between the house and the vehicles in the courtyard. The machine was systematically clipping the passenger side mirrors from each vehicle it passed, ripping them off with a screeching metallic grind. It wasn't long until the thrashing lights of the tractor caught up to him, swinging wildly to the left and the right. He glanced over his shoulder, realizing that the tractor had hit the hedge and was pulverizing it into the ground.

Seeing no alternative, Martin took a running leap, planted the sword, and vaulted across the waist-high hedge onto the hood of the convertible Melinda had been seen driving. He slammed down hard on the vehicle and rolled off, falling onto the courtyard paver stones. He scrambled to his feet. He wanted to see his adversary.

Martin looked up as the tractor passed him, shocked to see that the cab of the tractor was empty. No one was driving. A blinking remote control device guided the steering wheel. The tractor continued on its wild, destructive journey, plowing the remainder of the hedge flat before slamming into the garden outbuilding. Martin ducked down as the resulting explosion ripped the wood-framed building to sticks, fueled by the diesel tanks of the tractor and petrol cans stored in the small building.

Pieces of smoking wood clattered to the pavement and across the vehicles as Martin stood to his feet.

"Are you all right?" Chartwell called from the door.

"I'm going after Melinda!" he shouted. "Slight delay!"

"Well, what's keeping you?" Chartwell shouted back. "I've rung up the police. They're on the way!"

Chapter 46

As he rounded the bullet-chewed brick corner of the estate house, Martin looked past meticulous gardens through the sparse trees toward Stonehenge. He could see the joint-flashes of Melinda's black exo-suit through ground fog, even against the night lighting of Stonehenge itself. He took off running, trying to hold the sword he was carrying a safe distance from his body. The sword seemed ten times heavier holding it this way, as if the movement gave it life.

His mind raced, calculating a plan of action for when he caught up to Melinda. He tried to think what Hall would do. Of course, he would confront his opponent, and detain her until help arrived. What he did not doubt was his resolve to kill her, if necessary, to stop her once and for all. Someone had to. At the moment, it seemed, there was no one else to stop her.

Martin ran, a steady constant pace that moved the lower half of his body but created very little movement above the waist, save the flapping of black coattails behind him. His anger had cooled, galvanizing into a cold, hard shell that freed him to think only of Melinda's destruction. He blamed Melinda for Rebekah's death, for Hall getting involved, for everything that had gone wrong. He resolved to settle the score with her himself. Martin focused and continued on.

He regulated his breath as he closed the final yards leading to the great stones of the Stonehenge site. He felt hot sweat mixed with cold rain running down his neck, his heart racing faster, yet he did not feel out of breath. He slowed to a trot, trying to see Melinda in the gathering ground fog that lay low across the plain.

He narrowed down the options to a certain set of columns that glowed with the unusual blue glow of the exo-suit. It was at that moment that Melinda slowly stepped from behind one of the sarsen-stone columns of the great Stonehenge circle, sword raised as if expecting him, eyes lowered and glaring. Blonde hair pushed out from beneath a light fabric hood that covered her head. Martin was surprised to see that Melinda's hair color had changed.

"So you came all the way out here to bring me Ish-kalabar? Are you here to stop me or to join me?" Melinda taunted in an evil, song-like voice, as if she were trying to mesmerize him.

"You've changed your hair," he noticed.

"I'm changing my look to travel more freely," she replied. "The humidity is giving me a bad hair day, don't you agree?"

"The answer is, I'm not here to join you. I'm here to stop you."

Melinda stepped toward him, limping slightly. She pulled back her hood, exposing a full head of wild blonde hair. "You, Mr. Culver, will only come out of this alive if you make the right choice."

She threw off her coat, wearing only the body-hugging black exo-suit and black leather knee boots. The joints of the exo-suit blazed blue. The toe of one boot had been stuffed with a bloody piece of cloth at the toes.

Unzipping the front of the form-fitting exo-suit to a distracting level, she sighed.

"That's cooler. I told Uncle he designed the neckline too high on these suits," she stated, pushing a damp lock of hair away from her face. "But I do like how it buzzes against my skin."

Smiling, she stepped a circle around him.

"Your friends left you," Martin said. "The helicopter is gone."

"Oh, they'll be back. I told them I wanted to have some fun, to try out this suit, test its limits. I thought we could play a little bit."

Martin stayed focused on her eyes.

"You realize that if you challenge me," she said, "cutting into this suit will electrocute us both," Melinda laughed. "That will make things more intense."

"I understand the properties of the suit," Martin shouted. "I understand that it has batteries powered by the activity and heat of your movements, batteries that store that kinetic energy and give you back tremendous gains in physical strength and stamina."

"Then you must know that you cannot defeat me, not with that sword anyway. Even bullets would be of little use because of the Kevlar woven into the fabric. "

Martin approached closer, circling to the right.

"So you *are* foolish," Melinda said, belittling Martin's intentions. "Or naïve, and yet they call you an assassin. How do you expect to win?"

Martin did not answer, watching her as warily as he watched the sky behind her. Lightning flashed from cloud to cloud, building in intensity moment by moment. He raised his sword to strike from overhead.

"I am no assassin. You are the killer!"

"There is not one *drachma* of difference between us," Melinda said. "We both do what we do for money."

"No, that's wrong!" Martin responded. "I do what I do to stop vultures like you!"

Feeling his anger grow, Martin recognized he was about to lose control. Focusing on the sword, Martin lunged at her with all his might, drawing his blade up and over his head before bringing it down with enough force to cleave stone. Excalibur seemed to gain weight on the downward stroke.

Melinda raised her sword over her head and lateral to the wet ground. Their swords, like the skies, danced with electricity. Martin repeated his strike and moved closer to her.

"You are thoroughly unpolished," she grinned. "Your CIA master has not completed your training. Too bad because I have her now."

"Where has Director Hall been taken?" Martin shouted.

"Hall is in good hands. Eight of them to be exact. When she wakes up she will be headed home." Feeling drops of rain falling into her cleavage, Melinda glanced down to her exposed chest, then back at him from beneath her heavily painted eyelids. "I could teach you a thing or two, if properly motivated," she said.

"You are the last woman in the world I would ask to teach me anything," Martin stated. He then moved to bring his sword at her from the side. Melinda expertly stepped to one side and raised her sword in defense with a single, practiced move. Sparks flew as she stepped aside.

Lightning hit the ground just outside the trench surrounding Stonehenge, causing them both to cringe slightly. An intense ozone release cleared the air of every odor of sweat, of leather, of blood.

"With every movement I grow stronger," she mocked. "Each move you make leaves you weaker."

Martin noticed his injured hand was cramping. He changed his grip and continued to look for an opening.

"What style are you using?" he asked. "You are a rudimentary swordsman at best."

"All in due time, Mr. Culver. You have only seen me employ the most basic of defensive moves. When I eventually tire of toying with you, you will have ample opportunity to observe my skills."

Melinda forced a lunge in Martin's direction, causing him to sidestep her blade. He fended her off with a resounding blow of his against hers that reverberated oddly among the great stone uprights, as if someone were hammering on sheet metal. Again sparks lit up the darkness.

"What style are you using?" Melinda asked, sounding breathless. "I don't seem to recognize it."

"I have studied Japanese swordsmanship, and I have modified it to make it my own," Martin declared. "I have killed a half-dozen men and I won't hesitate to kill you, if it comes to that."

"I know what you want," she teased. "You want to run me through with your weapon, to punish me for all the things I've done. Then you want to finish me with that sword."

"What have you done that deserves punishment, Melinda? Tell me everything," Martin countered, dismissing her taunts as he moved, circling her for an attack vantage point.

"Well, I have been busy a busy girl since being back in London. First your friend Rebekah, and then my uncle, who deserved to die more than anyone I know, if not for atrocities against me, for defiance of the leader of our organization."

"Who gave the order, *hashashin*? Who paid your fee?"

"For Rebekah or for my uncle? Rebekah was on my own account, to hurt someone you love, to destroy your people the way you have destroyed my family."

"And the Professor?"

"That was an assignment from the man I work for. You do know who I work for don't you?"

Melinda lunged at him with snake-like reflexes, before realizing that she had over-committed and was off-balance. Martin brought his sword wildly around and down, forcing her blade point into the ground. Sparks flew, and Martin tasted fire.

"Who do you work for?" Martin asked, holding her sword stationary. He blinked rapidly to clear the flash from his eyes.

"I'll never tell you. You can't make me," she shouted defiantly.

He stepped back, bringing his sword up under hers in an attempt to gut her from bottom to top. She leaned sharply away, arching her back to escape the point of his blade.

"If you insist. I work for the Jackal."

"Some two-bit criminal in Istanbul?" Martin mocked.

"I'm surprised you haven't heard of him," Melinda said breathlessly. "You work for his daughter."

Catching the point of his sword in the material of her suit just above the buckle of her belt, Martin felt a surge of electricity pass into his sword. He heard the hiss of her sweat drops on his blade turn instantly into steam. He forced Excalibur upward as she dodged his lunge, his blade grazing her flat stomach as it forced through the fabric above her belt, separating the elastic material of her exo-suit with a satisfying ripping sound. Melinda stumbled but did not fall.

At the same moment, Martin's sword shot back and away from him due to the electrical surge. His arm went numb and gave off steam for several seconds.

"Carter Hall? Her father was killed years ago."

"You know nothing, Martin Culver. You are a liar believing a lie."

"You are the liar!" Martin shouted, mounting another attack. "You are evil, your sword is evil. *You* are hashashin!"

Martin wielded Excalibur with both hands, first up, then down, forming a figure eight motion that Melinda was unable to penetrate with her sword.

Melinda stepped back as Martin began to advance, raising her sword to defend against Martin's sudden flurry of strokes, sparks flying, his fury overtaking his judgment as he advanced steadily, forcing her to step back. Raising her sword in defense, Melinda felt the whirling Excalibur make contact with her sword like a whirring fan threatening to mow her down. Multiple impacts rang out across the plains, the sparks lighting up her face and nearly igniting her hair before she lost her grip on A'ish-kalabar.

Melinda snarled as she fell backward to the wet ground. Her suit was now split open from her navel to her neck, her belt all but falling off. She scrambled to her feet, cursing Martin's name as she attempted to hold closed the top half of the exo-suit.

"Lucky stroke, Martin Culver. Or else you missed. No matter, there are more suits. I shipped 500 to my boss on the same helicopter that is coming back for me. After I finish you I will burn this suit, along with your bones."

"The way your ISIS buddies roast their victims?"

"I am no heathen, Martin Culver, nor am I an ISIS convert. I am a woman of style and taste. I do, however, love ISIS money as well as the next woman."

"You're bleeding," he said, taking immediate advantage of her downward glance down to lunge toward her again. Her wild defensive stroke connected hard with his sword, knocking it from his hand and to the ground on his right. She stood defiant, blocking him from retrieving Excalibur.

Martin stepped back to put some distance between himself and her intentions. He ducked behind the stone uprights and waited. His arms ached. They were as heavy as lead. He watched for her approach.

Given away by the glow of her suit, Martin threw one arm around Melinda's neck, slammed her head against the rough surface of the upright sarsen stone, forcing her to drop her sword. She was sweaty and slippery, making it hard to maintain a grip. He could feel her damp exo-suit buzzing against his skin, the peculiar feeling she had described as pleasing.

Melinda reached her partially-gloved hands up and grabbed Martin behind both ears, unleashing jolts of powerful current beneath his scalp, searing his skin beneath the hearing devices. He broke her hold, slamming her to the ground, then scrambled back to where he dropped his sword, unable to find hers in the dark.

Chapter 47

Stonehenge
Wiltshire, England

Resounding metal clanged together in the night, the sound carrying across the Salisbury Plain, timeless echoes of another age. Hellish blue sparks flared with every strike from sword blades perfectly matched, perfectly deadly in their intent and purpose. Stray blows that fell against the brooding upright stone columns gave off sparks of silver and red.

Rain gathered in intensity to the North, hanging below the scudding clouds like ragged curtains in the windows of some ancient castle, pushed aloft by an intense, stiff breeze. Flakes of snow began to mix in. As the snow began, a rumble of thunder shook the ground.

Martin found the worst aspect of this modern battle with ancient weapons not to be the jarring impacts, which were painful enough, but the effects on his hearing, and specifically on his hearing devices. The sound of metal clashing against metal was unnerving. Every ringing blow vibrated his skull until his jawbone began to buzz.

Melinda powerfully thrust her blade past Martin's arm, slicing the sleeve of his coat, reminding him to pay attention. He stepped to the side, bringing his sword up to defend. Sparks exploded hot against his face as the two blades met again. Blinking back the light flash, Martin pushed up and away, freeing himself from her attack. Anticipating the Medina girl's next move, Martin turned and brought his sword up behind him, fending off her next parry. His foot did not slip on the wet grass. Martin swung Excalibur toward his opponent's neck, only to have his blade forced up and away.

Turning, Melinda brought the pommel of her sword against Martin's lower back, striking a jarring blow just above his left kidney. The sword fight continued, peals of death-dealing metal clashing against metal as each fended off bone-jolting hits.

Martin tried to catch his breath while maintaining his balance and his focus. He felt outmatched, once again forced to fight against impossible odds. Perhaps this is always how it would be, trouble around every turn, everything hingeing on the win.

Martin's mind clarified with each ringing sword collision, the stakes ever more certain. He had to take out Melinda, or be taken out himself. He knew that victory for his adversary would be a loss for mankind everywhere. Once the exo-suits were distributed and mass produced, there would be no end to the turmoil. A new age of evil would reign supreme.

Tapping into his anger, Martin swung Excalibur wide. He managed to knock Medina's sword out of her hand and into the deep grass beyond. As she scrambled hands and knees to retrieve it, he reached behind his ears and pulled off his hearing devices, jamming them into his jacket pocket. His world went silent. It was a world he had come to prefer.

Martin felt renewed, instantly freed from the distracting sounds of the sword-strikes. He focused more intently and paced himself. He began to sweat despite the cold, but it was not clear to him if his sweat was from effort or from fear.

He fought with every ounce of strength, according to all that he knew. His physical condition and energy were also working in his favor. So far he was not even out of breath.

Melinda's youth, her training and her determination were her strong points, not her strength or her skill, he calculated. Still, he was holding his own.

As the epic battle continued, Martin looked skyward to see clouds circling above the Great Stone Circle. Lightning struck at will on all sides. Inside the ring of stones, they seemed to be protected.

Martin listened, thinking he felt the rumble of thunder, sword held high, guarding against Medina's next attack. His hair stood on end, and then the lightning struck.

Two bolts of lightning descended from the sky, while between them, a circle of lightning revolved, directly over the Great Stones. Snow swirled within the circle, creating a surreal weather pattern reported in legend, but unmatched in reality anywhere in the world.

As he looked at the unusual weather phenomenon, Martin could see parachutists dropping from the sky, wheeling around and down. Each had a flare attached to their boot. There were at least a dozen that he could count. He hoped they were here to help him. He would be glad to have some backup.

The smack of metal flat against the side of his head brought him back from distraction. Medina had slapped him with the side of her blade in an unguarded moment. The slight smell of seared flesh registered as he turned to face her directly.

"I wanted to see what this suit can do," she said. "I am impressed. Plus, the more I move, the bigger thrill I get."

"You should see a tailor," Martin mocked. "Aren't you cold?"

"I am not worried about exposure. I am burning up, it's cooler this way. All this talk and no action means I need to use more energy. I will kill you in this outfit or out of it, but make no mistake, you will die!"

Medina charged Martin unannounced, wielding her sword ahead of her. She connected with Excalibur, sending a wave of current through both swords until Martin could no longer hold on. Falling away, Martin let go of Excalibur, and so did she. As Excalibur hit the ground, Medina fell toward Martin.

The torn top of her exo-suit fell open as she used both hands to brace her fall. Martin rolled away across the ground to the nearest stone column, where he scrambled to get his feet beneath him.

Medina stood to her feet, a double threat now possessing both swords. Her eyes lowered, her face glaring, she was taken over by rage, by adrenalin, by surging electrical current. Her body twitched uncontrollably as she absorbed one jolting shock after another.

Martin stood between two of the tallest sarsen stones, beneath one of the massive lintels. Careful observation quickly taught Martin exactly what to do. He had to wait, for the right time, the right moment. There was no winning against Medina as long as she held both swords. He understood that now.

Standing his ground, he watched the skies, counting to himself. He began to talk in an effort to distract her.

"You will never win, Melinda!"

"I have already won, Mr. Martin Culver. And this time, I won't leave my work to others. I will kill you myself."

Raising Ish-kalabar and A'ish-kalabar to the heavens, Medina once more claimed her victory.

"I am the victor now, I am the one who holds the balance, the keys to good and to evil," she shouted. With both swords raised, blonde hair damp and matted to her face from exertion, Medina looked down. She smiled a slightly evil smile on the realization she was spilling out of her torn top.

"Enjoying the show, Martin Culver?" she taunted. "Come over here, I will show you a finale you will never forget!"

Martin felt the hair on his neck stand up, but he did not run. At that moment lightning struck again. He stood his ground, framed by the sarsen stones.

The ground shook in the intense brightness, as the earth seemed to rise up in small clumps around Medina's booted feet. Electricity surged from the ground up into her body, causing her to quiver and to shake with urgent intensity. She threw her head back and tried to scream as the current surged up her body, causing every hair to stand erect, her head surrounded by a writhing halo. The bolt split in two and ran along her arms, leaping back into the sky at the end of each sword, Ish-kalabar in her right hand, A'ish-kalabar in her left.

Melinda's legs began to tremble, her lips moving, her voice a shudder of incoherencies as her eyes rolled back into her head. Her utterances merged into an unholy hiss as the untold voltage passed through her body. With stomach muscles convulsed in the throes of electrocution, her breasts heaved as she hung suspended, manipulated by the lightning, grounded to the earth through the hole in her boot, pulled toward heaven by the swords.

And then it was over. The lightning retreated, thunder rolling deep across the chalky plain surrounding Stonehenge. Snow fell thick following the thunder, as Medina's body crumpled to the ground.

Martin was surprised to find himself intact, standing only a few meters from where Medina lay dead. No doubt the great stones had insulated him or deflected the charge in some way. Perhaps the ancients knew this as well.

Medina's body lay face down, her exo-suit in tatters, her boots and hair still smoking, the hissing sound fading with the rising steam.

"It's over," Martin said to the soldiers, recoiling from the sound of his own voice. It was as if he were shouting. His ears popped as if he were descending from high altitude.

Beyond the stone uprights, Martin could see a heavily armed British soldier standing in every opening. He realized that he could hear sirens in the distance, the crunch of soldier's boots on the accumulated snow, the multiple clicks as they snapped their weapons into safety status.

Something in the electrical surge had changed his ability to hear. Perhaps it was simply time. Or perhaps his ears were healed due to something else entirely. Martin looked around. He saw a column of mist or smoke that had the appearance of a man with a beard, but it disappeared as quickly as he had seen the vision, if you could call it that.

Martin leaned down to retrieve the two swords, still warm from the recent electrical surge.

"You won't be needing these," Martin said to Melinda Medina's smoking remains. "And you were right. That was quite a show, a finale I will never forget."

Chapter 48

Kentworth Estate
Amesbury, Wiltshire

A stiff breeze whipped across the sectioned driveway, pushing light snow toward the southwest corner of each massive concrete square. Martin Culver did not flinch as snowflakes fell down his neck, coating the ancient trees rising high above him. The effect was cooling and welcome.

The British police had arrived, taking statements and cordoning off the areas of evidence. They had used up all the crime scene tape they carried. It had not been enough.

Chartwell watched as Martin handed over Excalibur and A'ish-kalabar to Captain Hargrove. As the MPS officer in charge of the investigation, he immediately carried the legendary swords to a waiting armored transport vehicle.

"Where are they taking the swords?" Martin asked Chartwell.

"To the vault with the Crown Jewels in the Tower of London, I would imagine," Chartwell speculated. "So what happened out there?" he asked.

"We dueled with the swords," Martin said simply. "I held my own, but nature decided to give me a hand. Good and evil has been balanced. Oh, and I may have caught a glimpse of Merlin or Myrddin as you called him."

"That was the hand of God, man. She was evil as they come."

"Did you find anything else in the house, before the police came?" Martin asked.

"I did," Chartwell said, slipping his hand out of his trouser pocket toward Martin. "Check this out."

"What is it?" Martin asked. "Your phone?"

"Not my phone, Martin. Her phone. Medina's phone. I found it beside a pile of her clothes. Apparently, when she changed into the exo-suit, the phone wouldn't fit. Or maybe a phone won't work with that much electrical current."

"This could be major," Martin said. "But it's evidence. We shouldn't take it. We can't take it."

"Martin, think about it. What happens to evidence? A year from now some barrister will pull that out of the evidence locker and the battery will be dead and everything it contained will be worthless or changed. Keep it, Martin. Use it."

Martin's phone rang. He did not recognize the U.S. number.

"Martin Culver speaking. Hello?"

"Can you hear me, Mr. Culver? This is Stoner from Director Hall's office. It's urgent that we speak. I hope I am not disturbing you."

"It's ten o'clock at night. I've just finished an exhausting sword duel, but other than that…"

"I don't have time, Mr. Culver. It's two in the morning here. Director Hall has been kidnapped. Have you seen her?"

"What? No, she hasn't been here since we arrived."

"Yes, she was. She was taken away from there by Medina's henchmen minutes ago. She tried to call you. She is on a helicopter that we are trying to intercept."

"How do you know all this?"

"She has her phone and has been drugged and maybe hit with a stun gun. They have her in some kind of box. She is sending me coded texts and location updates."

"Not a stun-gun," he corrected. "An exo-suit charge."

"Spare me the details, we've no time to lose," she interrupted. "Are you in a position to help me if needed?"

"Yes, just get me a way out of here. I might have to answer some questions first."

"Why?"

"I just witnessed Melinda Medina's death by electrocution. The Professor is dead. I am armed and I shot one of their bad guys. There will be questions."

"Good work, Culver, the fewer bad guys to worry about the better. Now listen, find the captain of the operation there, and put them on the phone with me."

"He is standing right here, hold on a second," Martin said.

"Here," Martin said, handing him the phone. "Inspector Candy Stoner, CIA. She asked to speak to you."

"Captain Hargrove here," the policeman said.

Martin watched as the MPS captain nodded to Stoner's words. He watched as the man tried to get in a word, unsuccessfully. Soon, he handed the phone back to Martin.

"You are free to go, sir."

"Culver, are you there?"

"Yes, I'm back. Here is the deal. Head back to your hotel. I will have someone meet you there to bring Sandra back to the U.S. The contact's name is Iyanah. She can be trusted. I will also have an ammo delivery for you from the armory and some more suitable clothes sent over."

"Where am I headed?"

"No time for that now, just follow orders. It will take me 4 hours to get where you are now. I want you with my team when we intercept the helicopter. If we can't take the helo safely in the air, we have made plans to follow it. It will have to refuel sooner or later."

"Why did Hall come to London?" Martin asked. Behind him, he heard the whine of one last helicopter, then watched as it lifted off, illuminated by the Stonehenge lights. The snow had finally stopped.

"She was trying to warn you, to stop Haddad, to stop the Medina's daughter Melinda. A real bitch, that one. You're lucky you came out on top."

"Hall was by herself? No other agents with her?"

"She wanted to maintain a low profile, then we had communications issues. She even flew commercial to keep it quiet. That's where we think she was drugged," Stoner said.

She collected her thoughts before continuing. "Culver, there's more. We found out who was behind Haddad *and* Medina's artifact smuggling, the mastermind behind ISIS' antiquities sales. We found the boss, the real head of the snake. Suffice it to say Hall's father isn't dead."

"What are you talking about?" Martin shouted. "Medina said the same thing. Hall's father is buried at Arlington. Hall told me that she always said goodbye to him when the plane passed over the cemetery whenever she flew out of DC."

"Everyone *thought* he died. Investigators never found enough DNA to make positive identification. The assumption was that Hall's father was blown to bits. Instead it looks like he got away, badly injured, but a survivor nonetheless. But it gets worse."

"How can it get worse?" Martin asked, a puzzled look crossing his face.

"Hall's father had her kidnapped tonight. She's on that helicopter. We have received her encrypted cell phone signals."

"Culver, we lost a U.S. Senator last night. The Senator was a close colleague of Hall's father for many years, before they had a falling out over peace overtures to the Arab world. The Senator was killed the way your employee was killed at your Foundation, Mr. Culver. The car he was getting into was bombed. We believe Hall's father is to blame. The battle has come to DC."

"But why?" Martin asked.

"Because the Senator ordered the hit on Hall's father, to try to kill him, to silence him."

Martin listened, distracted by the crystal clarity of her voice. His hearing felt fully restored.

"Culver, we haven't any time to lose. Hall's father is known as the Jackal. From all indications, his plans won't stop with this. He wants to see a world bathed in fire, purified from opposition to his designs. Whether or not we get Hall back, we have to stop him."

"Culver are you still there? If you are in, I will send you a copy of my intel."

"Send it," Martin said quietly. "I'm in."

"I have a plane to catch, Culver. We have to stop that helicopter. I will catch up with you in Italy if not before."

"I'll keep in contact," he said, disconnecting the call.

Chartwell watched Martin's face.

"What is it?" he asked Martin. "You have that look."

"Hall's father is the head of the smuggling ring. He had Hall kidnapped. They are taking her to him now. They need us to help."

"Mr. Culver, Mr. Culver sir," the police captain called out.

"Yes, what is it?"

"Are you about to leave sir? I have a few questions. This won't take much time."

Martin looked at the man's appearance, doubting if the captain ever spent much time on anything, especially his personal grooming. The detective had the hairiest facial features Martin had ever seen.

"Captain Hargrove, Mr. Culver, Harry Hargrove if you please. So sorry for the intrusion. I have to ask this. Did you say that a body was left at Stonehenge between the sarsen uprights?"

"Yes I did. Melinda Medina. She died when the lightning struck. I watched her fry."

"Sir, there is no body. We cannot locate it."

"What do you mean, there is no body?"

"It's simply not there, sir. We've combed the entire area."

Martin remembered the helicopter that he had seen lifting off over Stonehenge.

"Lieutenant, do you have a helicopter on scene?"

"No, but we can get one if necessary. You give the word."

"The helicopter I heard," Martin said. "The helicopter I heard came back for Medina's body! They've got Hall too!"

"That was the same bloody helicopter? Is there anything I can do, Mr. Culver?"

"Yes, Hargrove! Bring in your helicopter! Alert your air patrol! The helicopter that just left Stonehenge has the kidnapped Director of the CIA onboard! We have to stop them!"

From the cool quietness of his underground lair, the Jackal's eyes searched a wall of video monitors until he found the specific feed he was searching for. With a trembling index finger, he punched the button to enlarge that particular screen.

Watching the green light moving steadily across France, he reached for the controls, then removed the image with one push of a button.

"A cloak of privacy for your travels, my daughters," he said aloud, enjoying the slight echo that the expansive room created, no matter how low his voice.

Bringing up another monitor, the Jackal gazed at the scene of smoke and mayhem in the U.S. Senate building garage. He focused through the smoke on the scorched stall containing the smoking remains of an official government vehicle.

"So it begins!" he wheezed, his scarred lungs straining for breath. The rain of fire would soon reach every city on every continent. Only then would his mission be complete.

LINKS PAGE

All novels in The Martin Culver Series can be found here:

http://www.amazon.com/author/malcommassey

Read the author bio, check out other great novels, watch video book trailers, see upcoming events, and catch up on the latest author news.

Made in United States
North Haven, CT
03 June 2024

53268627R00157